The Whole Enchilada

The Whole Enchilada

Diane Mott Davidson

HARPER LUXE

An Imprint of HarperCollins*Publishers*

THE WHOLE ENCHILADA. Copyright © 2013 by Diane Mott Davidson. All rights reserved. Printed in the United States of America. No part of this book may be used or reproduced in any manner whatsoever without written permission except in the case of brief quotations embodied in critical articles and reviews. For information address HarperCollins Publishers, 10 East 53rd Street, New York, NY 10022.

HarperCollins books may be purchased for educational, business, or sales promotional use. For information, please e-mail the Special Markets Department at SPsales@harpercollins.com.

FIRST HARPERLUXE EDITION

HarperLuxe™ is a trademark of HarperCollins Publishers

Library of Congress Cataloging-in-Publication Data is available upon request.

ISBN: 978-0-06-227847-0

13 14 ID/RRD 10 9 8 7 6 5 4 3 2 1

To the readers of the Goldy series,
with much affection and many thanks

For had it been an adversary who taunted me,
then I could have borne it;
or had it been an enemy who vaunted himself against me,
then I could have hidden from him.
But it was you, a man after my own heart, my companion,
my own familiar friend.

—PSALM 55:12–13

Prologue

My friend Holly Ingleby died after a party I'd organized. She collapsed while walking with her son, Drew, to her car—less than a block from the house belonging to another close friend, Marla Korman. I knew I shouldn't have blamed myself. But I did.

The seventeenth-birthday celebration for Drew and my own son, Arch, was not an official event put on by my business, Goldilocks' Catering, Where Everything Is Just Right! It was a Tex-Mex potluck featuring sizzling-hot enchiladas, crunchy salted tortillas, cool guacamole, fresh-baked corn bread, and chile relleno tortas, those quivering, picante-laced custards brimming with lakes of cheddar and Jack cheeses. For dessert, there was *dulce de leche* ice cream accompanying a birthday cake with sparkler-style candles.

The whole thing was supposed to have been carefree and fun.

What was the opposite of *carefree and fun*? That party.

Years before, Holly, Marla, and I, along with a few other women, had been in a support group, Amour Anonymous. We'd all given love to the wrong men for the wrong reasons. With a few banjos, we could have played Nashville. Ha ha, so funny I forgot to laugh.

More important, we kept each other upright as we marched through hell.

When I saw Holly lying inert on the pavement, an icy abyss opened in my chest. Tom, my second husband—as wonderful as the first one had been horrific—grasped my shoulders to keep me from pitching onto the concrete where Holly lay.

Afterward, I thought, *That could have been me.*

I knew people differed in their opinions of Holly. In our mountain town of Aspen Meadow, Colorado, perched at eight thousand feet above sea level, forty miles west of Denver, the charitable called Holly a loving mother who'd come from nothing, then shared her creative gifts with the world. The uncharitable called her an untalented slut who chased rich men and charged too much for her work.

Marla and I always stuck up for her—not that it did much good.

Still, no matter what the charitable or the uncharitable said about Holly's personality and ability, they all would have agreed that she worked hard to maintain her slender, muscled body. At thirty-eight, she was still leggy, still blond, with a bright-eyed, surgically enhanced face and a vivacious personality. She had no history of disease and was not on medication.

As it turned out, there were many uncharitable people around my old friend. At the time, I didn't know who these individuals were. Nor did I have an inkling as to their motives.

Most people were stunned by her death. Most. Not all.

SEVENTEENTH BIRTHDAY PARTY
FOR
ARCH KORMAN AND DREW INGLEBY

Tex-Mex Potluck Buffet
Friday, June 15th
Marla Korman's new house
Meadowview, Aspen Meadow Country Club,
Aspen Meadow, Colorado

We'll provide:
Tortilla Chips and Guacamole
Enchiladas Suizas
Vegetarian Chile Relleno Tortas
Refried Beans
Corn Bread
Sour Cream, Sliced Black Olives,
Chopped Tomatoes,
Scallions, and Lettuce
Birthday Cake
Dulce de Leche Ice Cream
Soft Drinks, Coffee, Tea
(*And if you're over twenty-one and not driving,*
Beer and Wine)
If your favorite dish isn't here, feel free to bring it.
Suggestions:
Gazpacho
Tamale Pie
Tostadas
Arroz con Pollo
Flan

1

Before Holly died—before everything went south—I enjoyed the prep for the boys' party.

As I grated cheese for the enchiladas, I remembered meeting Holly on the maternity ward when our sons were born. She was standing very still outside the newborns' nursery, staring through the glass as tears dropped from her high-cheekboned face. I put her despair down to postpartum blues, and hugged her. She was quite a bit taller than yours truly, so we made an odd picture.

Within moments, Holly and I also discovered that neither of our doctor husbands had bothered to show up. She dabbed her eyes and said, "I feel so sorry for Drew. He has to know his own father doesn't care."

For a change, I bit my tongue. I hadn't been surprised that Dr. John Richard Korman had not made an appearance. Later, I dubbed him the Jerk, both for his initials and his behavior, which included breaking my right thumb in three places with a hammer.

I set aside the shredded cheddar and veered away from that memory. I touched my thumb, which still wouldn't move properly. Then I tore the skin off rotisserie chickens and ripped the meat from the bones. Who says cooking isn't cathartic?

Drew and Arch had been in the same Sunday School and attended Aspen Meadow's Montessori preschool. There, Holly enthusiastically helped students with their clay sculptures and tempera paintings. I felt lucky to have known Holly before her artwork made her famous.

I blinked at the pan of softened tortillas, then stacked them between paper towels to remove excess oil. Next I mixed *crema*—homemade sour cream— with the chicken, cheddar, and a judicious amount of salt. I began rolling the tortillas around spoonfuls of the filling and carefully placing them in buttered pans.

Goldy and Arch; Holly and Drew. I had a sudden image of Drew, Holly's darling son, at age five, his face splashed with freckles, his mop of strawberry-blond curls blowing in the breeze beside Cottonwood Creek. After church, Drew and Arch would hunt for garter snakes by the water. When they held one up for our inspection, we would shriek.

When the boys finished kindergarten, I put Arch into public school. Holly enrolled Drew at Elk Park Prep, an expensive local private institution. But the boys remained church pals until they were nine. Back then, Holly swooned over the cookies I brought in for the Sunday School class; she even begged for the recipes. She gleefully admitted she never made them herself, but gave them to the cook who worked for her mother-in-law, Edith. The cook was one of the benefits of living in the red-brick plantation-style house that Edith's deceased husband had built. George the First, as Holly called him, had made millions as a genuine oil baron. When I said it must be nice to have somebody else prepare meals, Holly replied that living with Edith wasn't worth a dozen chefs.

Holly also confided that she'd discovered, too late, that her husband—George the Second—was a mama's boy and a cheapskate. Despite Holly's pleas, George refused to buy a house for their little family. His mother might get sick, he maintained. She might fall down the stairs. No, George wouldn't hear of it. Worse, George and Edith put Holly, who had to look up the word *profligate*, on a stringent cash budget. Humiliated and furious, Holly came to hate them both. The boys were in fourth grade when she began divorce proceedings.

As I chopped onions for the enchilada sauce, the tears filling my eyes may have come from the onion. Still, I didn't enjoy recalling how much I'd missed my friend when she bought a house in Denver. I hated remembering how Arch had pined for Drew.

I found a tissue, blew my nose, and washed my hands again. I heated oil in a Dutch oven, then tossed in the onion. When it was almost done, I ladled in minced garlic. I stirred and inhaled the luscious scent. Next I added chopped Italian tomatoes, chiles, and oregano to the enchilada sauce, gave it a good stir, and smiled—for this was when the memories started their trajectory back up.

Not much more than a year after Holly left George the Second, the boys had an opportunity to get reacquainted. Holly sold the place in Denver. She purchased a fire-engine-red four-wheel-drive Audi and a house in Aspen Meadow Country Club, then called to say she was back.

By then, Marla Korman, the Jerk's second ex-wife, and I had become pals. I invited Holly to join Amour Anonymous. While the group met, Arch and Drew moved from remote-controlled cars to board games. In winter, the two of them sledded down nearby hills.

Drew, tall and athletic like Holly, began to tower over Arch. Sometimes the boys would build a jump for their sleds and plastic saucers, and laugh themselves silly when one of them wiped out.

At the beginning of each Amour Anonymous meeting, we would check in with a brief description of our current physical and emotional health. Then we took turns choosing discussion topics. I was the secretary. This was all before laptop computers became commonplace, so I wrote the notes by hand.

I sighed, poured the sauce over the first pan of enchiladas, and put them in the oven. I made myself an espresso and sat down. What came next was my best memory of Holly from those dark days.

Not long into my own years of singlehood, Marla was out of town when a sudden snowstorm postponed an Amour Anonymous meeting. Arch was spending the night with a friend, whose parents invited him to stay on. I couldn't have picked him up anyway, because my tires had once again been slashed. I suspected the Jerk, of course, but could prove nothing.

Holly called to check on me. I told her I'd gone back to bed. And I stayed there, as the blizzard raged on, day after whiteout day, with school canceled and Arch remaining with his friend. Holly called, and called, and called again. When I said I was too tired to talk, or even to get out of bed, she showed up on our street. She banged on the door. Cursing, I answered, still in my pajamas. Holly whirled inside and said she'd left Drew with a helpful neighbor. Looking me up and down, she tossed her long blond hair over her shoulders and ordered me to shower and dress. Meanwhile, she arranged for my car to be towed to the local tire place. Then she dragged me out of the house.

The roads had been plowed by then, so she sped down the interstate to Denver. Along the way, she caught sight of my raggedy, torn purse, which wasn't going to do me much good anyway, because I was low on money—the Jerk having once again "forgotten" to send the monthly check for child support.

Holly shot me a grin and asked, "Why do elephants have trunks?" When I said I had no idea, she said, "Because they'd look silly with handbags." I was so tired and depressed, I couldn't even smile.

Holly announced we were having a spa day. After our manicures and pedicures, her favorite colorist put highlights in my hair. While my hair was "processing," a word I'd always associated with curing pork, the colorist went to work on Holly's elegant mane. Holly, meanwhile, chatted about how she was seeing two men just then. She was skiing with one in Aspen the next week, in Vail with the other the week after.

The hairdresser looked at me and winked. Afterward, Holly and I gazed in the mirror. My friend hugged me, laughed, and asked if we were having fun yet. I couldn't help it: a grin creased my face.

Holly then piloted the Audi through slush to Cherry Creek Mall. She insisted on buying me a new leather purse and several outfits. The clothes were much too chic for the reduced circumstances of my postdivorce life. I didn't go out for lunch anymore; I didn't ski in winter or play tennis in summer. Worse, my catering business had barely gotten off the ground. But that day, none of those issues mattered. Holly drove me back to my car with its new tires, which she insisted on paying for, as she had for everything else that day. She waved my thanks away.

"I have money and you don't," she said. "It's that simple."

For Holly, it *was* that simple. In our group, she flatly stated that at age twenty-one, she'd married George—ten years her senior and smitten with her—because he was loaded. With no close relatives, she had been working two jobs while attending art school on scholarship. She loved being creative, but had trouble making rent. George was a cardiologist, so even if Edith's oil wells ran dry, they'd be set. Anyway, Holly reasoned, Edith was a sixty-seven-year-old widow, so how long could she actually live? *Forever,* she told us acidly, years later.

I softened the tortillas for the next pan of enchiladas, and thought back.

At another meeting, Holly told us that while she was with George, she'd thought she could make her own money if she established a career. That did not work out—at least, not during the marriage.

When Holly didn't make a fortune from her paintings, it surprised her. She was into astrology and had had her chart done. The stars had apparently predicted that she was going to be a very successful artist. I'd found this interesting. Whenever my catering business teetered on the brink of collapse, I was afraid to consult anything but a cookbook.

By the time Drew was seven, Holly had sold only three canvases. I learned this not from Holly, but from Edith, who'd begun telling anyone who would listen that her daughter-in-law was a dilettante who couldn't be bothered to raise her own son. Inevitably, some of this was reported back to Holly. Holly told us she confronted Edith for talking behind her back, and that the older woman loudly retorted that Holly sure had an *awfully expensive hobby!*

But I had to give Holly—or her chart—credit: after divorcing George, she started over. During her year in

Denver, she went back to art school, and started fashioning something she called portrait-collages. She sold so many works she developed a lengthy client waiting list.

When the *Denver Post* interviewed Holly, she gleefully repeated Edith's *expensive hobby* comment. Intuiting a sensational story, the *Post* sagely snapped photo after photo of Holly, as gorgeous as ever, posed seductively in front of her latest work. I wondered how long it had taken Edith, who now shared her mansion with George and his second wife, Lena, to tear that article into teensy-weensy pieces and burn it, maybe in a discarded oil drum.

Unlike what I was sure Holly's ex-mother-in-law thought, I was happy that my friend had found career success. We all seemed to be healing and moving on, and the meetings of Amour Anonymous became less frequent. Still, when we did meet, Holly would invariably confide that she was skiing, hiking, or playing squash with *somebody special.* She would say her latest client was making her *beaucoup bucks.* She would bring out photos of Drew scoring goals in soccer.

At the time, I wasn't seeing anybody, and Arch was giving me fits. In the career department, I found that my catering clients could be willful, demanding, or suddenly bankrupt. But I did adore my friend, and I was happy for her. The snowy day she'd pulled me out of a funk remained a high point of that painful time.

I took the first batch of enchiladas out of the oven, set them aside to cool, and began rolling the filling inside the new batch of softened tortillas. I frowned, because this was where my story about my friend went off track. Whose fault was that? I had asked myself the same question repeatedly, but hadn't yet come up with an answer.

In January of this year, Holly had abruptly pulled Drew out of Elk Park Prep—where she'd kept him all these years—and put him into Denver's Christian Brothers High School. CBHS was an enormous Catholic school that was not nearly as glamorous or expensive as EPP. But Arch had found a home there. He'd made friends, discovered a sport—fencing—and made the varsity. Drew tried out for the fencing team and made it. And the boys, who could drive themselves to school, began carpooling. They again became close pals.

I phoned Holly several times after Drew transferred to CBHS. But she returned fewer than half my calls. She finally agreed to come to a reunion of Amour Anonymous. Everyone but Holly and Marla had moved away, and our conversation centered on the fact that Holly couldn't believe I had taken notes at all our meetings. Imagine, in this day of every imaginable technological device! She said she "wasn't really in a relationship," whatever that meant. She drank a glass of wine, ate a cheese puff, and left.

Maybe it was harder to resume friendships when you were older. Even though Holly came back to St. Luke's, she rarely stayed to chat. She remained mum on why Drew had changed schools.

So, unlike the old days, Holly didn't talk about herself much. She didn't want to get together. She didn't talk about anybody *special*.

I found all this very odd.

Still, I'd been happy when Arch said he and Drew wanted a joint party. April, when their actual seventeenth birthdays occurred, was full of school commitments. If they held the party two months late, Arch worried, would that jam me up with the wedding season? Would a potluck work? Absolutely, I said. April in Aspen Meadow could be bitterly cold, extremely snowy, or both. This year, Aspen Meadow Lake had stayed frozen well into spring, delighting a small band of risk-taking skaters. May had brought snowfall, followed by rain, which brought hopeful anglers.

By mid-June, though, daytime temperatures were reaching the seventies. Brief showers punctuated the afternoons. Those same fishermen were happily pulling wriggling trout from the still-frigid waters. The risk takers had shed their blades and were riding their twelve-speeds too close to the tourist traffic.

Once the boys decided on their bash, as they called it, Holly phoned me. She apologized, but said she was too busy with her work to help with the festivities. I told her that was fine, and not to worry about it.

Marla, bless her, had insisted the celebration be held at her new house in the Meadowview area of Aspen Meadow Country Club. The boys wanted Tex-Mex food, and I'd volunteered to put together chips, guacamole, enchiladas . . . or whatever they wanted. Arch said he didn't want me to do it *all*. I replied that other parents had offered to bring Mexican dishes. And I loved not having to clean and set up our house, or my nearby conference center, which was, thankfully, almost fully booked for the summer season.

So here I was the day before the party: reminiscing, sashaying around our home kitchen, beating golden corn-bread batter, and making enchiladas. They weren't the typical beef-bean type one had at restaurants, but my own variation of *enchiladas suizas*. They were a favorite of Arch's. When I tried to explain to him that the dairy-rich dish had been developed in Mexico for the Sanborn coffee shops, he'd said, "Great, Mom. Thanks." His pale cheeks flamed and his toast-brown eyebrows quirked. "And *please* don't string up a piñata. I'm not five."

"Oh-*kay*."

No matter that my own son had no interest in piñatas or the provenance of dishes, no matter how problematic my regular clients occasionally were, I still loved cooking. With my business, I'd finally managed to turn my passion for feeding people into a moneymaker. Or at least, it was a moneymaker most of the time. I still had the occasional drunken host or crazed bridezilla, either of whom could cause a scene or have a full-fledged meltdown.

Lucky for me, Tom packed a gun in his work with the Furman County Sheriff's Department. Of course, he wouldn't bring it out at one of my parties. Whenever anything threatened to go wrong, if Tom was there, he used that *tone of voice*. It scared the innocent and the guilty alike.

I was happy that the boys' party would give the fencing team and parents, plus friends, a chance to get together before summer began in earnest. And would Arch really kill me if we strung up a piñata? I asked Tom. Yes, Tom replied. He would.

For the Tex-Mex celebration, my vegetarian assistant, Julian Teller, had set himself the task of making chile relleno tortas. In his midtwenties, Julian was compact, muscled, handsome, and perpetually grizzled-looking. Although I tried just to taste my own cooking to season it, when Julian tossed together cheeses, picante, and chiles, then poured a smooth mixture of eggs and cream on top, my mouth watered. Once the first batch of pies came out, I knew I would want to find a large spoon and dig in.

That Thursday afternoon, as Julian waited for the first two tortas to finish baking, he tapped the toe of one of his high-top sneakers on the floor. He said, "I'm just going to check what else we have going on this weekend." The third and fourth tortas sat on the counter, awaiting their time in the oven. I spooned the corn-bread batter into buttered pans and checked the timer for when they could go in. All the dishes would be made that day, to be reheated the next, at Marla's.

"In the computer," I replied. Yes, we now had several laptops: one in the kitchen for my business, one for Tom in his basement office, and one in Arch's room. Times did change, but I still wrote things down, as did Tom when he worked crime scenes. *Any little thing could help you find a murderer,* he always said. *Specks of dropped ash. A forgotten print. Some detail that, if you didn't record it, could let a killer get away.*

Julian clicked through screens to get to my calendar. He perused one, then zipped to the next. Kids' tech skills always amazed me.

"We have that church dinner Sunday night," he said. He squinted as he read. "*Plan Your Funeral?* Really?"

"Father Pete figured saying he was going to discuss death would drive people away." We all loved Father Pete, the rotund priest at St. Luke's, even when he was bent on talking about the hereafter.

Julian regarded me quizzically. "Well, it did. Only a dozen people have signed up."

I shrugged. "We extended the reservation deadline to Saturday, and opened the dinner to the community at large. So blame him if it's a flop."

Julian did not take his eyes off the computer. "I'm not going to blame Father Pete for anything. The man is obsessed with my fudge with sun-dried cherries." He clicked to a new screen, then another. "Hold on. We have Arch and Drew's party tomorrow night, then Saturday we're off, then we have the church dinner the following night, and then *another* party, Monday night?"

"Yup. Better still, for the rest of the summer, Goldilocks' Catering is *booked.*"

"The next few days will be packed." Julian sounded dubious, but was interrupted by the doorbell. I asked him to get it. He trotted down the hall, peered through the eyehole, then raced back. "It's Neil Unger."

There was a gentle knocking on our front door. Julian and I cringed.

"Better let him in," I whispered. The party we were doing Monday night was a surprise twenty-first-birthday celebration for Neil's painfully shy, awkward daughter, Ophelia. At that moment, I really didn't want to talk to Neil, or rather, listen to him. In his midfifties, barrel-chested, and charming, Neil had formed a group that was supposed to be working on bringing morals back into our culture. During the planning of Ophelia's party, I'd nodded politely as Neil gave me his homily on *The Decline of Everything*. I'd kept my lips buttoned, which showed unusual restraint on my part, if I did say so myself.

"I know you," Neil said to Julian, who had opened the front door. "Boulder, right?" He said it like, *You're from hell, correct?* When Julian murmured in the affirmative, Neil asked, "Could you please take my driver a snack? He didn't have time for breakfast. I need to talk to Goldy."

"Yes, sir," Julian said, waggling his eyebrows at me as he followed Neil down our hall. Julian unobtrusively slipped into the walk-in, pulled out some chocolate-filled croissants, nabbed a bottle of sparkling water, and disappeared.

When Neil smiled at me, I swallowed. He had a handsome, chisel-cut face, with charisma to match. But I was in no mood to find out why he was in my kitchen. I caught a whiff of his spicy aftershave, then blinked at his perfect steel-gray hair, which looked as if it had been set in wide furrows that morning with a wide-tooth comb and an entire can of gel. He said gently, "I was hoping you could help me."

"Help you—?"

He rubbed his dimpled chin. "I'm afraid my daughter knows about the party."

"Not from me," I said.

"Could you please check your computer?" His tone was plaintive as he waved a hand at the screen. "Maybe you've been hacked."

"I have *not* been hacked."

"How would you even know? Could you check? Please?"

Neil belonged to the country club and was influential in Furman County politics. I couldn't afford to alienate him. I clamped my mouth shut, tapped keys to run a virus check, and hoped I was doing it correctly.

"I wanted to give Ophelia a book on fiscal responsibility," Neil said as he ranged around the kitchen, nervously opening cabinets, then closing them. "But her stepmother vetoed that idea. So I bought her a gold bracelet. With charms."

"That sounds wonderful." I squinted at the screen and cleared my throat.

"My first wife died of cancer when Ophelia was very young." He exhaled. "I just want the party to be a success."

"It will be. Please sit down."

Neil Unger continued moving around my kitchen. He was behind me, so I ostentatiously took my hands off the keyboard. He finally scraped back a chair. He said, "I think my daughter's fiancé is a rhino."

"A rhino?"

"Republican in name only. I haven't said anything. I just worry for her."

"Um," I said, still staring back at the screen. I prayed the virus scan was working its way through my files. "Do the fiancé's politics really matter?"

"I suppose not. Ophelia just seems so . . . unhappy."

I thought back to Arch's years of misery. "I'm a big believer in counseling—"

"The talking cure?" He groaned. "We tried that once. She refused to speak."

The scan ended, with no viruses detected. I turned around and looked at Neil Unger, who at that moment resembled a puppy who'd just been rescued from drowning. He seemed to want to talk to someone. But right then, I didn't want to listen.

Julian reentered the kitchen and took in our little tableau: short caterer looking sympathetic, political heavyweight looking pathetic. I said softly, "My computer hasn't been hacked. If Ophelia knows about the party, she heard it from someone else."

Neil quirked his silver eyebrows, glared at the floor, and shook his head. He nodded at Julian and me, then left as quickly as he'd come in.

"That guy's a jackass," Julian said as he slid the last two tortas into the preheated oven.

"A jackass with a big checkbook and lots of friends."

"They're the worst kind." Julian set the timer. "Boss, we have a full schedule for the next few days. You can hire another caterer, give him or her the food you've ordered, and forget Unger. When I did a party for him, I had to listen to his political views. It's not an experience I'm going to forget anytime soon."

"We'll be fine."

"We have three parties in four days." Julian paused. "Are you sure you know what we're getting into?"

I actually laughed.

2

When I woke the next morning, gray light suffused the bedroom curtains. Tom was still asleep, so I moved through my yoga routine, then tiptoed to the kitchen. A mountain breeze moved languidly through the pines and aspens surrounding our house. I opened the back door for Scout the cat and Jake the bloodhound, and reminded myself that today we were celebrating my only son's seventeenth birthday. Okay, we were two months late. But, so what? I smiled and reflected that it was probably a good thing that I'd stayed up past midnight to frost the cake.

Tom had recently said he wanted us to have a baby. I would welcome an addition to our household. But I worried: catering, not to mention being the mother of a teenager, often left me feeling old and tired.

I pulled myself a double espresso, sat at the kitchen table, and stared into the dark liquid. I sighed. Among other things, I'd long been in denial about my intake of caffeine. Even though Marla, Holly, and I frequently referred to our knowledge of health and disease as coming from what we called Med Wives 101, I somehow never thought that knowledge pertained to *me*. My doctor had sternly ordered me to cut back. After my primal scream, I'd promised to switch to decaf on the third cup. It was the best I could do.

I chugged the coffee, let Jake back in, and put him in the animal containment area. Scout had disappeared, as usual. When I was washing my hands, Julian pushed through the swinging door to the kitchen and took in my dour countenance.

"Do I detect a negative vibe?" he asked mildly. To my surprise, he'd shaved. In a few hours, his heavy beard would begin to darken his lower cheeks and chin. But at least he'd made the effort. He wore a pale blue oxford-cloth shirt and khaki pants, purchased, he'd proudly told me, from Aspen Meadow's secondhand store.

"Negative vibe?" I echoed. "You're not in the People's Republic of Boulder anymore."

Actually, Julian had come back to live with us in late May, when the vegetarian bistro where he had been performing his culinary miracles had unceremoniously shut. Our first party would be the boys' Mexican fiesta. Julian's calming presence, brilliance with food, and efficient help made short work of the chores.

His high-top sneakers squeaked across the floor as he hustled around me to the espresso machine, clattered a cup into place, and pressed buttons. As the stream spiraled downward, he hunted for the sugar bowl. Then he doused his espresso with so much of the sweet stuff that I had to close my eyes.

My business line rang: Marla.

"Some guy called me late last night," she began without preamble. "I'd just supervised the lawn being mown and the delivery of a volleyball net and new lawn furniture—"

"Marla, you didn't have to do all that—"

"I'm just trying to explain," her raspy voice went on, "why I'd drunk three glasses of wine, okay, maybe four, had dinner, and gone to bed. The phone woke me up. This man said he needed directions to the party."

Julian cocked his chin, but I shook my head. "A fencing-team parent?"

"That's what I thought," said Marla. "I was a little out of it, and actually, I thought *he* was a little out of it, like he'd lost his directions, or didn't have access to the e-mailed invitation. So I told him how to get here, then asked for his name. He wanted to know if Holly Ingleby was going to be a guest at the party. I said yes and by this time I'd grabbed a pen. I asked him again who he was. But he hung up."

"Caller ID?"

"Unavailable. Maybe he was an old boyfriend of hers." I shook my head. Marla said rapidly, "The diggers for the horseshoe pitches just arrived. Sorry, Goldy. See you in a bit."

I hung up, groaned, and told Julian about an uninvited guest showing up that night.

"Nothing we can do." His voice wrapped around the door to the walk-in, where he'd disappeared to bring out the first pair of tortas. When he reemerged, he put down his load and gave me a look. "Tom will be there if there's a problem. And I'm sure we have more than enough food." As we placed more covered pans and bowls into cardboard boxes, I admitted to myself that Julian was right.

"For a kid, you're awfully wise."

"It's from all that time being laid-back in Boulder."

"Please don't say *being laid-back* to me."

We packed my van with the boxes of Mexican food, the birthday cake, the gifts for the boys, and a dozen gallons of *dulce de leche* ice cream, kept ultracold in coolers. I backed out of the driveway, and we took off for Marla's house.

At ten o'clock, the tourists hadn't shown up in Aspen Meadow yet, so there were few cars on Main Street. The sun shone on the cloud of chartreuse pollen that shimmered between us and the Continental Divide. Cottonwood Creek, swollen with snowmelt, roared and splashed over the rocks submerged just below the surface. As we passed the falls and began skirting the lake, Julian craned his head to peer upward.

He asked, "Don't Holly and Drew live around here somewhere?"

"Holly and Drew? No way. Holly has a big house in Aspen Meadow Country Club."

"Not anymore she doesn't. Marla told me she recently moved over by the lake, near town. She and Drew are in one of those rentals where you don't have to pay much if you keep it nice while it's for sale." Julian's brow furrowed. "Come to think of it, I might not have been supposed to tell you that."

"When did this happen?"

"Um, I don't think I have permission to—"

"You might not have permission from *Marla* to tell me our friend *Holly* is renting near the lake?" How could Julian know more about where Holly lived than I did? "How could Marla possibly have told you and not me—"

"Okay, here's the deal, but you can't tell anybody. Holly lost her house in the club." Julian's tone was matter-of-fact.

"But," I protested, "that's simply not possible. She's rich. And anyway, I assumed she bought that place in the country club with the profits from selling her Denver house. Plus, she should still have some money from George the Second." I stopped talking and allowed my mind to grind through what, exactly, I knew about Holly's financial situation. "Okay," I said, as much to myself as to Julian, "when Holly divorced George, she moved out of Edith's mansion and bought a big place down below. But driving Drew back and forth to Elk Park Prep in the winter, she landed her Mercedes in ditches filled with snow more times than she could count. So she sold the Denver house, bought a place in the club and a four-wheel-drive Audi, and moved back up here. When did she lose the house?"

"You're asking the wrong person."

"I mean," I responded, "her ex is wealthy. Yes, he was a skinflint with Holly, and so busy with his work he didn't give her enough attention. So he wasn't a super husband. But I don't think he'd let her lose the

country-club house where she and his *son* were living."
I shook my head. Did *I* think George would do that?

"Well," Julian replied, "I don't know if George was
involved in it. According to Marla, Holly refinanced
the place in the club. Then she couldn't make her payments. She tried to do a short sale, with no luck. The
bank foreclosed."

"How do you know so much about Holly?"

"Watch where you're driving, boss." Julian's revela-
tions had so disconcerted me that I'd drifted into the
wrong lane. I corrected the van and glanced over in
time to see a grin pleat Julian's cheek. He said, "Marla
told me about Holly's situation because I *asked*. And
anyway, I care about my very first food client."

"Your first client? What in the world are you talking
about?"

"I met Holly when I got to Elk Park Prep," he said
simply. "I was a boarding student, remember? I was
fifteen and on the swim team."

"You were at EPP when you were fifteen? I thought
you arrived later."

"Nope. I was a scholarship student beginning at age
fifteen. Anyway, I'd get hungry after practice, before
dinner was served to the boarding students. Since I was
a vegetarian, I got permission to use the kitchen to make
my own meals. One time, when Drew was, oh, nine or

so, he suddenly appeared beside me, said he'd smelled something yummy, and what was I doing? He said his mother was late picking him up, and asked if he could have a plate of whatever I was fixing. So I gave him a bowl of vegetarian chili. He raved about it to Holly. She came into the kitchen the next day, all breathless, saying her husband, George, was a vegetarian, too. She hated having to prepare food for him on Edith's cook's one night off. So she paid me, each week, to make a vegetarian dinner for the four of them. Which I did, until the Inglebys got divorced and I moved in with the Farquhars."

It had been at Adele and Bo Farquhars' house, where I'd briefly been a live-in cook, that I'd met Julian. "You're telling me Edith never figured out that it wasn't Holly making the food on her cook's night off?"

Julian shrugged as we zoomed through the stone walls marking the entrance to the Meadowview area of Aspen Meadow Country Club. "Maybe Edith knew it wasn't Holly cooking, maybe she didn't. But if Edith suspected her daughter-in-law wasn't actually making that meal each week, she didn't say anything about it. Holly wasn't a very good cook, I guess. It was worth it to Edith to keep mum, if she was going to get a decent dinner on the one night a week when the cook wasn't there."

I reflected on all this as my van turned onto Arnold Palmer Avenue, and we sailed past gigantic gray, beige, and white homes, all dusted with pollen. Holly had lost her house after refinancing. I had not known that. What I *had* known was that she'd transferred Drew from Elk Park Prep to the Christian Brothers High School, and had not been forthcoming about her reasons. I'd put it down to a problem caused by Edith, not something related to money. The tuition for the Christian Brothers High School was half that of Elk Park Prep. But . . . could Holly really be having financial problems? How could Marla not have told me? And anyway, how was it possible?

After all, Holly was an artist whose works reportedly commanded large sums. She'd been at pains to point out to me that she had lots of clients. Plus, Drew was only seventeen. Holly had told us—I knew it was in the Amour Anonymous notes somewhere—that George had had to give her a big settlement, and was duty bound to pay child support until Drew was *through college*. And George made loads of money. There was always the Ingleby oil fortune, just in case. So what was going on?

"Boss, you just passed the turnoff to Marla's. Yo," he howled, "look out!"

A man darted out from behind a chokecherry bush beside the road. I swerved to avoid him. With a fierce thud, the van hit a boulder. I shrieked to Julian to check if the guy was okay.

"Hey!" Julian shouted. He jumped from the van. The sandy-haired, beefy man, dressed in jeans and a sweatshirt, ran off. Julian tried to give chase, but the guy had too much of a head start. "Are you all right?" Julian hollered after him.

"Come back!" I cried. I yelled at the disappearing figure, "I'm sorry!"

The man did not come back, or even turn around.

Cursing, I returned to my van, which had sustained damage to the bumper. Worse, at that moment, someone's ground-level irrigation system started up.

I said, "I feel so stupid."

"It's okay, boss," said Julian. "It was my fault. I should have waited until we got to Marla's to ask you about Holly. Or really, I shouldn't have told you any of that stuff at all. I mean, obviously, it upset you."

"It wasn't your fault. I should be able to listen and drive."

Water was pelting both of us, so we stopped arguing. We kept entire changes of clothes in the van, for just such eventualities. Julian insisted I go first, so I got back inside and quickly slipped into my dry outfit. There was nothing I could do about my bedraggled hair, but we were less than a block from Marla's place.

I leaped from the van, thanked Julian, and told him to go ahead.

Meanwhile, I sat on a patch of grass well away from the sprinkler system. I puzzled over what Julian had told me. But I was not about to wonder aloud about Holly's financial situation, even to my trusted assistant.

When we got back in the van, I asked companiably, "Did Holly have a favorite dish that you made?"

He grinned and shook his head. "She loved chile relleno torta. Said it was better than actual chiles rellenos from the best Mexican restaurant in Denver. That's why I made four of them for tonight. Not that she'll eat that much. She never does."

I turned around carefully, made it onto Marla's street, and signaled to pull into her driveway. The pitch diggers, riding in the back of an enormous, exhaust-burping truck, waved to us as they left.

"Hoo hoo!" Marla called, waving from her garage doors. After losing forty pounds on a low-carb diet, she'd been "forced," she'd told me dramatically, to buy all new clothes. Today she wore a royal-blue short-sleeved turtleneck and black pants. Sapphire barrettes sparkled in her hair. She looked us up and down as we hopped from the van. "Did it rain and I missed it?" she asked, smiling. When she caught sight of my face, she said, "Uh-oh, you're pissed. Look, I know I should have gotten that mystery guest's name, but I just . . . what happened to the front of your van?"

"I almost hit a guy when Julian was telling me about your friend and mine, Holly Ingleby, and her recent financial problems."

"*What* guy?" Marla peered at my van. "You hit *something.*"

"Yeah. A boulder. Then somebody's sprinkler system started up. That's why we're soaking wet."

"Think I'll make myself scarce," Julian said quickly. He slid open the van's side door and heaved up the first ice-cream cooler. "Front open?" he called to Marla.

"Yes. Look, Goldy," Marla began, "don't you want to have a shower? Julian?" But he had disappeared. "I'm sorry you hit a boulder, and I'm sorry I called you so early, but I figured you would *want* to know—"

"About some guy who may or may not turn up, looking for Holly? D'you suppose he's a creditor? Maybe he's the one I just about killed, down on Arnold Palmer Avenue."

We were interrupted by yipping, barking, and howling from the three beagles Marla had adopted from a puppy farm. The trio of females—named Madly, Sadly, and Gladly—had grown exponentially in the past year. As they raced outside, they greeted me with enthusiasm and sniffed the air, hoping for treats. But with their canine sixth sense, they knew something was wrong. After I gave them obligatory pats, they looked to Marla for a signal.

Marla's face, meanwhile, had turned bright pink. "Holly didn't want me to tell you about her money issues."

"Why not? The three of us were, and I hope still are, *friends*, Marla. Besides, you told *Julian*. What's with that? Holly isn't paying me to do this dinner tonight, so it's not as if I would worry her check would bounce."

Marla put her hands on her newly slim hips. The dogs began to whine. "Julian wasn't supposed to say anything to you. It's just . . . I learned these things, and when Julian asked me about Holly as soon as he moved in with you, I told him. Next time I saw Holly, I asked if I could tell *you*. She said no. She didn't want anyone to be aware of her financial issues."

"But why is it a secret, even from me? You and Holly and I were in Amour Anonymous together. We took care of each other and talked about everything. We just had a reunion, for God's sake."

Marla held out her hands. "She's ashamed."

"Of what? Why isn't she going to a lawyer and demanding a bigger child-support check from George?" I pulled out the cake and made for the front door.

"She is, I think. Or I'm guessing. I know she sold her Audi, as well as Drew's, to raise cash. Plus, don't think I haven't asked if I could help her. I did. She refused. All right, girls," she said to the dogs, "let's go."

I held the door open for the beagles as Julian came back out. The house, or the property it sat on, had belonged to Marla's sister, Adele Farquhar, now deceased. That had been a different, sad story. The residence next door, empty and unsold for years, had been reputed to be jinxed. *That* house, Marla had plowed under. I shuddered.

Marla's new home only resembled the Farquhars' in its footprint. The exterior was clad in creamy beige stucco, the roof topped with copper-colored steel tiles. Inside, Marla had chosen soaring ceilings, three stories of windows overlooking the far mountains, acres of blond wood, a river-rock fireplace and hearth, and of course, a state-of-the-art surveillance system. In all, the whole place was as soothingly modern as Adele's had been green-and-pink traditional.

In the kitchen, Julian had already stored the second ice-cream cooler. He marched in behind us with boxes that he piled on the granite-topped island, then threw me a quick glance. I still must have looked thunderous, because he opened a box and began moving silently between it and Marla's oversize, stainless-steel refrigerator. Marla, meanwhile, shooed the beagles into their fenced dog run outside.

"Look, Marla," I said when she returned, "Holly is my friend, too. She was in our group. She belongs to our church. Why keep her problems secret from me?"

"You can ask her if you want," Marla said flatly. "She absolutely, positively will not tell me anything more about it. And, Julian, you shouldn't have said anything, either."

"Sorry," muttered Julian. "I guess I thought Goldy would know, like from Arch or something. I mean, don't Arch and Drew carpool to school?"

"Yes," I said acidly, "but Arch doesn't keep me up-to-date on the real estate market. He also refuses to share any gossip at all."

Marla held out her hands again in explanation. "The *only* reason I found out about Holly's house in the club is that it's a matter of public record. When I was thinking about moving over here, the house I was selling had to compete, pricewise, with her attempted short sale. You want a shower? Then some coffee?"

"Sure," I said. "Thanks. Decaf." I groaned.

"Killing a boulder, getting soaked, and no caffeine. No wonder you're in such a bad mood."

I had a quick shower, dried my hair, and drank Marla's iced decaf, which was marginally better than what I had at home. Julian said he would shower after he'd had a swim in Marla's pool. By the time I came back to the kitchen, he'd schlepped in all the boxes.

As we unpacked, Marla said that at the country club, she had gleaned the tidbit she had told Julian, who in turn had shared it with me. Yes, Holly was living almost rent-free in a house over by Aspen Meadow Lake. It was a place she just had to move her nice furniture into and keep tidy, in case potential buyers dropped in. Marla added that she'd learned from me about Drew transferring to CBHS from Elk Park Prep. And how come *I* hadn't asked Holly the reasons for her actions?

"Oh," I replied, "I assumed Edith had gone on one of her ball-busting campaigns. I asked Arch, and he refused to grill Drew. Plus, I . . . was trying to be polite."

"A-*ha*." Marla pointed a red-painted nail at me. "And after all, I *am* famed for my rudeness."

"Marla, I didn't mean—"

She grinned. It was noon. She asked, "Would you and Julian like some salads for lunch? I just bought some fresh Chilean sea bass—"

"I'll fix it," Julian interrupted.

Half an hour later, we were diving into thick slices of bass poached in butter and garlic, topped with a chiffonade of basil, and perched on a salad of microgreens dressed with a freshly made lemon vinaigrette. I felt revived. Julian asked if he could do the dishes, then swim his laps. Marla told him to skip the dishes and go ahead.

After Marla and I cleaned up, I checked in with Tom. He'd gotten the all-clear, and would be at Marla's at five. I put my previous funk aside and concentrated on the coming party.

The *slap-slap* of Julian's methodical swimming gave me extra energy as I bustled around checking my lists, fluffing linens out over rented tables, and setting the buffet with what Marla had insisted on: china and flatware, with plastic cups for drinks, so that the kids and parents could have their beverages out by the pool.

The sun began its long slide between thin layers of pink cloud on its way to the Continental Divide. Those jagged peaks above the timberline, still sheened in snow, glowed in the afternoon light. When I answered the door—to pick up sword-shaped floral decorations thick with red carnations and dark blue delphiniums— playing children were calling to each other from the street at the end of Marla's driveway. The sweet mountain air was cool, perfect weather for energetic teenagers wanting to *par-tay*.

Marla nodded at the arrangements before placing them on her long dining room table. "I told the florist to make them masculine. Okay, look, Holly called. Afraid I have some bad news."

"Not about the party."

"No. You know a local caterer named Kathie Beliar?"

"I thought Kathie Beliar was a substitute teacher."

Marla shook her head. "Not anymore. She's opened a catering company she's calling Goldy's Catering."

"*What?*"

"She phoned Father Pete when Holly was in his office, and offered to do the church dinner for half of whatever you were charging."

"But I'm not—"

"I know. Holly told Father Pete, who was confused, that I was still paying for that meal. So Holly left a scurrilous message on Kathie's voice mail, telling her not to try to undercut you. Kathie then called Holly back, saying she would do tonight's party, which she'd heard about from somebody at the club, for half of whatever you were charging."

"But I'm not—"

"Wait," said Marla, motioning to her own laptop, which she kept on a desk in her kitchen. "Did you not register your business as a domain name?"

I shook my head while looking in wonder at www. goldilockscatering.com. There was Kathie Beliar, whom our local librarians had often said looked like me, with her hair cut and curled like mine. Why anyone would want to look like an aging Shirley Temple was beyond me. But there was my doppelgänger, standing in front of a van that had been decorated to look like mine, with a phone number only one digit off mine.

I said, "But her name's *Kathie.*"

Marla said, "So? Your actual name is Gertrude."

I sighed. "I can't deal with this right now. My business is almost booked for the summer anyway."

Marla said gently, "I know. I just thought you should know, in case anyone brings it up tonight."

"Thanks." I swallowed and tried to refocus my attention. "Now, where are you going to put the drinks?" That's when we discovered that each of us had bought plastic cups. Unfortunately, we both thought the *other* one was providing beverages.

"Not to worry," Marla trilled, as she bounded off for her Mercedes. She called over her shoulder that she would buy cases of nonalcoholic drinks for the kids, and beer and wine for the adults. She promised to be back before the food was served.

Tom, handsome and smiling, appeared just before five. Julian, his hair wet from his shower, joined us. A few moments later, Arch piloted his Passat up the driveway, and the first batch of his pals spilled out.

"Drew's mom is bringing him," Arch announced. He wore flip-flops, khaki cutoffs, and a T-shirt featuring the logo of a band I'd never heard of. "The rest of the guys are parking down on the street." He nodded to me, but his eyes contained a warning: *Hug this birthday boy at your peril.*

I hadn't been paying attention to my driving and had almost hit a guy in Marla's neighborhood. I'd run my van into a boulder. A rival caterer in town was trying to steal my business, starting with the name.

But at least I hadn't strung up a piñata.

3

By half past five, most of the fencing-team parents and kids, plus assorted girlfriends, had shown up. The boys' bald heads always gave my heart a jolt. They'd all shaved their scalps in sympathy with one of their teammates. He'd been stricken with leukemia and was going through chemo. The boy was doing well, but wouldn't be at the party.

The parents marched through to Marla's kitchen, proudly holding their favorite Mexican dishes aloft. Tom asked them how long their entrées needed to heat, and if anything ought to be refrigerated. Then, as carefully as he took notes at a crime scene, he wrote down everything in his notebook.

Marla honked the announcement of her arrival. Parked behind other vehicles in her own driveway, she called for Tom to push out a dolly so he could haul in three cases of Dutch beer, two of nonalcoholic brew, a case of wine, and several twenty-four-packs of juice, water, and pop. Tom placed all the drinks in Marla's second refrigerator, located in the garage.

"I'm having a shower and getting dressed," she said, then disappeared. Fifteen minutes later, while Julian and I were assembling the chips and guacamole, she trotted into the kitchen. That had to be another record. She flicked her highlighted gold-and-brown hair back from her ears to reveal dangling chocolate diamond earrings. She cocked a hip and presented herself, swathed in a leopard-print pantsuit with a sequined belt.

"You look fantastic," I told her. "Anyone who can lose that much weight—"

But I didn't finish the thought, because Marla wasn't listening. Suddenly distracted, she gazed over my shoulder, through the kitchen windows with their magnificent view of her pool and her flat land, and beyond, the mountains. She asked, "When did Bob Rushwood and Ophelia Unger arrive?"

"Bob Rushwood?" I asked, puzzled. "The trainer from Aspen Meadow Country Club? What's he doing here? Why is Ophelia Unger here? Her party isn't until Monday night."

"They came while you, boss, were helping the Smythes bring in their dishes. You were out getting the drinks, Marla." Julian tilted his head to indicate the windows. "Ophelia is engaged to Bob. They're going to do their pitch when I'm trying to make my first round with the appetizers the parents brought."

"*What* pitch?" I asked.

"Okay, this was not my idea," Julian said defensively. "Arch came in and said Drew had worked with Bob last summer digging trails. You know, Pails for Trails?"

I nodded, recalling the bright red pails beside cash registers in every store in Aspen Meadow. Glued on the front were photographs of kids in wheelchairs being pushed up mountain trails that had been widened by a large cadre of volunteers whose tools were bought with the change people dropped into the pails. Okay, great idea. But I didn't want anyone making a *pitch* for *anything* at my son and his friend's party.

"He promised just to talk for five minutes," Julian went on. "He's looking for kids to help with the trails this summer. One mother told Bob it was *unseemly*— I'm quoting here—for Bob to be trying to sign up trail-building volunteers at a birthday party. And Bob said, first of all, Drew had invited him. Second, Bob said, he'd had one kid work on the trails for two summers, then Bob wrote him a recommendation, and the kid got into Harvard. And did this parent want her kid to go to an Ivy League school? The mother practically fell over herself ushering Bob out back."

Marla rolled her eyes at me. "Has he started talking yet? Set the timer. I don't want muscle-bound Bob and dreary Ophelia talking more than five minutes."

"She's not dreary," I said. "She's shy."

"Not to mention totally clueless in the fashion department."

"Marla, that's—"

"Did you set the timer?"

I obligingly set the stupid timer and peered out beyond the newly dug horseshoe pitches. I knew Bob Rushwood only by sight. With a black Spandex top and leggings showing off his wide shoulders and brawny legs, he was one of those ageless athletes who looked thirty but could be forty. I frowned. And who would choose to put beautiful dark brown hair into dreads?

Tom appeared from behind me. "What are you looking at? Or are you looking at a person?"

"Do any fortyish white athletes you know wear dreads?" I asked.

Tom peered out the window and saw Bob. "Absolutely."

"But don't big, manly athletes avoid hairdressing salons?"

"Miss G., if you make the kind of money professional athletes do, you can pay for a hairdresser to come to your *house*."

At Bob's side, Ophelia Unger was shorter than her fiancé. She wore black-framed glasses, and was thinner than I remembered. Her shaggy dark hair was longer than I recalled, too. Her attractive face was set in a bored expression. Clearly, the trail-digging enterprise didn't make *her* want to go to Harvard. Where Bob's tight outfit stretched across his pecs, abs, and other muscles I didn't have, Ophelia sported a lime collared shirt, lime Bermuda shorts, and sandals. I wondered about what Neil had said, that Ophelia seemed so unhappy. She certainly *looked* miserable enough.

On Marla's grass, the kids and parents listening to Bob lounged in various states of repose. Two boys appeared to be asleep.

I said, "Apparently, the idea of building trails isn't meeting with enthusiasm."

"D'you think?" Marla replied from beside me. The timer hadn't gone off, but never mind. With the parents watching, she pulled out a frying pan and a metal spoon and raced onto her back porch. Julian snorted with laughter as she banged on the pot and shouted to Bob and Ophelia that their time was up.

I glanced around for Tom, who had disappeared. Then I spotted him, setting up Marla's new volleyball net next to the horseshoe pitches. What a guy.

It was time to start baking the entrées. Tom had preheated Marla's ovens and left the schedule where I could see it. I put dish after dish onto the racks: Julian's foil-covered chile relleno tortas, my *enchiladas suizas,* the Boatfields' tostadas, arroz con pollo from the Smythes, empanadas from the Mikulskis.

The adults who hadn't been listening to the presentation on trail digging were milling about Marla's kitchen, stirring gazpacho, grating cheddar, *queso,* and Monterey Jack cheeses, spooning soft dollops of sour cream and guacamole into crystal bowls. A few of them wandered into the backyard to help Tom with the net.

With her usual fanfare, Holly arrived. She dinged unnecessarily and repeatedly on Marla's doorbell. *Summoning her audience,* I thought, with a smile. It was twenty-five minutes after the party was supposed to have started. I'd never known Holly to be on time for anything.

When I opened the door, instead of seeing her smiling face and hearing her humor-filled voice, I saw only Drew, who had high cheekbones, was six inches taller than his mother, and sported the same shaved head as his teammates.

"Where's your mom?" I asked.

Drew pointed, and I looked around. Holly, huddled beside Marla's door, wore a sparkly silver designer pant-suit with complicated folds and creases. The shimmery fabric had been skillfully cut away to show off her tanned, buff shoulders, which she'd draped loosely with more glittery fabric. She'd swept her blond hair back. Holly didn't look like a parent; she looked like a model who'd been given the wrong outfit for a backyard barbecue. Stringed bags hung from each of her hands. She glanced fearfully down the driveway, where, I now realized, a tall, well-built, balding man was standing. I was willing to bet his male-pattern baldness was owing to age, not choice.

A fringe of sandy hair around the man's collar made me look twice. Was this the guy I'd almost hit that morning? If so, he was no longer wearing jeans and a sweatshirt. Oh, how I wished I'd gotten a good look at him . . . before I hit the boulder.

"Let me in quickly," Holly said to me.

"Mom," said Drew, "who is that guy?"

"Nobody," she said. It was clearly a lie. "Goldy, don't look. Don't give him the satisfaction."

I couldn't help myself; I craned forward to get a better view of the stranger. But in the gathering gloom, I could only make out an unmoving male. Apart from the bit of sandy hair, all I could tell was that he was perhaps in his early fifties. He had a pale, moon-shaped face. He may have been tall and brawny, but his ill-fitting, long-sleeved shirt and rumpled pants did him no favors. His expression was gloomy, as if someone in his family had just died.

"Holly," I began, "what the—"

Holly slipped through the door. Drew quickly followed. I continued to stare at the odd-looking man until I heard Holly's bags hit the floor. One of her powerful hands pulled me back inside. She firmly shut the door.

"He's a son of a bitch," she hissed, her blue eyes ferocious.

"Is he a *dangerous* son of a bitch?"

Holly looked unsure, and I recalled the moon-faced man's unhappy expression, his body slouched in apparent defeat. Was this the guy who'd wanted to know where the party was, who'd wanted to know if Holly would be here? Had he been lurking on Arnold Palmer Avenue that morning? And could he *really* have been one of Holly's former boyfriends? He hadn't been particularly good-looking. Like Ophelia, he lacked fashion sense. Even George Ingleby was handsome, in a broad-faced, bearded, Russian-army-officer sort of way, and always dressed in khaki slacks and a tailored shirt. The guy in Marla's driveway looked like an advertisement for Goodwill.

Yet there was something about Goodwill Man that had appeared familiar, apart from the fact that I thought I might have almost mowed him down that morning. What was it? I grasped for the memory, but it was just out of reach. Had I catered an event where he'd been a guest? If that was the case, the party lay in the distant past.

Holly said, "You should tell Tom to get out his service revolver. Just in case."

"Holly," I demanded, "who *was* that guy?" Even florists, I thought, send sterner-looking individuals.

"See if he's gone," she commanded.

I scanned the driveway. The man had turned his back on Marla's house and was slowly, carefully, making his way toward the street.

"Crisis over," I said, my tone reassuring. "Come see Marla's kitchen." I hugged Holly, but she remained stiff. I added, "Really, Holly, that guy looked as if he'd rather be anywhere than standing out in the driveway."

"You have to trust me. He's crazy."

"I don't know about crazy. He certainly didn't look *happy*." I tried to make my voice comforting. I picked up her bags as she scooted into Marla's living room and peered back down the driveway.

"Dammit!" she exclaimed. "He stopped walking. What a nightmare."

Pink with embarrassment, Drew hovered in the foyer. "Where is everybody?" he asked, his voice fretful.

I said, "Out back. Tom's there, too, Holly, so if you'd be more comfortable being near my big, strong, police-officer husband, you could follow your son."

"No, no, that's all right. Sorry," Holly said, as she lifted the glittering wrap off her shoulders, shook it out, then rearranged it over her shoulders, like wings. She smiled at us, and for a moment it was the old Holly, mischievous and jokey. "Did you hear about the guy selling chickens? He ended up with egg on his face." Drew rubbed his scalp, gave a sideways grin that revealed a dimple in one cheek, and opened his eyes wide. *Watch my mom being her usual self!* He shifted from foot to foot, impatient to be away. "All right, Drew," said Holly, "go ahead."

"Are you going to tell me who that man was?" I asked.

"I really don't want to talk about him," said Holly.

"I'm more worried about you," I replied softly. I didn't mention losing her house or transferring Drew, but I wanted to give her an opening. "Are you all right?"

"Yeah, I'm fine." She smiled again, but her tone was guarded. She came close to my left ear and whispered, "I need to talk to you. In private."

4

Holly and I walked quickly into Marla's kitchen. She greeted friends. Then she stepped out to the screened porch, where she scanned the group out back. I wondered if she was looking for the man from the driveway.

I slid up beside her. "Let's have some wine," I whispered. "Then we can talk."

"Okay." Her velvety-blue eyes darted right and left. She said under her breath, "I'm in a relationship mess."

"With that guy out front?"

"Not him, not . . ." She seemed about to add, *anymore,* but changed her mind. "That guy's just a nutty manipulator who's trying to get money out of me."

"A nutty manipulator?" I repeated, trying to think of a place in Marla's new house where we could have a confidential conversation. At the same time, I wondered if I could hand over the timing of the oven to someone reliable. Ever eager to glean gossip, Marla spotted us and hurried out to the porch.

To Holly she said, "Does this have to do with George?"

"God, no," said Holly.

"Bull," said Marla.

"I wish George were dead," Holly said.

"I can't wait to hear *this*," Marla murmured.

Ignoring curious glances from the folks in the backyard, Holly put her strong hands around Marla's and my upper arms and pulled us close.

"Why do you wish George were dead?" Marla asked, sotto voce.

"Did you hear the one about the farmer who slapped a mosquito off his donkey?" Holly replied. "The bug was a pain in the ass."

I thought, *Not again.*

"Don't say another word," Marla warned, as she turned back to the kitchen. "I've got a good Cabernet in the kitchen. And no more jokes. I want the whole story."

While Marla poured us glasses of wine, I wondered where, in fact, George Ingleby was. Had Holly seen him, hence the whisper? All the guests seemed to have arrived, and yet I had seen neither George nor Lena.

As Holly checked out the people standing around the pool as well as splashing in it, I reflected that I did not like or dislike Dr. George Ingleby. Years ago, he'd been a legend in his own mind, never less than an hour late for any appointment, intent on impatiently interrupting patients as they related their tales of woe. He'd marched importantly down every hospital corridor he'd ever found himself in. But after he'd stumbled badly in the relationship with Holly, it was my guess that he'd gone into therapy. George seemed to be living proof of another of Holly's favorite riddles, an oldie but goody: *How many psychologists does it take to change a lightbulb? One, but the lightbulb has to be willing to change.*

George had actually started showing himself to be a good dad to Drew. He may not have taken his son to church, but he came to every fencing meet this spring. He even attended some of the practices. He must have reworked his schedule so he could be present at CBHS parent-teacher conferences, with Holly sitting stiffly on Drew's other side. At these events, George did not smile at me, or even acknowledge that he knew who I was. But so what? Okay, he hadn't been a good husband to Holly. But I didn't think that any of us, especially Drew, would be better off if George were no longer alive. This I kept to myself.

"Actually, you know what, Holly?" Marla said, after she returned and we toasted with our plastic cups. "Ex-husbands don't provide any more fireworks once they're dead. Sort of deprives us of fun."

"Deprives us of fun?" I asked, disbelieving. Father Pete was out back with the other parents; Holly had invited him. But if our good priest heard us rejoicing over the death of a former parishioner, no matter how dissolute that churchgoer had been, he would not be happy.

Marla shrugged. "Not having an ex to complain about is sort of a loss."

"Like you know what I'm talking about," Holly said drily.

"Not at the moment," Marla replied smoothly. "But I'm hoping you'll tell me."

Holly did a careful survey of Marla's backyard. Her eyes seemed to catch on someone, or something, because her face turned tense. "Oh, God," she said. "What the hell is he doing here?"

"He who?" I asked. But Holly became suddenly quiet.

I followed her gaze. There was a group of about twenty adults beside the kids. Among them stood Dr. Warren Broome, his head above the rest. Patsie Boatfield had her arm protectively twined through his.

"Wait," I said. "I knew Patsie Boatfield was bringing her new husband. Did she marry Warren Broome?"

"You really don't keep up, do you?" said Marla.

Patsie was a member of St. Luke's. "They didn't get married at the *church*," I said, as if this excused my ignorance.

"I'm pretty sure Father Pete refused to do the service," Marla countered.

I groaned. Poor Patsie. Or at least, that was the way I saw it. Warren Broome. Oh, God.

He was a Denver psychiatrist who'd become infamous a couple of years before. The reason: he'd slept with at least one of his female patients. That patient had reported him, and claimed there were other victims. She'd gone to the papers, even asked for help from the public in identifying these other women. But no one else had come forward. Broome had been suspended for six months, as I recalled . . . and then he'd gone off my radar, which was not nearly as keen as Marla's.

At the moment, Broome was staring at Holly. He was quite tall, and, in addition to his sexual misadventures, was a reputed ace on the tennis court. He had the kind of straight, ash-blond hair most women would kill for. Beside him, Patsie chatted amiably to the gaggle of guests. Warren, his thin-lipped mouth open, seemed to be ignoring her. If anything, as he stared up at Holly, he resembled a drooling kid who was pressing his face against the candy-store window.

"Focus, Holly," Marla ordered. "You're in a relationship mess, you're dealing with a manipulator, and you wish ill to your ex. And besides all that, you're going to explain to us, your *friends,* what your financial situation is. Goldy wants to know why you're in a rental, and we both need to find out the reason you transferred Drew from EPP to CBHS. I have money and Goldy is good with advice. So spill it."

Just at that moment, though, we were distracted by Tom announcing loudly that the volleyball net was ready for use. The kids burst upward like exploding confetti. They called to each other, tossed around the volleyball, and picked teams. A few of the kids— including Arch, I noted—moved to sign Bob's clipboard. Bob appeared crestfallen that he'd recruited so few volunteers. Ophelia had retreated to the shade of one of Marla's trees, where she sat on the ground, reading a book. Reading? It didn't seem like the most logical activity for a young woman to do at a birthday party, especially with her handsome fiancé just a few feet away. A squiggle of worry wormed its way into my brain: How would she act on Monday night? Sullen? Shy? Or studious?

"Oh, God, he's inside!" Holly said as her gaze traveled back to Marla's kitchen. The man from the driveway was hovering over the stove. With his sandy-haired fringe, he resembled a monk attending to a pan on one of the burners. "You have to get Tom to get rid that guy," she begged. "He's nuts, I'm telling you."

Marla's forehead knotted in puzzlement. "What's he *doing*?"

"Goldy!" Holly said sharply. Below in the yard, a bunch of kids looked up to see what was going on. "Do something. Get Tom."

"I'm here," said Tom. His voice was low but authoritative. When had he arrived at my side? I shivered. Had he been on his way up here, and heard Holly when she'd yelled about the balding man being inside? He said, "What's the problem?"

"There's an uninvited man by the stove—" I began.

"Oh, no!" Holly cried, pointing into the kitchen. "Now George and Lena are here, too." She gripped Tom's forearm. "You have to get rid of that balding guy in the kitchen. The one who looks out of place? He's wearing a shirt with long sleeves. And I don't know how in *the hell* my ex-husband, and his bitch wife, Lena, came to be here."

"Didn't you invite them?" I asked, bewildered. "It's Drew's birthday! He's your son's father, Holly."

Holly turned her face away, as if she couldn't hear me.

Marla said, "Oh, for heaven's sake, Holly," echoing my tone. "Goldy's right. You should have invited George."

Holly wailed, "Everything's falling apart."

"One thing at a time," said Tom. "Ladies, please dial it down several notches." He hustled into the kitchen, took the balding man by one elbow and George Ingleby by the other. Despite being well built, the balding man appeared to melt. But Dr. George Ingleby, his coarse black hair standing on end, put up a fuss. And once again, George reminded me of those old photos of Stalin: unyielding stance, upraised chin, proud demeanor. He even had a thick mustache. George strained against Tom's superior strength and raised his voice. Unfortunately, there were no closed windows between the kitchen and the porch.

"I should have been invited to this party!" George Ingleby hollered. "I'm his father. How dare your wife exclude me?"

"Out, out," Tom was saying.

"*Damned spot,*" Marla added gleefully, happy to have at least some ex-husband drama. Holly crossed her arms and ignored both of us.

"We're walking to the front door," Tom went on, wrenching George's arm and pulling the tall, balding stranger along as well. "We don't want a scene, do we?" Tom's cold tone scared even me. "In fact," he concluded, "we want no excitement here at all."

Then Tom pulled the stranger, who had not spoken a word, and George, who looked as if he worked out as much as his ex-wife did, toward the front of Marla's house. No matter what those guys' routines at the gym were, neither one of them was a match for my husband's strength. For the first time, I noticed Lena Ingleby, who was as short and curvy as Holly was tall and slender. A dark nest of curls surrounded her head and framed her pretty, perfectly made-up face, which featured a tiny chin and even more tiny turned-up nose. She didn't dare touch Tom, but she did squeal in protest.

"Holly had no right to exclude us!" she cried. "She's already sending Drew to Alaska, to see her sister. George was manipulated into giving his consent, but really . . ." Her voice trailed off.

"Yeah, like you care about Drew," Holly said under her breath.

"But *why* didn't you invite George to this party?" I asked, as gently as I could. We had divided the invitation duties in half; she was supposed to invite Drew's people, while I did Arch's. About twenty folks had replied to me; the rest had answered Holly, which was how we'd come up with forty-odd guests, many of whom now stood in Marla's kitchen looking at each other, openmouthed. Their expressions seemed to be asking: *How often do you witness adults acting like spoiled kids, at a kids' birthday party?*

"Oh, George is such a wuss," Holly said. "How could I enjoy myself if he was here?"

"Darling," said Marla, "it's not *your* party."

Holly shrugged. Meanwhile, someone had finally told Drew what was going on. He raced past us, calling to his father.

"Oh, *don't*, Drew," Holly cried.

Drew stopped long enough to give his mother a slit-eyed look. "You should have invited him."

"God," said Holly, tossing her hair over her shoulders. "Everybody always blames me when things go wrong."

When Tom, the stranger, George, and Lena had disappeared, the timer went off. I called to the parents, who remained rooted in place, directionless. "Everyone who has a dish heating, now is the time to check it. Dinner's in ten minutes."

And that, finally, was how we got things going. The parents began talking to each other and pulling their casserole dishes from Marla's ovens. Arch, who was in charge of leading the kids to the buffet table, knew his cue. Drew, his body slumped in defeat, slouched along behind him. All the rest of the guests—kids and parents alike—offered to get drinks, serving spoons, or whatever was needed. Marla asked that they make sure no one went outside with a china dish or glass bottle. We also needed more plastic cups lined up on her kitchen island. Soon everyone was busy with duties.

Considering the early fireworks, the party went off . . . well, okay, I suppose. When Tom reentered Marla's dining room, I cocked an eyebrow at him. He shook his head once, indicating that I'd hear later what had happened. Meanwhile, the dining room table was crowded with offerings. A pool of steaming cheese floated atop a tamale pie, while an inviting scent wafted from the enchiladas. A large tossed salad tantalized with its sweet cherry tomatoes and crunchy chips. But it was Julian's gorgeous colorful chile relleno tortas that had most of the guests oohing and aahing.

At Marla's insistence, I went through the line with the other parents. Julian, meanwhile, moved quickly and purposefully around the buffet and the guests' tables. He filled serving dishes, removed empty bowls, and asked if people needed something else to drink. Really, I wondered, how had I managed the past few years without him?

Drew seemed to recover from his father's unexpected appearance, followed by his swift disappearance. He and Arch blew out all the candles on the sheet cake. Julian and I scooped out *dulce de leche* ice cream until my arm ached. Julian's swimming-strengthened arms never appeared to be bothered by anything.

Even Holly, who had seemed unsettled by the appearances of the uninvited stranger, then George and Lena, began to laugh and enjoy herself. To be honest, I would have been upset, too, if my ex-husband had made a scene and I were being stalked by a "nutty manipulator." I did notice that Holly conscientiously gave Warren Broome a wide berth, even walked away when he leaned down to talk to her. I made a mental note to ask Marla about that. Could *he* be the one with whom she was having the relationship mess? For Patsie Boatfield's sake, I certainly hoped not.

Before I could stop him, Bob Rushwood, holding one of the red Pails for Trails, made the rounds of the parents, asking for donations. He'd given one to Ophelia, who stood resolutely beside Marla's fireplace. Well, I didn't blame her for refusing to be so rude. Several of the parents, including Holly, crossed the room to avoid being hit up for cash. I started across the room toward Bob, to ask him to stop trying to raise money at a birthday party for someone else. But Marla beat me to it, snatching the pail from him and taking the one Ophelia gladly handed her.

Holly giggled with friends and said *no thanks* to cake topped with ice cream. Then I realized I hadn't seen her eat any dinner. Maybe this was how she kept her svelte figure. When the boys tore into their last gifts, twin boxed sets of masculine soap and cologne, I noticed Holly spoon up a minuscule amount of Mexican food. Well, at least she wouldn't go home hungry. I still hadn't heard what the source of her financial problems was, or the nature of the relationship mess.

Summer nights in the mountains can be quite cool. Perhaps it was the chilling of the air that made the party break up early. Arch put on a mask of happiness, but I knew he was disappointed that it hadn't been more fun. Bob and Ophelia's presentation and panhandling, the bizarre appearance of the balding stranger, and the arrival of George and Lena had made the party develop a layer of unease. Even I had been unable to relax completely.

Holly and Drew were the first to leave. Holly looked a little green around the gills, but I put it down to the effort she'd had to put into avoiding the manipulator, George and Lena, Bob and Ophelia, and finally, Warren Broome.

"Goldy," she said, "I'm sorry. Maybe I should have invited George and Lena. I just . . . Let's . . . We'll get together soon, and talk."

"Sure," I said. I hugged her. She clung to me, just like in the old days. Then she turned away.

Sometimes parties go well, sometimes they don't, I reminded myself, as I helped people into their jackets. And then I and everyone at the party, everyone who lived on or near Marla's street, heard Drew screaming.

5

"Mom!" Drew yelled. "Mom, what's wrong? Wake up! Somebody help me! Mom!"

A human wave erupted down the driveway. Some of us trotted, some walked. The kids, worried about Drew, raced. But everyone suddenly stopped by Marla's mailbox. It was there that Julian, who'd arrived first, put out his arms. He ordered everyone to stay where they were, then called for Tom.

When I saw Holly sprawled on the street, I stopped breathing. I was close enough to know something was very wrong. The logical part of my brain was asking, *What?* But my emotions were way ahead of that, and I found myself gasping for breath.

Drew was screaming, "Mom! What's wrong? *Mom! Talk to me!*"

My knees buckled and I pitched forward. Tom grabbed me.

"Miss G.," he said softly. "Sit down. Don't move." He called to one of the parents to stay beside me. I barely registered Patsie Boatfield putting her arms around my shoulders.

Bob Rushwood was hollering something about knowing CPR. Tom called for him to help, and they dashed past us, as did Marla. I was having trouble getting oxygen into my lungs. Someone handed Patsie a paper lunch bag, and she ordered me to breathe into it.

I did so, then shakily stood. "I have to be with Holly," my voice squeakily announced.

"I'm coming with you," Patsie said. She felt my wrist, and I finally looked at her. She had curly red hair that she had allowed to grow into a long, attractive mop. Her clear blue eyes matched the sleeveless dress she wore. "Your pulse is thready," she added. "Goldy? Do you remember I'm a nurse?"

"Yes," I mumbled, mentally adding, *I think so.*

Patsie held me up until we got to the bottom of the driveway, where Julian let us through. Drew was kneeling next to his mother's prone body. Marla sat on the curb, stunned. Tom's presence gave me a chill of relief. Tears spilled down my cheeks. Bob Rushwood was performing CPR on Holly. *This isn't happening,* my logical mind said.

Tom took Drew's cell phone from him and began speaking to someone I assumed was the emergency operator. Drew, his hands empty, leaned in close to his mother and sobbed.

"Patsie, help me," I finally said. I choked up and couldn't speak for a moment. "We have to get Drew away from this. Holly needs air."

"I'll do it," she said authoritatively. "You go be with Marla."

This I did. Marla and I sat next to each other, shivering.

Despite Patsie's pleas, Drew would not move. Big-boned and strong, he barely registered Patsie, who finally gently pulled on his forearm. He wouldn't budge, even shoved her away with such force she almost toppled over. She righted herself, pressed her lips together, and came over next to Marla and me on the curb.

Arch, whom Julian had allowed through, tugged my sleeve. "What happened?" he said. "Is Drew's mom okay?"

"I don't know," I told him. We were about ten feet away from where Bob, his dreads incongruously hanging over Holly's shoulders, was still working on her.

Patsie spoke again, the voice of authority. "Arch? You need to help Julian keep everyone away from this. Tom and Bob have to work on Holly. The ambulance will be here soon."

"Father Pete," I said, my voice disembodied. "He's here. Let him through, if you can."

"Sure, I'll go get him," Arch said. "But . . . what happened to Drew's mom? Did she lose her balance on the driveway?"

When I didn't reply, Patsie shook her head grimly. "Please go get the priest, Arch. He needs to be with Drew."

I stood and motioned for Arch to follow me. The parents and kids were rubbernecking to see what was going on. "Something else?" Patsie called after us. "Make sure no one films this with a cell phone."

But Julian was already telling the guests to put their phones away *now*, or he would confiscate them. Arch walked to the driveway and added, "Can somebody please send Father Pete over to where Drew is?"

When I turned back, Drew had finally moved to the curb. He sat huddled next to Marla and Patsie. Patsie had a hand on his shoulder and was talking in a low tone. Paying her no heed, he was staring openmouthed at his mother. When he stood, he immediately leaned against a pine tree whose roots snarled the ground.

When he teetered, Patsie snagged him, then steered him away.

"Everybody better sit a little ways off so the ambo can get through." She corralled us to a small spew of stones. When I sat down, the gravel bit through my slacks. Drew watched Bob working expertly on Holly. I knew CPR, but I don't know if I could have been that good at it. I wondered vaguely if anyone had collapsed on the treadmill at Aspen Meadow Country Club, and Bob had had to bring the would-be athlete back to life.

Tom was holding Holly's wrist while he barked commands into the cell phone. Holly still had not moved on her own. Like everybody else, I wanted to ask Drew what, exactly, had happened. Was it possible Holly had lost her balance, fallen on the driveway, and been knocked unconscious?

Sirens sounded from far away. This sent Drew into a fresh torrent of sobs. "God! Oh, God!"

Father Pete, his olive skin glistening with sweat, trundled over and lowered himself to the gravel beside us. He shook perspiration off his black curls and put one of his large arms around Drew.

"We were walking," Drew explained, without any of us asking. "She usually goes faster than me. But she didn't this time. She was going so slowly that I asked her what was wrong. She said she was just so tired all of a sudden—" He dissolved in tears again, then wrenched himself away from us and lunged toward his mother. "Oh, what is the matter with her?"

"Come here." Father Pete caught the back of Drew's jeans. Despite being overweight, Father Pete, a former prizefighter, was still nimble. "Drew? Stay with me. Julian!" he called. "Please walk over to us."

Julian sternly ordered the parents to stay put, then traversed the short distance to us.

"Sit down next to Drew, please," Father Pete commanded. Julian did so, but his face, so animated when he'd talked about cooking for Holly, was completely drained of color and expression.

I swallowed my panic and swiveled my head in all directions.

Marla's neighbors' houses were set far back from the road, not chockablock the way they were on our street. Still, there had been kids who'd been playing out front when I set up. Had anyone besides Drew seen what had happened to Holly? Squinting, I could make out a couple of neighbors standing in their doorways, curious about the ruckus. But no one was approaching us, as they would, or at least as I hoped they would, if they'd witnessed something Tom should know about.

A sudden wind lashed the aspens and ponderosa pines lining Marla's driveway. The party guests, who'd edged nearer despite Julian's warnings, talked in hushed tones. The sirens became louder. Drew suddenly grabbed Father Pete's shirt.

"Father Pete! She trusts you. She trusts you!" he cried. "If she's dying, give her the last rites. You know, extreme unction. Or whatever it's called. Quickly! I know she'd want you . . . hurry!"

Without questioning this, Father Pete got to his feet. He asked Drew to accompany him. The two of them quickstepped over to where Bob Rushwood was still working on Holly. Bob's expression when he looked up at the priest was stricken. Tom, Bob, and Father Pete exchanged a few low words. Tom pressed his lips together and looked stoic as he pulled Bob up and away.

The ambulance careened onto Marla's street. Father Pete motioned for Drew to join him, and they crouched next to Holly. Father Pete said words over Holly, made the sign of the cross on her forehead, and said more words. She still did not move.

The paramedics jumped from the ambo and moved everyone away from Holly. They put up screens to shield the scene from inquisitive eyes. After a few minutes, one of them came out and confirmed what Tom, Bob, Father Pete, Marla, Julian, and I already knew, although I couldn't face it. None of us could.

Holly was dead.

Tom walked over, exhaled, and asked if I was all right. I said no, not really. His face creased with concern as he murmured that the ambulance was going to leave, but he needed to wait for the coroner's van. He turned to Marla and told her to ask the guests to go home. When Marla appeared dumbfounded, he asked Patsie to do it. Also, Tom said, he didn't want Drew to be around when the coroner's van arrived. So . . . a patrol car was on its way. If I felt up to it, could I drive into town with Drew, wait for someone from the sheriff's department, then take Drew back to Holly's house? Tom added that Father Pete and Julian could come with us. Father Pete had already told Tom he knew how to get to Holly's rental. I looked quizzically at our priest. How did he know how to get to Holly's house, when I had no idea?

"Goldy?" Tom asked, his voice still low. "Do you feel okay?"

"I suppose."

"Any stomach upset?" When I shook my head, he said, "How about the other guests? Anybody feeling sick? I'm just trying to cover the bases here."

"No, Tom. Except for this, this . . . I'm all right." I turned back to the driveway, where Patsie was dispersing the glut of people. "Nobody has reported anything."

Tom said, "All right, then. I have to call social services."

"Why?"

"Drew is a minor," he explained. "He has to be in foster care until we know what's what."

"What are you *talking* about?"

Tom's voice was barely above a murmur. "Keep it down, all right? After that fight between George and Holly, I can't let Drew go to George's house. We both know there was no love lost between Edith and Holly. Probably Lena hated Holly, too, so it's not a good environment for the kid. I don't know what's going on here. Neither do you. But unless Holly was under the care of a doctor, there has to be an autopsy." I closed my eyes and fought the urge to be sick. Tom said, "Miss G.? You with me?"

I opened my eyes and nodded. "Yes."

"Drew is a minor, so what I'm *talking* about is the *law*. I've already asked Drew if he has relatives in the area, even in the state, besides his father. He does not. So, listen. He has to be with an approved foster family for the time being. He'll be okay. We have families who help when kids' parents die suddenly. I can give the deputy directions as to where Drew should be taken after he's ready to go. But . . . can you take him home to pack? I thought it would be better if he had some people around who know him, instead of just a department deputy."

I swallowed. "I can do it."

Tom still kept his voice very low. "Somebody said something about Drew taking off for Alaska?"

I nodded. "Lena did. But I'm sure he won't . . . I don't know when—" I choked up again, and worked to get control of myself. "Do you know what, what"—I couldn't bring myself to say *what killed Holly*—"what happened?"

Tom said, "No, I don't." He took a call on his cell, then said, "The cop will meet you outside the Grizzly." He pressed his lips together, then asked, "What did Drew say Holly said? Right before she collapsed, how did she act?"

"He didn't elaborate," I said, "but apparently Holly said she was suddenly very tired—and then she fell."

"Overwhelming fatigue. For a woman, that's classic for a heart attack," Tom said. "We'll know more later. Goldy? Are you all right?" I must have looked awful, and there was a sudden roaring in my ears. But I nodded. Tom made a quick call on his cell, disconnected, then turned to me. "Do you suppose Julian will be able to help Drew get ready?"

"Of course," I whispered. I would have to summon strength. If something had happened to me, Holly would be here, bustling around energetically, offering to take care of Arch.

Tom went on, "I'll ask him about this trip to Alaska, when he's supposed to go. If it's soon, he should go. It'll be a few days before we know anything." He seemed to think of something, then reached into his pocket and gave me a set of keys. "These go to Holly's car. She had them in her hand when she collapsed. She also had a small purse, but I'm taking that down to the sheriff's department."

"What about her cell phone?"

He shook his head. "We don't have it. I just have a prepaid cell of Drew's. He used it to call emergency services. Goldy, please tell me if you are all right to do this."

"Yes," I said, trying to sound stronger than I felt. "I'm okay."

The crowd parted as Tom walked quickly to Father Pete and Drew. The three of them made their way back up Marla's driveway. I motioned for Julian to accompany me. Arch hurried over.

"Mom. Where are you all going?"

"To Drew's house, so he can pack. He . . . has to . . . well, he has to stay someplace safe. Do you know when this Alaska trip is?"

"No, sorry. But, please. Let me come with you. I want to be there for Drew." His pale forehead, a pasty gray in the early evening light, furrowed. "Drew will want a friend with him. You know, somebody his own age."

I took a deep breath. "For sure. Thanks, hon."

When asked, Drew told Tom that he was due to leave the following evening for a fishing trip with Holly's sister and her husband, who lived in a remote part of Alaska. He seemed confused. Should he still go to Alaska? Shouldn't Holly's sister stay here in Aspen Meadow, to . . . make arrangements? No, Tom said. If Drew felt up to it, he should stick with his plan. It would be good for him to be with Holly's sister. Drew gave Tom the number of the sister. Yes, he was sure she would fly to Denver to get him. No, Tom reiterated that he would be staying somewhere safe until his aunt arrived. Drew nodded, then pressed his palms into his eyes.

I looked up and down Marla's street for Holly's vehicle. Marla had said Holly sold the Audis, but what had she bought instead? I finally got the bright idea to press the remote on her key ring. This led me to a dusty-black Honda Civic. I exhaled.

Arch, Julian, and I followed Father Pete, who used his own car to drive Drew. I'd told our priest about the cop needing to be with us, and he nodded sadly.

A prowler flashed its lights at us when we pulled up in front of the Grizzly Saloon, our local watering hole. Father Pete took the lead.

Arch and Julian conversed in low tones. I couldn't talk; I could barely even breathe. I kept seeing Holly's lovely face, her last words: *We'll get together soon, and talk . . .* My heart pounded, and I ordered myself to pay attention to my driving.

Relax, I told myself. *Relax. Think about something else. Put your attention on anything that will get your mind away from what just happened.*

Traffic stopped us in sight of the spillway below Aspen Meadow Lake. *Don't think about Holly,* my mind ordered, *put your attention elsewhere.* I blinked at the hills, thick with evergreens, that rose from the lake's man-made shores. The body of water itself had been formed when engineers constructed a dam separating Upper and Lower Cottonwood Creek. Above the falls, the engineers excavated a meadow. The flooded part became the lake. As a result, the town of Aspen Meadow benefited from a reliable water supply, and summer and winter recreation seekers, as well as tourists, enriched the town's businesses.

A bloop siren from the prowler reminded me I had failed to accelerate when the traffic had cleared. I stepped on the pedal to follow Father Pete.

"Mom?" Arch said. "Do you want Julian or me to drive?"

"No, no, I'm okay." Which I wasn't. I turned left, then made a quick right behind Father Pete, onto a narrow road.

I frowned. Where the engineers had had to blast the bottom of an actual mountain when they created the lake, they'd left a large cliff overlooking the water. As I followed Father Pete, I realized that was the hill we were driving up. The engineers had, perhaps intentionally, created a cove where, it was rumored, trout liked to hide.

Much-desired sites that truly command vistas of the lake are hard to come by. So I was surprised when we finally finished climbing the winding road to the top of the hill that looked out over the water. The long lake view was stunning. The architect who had designed Holly's rental had been fortunate to find a site with a rock outcropping that formed a thick precipice. Through a series of ingenious outdoor staircases, the architect had even afforded the homeowner a way of getting down to the path that circled the lake. Two dramatic wooden decks were cantilevered out over the water.

Just looking at those protruding structures made me dizzy, and I averted my eyes.

When Julian, Arch, and I got out of the van, Father Pete was holding on to Drew, right in the driveway.

Drew, his tall body leaning into Father Pete, was sobbing. The priest gave an almost imperceptible shake of his head.

The cop was a tall black policewoman named Sergeant Jones. She had a head of black ringlets that didn't seem to go with her being thick and muscular, which she certainly was. I was willing to bet she could take down any criminal, anytime. After she introduced herself to Julian, Arch, and me, she walked over to Father Pete and Drew to do the same. She took the keys I handed her, and she and Drew climbed up to Holly's front porch.

"Poor Drew," said Arch, his voice low. "I don't know how he's going to make it. He loved his mother so much. Oh, Mom," he said, and unexpectedly hugged me. And in that gesture, he seemed to say—or maybe it was my imagination—*I know that I can be difficult, but I would miss you so much . . .*

I clung to him a moment longer than necessary. When he pulled away, he was looking at the ground.

"It's okay, hon," I assured him. "Does . . . Drew get along with his dad?"

Arch replied in a low tone, "I suppose." When I waited, he elaborated. "Drew doesn't talk much about him. But I know you've seen how George comes to all the meets, so it's not like he's, you know, absent. Drew told me that Lena, George's new wife? She's always criticizing him. But his grandmother, his dad's mom, makes up for it by smothering him with love, which drives him just as crazy."

We arrived on the porch, which was cluttered with lawn furniture. Sergeant Jones was inspecting the front door. She pointed to a panel of buttons. "Was this installed with the house?"

"No," said Drew, his face blank. He stared at the panel, as if trying to remember the code, or even why we were there. "The architect went bankrupt building the place. No system. But we had a break-in a little over a week ago. Mom insisted the owner pay for a security system to be installed, even though the guy's already reduced the price, and the place is still for sale."

"You had a break-in," Sergeant Jones repeated, deadpan. Her large brown eyes regarded Drew. "Did you tell Investigator Schulz about that?"

Drew shook his head. "Nothing was taken, and only a file cabinet was wrecked. But Mom said she had antiques that were more valuable than a bunch of files. There's a panel for the outside, and one right inside the door." He rummaged through his wallet and handed Sergeant Jones a ragged piece of paper. Sergeant Jones painstakingly entered the exterior numbers—zero-nine-zero-four—and threw open the front door, then entered the second code—zero-four-one-five—inside.

"Everyone wait here," she ordered us curtly. She drew her weapon, which did not give me a good feeling.

"Wait a minute," said Drew. He pointed to a large rectangular cardboard box leaning in front of some chairs against the far wall of the porch. "Oh, jeez. That's one of my mother's collages, back from framing."

"Well," I began, when no one said anything, "what should we—"

"No, no, no, I don't know what to do with it!" cried Drew. "I don't know what to do with anything!"

I walked over to the box, which was the size of a dining room tabletop, and read the label. It had come that day, addressed to Holly.

Father Pete said mildly, "Not to worry. We'll put it in the living room, in case it rains." He still had one arm around Drew when Sergeant Jones returned and said the house was clear. Father Pete addressed his remarks to her. "Drew is still leaving for Alaska tomorrow. Investigator Schulz explained to Holly's sister that no arrangements could be made for a memorial service, or anything else, for at least a week. He gave her my number, and she called on our way over here. Drew does not want to stay with a foster family any more time than necessary. So the sister is getting the first flight out of Anchorage. Drew wants to be with his aunt and her husband, the way they planned." He gave the policewoman a significant look, so she would understand the emotional importance of following this course of action. "Meanwhile, Drew has to finish getting ready for his trip. We're going to sit in the kitchen for a couple of minutes first. Can someone manage the carton?"

"Yes," said Julian, who was blinking. He had that quirk, opening and closing his eyes quickly, whenever his attention had been derailed and he needed to get it back on track. He picked up the package and shuffled inside with it.

Drew, Sergeant Jones, and Father Pete settled in the kitchen, which caught the last of the light from the setting sun. Bits of their conversation floated out to us in the living room: *Were there relatives or other people to be notified? Did they have a pet to be cared for? Did Holly have end-of-life plans . . . ?*

Arch and I sat uneasily in the living room, which was very neat but was even more cluttered than the porch. In addition to all the furniture from Holly's former spacious home, there were numerous tables and shelves holding religious objects—small, ivory-colored sculpted Madonnas, mounted crystal crosses, tiny wooden statues of saints, ceramic lambs and fish, both symbols for Jesus, and lots of baby Jesuses themselves—plus other items I recognized from Holly's previous residence. We knew Father Pete would call us when we were needed. Julian laid the box against the front wall and mumbled something about asking Drew where Holly's studio was. He returned a moment later, shaking his head.

"Drew says his mother never worked at home, even before they rented this house. She always leased space down in Cherry Creek." Julian's handsome face contorted in puzzlement. "Does that make sense to you?"

I thought about Holly, about her financial problems, about a recent break-in at this rental, about haggling for a security system, about the price of real estate, any real estate, in that phenomenally expensive part of Denver: Cherry Creek.

I said, "None of this makes sense to me."

6

Julian stared in the direction of the kitchen, where the murmur of Father Pete, Drew, and Sergeant Jones's voices were indistinguishable. After a moment, he sat down beside the china cabinet, on the Bidjar rug covering Holly's living room floor. The rug, which I remembered Holly had inherited from her grandmother, was a gorgeously intricate maroon, navy, and cream design. She'd also inherited the furniture: the cherry end tables and butler's tray, now covered with statuary, plus a china cabinet, whose shelves displayed rows of Holly's plates. I recognized a pattern we'd eaten off of once: "some of Granny's Haviland," Holly had airily called the dishes, with their sprays of tiny pink flowers on a white background. Interspersed with those plates were others with a religious, specifically a

Roman Catholic, theme: an angel on one, a lamb and fish on others. I couldn't bear to look at them, and turned away.

The room was also crowded with pairs of wing-back chairs and two love seats, all upholstered in a creamy satin to complement the jewel tones in the rug. The pale beige walls held the oil paintings from her old living room, plus one of her portrait-collages. The brass-and-crystal table lamps looked familiar, as did a square table pushed into one corner. All of this had worked well in the large living room of Holly's big place in Aspen Meadow Country Club. Here, it resembled a jumble sale.

Why, it occurred to me out of nowhere, would a thief want your file cabinet, but not Granny's Haviland or your precious Oriental rug?

I swallowed and sat in one of the chairs. Holly was never going to be back here. She would never sweep in with the energy of a tornado, she would never tell me a joke and fling her blond hair over her shoulders. She would never look with concern, pride, or exasperation at Drew. The realization hit me hard.

Julian got up from the rug and sat gingerly on one of the love seats. As he scanned the room, it seemed his thinking was going along the same lines as mine. I blinked at the Italian oil paintings of bucolic scenes that hung on three of the walls. They were probably copies, but Holly would never . . .

Pull yourself together, I ordered myself.

In the corner of the room stood that square mahogany table. I noted that it had carved legs. Two dining room chairs had been drawn up to it.

"Boss," said Julian, "you don't look too good."

Breathe, my inner voice commanded. *Get up and move.*

With effort, I hauled myself up and walked over to the table. A handmade wooden jigsaw puzzle lay on top, with most of the border done. It looked like one of the puzzles Holly had made for the Montessori school.

The pieces to this one lay about higgledy-piggledy. Had Drew and Holly started on it—it was a colorful map—and just not finished? That would explain why there was no TV in evidence. But Drew and Holly had only gotten so far. This detail of family life, forever unfinished, made my heart lurch.

Arch said he was going upstairs to help Drew pack. I looked over at Julian, who had his lips pressed together and was still glancing nervously around the room. Finally, he said, "If she was having money issues, why not sell some of this stuff? Why did the burglar not take these things?"

"I don't know."

My gaze fastened on the living room's fourth wall, the one that contained the portrait-collage. Like all of her works, this one contained pieces from the person's life—bits of clothing, mementos, photographs—as well as painted images applied here and there. I walked away from the puzzle table and stepped up close to my old friend's work. The collage was not framed, but hung inside a Plexiglas box. I almost gasped when I realized the subject was Drew, from when he was little.

There were six different squares inside the Plexiglas. They contained two photographs, one of Drew as an infant and one from the time when I remembered him best, as the tyke who loved Hot Wheels. Holly had put one of the miniature cars into a square. Another held a swatch of the denim jacket he was wearing in a birthday-party photo as he proudly held up an empty goldfish bowl that he had just unwrapped. There was also a tiny stuffed gray kangaroo, and a gold-and-blue badge from Scouts. Holly had painted fanciful shapes—blue rams, more angels, and pairs of goldfish—in each of these colors around the squares, pulling them into an aesthetic whole. Tears bit the back of my eyes.

I fumbled in my pants for a tissue. The piece looked vaguely familiar. Had I seen it before? I couldn't remember. Probably I had, when I'd visited Holly's country-club house, after she'd started making the collages. I blew my nose and again ordered myself to get my act together.

Julian came over to stand next to me. "Are you all right?"

"Not at the moment. But I'm going to be. We have to help Drew."

Julian leaned in close to the collage. He whispered, "This is Drew, isn't it?"

"Yes."

I glanced at Drew, who was looking disconsolate as he stood next to Sergeant Jones. He was emptying his pockets. I caught a bit of what he was saying, something about needing to wash his shorts before he could finish packing. Arch called from upstairs, asking if Drew was taking fishing gear to Alaska.

While Drew and Sergeant Jones ascended the stairs to join Arch, Father Pete lumbered back toward Julian and me. At the sight of him, I reminded myself, *You're here to help. Remember?*

What could I do? Well, there was the box with the framed collage. What about asking Father Pete if it was ethically okay to open it? What if it did indeed contain a collage that someone was expecting to be delivered? Wouldn't that help with the money Drew was sure to need?

Father Pete said, "Drew's aunt got a flight. She has a layover in Spokane, but that shouldn't be too bad. Drew has his ticket. He's supposed to stay at his aunt and uncle's cabin for a week. George already gave his notarized consent. Drew is still torn. I told him he should go, that it was the normal thing he would have done, and that being with Holly's sister would bring him comfort. I didn't say that it'd be better than moping around here, imagining an autopsy on his beloved mother." Father Pete's wide brow wrinkled. "Drew most definitely does *not* want to stay with George, Lena, and Edith. The mother from the foster family is on her way here." He fingered a piece of paper. "Drew gave me a list of people to call. The only immediate problem is that Holly was supposed to give Drew cash for the Alaska trip, and she hadn't done that yet. Drew doesn't know Holly's ID number for the ATM. He's a minor, and doesn't have power of attorney, so he can't get a new one. He's adamant about not asking George for cash." Father Pete shook his head. "He won't tell me what the financial bad blood is between his mother and father. He's so vulnerable at this point, I'm not going to press it."

"I will—" Julian began, but Father Pete stopped him by holding up his hand, which resembled a bear's paw.

"Back in the old days," Father Pete went on, almost apologetically, "I could have given, or at least loaned, Drew money from my discretionary fund. But with so many priests using their discretionary funds to send themselves to Europe or to buy new Volvos, now the government says all funds in those accounts have to go to the genuinely, verifiably poor. I'm pretty sure Drew and Holly are not actually poverty-stricken, even if they were going through a bad patch. I know *George* doesn't have financial issues—"

"I'll give Drew money," Julian piped up.

"So will Tom and I," I said. "How much are we talking about?"

"Let me do it!" Julian said, his grief momentarily flashing as anger. Julian had inherited money that he seemed hardly ever to use, except when his friends needed to be bailed out of a fix. And the IRS wasn't asking questions. "How much does he need?"

"About a thousand," Father Pete said, his tone still remorseful.

"No sweat," said Julian.

I said, "Why don't I give him five hundred, and you can do the other five?"

Julian rubbed his now-scruffy chin. "I'll tell you why not. It takes forever to settle an estate these days, what with filing a will, going through probate, you name it. So a year or more could pass before you're paid back. And with Arch going off to college next year—"

"Rather than you two arguing over who gets to be more charitable," Father Pete interrupted, "I'm making an executive decision that Julian will give him the money."

"Good," said Julian. "I have my checkbook right here." He drew a checkbook and pen out of one of his deep pockets and began writing furiously.

Father Pete waited until Julian had ripped the check out and handed it to him. Then our priest said, too casually, "Julian, why don't you go upstairs with the boys and the sergeant, and help Drew pack? He said all he's done is get the suitcase down. He also needs to get his phone and charger, finish his laundry, find his hiking boots, and pull together whatever else you, he, and Arch think he'll need for a fishing trip in Alaska. Goldy and I can go out to the kitchen to discuss arrangements for Holly."

I shook my head vigorously. I did *not* want to talk about arrangements for Holly.

"What about this box?" I asked. "Drew said it was a collage for one of Holly's clients." I glanced over at the carton. From not far away, the washing machine began to chug. When someone dies, survivors have to deal with the minutiae left behind by the deceased: with their children's laundry, with their paperwork, with planning a liturgy. Sometimes these tasks can be comforting. Other times, they send survivors like yours truly into a state of bewilderment. Beside me, Julian, too, seemed frozen.

I'd become fixated on the box simply because it seemed like something we could *figure out.* If Drew was going to be gone for a week, shouldn't we open it to see who was supposed to get it?

"I'll ask Drew about it," I said.

"Let Julian do that, Goldy," Father Pete said gently. "Please, come out to the kitchen with me. You could help by cleaning out Holly's refrigerator. If no one is going to be here for a week, food shouldn't be left to spoil. Then you and I can talk about pulling together a memorial service, for when Drew gets back."

"Okay," I said, feeling unsure. But Father Pete was right. I needed to do something with my hands.

"First?" said Father Pete, once he was settled in a kitchen chair. "Could you see if Holly has some of the bourbon I had the last time I was here? It's in the pantry." He took a deep breath. "Just because I see death often doesn't mean I'm used to it. Strokes, heart attacks, cancer in the young, it happens more than you'd think. Plus, Holly was so kind, so funny . . ."

He didn't need to finish the thought. I located a small bottle of Kentucky's signature liquor in Holly's pantry and poured Father Pete what he asked for: an inch of bourbon with no ice, no water, and for heaven's sake, he added, no ginger ale. I poured myself a tiny bit of the golden liquid and without thinking slugged it down. It hit my brain like fire.

While Father Pete sipped, I opened Holly's refrigerator. It contained very little: only two opened packages of supermarket cheese; one cheddar, one Swiss, both well wrapped in plastic. A quart of milk felt half empty, ditto a pint of supermarket-brand cottage cheese. The crisper held only a quarter of a head of iceberg lettuce. I guess when you lose your house, you also lose the Brie, the Gruyère, the asparagus, the strawberries, and the fresh fish you always swore by.

Father Pete finished his whiskey and asked me to give him a refill. I'd never seen him have more than a single drink over the course of an entire evening. As he started on his second, he asked if I knew what hymns Holly liked.

"Hymns?" I chucked the cheeses into the trash. "I don't have a clue."

Father Pete fretted. "This is why people should plan. It's good we're having that dinner. The music director will be making a presentation."

I took a deep breath. I couldn't think that far ahead.

I poured the milk down the drain and put all the rest of the refrigerator contents in a large plastic bag that I tied shut and took out to the garage. There, I unfastened the chains on a wheeled bear-proof trash can. With all the bears raiding our neighborhoods, the Denver outfit retrofitting trash containers with hooks and chains must be making a mint. I unfastened the clips and dropped the bag into the half-full can, then dragged the thing to the curb.

Without forethought, I sat down on the pavement. I felt Holly's passing now like the unexpected ocean waves that used to knock me down when I was a kid. Instead of a mouthful of grit, I felt dizzy. Maybe I shouldn't have had the bourbon. Maybe I should have had some more. I ordered myself to get up and go back into the house.

Back in the kitchen, Father Pete was refilling his glass. When he saw me, his large face reddened. He began to talk about the readings for the Burial of the Dead, Rites I and II. Was this the way he dealt with his own grief? I wondered.

I was fidgety and simply could not listen. I opened the freezer. It held only frozen spinach, peas, and beans, all supermarket brand, and frozen chicken thighs that had been divided into freezer bags. From the quantities, I guessed Holly had bought everything in there on sale.

Questions about Holly's financial situation niggled at the edges of my brain. Marla hadn't known anything apart from the fact that Holly had lost her house in the country club. Our friend hadn't had time to share what was going on. I saw her pretty face again, heard her earnest words: *We'll get together soon, and talk . . .*

Did Drew know what was going on with Holly's finances? Or had he just picked up on the animosity between his parents, and didn't want to agitate George or Lena? I doubted that he knew the particulars. I'd learned from experience that the last thing you wanted to trouble a child of divorce with were discussions of your financial problems.

From behind me, it sounded as if Father Pete was talking to himself. He concluded, resignedly, that he supposed he should hold off on setting a date for the memorial service until after Drew returned. No matter what they initially thought the cause and manner of death was, there was that autopsy to contend with. Those always held things up.

I picked up the bottle of bourbon, as much to get it away from Father Pete as anything else. I said, "Why don't we go out on the deck, where Drew won't be able to hear us?"

"Good idea. I'll just go up to his room to tell them we'll be outside."

After he left, I poured myself a half inch of bourbon in a plastic cup. It occurred to me that Drew might need me to do errands for him. But if I went up and asked, Arch might glare at me for hovering or intruding. So I glanced at the detritus that Drew had dumped from the shorts he'd needed to wash. It contained a cell phone. Hadn't Father Pete said Drew needed to take his phone and charger to Alaska? And hadn't Tom told me that Drew had called 911 from a disposable, which deputies had taken down to the department?

I picked up the phone. On the back was a piece of adhesive tape where Holly had penned *Mom's*. This was a cell phone Drew had had in his pocket? Or maybe Holly had had it, and he'd used it . . .

Curiosity cut through my brain's fog. The whole thing had happened so swiftly, and been so odd, so heart-wrenching. Feeling only slightly guilty, I pressed the button for *Recents*. There were calls to the church, to me, and to Marla. There were no voice-mail messages. I tapped the icon for text messages. What harm could it do? I wondered. Holly was dead.

There was only one: it was from a cell-phone number I did not recognize. I stared at the message. *Not another cent. Don't ask, or you will regret it.*

I blinked, then took a small sip of the whiskey. The bourbon burned my throat, then my stomach. I glanced at the lake. Would Tom want to know about this? *Yes.*

Yet I did not want to call attention to the message, to arouse more grief and curiosity from Drew, by taking the phone upstairs to Sergeant Jones. My own cell was in the van. Better to call Tom from Holly's cell, I figured.

Would Drew be able to hear me from the kitchen? What if he made a sudden appearance? No matter what, I did *not* want him to hear me phoning the sheriff's department. I slid through the glass doors to the upper deck, doubting I would be audible to Father Pete and the boys. The window on the second floor must have been to a hallway. The voices inside were muffled. Outside was better than the kitchen, but I would still have to whisper.

Holly had planted long containers of pink and purple petunia blossoms at the far end of the deck. The blooms fluttered in the breeze, now sharpening with the advent of evening. Sticking up from the planter was one of those plastic holders that florists put in bouquets. Instead of a card, though, was a business envelope.

I punched in the numbers for Tom's cell as I walked to the planter. Words on the envelope, written in marker pen, were legible: DREW! HERE'S YOUR MONEY! Oh, good, I thought, there was one problem solved.

A few steps onward, there was a horrific cracking noise. What the hell was that? I wondered. Then I felt myself losing my balance. As my body slid sideways, I tried to reach out for something, anything.

But the deck railing was too far away. The boards under my feet gave way.

Down I plummeted, down past the second deck, down past the outside staircases, down, down, down, for what seemed like forever, or a blink. I could hear my own scream, but as in a nightmare, wasn't sure anyone else could. I choked on my shriek once I plunged into the icy lake.

My leg hit something hard under the lake's surface. I screamed and inhaled way too much water. Then I blacked out.

7

Julian, that champion swimmer, hauled me out of the water. At least, that's what the paramedic told me in the ambulance, when I awoke, shivering, with excruciating pain running down my left leg. I was on my stomach, and the medic was tending to my thigh. An IV drip snaked into my right arm.

"How did you know Julian was a swimmer—" I began, before the ambo swayed precipitously. I leaned off the narrow stretcher and was sick.

"Don't talk," the medic commanded. His gloved hand offered a wipe for my mouth. Actually, the guy looked familiar. Did I know him? I couldn't remember.

"There was a note," I said, defying his command. "On the end of the deck. That's why I walked out—"

"Stop talking." He finished taping my leg.

"You have to call the sheriff's department," I ordered him. He was right: talking made my leg shriek with pain. "Sergeant Jones was with us." And . . . what? "My husband is an investigator at the department. Tom Schulz."

"I know who you are, and I know who your husband is," the paramedic said, trying to sound kind. I noted that my wet clothes had been cut away and I now was ensconced in a hospital gown and warm blankets.

"Call Tom *right now.* Tell him there was a note on the deck." I couldn't say please. Despite the blankets, my whole body was trembling.

The paramedic exhaled, but used a cell phone to call the Furman County Sheriff's Department. After a delay in which he was patched through to someone, he relayed the news about the note on the deck, and how I was sure the deck had been sabotaged. After a few moments, he snapped the phone closed and announced, "Your husband is meeting us at the hospital. He said to tell you everyone else is okay."

I was dimly aware, or afraid, that that bit, *Your husband is meeting us at the hospital,* was one of those good-news, bad-news things. Tom loved me, no question. He would be worried for me. I was also keenly, embarrassingly aware of the look he would give me:

Can't you even take a kid home without getting into a mess? Or plunging into the lake?

I sighed.

A few minutes later the ambo arrived at the emergency room of Southwest Hospital, the closest major facility to Aspen Meadow. That certainly hadn't taken long. I wondered, *How long was I out? When is my leg going to stop hurting?* And, most illogically of all: *Have I gained so much weight this winter that I could collapse the boards of a deck?*

No, no, I told myself. *Something was wrong with that damned deck.*

But who was the intended victim? Drew?

The ER staff repeated the news that my husband was on his way. A policewoman was already there, they also said, and she would be staying with me. *To make sure you don't get into more trouble* was the unspoken message. I breathed again and allowed myself to be wheeled into a cubicle. Not that I could have done anything about it.

A policewoman, tall, thin, with brown hair pulled into a bun, introduced herself. I assumed Sergeant Jones had stayed with Drew. But my mind was so muddled that I couldn't remember this policewoman's name thirty seconds after she'd given it. She would be outside the curtain, she said, if I needed her.

A doctor pulled back the curtain, and this time I thought to look for a name tag. *Walter Smith, M.D.* That was a name I hoped I could remember. Dr. Smith, who was short and wide and had silver hair that he combed back over thick curly black hair, said that the force of hitting the lake and suddenly inhaling water had caused me to lose consciousness. He told me that I had abrasions on my left leg, and that the skin on that leg was badly scraped. *Scraped,* I thought. *Is that a medical term, doc?*

Apparently, Dr. Smith went on, my leg had hit something submerged beneath the water. Still, because I'd blacked out when I hit the lake, he wanted to check for a concussion. He also wanted to check my lungs, because I must have inhaled lake water.

I took a blow to the leg, but did not get my leg blown off, I thought again. But I kept my mouth shut.

Smith listened to my lungs and nodded. He had me follow a minilight from one side to the other. I guess I passed, because Smith began speaking in reverential tones about "Investigator Schulz." Honestly, it seemed as if even the mere mention of my husband had people bowing at his feet.

Smith asked me what month it was, who the president was, and what the main ingredient for bread was.

I answered the first two questions, then said, "Do you mean the most important ingredient in bread? Or the main ingredient?"

He shook his head, smiled ruefully, and said everything he had heard about me was true. I did not find this reassuring.

I asked him for a half dozen aspirin, please. He said he would put something into my drip. Meanwhile, he needed to examine my leg. The medic had wrapped it well, he concluded admiringly, after a moment of painful pressing. They were going to unwrap it, though, put antibiotic cream on it, then rewrap it. All in all, Smith concluded, I was pretty lucky.

"I don't *feel* very lucky," I said.

"The leg will turn black-and-blue," Dr. Smith said crisply. "It will be sore. Give it a week of rest, and you should be fine."

A week of rest? Clearly, Dr. Smith had never worked as a caterer.

"You must have hit a rock when you fell into the lake," Smith mused as he was leaving. "Did you see it?"

"You know what? As I fell, I didn't get that good a look at what was *underwater.* Now, how about that painkiller?"

Smith disappeared. A nurse swished in and put what I hoped was a very strong opiate into the drip. She then stayed to keep me awake. I told her that Dr. Smith had ruled out a concussion. She flipped through the notes on the clipboard, and said he had *not* ruled out a concussion, and she was there to keep me awake.

Which was too bad, because within a few moments I wanted nothing more than to drift off to sleep. The nurse asked if I liked living in Aspen Meadow, were we really getting a lot of bears this summer, and was climate change affecting us? I finally gave her my full attention only because I was fantasizing about the amount of strength it would take to strangle her with my IV cord.

"Shut *up*," I snarled unkindly.

"Oh, dear, they said you were difficult," she commented.

"They were right!" I cried.

"Do you want another warm blanket?" she asked, unfazed.

I realized I was shaking—from cold, from despair, from stress, I did not know. "Sorry. Yes. I'm so sorry."

"Miss G.," said Tom, suddenly beside me. The nurse whisked away, then returned with a warm blanket, which she tucked around me. Was it my imagination, or was she opening her eyes wide at Tom, as if to say, *Poor you, to be married to this harpy?*

"Goldy," said Tom, once the nurse had left. "How're you doing?"

"Better now that you're here. And I *don't* need a policewoman to keep me out of further trouble."

The skin around Tom's green eyes wrinkled. This was a small indicator, a tell I had learned, that he was in emotional pain. "The deputy is here because I was worried about keeping you safe. Sergeant Jones found the empty envelope addressed to Drew. It was floating on the lake surface. There was no money anywhere. Then the medic called, telling us that the envelope was what had lured you to the end of the deck. I would have been here earlier, but I wanted to get a look at the structure, or what's left of it. I also wanted to check out the lake underneath it."

"The lake—" I seemed incapable of finishing a thought.

"Our guys found pieces of the deck floating in the lake. But no *supports* for the deck. We've got a certificate of occupancy on file from the architect, plus photos, so there *used* to be supports there. We're thinking whatever had been cantilevering that deck out over the water had been removed. No easy task, but you could do it. And the lake there is very shallow. The rocky bottom hit your leg."

I tried to absorb this information, but could not. They found the envelope . . . the supports removed . . . the rocky bottom in shallow water . . .

Wouldn't someone have seen a person removing the supports? I wondered.

"Julian," I said.

"If Julian had not been there," Tom said, his tone matter-of-fact, "and had not been such a strong swimmer, you would have hit your leg, inhaled even more water than you did, and probably drowned." He paused. "We don't think you were the intended victim."

"I was wondering about that."

"It was probably either Holly or Drew."

"The envelope was addressed to Drew."

"Maybe he was a target. But it was a setup of some kind, no matter which of them was the target." He waited a moment, then said, "We're now treating Holly's death as a homicide." He lifted the warm blanket and touched my sleeve. "Hey!" he called in the direction of the curtain, using that commanding tone of his. "Can someone please get my wife another blanket?"

"Tom," I managed to say, "Drew said Holly recently had a break-in."

"A burglar? Did they report it?"

"I don't know. Whoever it was didn't take anything valuable. Just . . . something about a file cabinet. Then Holly got the seller to install a security system. Ask Drew about it."

Tom nodded. "Anything else?"

"Holly's cell phone," I said. "Drew had it. He must have forgotten . . . when he was on Marla's street. It had a threatening text . . ."

"A threatening text," Tom prompted.

I grasped back into the far reaches of my brain. " 'Not another cent. Don't ask, or you will regret it.' Something like that. I was holding the cell when the deck gave way."

"Miss G.," said Tom. He squeezed my shoulder very gently. "This is very helpful. Please get some rest."

I finally succumbed to a half sleep.

Sometime later, I was wheeled away. Nausea rolled through me. *If I can realize these things,* I thought, *then my brain must be coming back.* Did I want my brain back?

My thoughts, such as they were, reverted to Holly. Tears pricked my eyes as I recalled her limp body on the road. Tom had actually used the word *homicide.* But there hadn't been a shot, or stabbing, or . . . would the cops have talked to Drew already? Who, besides George, Lena, and George's mother, didn't like Holly?

Oh, God, I had a headache.

When I opened my eyes, Tom was sitting beside the bed, holding my hand.

"Time?" I asked.

" 'Bout midnight. Arch is out in the hall with Julian. Do you want them to come in? Arch is asleep in a chair," he added.

"First," I said. "Wait." My mouth felt full of fur. "Cell phone. Holly's."

Tom said, "Our guys found it in the lake. The lab's working on it."

I said, "Drew?"

"He's with the foster family now. His aunt will be here today—it's technically Saturday—in the afternoon. Then she'll take him to Alaska. Julian gave Drew a check for a thou, to use as spending money? Said that was what you agreed?" When I nodded, Tom went on, "Drew and his aunt will be taking a flight together, changing planes at Sea-Tac. One of our guys will drive them to DIA. Get this: Drew wasn't sure he wanted to leave. He was worried about *you*. Also, he confirmed your report about a break-in, the sixth of June. Holly did call the department, but the deputy who wrote down the details said nothing of value was taken. The only things that were busted were the back door, which the owner had repaired, and a filing cabinet. Holly told our guy she couldn't tell if anything was missing. After that, the security system was installed. Oh, and she told Drew she was taking out an insurance policy. But the only thing she did was unpack some boxes and put out a bunch of religious statuary." Tom gave me a puzzled look. When I nodded, he said, "So that makes no sense. We got a warrant, and our guys are going through her stuff now. So far, there's no policy, nor anything else of interest." Tom stopped talking, then fidgeted a bit in his chair.

I said, "What?"

"We just got an anonymous report that Drew and his mother had a big fight this week."

"An anonymous report of a fight between a teenager and his mother? Please. Arch and I have disagreements all the time."

"A friend of mine is an Alaskan state trooper. Used to be one here. He's going to set up camp near the cabin where the aunt, uncle, and Drew will be."

"To protect Drew?" I asked. "That's good. I'll bet you're right, that note was meant for—"

"Yes, to protect Drew. But there might be something else," Tom added tentatively.

"What?" I asked.

"It's a long shot, Goldy." Tom would not meet my eyes. "But we have to consider the possibility that Drew poisoned or otherwise harmed his own mother."

"That's insane," I said.

"Really? One of our guys interviewed him at the foster family's house, and couldn't rule it out."

"Your guy must be new."

Tom ticked off points on his fingers. "Holly pulled him out of Elk Park Prep, where he had numerous friends and was a star athlete. She put him into a big Catholic high school, where he may or may not have been so adored. Going back to the divorce, Holly dragged Drew out of Edith's mansion in Aspen Meadow, then moved to a place in Denver—"

"You don't know that she *dragged* him. He was a kid, for God's sake. If you move, you move."

"But a while ago you told me he was all broken up about it." When I did nothing but nod, Tom said, "Then she schlepped him back to Aspen Meadow, we don't know why—"

"I know why. She couldn't take driving Drew back and forth to Elk Park Prep all winter. She slid her Mercedes into one too many snow-filled ditches. She bought a four-wheel-drive Audi. Elk Park Prep *is* in Aspen Meadow."

Tom spoke as if I hadn't said anything. "She bought a big house in the country club, got a second mortgage and spent that money on God knows what, then subsequently lost the place to foreclosure. After that, the two of them moved into a house where the rent was kept low, because she'd agreed to put her nice furniture into it. She kept it neat in case someone decided to buy it. We don't have all her financials yet, but we have to assume she didn't have much money, or that she wasn't giving *Drew* much money. And then they reportedly had a big argument." His green eyes finally met mine, and they were resigned. "We *have* to keep an eye on Drew. Teenagers can, and have, come up with all kinds of reasons to kill their parents."

"I don't believe it. Drew adored Holly."

"Maybe so. It's just a possibility we have to consider."

"You're thinking she was poisoned? You said her symptoms were classic for heart attack. Did anybody else from the party get sick?"

"Not that we've heard."

I sighed. "What have you been able to find out about Holly?"

"I ordered a full tox screen, but the medical examiner won't be able to get to the autopsy before late Monday, possibly Tuesday. I wanted to know what kind of medication she was on, just in case what we're looking at here is an adverse reaction that precipitated a heart attack. Aspen Meadow Drug cooperated, said they didn't need to wait for a subpoena. Holly wasn't on any meds. Her GP is in Hawaii, out of cell range, unfortunately. But we'll get hold of him. Still, Drew insisted over and over that Holly hardly ever went to the doctor. He said she didn't believe in them." He paused. "Was there anything else? That you noticed, I mean?"

Tom trusted my powers of observation, and now that I knew I wasn't going to be bawled out for splashing into the lake, I tried to focus on what I'd seen at Holly's. Tom, I knew, would not want me to get overinvolved in this case. *That only happens from time to time,* I would have insisted. *It happens all the time,* Tom would have said. But Holly had been my dear friend. So I was going to get involved. But I would have to be careful.

"There was a box," I said. "On the front porch. Drew thought it was one of his mother's collages, back from the framer."

"We have it," said Tom. "The collage is of Patsie Boatfield. She's wearing a blue-striped dress in a photograph in one of the squares, and some of the cloth is in another."

"Oh, I know that dress," I said. "She used to wear it to the fencing meets, because she had this idea it was good luck for the team. Then she spilled bleach on it somehow, and she told me she couldn't wear it anymore. What other materials were in the collage?"

"Bits of jewelry, seashells, photographs of Colorado ghost towns, and some pressed flowers. Patsie said she had the collage made for her new husband, Warren Broome. Said we could keep it as long as we needed it."

"Was there anything else in the box?" I cocked my head at the wall in front of me. Did hospitals really think pale green was restful? The color was that of mold ruining a good piece of cheese.

"Yup," Tom said. "There was a note in the bottom, with a number on it. Typewritten, so it's no help. It said, 'Twenty-five K.'"

"Twenty-five thousand? Dollars? For *framing* a collage?"

"The collage wasn't framed. It was in a Plexiglas container. Our guys are trying to track down who sent the carton it was in . . . What are you doing?"

"I want to get out of here," I said impatiently. I swung my legs over the side of the bed. Pain flooded into the left thigh. I pulled the IV out of my arm.

"Goldy, don't. You've had all the tests, but they want to keep you for observation."

"I'm fine. And if there's one thing I learned in Med Wives 101, it's that as long as you pay your bill, you can check yourself out of the hospital whenever you want."

8

Alas, if only it had been that easy. Within forty-five minutes, I was ready to scream.

Granted, I had physical aches. But waves of psychic pain—the memories of Holly; the regrets; the new information from Tom: *We're treating this as a homicide, we have to consider the possibility that Drew poisoned or otherwise harmed his own mother*—threatened to engulf me. These were heavier, more tangible somehow, than my sore leg and throbbing head. They made me feel vulnerable. Any little thing—Tom's absence while he dealt with the cashier, Julian's disappearance to pick up my prescriptions, Arch locating Tom's car and bringing it to the exit, then rushing off to get his Passat—threatened to put me over the edge. Sitting in the insisted-upon wheelchair by the exit, I stewed and considered hollering about the injustice of it all.

One thing Tom had given me was my cell, which the nurse's aide said I could use. I checked my voice-mail messages: three, all from Marla.

"How are you?" said her disembodied voice. "I feel like hell. I need you to tell me it was all a bad dream."

The second: "Goldy? Where are you? Pick up your phone!"

The third: "Okay, now I'm both worried and pissed, and I'm going to stay up until you call! And it doesn't matter if it's in the wee hours. Patsie Boatfield stayed and helped bring stuff in from outside. She never really knew Holly—"

The message cut off. I checked the time on my cell: just after 1 A.M. My watch had magically disappeared. Even while reluctantly conceding that removing a patient's watch might be hospital policy, or that my discount-store timepiece might not be working so well anymore, now that it had spent some time—*Don't start screaming,* I told myself—underwater, I punched in Marla's number.

"Where in *the hell* have you been?" she demanded before the phone had even rung one full time.

I gave her an abbreviated version of falling into the lake. Since Tom was ultrascrupulous about people listening, precisely because folks *did* gossip, and since the nurse's aide was still at my side, I omitted any mention of being at Holly's rental, or the note that had sent me into the water. I just said I fell off *a* deck . . . into Aspen Meadow Lake. I tried to put warning in my voice, and she caught it.

"You're somewhere you can't talk."

"Yup."

"Call me when you're alone. I'm making slow progress with these dishes." She moaned. "The fencing parents all wanted to pitch in, but I said, 'No, no, just wrap up any leftovers you want, and take your kids home. My cleaning lady will be here in the morning,' and of course I forgot that the cleaning lady took off the entire month of June. Patsie was great, though—"

"Wait," I said. Tom was approaching from the end of the hallway. I bade Marla a hasty farewell with the promise, cross-my-heart-and-hope-to-die, that I would call her as soon as I was free of the hospital.

Which, unfortunately, I forgot to do, because Tom signaled for me to go with him. Arch and Julian were following in the Passat. I wanted to hear what Tom had in mind, although if it contained the news that they were indicting Drew for the murder of his mother, maybe I didn't.

"Tell me what you're thinking about Drew," I demanded as soon as we pulled away from the curb.

Tom's tone turned wary. "I sent another deputy over to question him in foster care."

I made an exasperated sigh.

Tom flicked me a glance that I could just make out from the streetlights. "This deputy's been an investigator for a while. He said Drew was very upset. He also said we shouldn't rule him out yet."

It felt as if my throat was closing. I croaked, "Did he give a reason?"

"Said it was just a gut feeling. He couldn't ask Drew specifics about poisons, or anything like that, because we don't know what we're dealing with."

"Do you have *any* idea what killed Holly? Do you have a theory about the note that sent me into the lake? Or the text message to Holly?"

"No. But I need to know a couple of things from you. And maybe Marla."

"Go ahead."

"But Marla can*not* talk to anyone else about this. I can trust you. I'm not at all sure about her."

"Tell me, will you?" I ripped into the bag of prescriptions Julian had solemnly handed me, to see if Dr. Smith had ordered a painkiller in addition to the antibiotic cream. He had not. My leg was burning with pain, so I clawed through the glove compartment of Tom's car, landed on a bottle of ibuprofen, and took two without water.

Tom said, "Gosh, Miss G., don't you think we should turn around and go back to the hospital?"

"No." My voice was still cracking. "Bring me up to speed."

"Our guys are out canvassing the party guests and Marla's neighbors. So far, almost everyone was willing to give up cell phones. We're hoping someone snapped a picture of that stranger who showed up unannounced. I'm angry that I didn't get his name. Would Marla have it?"

"Nope, he wasn't invited. But that didn't stop him poking around in Marla's kitchen."

"I remember. Do *you* have any idea who he was?"

I paused. "Well, actually, he *did* look kind of familiar. But from a long time ago."

"Your banged-up leg messing with your memory?"

"No," I said crossly. "If a parent took a picture of him, and I see it, maybe it'll jog something. But Holly was afraid of him. She said he was a son of a bitch, and she wanted you to get out your service revolver."

"And you didn't think to tell me this?"

"I just—" I had to clear my throat. "I just thought she was being her usual dramatic self."

Tom exhaled. "Marla didn't know him. But you think you do."

I closed my eyes and saw the balding stranger, but could not come up with a name. "Maybe something will jog loose. What about Marla's surveillance system?"

"She says she turned it off before the party."

"You said almost everyone gave you their cell phones. Is that your way of saying someone refused to?"

"One. Warren Broome. Alexander Boatfield's stepfather? The guy who was caught with his pants down? The woman who exposed him—"

"Tom."

"The woman who went public with his misdeeds said she was sure there were others like her. Okay, so Broome recently got back his license to be a practicing psychiatrist. I don't know how many patients he has, but he said he had confidential messages from them on his phone. If he gave us the cell, he'd be violating privacy laws. Which I understand. We'd have to get a court order to find out his patient list, and we don't have enough evidence to satisfy a judge that we would need that."

I said, "Womanizing Warren is full of it. If he just started working with patients again, he shouldn't have that many confidential messages."

Tom lifted one of his large hands, a gesture of exasperation. "We don't have enough for a warrant, Miss G."

"And Holly's money problems?"

"We're still trying to dig into her financials." Tom bit the inside of his cheek. "Did Holly and George have a tiff about child support?"

"I don't know. You saw how they fought. Maybe he cut her off for some reason, and she was retaliating by not inviting him to the party. But unless I'm a complete incompetent at judging character—"

"Which you most definitely are not."

"George is *devoted* to Drew. He's been a faithful father, coming to parent-teacher conferences, attending the fencing meets." I paused. "The rest of what I know is old. I remember from Amour Anonymous that George was ordered to pay Holly a big settlement, plus support, for a long time. Until Drew was through college, I think. That's what I don't get—"

"Big? How big?"

"I'd have to check the Amour Anonymous notes on that."

"You still have those?"

"I was the secretary," I said proudly. "They're all in a file in the basement." I added, "Handwritten, though."

"Oh, great. They'll be unreadable, and tucked between your college French notes, your notes from teaching Sunday School when Arch was seven, and your art history textbooks. Honestly, Goldy, do you ever throw anything out?"

"Art!" I squealed, and moved my bum leg too fast. Pain shot up my spine. "That's it."

"Art," Tom prompted.

"The stranger is an artist."

"Name?"

I searched my memory bank, but came up empty. "Let me try to remember." Even to my own ears, my voice sounded feeble. "Now, what about George and Lena at the birthday party? What was the big fight about?"

"They hadn't been invited. Country-club friends asked them what they were taking to Drew's party," Tom said simply. "If I'd known Holly was going to drop dead an hour after George and Lena left, I would have gotten more details. But as it was, I was trying to get rid of the man you now say is an artist, plus two frustrated people, one of whom was the father of one of the birthday boys. Their tempers were frayed, and I just asked them to leave. A pair of deputies was due to talk to George and Lena tonight, but I haven't heard anything yet. Okay, let's get back to Holly's money. She lost the house, transferred Drew, sold their cars, all while supposedly getting big money from George and having lots of collage clients. Anything else?"

"There wasn't much food in her house. She never liked to cook. Julian used to help her out, providing weekly meals, back when she was married to George. But that was a *long* time ago."

"So how were they eating?"

"No clue. Presumably, Holly was making money on the collages, so even if she and George were fighting over finances, they'd have enough to eat out. Cheaply."

Tom took this in. "What did Holly have to eat and drink at the party? Did you notice?"

I shook my head and exhaled. "She drank some wine, but I don't think she ate very much. She did try some of one of Julian's chile relleno tortas. He made torta especially for her, because it was her favorite dish from the ones he used to cook for her family. It's vegetarian, so back in the day, George would eat it. She turned down the birthday cake and ice cream."

"All right. Maybe there will be some leftovers we can test." He thought for a moment. "Do you know of other enemies Holly might have had? Besides her ex-husband and his difficult new wife?"

"Edith Ingleby has always hated her."

"I'm not ruling anyone out at this point, but Edith wasn't at the party. How about the people who were there?"

"It might have been my imagination, but she seemed to be avoiding Warren Broome."

"Got it," said Tom. "Anybody else?"

I scrolled back through what I knew of Holly's history. She'd lived in Denver, then married George and moved to Aspen Meadow, which we were now entering. Fog blurred the streetlights. The digital thermometer on the bank said it was forty-eight degrees. *Think about Holly,* I ordered myself, and shivered.

After Holly moved out of Edith's mansion, she bought a house in Denver. At the time, she'd said she didn't relish the idea of commuting to Elk Park Prep for Drew, but she figured he needed to stay with his friends, the teachers he knew, that kind of thing. Once settled in Denver, she'd added, she wanted to go back to art school.

Still, Aspen Meadow was spread out over thousands of acres of mostly forested, mostly hilly terrain. Holly could have taken her art classes during the day, and still been up to EPP in time to pick up Drew. She could have had his friends over to visit. She could have stayed at St. Luke's. So why move to Denver? Had she really so desperately wanted to get away from George and his dragon-lady mother, that she'd felt the need to be forty miles away? If so, then why, after a relatively short period of time, move back to Aspen Meadow? Could it really have to do with what she said, spinning out in the snow? Selling a house in Denver, and moving back up here, seemed like a lot of upheaval . . . just to make your drive easier. In retrospect, Holly's explanation sounded pretty feeble. I shared all this with Tom.

"Okay, good information, thanks. Anything in your mind about former boyfriends, things like that?"

"I don't know. After she divorced George, she always seemed to have boyfriends. But none of them panned out."

"Do you know any names of former boyfriends? Do you think that artist might have been one of them?"

"I don't know any names. I didn't put that kind of information in the Amour notes. Mostly we checked in on each other, made sure we were taking care of ourselves, that kind of thing. And we had discussions."

"What kind of discussions?"

I thought for a minute. "We alternated between blaming our ex-husbands for all our problems and blaming ourselves for things falling apart. The main thing was, we wanted to support each other while we became better people. So we looked at issues having to do with . . . well, character. Why? Do you want me to turn over my notebooks to the department?"

Tom said, "Not yet. But once you know the child support data, and if you find out medical information on Holly, I do want to hear."

We pulled into our driveway right behind Julian and Arch. The single-car garage was given over to my van, which I was thankful someone had driven home. I was suddenly so exhausted I just couldn't call Marla back.

My business line rang at 6 A.M. I threw off the covers and started to stumble out of bed. My plan for getting to my insistently ringing phone failed though, as pain seared my left leg and I fell on the floor.

"You need to let me get that," Tom scolded. He had just come out of the bathroom. He was dressed, looking as sharp as any investigator had ever looked, in a white shirt, navy tie, khaki pants, and charcoal jacket that I'd picked out myself. "We're starting early on the investigation into Holly's death and the sabotage of her deck. So I need to go in. You, on the other hand, need to stay in bed." He helped me up at the same time that he answered the phone. "This is Goldy's Catering, who is this and what do you want so early in the morning?" He was silent for a while, then looked at me with lifted brows. "Really? You and your husband both? Are you all right?" More silence. Then, "Do you remember what you ate and drank at the dinner?" He dug into his pocket, pulled out his notebook, and wrote in it. "Okay, thanks for calling."

"What?" I said, panting.

"That was Doreen Smythe. She told me she and her husband had terrible nightmares. More like hallucinations. They ate chips and guacamole, tamale pie, torta, enchiladas, and cake. They drank wine. Their son ate chips and guacamole, then arroz con pollo, and cake. He had no problems." I shook my head, confused. Tom jotted in his notebook, then observed me trying to get dressed. "Miss G.," he said, "let me help you with that." He gingerly pulled up the right leg of my biggest sweatpants, then my bandaged left leg. "Since their son didn't have any trouble, Doreen thinks their drinks at the party might have been spiked with a hallucinogen."

"We had beer, wine, and soft drinks."

"Doesn't mean it couldn't happen. People can pour stuff into plastic cups just as easily as anything else."

I thought about this, and envisioned the line of plastic cups in Marla's kitchen. The reason she hadn't wanted anyone to go outside with bottles was in case one broke and a barefoot kid stepped on the glass. I already knew why she hadn't bought canned beer: she thought it tasted funny.

Tom told me his guys had completed the canvass of Marla's neighborhood, with nothing to report. Now they were at work over near Holly's rental, to see if anyone had noticed somebody sawing out a load-bearing beam under the deck. So far, two people had reported observing what looked like a tallish person, a man, they thought, wearing a uniform and a cap. He was working under the big deck the previous day. They'd guessed the guy was a window washer.

"With a saw."

"What are you planning on doing today?" Tom asked, a note of warning in his voice.

"Tom, it's just past six o'clock, and I have a bum leg. I have no idea what I'm doing today."

"No cooking," he warned.

"Okay! No cooking! I'll talk on the telephone and see if I can find those Amour Anonymous notes, how about that?"

He eyed me warily. "Listen to me. If the department is treating this as a homicide, then that means there is a killer out there. Do you understand what I'm saying?" When I nodded, he went on: "When you talk to people? You reveal nothing, no matter how much you trust that person."

"Marla?"

"Okay, you can talk to Marla. Make sure she knows to keep her mouth shut, though. Ditto Julian."

"All *right*," I said. I wished Tom luck. Breaks in a case usually came fast right after a crime, and Tom had a crack team.

But if I couldn't reveal anything, and had a bum leg to boot, what could *I* do?

I desperately wanted to find out what had happened to my dear old friend. I also needed to know why I'd taken that plunge into the lake.

Okay, I would talk on the telephone. I would scour the Amour Anonymous notes. But, somehow . . .

"Miss G.?" Tom asked mildly. "Holly was your friend, and no matter what I say, now you want to go talk to people, right?"

I sighed. "I suppose so."

"You can go places, and you can talk. You can ask questions of people you know. I figured you would want to, but Sergeant Boyd is going to accompany you on every venture out of this house. I know you so well, I already called him. He agreed, and now he's outside waiting."

"I don't want his presence to intimidate people—" I began.

"Oh, no?" Tom replied, his eyebrows raised. "I don't want you dead. You can get Marla to drive you. But Boyd is accompanying you, wherever it is you plan to go. Got it?"

9

I let out a resigned sigh and agreed. I didn't even know
exactly what I was going to do yet, but I knew that
the only way to lift the psychic pain from my shoulders
was to do *something.* Anything. Tom took off. I did
as many yoga stretches as my banged-up body would
allow, then limped down to the kitchen. Julian was
already there, dousing his espresso with sugar.

"I suppose that phone call woke you up," he said,
his voice full of sympathy. "Me, too."

"Arch?"

"Slumbering deeply," Julian replied. "Which is
good. I know he was worried sick about you."

"I'm glad he's asleep." I went to the front door and
waved to Boyd, who signaled back. Apparently, he
didn't want to leave his patrol car, which was running.

Back in front of my espresso machine, I asked Julian, "Did you have any weird dreams? The woman who called said she and her husband did, and they were like hallucinations."

He frowned. "Hmm. No. Did you? I mean, if you did, it would be only natural . . ." He didn't finish the thought. Instead, he drained his coffee, fired up the countertop computer, and scrolled through screens until he brought up the menu for the church dinner. He perused it, then set off for the walk-in.

I said, "You can't be serious about cooking now."

"I'm totally serious. I'm awake, aren't I? We have an event tomorrow night, don't we? My boss has a banged-up leg, doesn't she? No time like the present to get going with prep." He pulled out bags of frozen jumbo shrimp.

"That's *prep*?"

"I'm going to change your menu a little bit."

I groaned. "Father Pete wants people to give to the church. Please don't make anything weird."

Julian gave me a blank look. "Forget it. I'm making Weird Shrimp." He paused, then said, "Just kidding."

I shook my head, put together my own quadruple espresso with cream, plunked in ice cubes, and snagged my cell. On our front porch, I waved again to Boyd, who nodded.

Cool, sweet early morning mountain air moved languidly through the brilliant pink blossoms of my hanging ivy geranium. I drank some of the iced coffee and stared at the cell phone. Would Marla mind if I called so early? Probably not, if the call contained gossip.

"Oh, dear," Marla said. "My poor dishwater hands can barely pick up this phone. And my best friend, who promised to call me back last night, neglected to make said call, even though she *knew* I would need to talk to her. So I am not in a wonderful mood."

"This early in the morning? You're never in a wonderful mood. If you promise you'll keep this confidential—"

"Oh, you take out all the fun."

"—then I can tell you what happened last night."

"All *right.*"

"I was lured off the deck at Holly's rental."

"Lured?" Marla's voice was suddenly sharp. "Okay, I'm getting up. Wait a minute. After what happened here, with Holly?" She paused to blow her nose. "Oh, man, this pollen . . . I keep thinking about . . . you were *lured*? What is going on?"

"Somebody set a trap by removing the supports to the upper deck at her rental. There was a message at the far end of the deck. I think it was meant for Drew, but it could have been intended for Holly, if the first chance at killing her didn't succeed."

"So Tom is thinking homicide?" Marla said, disbelief audible in her voice.

"First of all, have you heard anything, even the tiniest murmur, about Holly and Drew fighting recently?"

"Well," she said tentatively, "I *did* hear that they were having disagreements, but only typical teen issues, especially when there's been a divorce. 'I need money and you're not giving it to me.' Also, I heard he wanted to spend more time with George, and Holly was opposed."

"And you gleaned this information where?"

There was a silence. "From Warren Broome," she said finally. "I think. At the party? He came over and asked me a question about the enchiladas. I think I told him to go ask you. Did he?"

"No."

"I'm so tired, Goldy, and the whole thing with Holly . . . I just don't recall. But tell me why they think Holly was killed, as opposed to having a heart attack."

"Wait. First, do you have leftovers from the dinner? The sheriff's department might want them, to analyze."

"No," she wailed. "I ground up everything in the disposal."

"Don't worry about it," I said, trying to hide the disappointment in my voice. "I'll give you all the pertinent facts when you come get me. I got scraped up when I hit the lake bottom," I explained. "I don't trust myself to drive. Also, we're going to have a police escort, wherever we go."

"Don't tell me. Boyd."

"You got it."

"So Tom doesn't trust you."

"Nope."

"Oh, what else is new?" She added, "Maybe he's trying to keep you safe."

"Yeah, yeah, that's what he said."

"I'll be there ASAP. But you better make me some of that iced coffee with cream. I know what you're drinking. And oh, do I need it. I had the worst nightmares last night."

"Wait. You had nightmares?"

"Yeah. The kind that are vivid, horrible, and in full color."

"What did you have to eat and drink last night?"

"Um . . . why?"

"Because you're not alone. The Smythes also had hallucination-type nightmares."

"Okay, let's see . . . I had guacamole, no chips, pollo, no arroz, one teensy-weensy enchilada, and chile relleno torta."

I swallowed. "Did you see anyone tinkering with the drinks or food?"

"Goldy, *everyone* was tinkering with the drinks and food. But I don't remember anything suspicious. If something occurs to me, I'll tell you when I get there."

I thanked her and signed off. I drank my coffee and thought again of the plastic cups lined up on Marla's island the night before. I had not seen anything already poured into the cups. Still, I went inside and started a new file on the computer. So far, three people had reported having nightmares: Marla and the Smythe parents.

When Marla pulled up twenty minutes later—a record—she was driving her new white Mercedes SUV. She'd said she'd bought the car because she wanted to plow through our big snowstorms in style. I had asked Boyd if he wanted anything to eat or drink, and he told me he was fine. When I informed him a bit later that we'd be heading out soon, and where we were going, he said that was fine, too.

"Thanks for coming," I said, handing Marla the iced coffee. "I brought you fontina," I added, and placed wrapped pieces of cheese between us. "I didn't think you'd have time to eat."

"Thanks. No, I didn't. You're the best." She glanced at her dashboard clock. "But where do you want to go at this hour, on a Saturday?"

I'd been thinking about this. "I want to tell you where I want to go second before where I want to go first."

Marla bit into the fontina. "I'm listening."

"All right, then, the second people I want to talk to are the Inglebys. Things didn't end well last night with them." I patted a basket I'd brought into the car. "Edith loves my blueberry muffins, and I had some frozen. While we're talking to Bob and Ophelia, they can be thawing."

"Bob and Ophelia?"

"You remember that Bob Rushwood is the trainer at Aspen Meadow Country Club? After I talked to you, I called over to their new fitness facility. Boyd is going to follow us there."

Marla revved the big car's engine and screeched away from the curb. "Go on."

"Bob has one client at this hour: Ophelia. She didn't seem like the athletic type, so I doubt she'll mind us interrupting her. Anyway, Bob was doing CPR on Holly right after she collapsed. I want to know how she seemed. Was she conscious? Was she having a hallucination? That kind of thing."

Marla raised her eyebrows. "You don't think Tom's guys have already talked to him?"

"I'm sure they did. But they didn't have clients calling early this morning saying they had nightmares and hallucinations after ingesting something questionable."

"Ah."

"Okay. Now a question for you: did you ever see Holly at Aspen Meadow Country Club?"

"Yes. But not recently. That doesn't mean anything."

I ignored this. "Holly was a fitness fanatic who, according to Drew, hated doctors. I've never seen her at the rec, or that much more downscale place, Aspen Meadow Fitness. *And* Holly belonged to the country club, or she used to, back when she had money. So . . . did she work out there, do you think?"

Marla said, "Goldy, I am the last person who would know this. Even after losing all this weight, I wouldn't be caught dead in the club's new fitness facility." She shuddered. "Skinny people with money, working out with their headphones on? How am I supposed to get gossip from *them*? I have a treadmill at home. Also hand weights, which I look at from time to time."

"Okay, but I was thinking—"

"Always a dangerous undertaking."

"Holly's doctor is in Hawaii somewhere, out of cellphone range. So if anyone would be likely to know whether she had *other* health issues, wouldn't it be Bob Rushwood? Or somebody else there at the club? You'll have to get Boyd and me in, though."

"Goldy, I don't *want* to. Those jocks at the club will *judge* me."

"You've never been *in* their new fitness facility. And you've just lost a bunch of weight! How can the athletes criticize you, if they don't recognize you?"

"Oh, all right. Plus, maybe one of them will be cute."

On the way to AMCC, I filled Marla in on my visit to Holly's, along with Tom's investigation so far. I reminded her everything had to be secret, and that we were to reveal nothing and trust nobody. I'd remembered the uninvited stranger was an artist. Had he not looked familiar to her? I asked. She said no.

"My sources did come up with something," she said as she zoomed along. "Ophelia's father, Neil Unger? He won't pay for her to go to college. He's only given her money for clothes shopping for the past two years. No money for tuition."

I thought of über-wealthy Neil Unger banging around my kitchen on Thursday, and trying to clean up America through his organization, The Guild. Now, back in medieval and Renaissance days, guilds had been good things, bringing together carpenters and stone masons and other folks engaged in the same professions. Guilds were the precursors of unions, and I'd often wondered if there was a caterers' guild.

But those weren't the kind of organizations Neil Unger had in mind. This spring, he had paid me to do a dinner for The Guild at my conference center. Even though I'd been well compensated, even though it had led Neil to contract me for Ophelia's party, his speech after the dinner had left me feeling queasy. He spoke disarmingly to an enthusiastic, all-white, all-male group about what he called "those people." And who were those people, exactly? By the end of the evening, I had concluded only that they were crooks. What they were doing or stealing was never clear to me.

Marla said, "Goldy? Hello?"

I said, "Sorry. My train of thought derailed. Why won't Neil pay for Ophelia's college tuition? He thinks college professors are crooks?"

"No, my sources say he's punishing her. It had something to do with the former fiancé being a crook."

"Neil is big on crooks."

Marla waved this away. "At the country club, he announced on numerous occasions that if his daughter couldn't figure out the man she was going to marry was a thief, then clearly she wasn't college material. According to Neil, his daughter concurs in the not-being-smart-enough assessment."

I said, "But you're not sure she actually agrees with him?"

"Does Ophelia seem like the stupid sort to you?"

"No," I admitted. "But actually, I've never heard her say much. She averts her eyes whenever she sees me. And maybe she's not the intellectual sort, but with all that money for clothes her father gives her, you'd think she could dress like she wasn't an escapee from the fifties. Clearly, her father's mind-set is stuck back there."

"Overbearing men with money," Marla said. "I think they're in every decade."

But speaking of the fifties, I was pretty sure that was when Aspen Meadow Country Club had been built. Never updated, its main building, with its stone-and-wood façade, always put me more in mind of a deluxe Holiday Inn than a country club. There was a neon-green golf course, kept pristine in our arid climate by sprinklers that were now swishing arcs of water in rhythmic circles. Only a few cars dotted the parking lot, which was no surprise. Who wanted to jump out of bed early on a gorgeous Colorado Saturday morning, and hightail it to an *indoor* place to run?

Five people, to be exact. When we entered the dungeonlike facility, Bob was working with Ophelia on what looked like a Tower of London torture machine. There were only three other people in the gym, two of whom were white-haired gents who looked as if they were retired. Those two, who were nearest to us, raised their eyes admiringly to Marla. She ignored them. The men were walking on treadmills, which, like the early-Saturday workout phenomenon, was another thing I didn't understand. Okay, Marla walked on a treadmill, but her neighborhood was hilly, and she had had a heart attack. With our state so lovely and leafy in summertime, why would these men walk on treadmills in a windowless, neon-lit, mirrored room that still smelled like its newly installed carpet?

As Boyd, Marla, and I paced carefully toward Bob and Ophelia, I reflected that there were a lot of things about Colorado's health obsession that I didn't understand. That was why it was the fittest state in the nation, and I was the one supplying the butter and cream.

I checked in with myself. How did I feel? My leg hurt. The emotional ache caused by losing Holly was still there, like a bruise you're afraid to touch, but do anyway. You want to see how the pain is compared to the last time you felt it. I was doing only slightly better. I put this down to wanting to be helpful in the investigation into Holly's death. My jaw set. *I owe her that much*, I thought.

I glanced over at Boyd, who wore the green-and-brown uniform of the sheriff's department. He looked uncomfortable with the training facility, but not nearly as out of place as he'd appeared the few times Tom had told him he had to cater with me.

"Bob Rushwood!" Marla called, as if they were old friends. "We need to talk to you for a minute."

Before we could get over to Bob and Ophelia, though, the third man in the gym trotted up to Marla. She squawked, then recoiled and got hold of herself. "Oh, Neil. I didn't recognize you without your clothes on. Your usual clothes, I mean."

Actually, Neil Unger was wearing workout wear: a white T-shirt and white sweatpants, both emblazoned with the navy-blue logo for The Guild. My heart did a nosedive. Why had he stopped us? I did not want to talk again about Ophelia's party. Instead of addressing Marla, though, Neil nodded at Boyd, who gave him a slit-eyed look. Then he turned to me. Like Marla, I involuntarily leaned away.

"I was sorry to hear about your friend," he said in that raspy voice of his.

"Um, thank you."

He sighed. "I knew her, you know."

"No," I said, trying not to betray sudden interest. "How?"

"Oh, just . . . from the club." His smile was all charm. "Her death won't affect your ability to do Ophelia's party, will it?"

I tried not to sigh. Even after all my years catering, the narcissism of the wealthy still took me by surprise. "No. We'll be fine."

"You're sure?"

"Yes, Mr. Unger," I said, my tone deferential.

"I'll be coming with her," Boyd said, his tone so low I had to strain to hear it. Now what, I wondered, would possess him to offer that nugget of information?

"Is that necessary?" asked Neil.

"I'm just giving a helping hand," said Boyd. "As will her assistant, Julian, who has been to your place before, I believe."

"Took food out to my driver the other day?" Neil said. "Kid from Boulder?" His tone filled with distaste. I waited for him to say that everyone in Boulder was a crook, but he only whispered, "I think maybe you were right." He glanced over at Ophelia, then back. "I think perhaps she doesn't know about the party."

"I hope not."

"Please don't be late," he said.

"Yes, sir," I said to Neil's backside as he slid off in the direction of the men's locker room.

"Yes, sir?" Marla echoed. "What, are you an army private now?"

"No," I said. "The guy just scares me."

"Come on," Boyd said jovially. "He's going to clean up America. Let's do what we came here for."

"Bob?" Marla called. "Can we talk?"

Bob looked up from where he was guiding Ophelia on a machine designed to strengthen biceps. The poor girl's scarlet face streamed with sweat, and she seemed very glad to be interrupted. Her thin dark hair was pulled back in a ponytail from which many strands escaped. She wore oversize dark sweatpants along with a graying NHL T-shirt that I recognized as a giveaway from a Colorado Avalanche game. She certainly didn't *appear* to be a wealthy young woman, excited about her twenty-first birthday, just two days away.

Bob reluctantly let her off the machine. Ophelia looked warily at Boyd, then said she would allow us to talk in peace. She put plugs in her ears and flopped onto a nearby bench, where she picked up an oversize book she'd left tented there. I wondered if the interest in muscle building was hers or Bob's. I suspected the latter.

Still, I wanted to make nice, if for no other reason than that I would be catering her birthday party, and, hopefully, her wedding. I limped over and smiled at her, but she assumed a blank face and pulled out one plug.

"I love to read," said I. "What book do you have there?"

She reluctantly held up the spine of her thick volume: *Architectural Planning.* Hmm, not on my night table. She didn't want to elaborate, and I couldn't think of anything else to say, so I walked cautiously back over to the others.

"What's the matter with your leg?" Bob asked, worry creasing his handsome face as I approached Marla's side of the machine. He brushed back the dreads and peered into my eyes. "You're in pain."

"Kitchen accident," I said, acting grieved at my own clumsiness. "Spilled grease on the floor, slid in it, fell. I'm fine," I lied.

"We want to talk to you about Holly," Marla said earnestly. "She was our friend. A dear friend. Did she work out here?"

"Look," Bob wearily replied, crossing his arms across his black Aspen Meadow Country Club Spandex top. "I had the cops at my place until ten last night."

"Hi," said Boyd suddenly, moving forward and offering his large paw. "My name's Sergeant Boyd, also with the Furman County Sheriff's Department. I'm just helping Goldy and Marla deal with the death of their friend. Could you help them out? They want a better understanding of what happened."

Bob's forehead furrowed. To me, he said, "To answer your question, Goldy, Holly used to work out here at the club, but then she quit. That was last fall. I know her mostly through her son, Drew, who helped build trails with our crew out in the Preserve last summer. I don't *know* what could have caused her to collapse like that in your driveway, Marla. I mean, she was just, I don't know, strolling along, right?"

"Right," Marla confirmed. "Was she conscious when you started working on her?"

"No."

"When she worked out here, did she tell you she had a history of heart disease?" I asked.

"No." Bob sighed as he rubbed his eyes. "Like I told the sheriff's department investigators, back when I saw her here, she just did strength training. She knew which machines she was planning to use and she kept charts of her progress. She didn't want any guidance from me. I don't know where her charts went, because we clean out the lockers of people who quit the club as soon as they leave."

"Before the party, when was the last time you saw Holly?" I asked sharply. My leg was beginning to hurt badly, and I wanted to get out of there. "Did she seem ill or tired or anything?"

"I talked to her on the phone on Thursday about doing the presentation for the trails project at your sons' birthday party. But I hadn't seen her in person before the party since the last time she worked out at the club." Bob gestured in the direction of his fiancée. Absorbed in her book, she didn't even notice him. "That's when I started working out with Ophelia," he said, a tad too loudly. "And it turned into something else. My sweet girl and her books. She's really smart, you know."

Ophelia looked up at him, then went back to reading. Most women would have beamed at flattery rained on them, especially from a handsome fiancé. Instead, Ophelia did not look up when she said loudly, "I'm almost done with this chapter." Aha, maybe the earplugs didn't block out the noise, after all. She asked, "Can we skip the rest of the arm curls?"

"Nope," said Bob. "But we won't make these as hard." He winked at us.

Ophelia pulled out the earplugs, inserted a bookmark, and walked back to the machine. Before getting on, she gave us a sour look.

"You know," I said thoughtfully as I hobbled back to the Mercedes next to Marla and Boyd.

Marla said, "I know what you're going to say."

"Okay, mind reader, what?"

"That Ophelia, who's reading some book that makes you involuntarily sneer in disgust, is not the kind of person who would willingly forego college."

"Why, *Marla*," I said admiringly, "I think you'll do okay in this investigating business after all."

10

"Are you sure you want to take on the Inglebys?" she asked, revving the engine. "You really do look as if you're in pain."

"I'm not taking on the Inglebys," I said lightly. I rearranged my legs so the weight was off the bandaged one. "You and Sergeant Boyd are accompanying me as I deliver blueberry muffins."

"And what was Ophelia reading?" Marla asked as she whipped her Mercedes out of the country-club parking lot. When I told her, she said, "*Architectural Planning?* I heard AMCC is going to tear down the existing ugly-ass clubhouse, and build something new. Maybe Ophelia could help them out."

"Just drive." Meanwhile, I punched in 411, got the number for Aspen Meadow Country Club, where I left a message, asking for someone to call me back.

"Why are you doing that?" Marla asked.

"I want to know exactly when she quit the club."

"What difference does that make?"

"Presumably she was either beginning to have, or was in the middle of having, a financial meltdown. So what I'm wondering is, when in the fall did that start?"

Marla said, "The club won't tell you anything. But one thing is certain. She sure wanted me to keep what I knew about the foreclosure to myself."

"Right. I'm just trying to figure out the time frame for these problems starting for her in the financial department. She quit the club. She sold her luxury cars and bought old used ones. In the middle of the year, she pulled Drew out of EPP and put him into CBHS. If an outsider were putting these events together, he or she would say, 'She's short on funds.' And so she was trying to get those funds, or more of them, from someone who wasn't happy about it, and sent her that text message. Maybe it was George or someone else, a client for the collages, say, or somebody who owed her. It could have been from someone who had loaned her money before."

Marla decelerated as she approached a curve. "So. Where did all the wealth she used to have go?"

"The woman loved to shop. And then there was a recession. Where did any of our money go?"

Marla shook her head. "She was having severe financial problems. She tried to extract money from somebody. Then she was killed. What does that tell us?"

Grief reemerged and wrapped itself around me like a heavy cloak. I gripped the basket of muffins and said, "I don't know."

We pulled up to the entrance to the Ingleby mansion fifteen minutes later. Too late, I remembered the last time I had visited Holly here. A high fence surrounded the property, complete with a gate and intercom. To my surprise, though, the gate was open, and we did not have to wait to be allowed entry. At the same time, Marla and I wondered why this was so. Marla zoomed up the driveway. Boyd followed us through.

When we got out of our cars, Boyd came over to us. "Now remember," he said, "we didn't let Drew come over here, because George and Lena had a fight with Holly right before she died under mysterious circumstances . . . and you fell through a trap into the lake. So if they push you to know why Drew isn't staying with them, you just let me say it was department policy, okay?"

"Sure," I said.

Marla complained, "This investigation work doesn't allow me enough latitude to dig for gossip."

Boyd smiled. "Deal with it."

Meanwhile, the answer to the open-gate question came in the form of the sleepy-looking woman who answered the front door of the immense house, built from red brick in complete defiance of Rocky Mountain style, which deemed that all houses above the elevation of Denver should look either like ski lodges or Mexican restaurants.

"I'm the maid," the woman said, blinking. She was tall, white, midfifties, with gray hair like steel wool. She did not seem hostile so much as exhausted. "Who are you? How did you get in here?"

Boyd stepped forward, showed his ID, and introduced himself. "I'm from the sheriff's department. We drove through the open gate."

The maid eyed Marla and me before saying, "Don't tell me you're from the press." She wore jeans and a faded T-shirt that had been silkscreened with a picture of a red Ford Mustang.

"We're not," Marla replied. "But why would you think we were?"

The maid, who had not given her name, stifled a yawn. Then she stared at the firearm in Boyd's holster. "Some other deputies from the sheriff's department were here until late last night. They said journalists might start poking around because George—Dr. Ingleby," she immediately corrected herself, "used to be married to Holly. You still haven't told me who you are."

We introduced ourselves as Goldy Schulz and Marla Korman, friends from the church who'd brought blueberry muffins. Sergeant Boyd was accompanying us to be helpful, I added, although it was clear that bringing muffins did not require a law enforcement escort. We wanted to speak to George, Marla said. We did not mention we were friends of Holly. The maid said her name was Sally, and if we wanted coffee, she would make us some in the kitchen. Oh, I got it: Mustang Sally.

I said we would *love* some coffee. Tall, thin Mustang Sally led the way to the kitchen. My enthusiasm prompted her to say the only coffee Edith would allow her to buy was a discount brand called Frank's. I tried not to groan.

The kitchen was not large. Maybe Holly's energy and vivacity had so filled the place when I'd visited before that I hadn't noticed how dated the house was. I did know one thing: this particular residence had not changed in seventeen years, and maybe it had been this way for the past three, four, or five decades. Laminate wooden cabinets were peeling. Some pulls on those cabinets were missing; the ones that remained featured ceramic roosters and other barnyard animals. I averted my gaze when Marla rolled her eyes at me.

I sat in a chair with red vinyl splitting up the seat. It was one of six at a wood-laminate table beside the kitchen wall. Boyd pulled out the chair opposite mine for Marla, scraping the metal legs across the puckered, pale lime linoleum floor. Then he walked purposefully to the far, shadowy end of the kitchen, where he stood stock-still.

"I've never been here," Marla said under her breath. "Do you think it's changed since 1958? No wonder Holly wanted to be an artist. She could start by fixing this place up."

Mustang Sally began purposefully preparing coffee in an ancient drip machine that sat, tilted, on a buckled laminate counter. "Dr. Ingleby," she called into the chipped plastic intercom. When George didn't respond, Sally waited for the coffee to finish, then poured the dark, viscous fluid into two ceramic mugs emblazoned with the words *Frank's Discount Coffee,* probably free when you bought fifty pounds' worth. When George Ingleby did not answer the intercom a second time, Sally glugged nondairy creamer into a little glass pitcher and put it out with a bowl of sugar.

"I don't think he heard you," Marla said brightly. She sipped her coffee. Her lips formed a moue of despair, and she kicked me under the table. Well, I'd already had my caffeine for the day anyway.

"Dr. Ingleby," Sally said loudly into the ancient box on the wall. "You've got visitors from the church." She turned to us, her face registering surprise for the first time. Clearly, she hadn't had any of Frank's finest caffeine-delivery system yet. "Why do you want to see him? It's his mother who—"

But it was too late. Edith Ingleby slammed open the door to the kitchen. "What are *you two* doing here at this hour?" she cried. Edith Ingleby, whose short curly hair had been frosted, had a frosty disposition to match. Even at this early hour, she wore a floral suit that looked as if it, too, had come from 1958. I recalled Marla had said Edith was eighty-four. But even wearing low heels, she moved quickly across the floor, as if she were used to its wrinkles and dips. "Already out collecting for St. Luke's? The dinner's not until tomorrow night. And in any event, *I* am in charge of fundraising for the columbarium."

"Mrs. Ingleby, they've brought you blueberry muffins," Sally said meekly. The hapless maid seemed to be trying to avoid a storm. "Your favorite."

"Your husband," Edith Ingleby said as she shook a gnarled, beringed finger in my face and advanced toward me with reptilian speed. I leaned back.

"My husband what?" I said.

"He sent my baby away before we could say good-bye." Edith Ingleby fished a muffin out of the basket and put it on the plate that Sally quickly slid underneath. "I don't know why I put up with this. Gone. Gone." She sighed dramatically, then sat down and turned her attention to the muffin. "My daily miracle."

"Your daily miracle?" asked Marla, genuinely puzzled. "Goldy's muffin?"

Edith had sunk her large yellow teeth into the muffin and merely nodded. Marla turned to me. "That's an endorsement for baked goods with blueberries."

"Mother?" exclaimed a startled George Ingleby from the doorway. His black hair stood on end. *Bedhead*, Arch would say. George wore wrinkled khakis and an equally wrinkled yellow golf shirt. He blinked and took us in. Well, it wasn't quite eight o'clock on a Saturday morning. "Why are you here? Something to do with the church?" His voice was calm, but his eyes accused, much as his mother's had.

I introduced Sergeant Boyd, and said we were here to bring muffins to Edith.

George's voice went very quiet as he said, "That's not what it looks like. It looks like you're trying to confuse my mother."

"We have no intention of confusing her," Marla said smoothly. "We were just sitting here, drinking coffee that Sally made for us, and your mother came in and—"

"Oh, it's you all," Lena Ingleby said from the doorway. Her tiny mouth pulled itself into a pout. "Plus a police escort? Why are you here, so early in the morning?"

"Gosh," said Marla, shaking her head at me. "Can't anyone in this house make us feel *welcome*?"

"Here's the deal," I said, aiming my words at George. "We were friends of Holly's—"

Pain crossed George's face, but he only said, "I know."

Lena sighed and held her fingers out at her side. "You haven't answered my question. Are you here to say you really *meant* to invite us to Drew's birthday party last night? And you forgot?"

"Lena dear," George began, but again could not find words.

"But you wanted to go, sweetheart," said Lena, her voice trembling. "And they didn't invite us. You were so hurt."

"It's all right," said George.

Lena dropped her hands and shook her head. "Goldy? Marla? You two should be ashamed. Then there's your friend Holly. That *slut*. And you call your-selves *Christians*."

Boyd, I noted, moved out from the shadows beside the cabinet. Alert and suddenly more present, he took in the scene now unfolding.

Even if we were there too early, even if our appearance was unexpected, even if Holly had spitefully left George and Lena off the guest list, what Lena had said made my mouth hang open. Our friend Holly was *dead*. Yet here was Lena, whom I only knew as a receptionist who had once worked for George, criticizing her.

Lena's verbal blow was too low for Marla. She stood up, put her mug into the dented, stainless-steel sink, and turned to go.

"You're washing that cup!" Edith said, raising one hand, as if she'd just scored a goal. Mustang Sally raced out of the kitchen. It was as if she believed her duties had been discharged, and nobody could make her stay. Or else she couldn't take any more conflict for one day. Meanwhile, like Marla, I wondered about the common courtesy that seemed to be absent here. What was I missing?

"Let's go," Boyd commanded. But for whatever reason, I couldn't move. "*Now,*" he added. Marla stood expectantly, waiting for me. I reluctantly scraped my chair back.

"Darling," George said to his wife, attempting to pacify in that quiet way of his. "Please don't worry about me."

"But I do worry about you," Lena said, her voice low. She turned to us. "Failure to invite father, step-mother, and grandmother to birthday party." She used her fingers to tick off points. "Arriving uninvited, early in morning, at *my* house, to collect money for the church."

When Edith stood, her chair fell over. "This is *my* house!" she howled. "Not yours!"

"Of course it's your house, Mother," said Lena, squatting quickly to right the chair.

"I am not your mother!"

"Let's go outside," George said calmly, pointing to Marla, Boyd, and me.

"Gosh, that was interesting!" Marla said, once the four of us were out in the fresh air. In an attempt to clear my head, I inhaled deeply, once, twice, three times. I was wondering if I should say, *Remind me why things didn't work out between you and Holly, George?* But of course no such words issued from my mouth, because we were there to obtain information, not offend people. Which we'd managed to do anyway, apparently.

"I am not going back into that kitchen to wash a mug, George," Marla warned. She looked at me. "If

I did, that would be a miracle. Like Goldy's muffins, right? What was your mother talking about?"

"Nothing," said George, rubbing his forehead. "She gets addled," he said in that low voice of his. I wondered if he used it on cardiac patients. "First the cops came last night. Then the three of you, arriving this morning, just . . . made it worse. And Lena really is very nice. She's just always been protective of me."

"Look, George," I said, trying to match his soothing tone, "we're only here because we were friends of Holly's, and we're trying to understand how she could have—"

"Oh, please don't," George interrupted. His voice shook, and his brown eyes filled with tears. "I loved her. I did." He pressed his hands over his eyes and sobbed. "I love Drew. I bleed for my boy. I don't know how this could have happened to his mother."

"Nor do we," I said gently. "We're only trying to find out about Holly's . . . situation." I paused. Could I bluff? I wondered. "I kept the notes from a support group we were all in, and I know the details of your, er—"

George looked up abruptly. No, I could not bluff. We should not have come.

"The details of what?" he prompted, rubbing his mustache. When I didn't reply, he said, "Why did your husband send my son off to Alaska so quickly?"

"That's not what happened," Boyd interjected. "Drew had permission from you to go to Alaska." He did not want to tell them about the department's investigation, of course, or that Drew himself had not wanted to stay with George and Lena. He certainly didn't mention that Tom was considering Drew as a person of interest in the case. "Our department has a policy about minors traveling after the death of a parent, and we adhered to it—"

"But I'm his parent, too!" George cried.

Boyd held up his hand. "The victim's sister flew into Denver this morning. They departed together. We just wanted to keep Drew safe until he had packed and taken off. That's all."

At this point, Lena pushed through the front door. Apparently, she didn't want to be left out of anything. She put a protective arm around George.

"We have a policy, and we adhered to it," Boyd repeated.

George said, "I tried to call him, but only got voice mail. The police were *here*"—he pointed at the big house—"so I didn't have a chance to call him more than once."

I said, "I'm sorry this has happened. I'm sorry you couldn't reach Drew when the police were here."

Lena said, "You didn't know the police were here when George was trying to reach Drew? Goldy, I thought you were privy to *all* the investigations of the sheriff's department. Isn't that the rumor around town?"

"Ex-*cuse* me?" said Boyd.

"Ah-ah-ah," Marla warned Lena, singsong fashion, wagging a finger in Lena's face. "Don't you go listening to rumors."

"Says the town's most notorious gossip," Lena replied acidly.

"Well," said Marla, "I think I've had enough insults for one day. How 'bout you, Goldy? Sergeant Boyd?"

I said, "We shouldn't have come. Let's go."

Boyd said something under his breath that sounded a lot like "Thank God."

I waved to Lena as we climbed into Marla's Mercedes. "You all can keep the basket."

"Holly screwed Warren Broome!" Lena hollered after us. "I'll give you that gossip for free, Marla!"

11

"Interesting," said Marla. She was zooming toward the open gates, whose doors began juddering closed before Boyd was even through. Someone had been watching to make sure we actually left—and didn't come back. "Did you know that about Holly and Warren Broome?" Marla asked.

I thought back to Warren Broome's forlornness at the birthday party. He had seemed to be feeling uncomfortable, as if everyone there knew his sordid history. But more important, he had stared, unblinking, at Holly.

"Yes, okay, maybe he appeared lovesick. I wasn't aware of any affair between Holly and Warren. You know I depend on *you* to keep me up on these things. Warren *was* gaping at Holly at the party last night."

"Was she gaping back?"

"Not really," I said. "She seemed to be avoiding him."

"Patsie Boatfield's son goes to Christian Brothers High School," Marla protested. "How come you don't know about this?"

"I'm a full-time caterer—"

"When you're not nosing into investigations."

"Thanks. That, too. But there's no way I could or even would be aware of what goes on between the thousand-plus sets of CBHS parents."

"Well, what *do* you know?"

"Not much. Patsie is one of those parent-type friends whom you see at your children's activities but don't really see outside of them. I'm figuring she and Warren married quietly, probably because they didn't want to alert the press. Warren and Patsie can't have been married that long. And anyway, how come *you* haven't heard about this supposed affair between Holly and Warren? Patsie's house is in Flicker Ridge. What do we know about Warren Broome, anyway?"

"Not a whole lot," said Marla, "apart from the fact that he was only temporarily disbarred or whatever it's called when a shrink can't shrink people for a while. But when we get back to your place, I'll make some calls. What were you going to ask George?" Marla asked. "Details about the child support?"

"Yes. But apparently even *I* have qualms when it comes to digging for information."

"But if I know you," Marla said, "you have the details of Holly's settlement and child support situation somewhere, because you took the Amour Anonymous notes, and have kept them all these years."

"I did indeed." I thought of George's face as it crumpled in grief. "Poor George," I said.

"Oh, dammit. Damn *this*," said Marla. A cry escaped from her lips, and she signaled to pull over. When her tires crunched on the dirt, she turned to me. "Holly's dead, isn't she? She's never coming back—"

I held my friend as she cried. Boyd hustled up.

"What's wrong?" he asked through the open window.

"We're just mourning our friend," I said, and then Marla and I cried together.

Once we reached home, Boyd said he would stay in his car. We were to call him if we wanted to go out again.

In the kitchen, Julian was grating a block of cheddar so orange it had to be for Arch. My son didn't like the sharp, white variety. An omelet pan, butter, and beaten eggs stood at the ready. Arch was sitting upright at the kitchen table, his face drawn. It had been a hard twelve hours for him, too. A pristinely laid place—Julian's doing, no doubt—was in front of him. Arch wore a rumpled navy sweatsuit that I suspected he'd grabbed from the hamper.

"Clothes are clean, Mom," he said, to my unasked question. He sighed deeply. "How's your leg?"

"Hurts," I said as I propped my left foot on a chair. "How about you? Are you all right?" I asked.

"No, Mom. I am not all right."

"Well," I began, "what can I—" I stopped myself. It might be okay to question other people on their states of mind; it was definitely not okay to interrogate Arch, much less to see if he wanted a hug, or anything else.

"Should I add another couple of eggs to this omelet?" Julian asked us. He plopped a chunk of butter into the pan. It hissed as it slid sideways.

"Oh, yes, please," said Marla brightly.

Arch groaned. "I'm starving here."

"All right, never mind, I'll make a separate one for you and Goldy," Julian said to me, winking at Marla. "Need to feed Mr. Starving here. How about Sergeant Boyd? Should I ask him in to have food?"

"He said he wants to stay in his prowler."

Arch gave me a puzzled look. "Where have you been?"

"Just . . . over to see George."

"Drew's dad? Why?"

I shook my head as my throat closed up. I rubbed my forehead. "Trying to figure out what happened to Holly. He . . . couldn't help." Remembering Lena's parting shot, I weighed whether to ask Arch if he knew anything about Warren Broome, the stepfather of Alexander Boatfield, his teammate. My son might not want to talk about his own emotional state, but would he know anything about the Boatfields? Probably not. Arch was generally clueless on these matters, and even if he were *not* clueless, he would say he was.

While Arch ate—forking up huge mouthfuls, so he must have truly been hungry—I checked our voice mail, which showed I had two messages. The first was an anxious one from Father Pete: Had I thought about working with Kathie Beliar on the church dinner? Did I really think she could bring a dozen more people to the dinner . . . and the church? Miss Beliar had called him again, he said. St. Luke's *so* needed new parishioners, he added apologetically, and we could use the extra money for the columbarium. Did I, Father Pete tentatively asked, possess the advertising resources that Kathie Beliar claimed to have? She'd said I did *not* have advertising resources.

I shook my head. Poor, naive Father Pete.

When Marla announced she would put the kibosh on the co-catering bit, I hit pause on my machine. Marla called Father Pete as I washed my hands and set two more places. Once Marla was connected to the church's voice mail, she said that no, Kathie Beliar could not co-cater the church dinner the next night, because she, Marla, was paying for the meal, and if Father Pete was going to hire another caterer besides her friend Goldy, then the church could pay for it.

"That ought to take care of Miss Beliar," she said, pressing her phone's power button. She watched Julian mince scallions, grate Gruyère, whisk eggs, and melt more butter. Arch, meanwhile, washed his dishes and made himself scarce. "Go ahead," Marla said, satisfied, once our omelet was cooking. She nodded at our message machine. "What else have you got on there?"

Julian and I smiled at Marla's nosiness, but she was doing the driving, paying for the church dinner, and most important, helping gather information on what might have happened to Holly. We—I—owed her.

On my machine, Patsie Boatfield asked if I could call her.

"My, my," said Marla as she washed her hands. "Maybe she heard the gossip about her hubby, too."

"What gossip and what hubby would that be?" Julian said, sliding a heavenly scented omelet onto a platter between us.

"Oh, nothing," Marla said, uncharacteristically closemouthed for once. She picked up the platter and made for the door to our basement. "Girls' Club meeting in the basement! Julian? Could you please bring down plates, napkins, and flatware?"

"Thanks, Julian, really," I said as he gathered up what we needed onto a tray, then added glasses of water.

With genuine concern, he asked, "What's the matter with Marla?"

"Oh, Lena and Edith Ingleby were mean to her."

"People have been mean to Marla forever." He heaved the tray onto his shoulder with the professionalism of the restaurant-trained. "It never upset her before."

"It did this time," I said firmly, then followed him down the stairs.

As I limped carefully toward our cellar, I remembered when Tom had moved from his cabin outside Aspen Meadow into our house. He'd lived with us a few months before tentatively asking if we could take on some home-improvement projects. He promised we would have to agree on everything before he started.

At first, I suspected he wanted to toss all our old furniture and replace it with his lovingly maintained antiques. But as it turned out, the antiques had found pride of place in the house, and I was more than willing to donate the furniture that Tom's pieces had displaced. Our first big project had been cleaning out the garage so Tom could store his tools. Luckily, we'd ended up with so much extra space that when Julian moved in with us, he had been able to store his few boxes next to Tom's shelves.

After the garage project, Tom and I started on the basement, with the idea that we would make room for his computer and files. Since that meant sorting through much accumulated stuff, I agreed, albeit reluctantly. The garage had been a piece of cake, so to speak. The basement was a whole bakery's worth of issues.

Over Tom's ensuing days off, though, we filled dozens of bags with discarded toys, outgrown clothes, and assorted gewgaws. We saved what I was desperate to hang on to—all the notes and files I'd had forever—then donated what was usable, closed my eyes, and tossed the rest. Nevertheless, I'd looked with despair at the new space. It seemed dingy and barren until Tom suggested we paint it white, which we did. Then we put up bright red-, yellow-, and blue-striped curtains in the half windows above the washer and dryer, his desk, and our combined bookshelves and file cabinets. In the end, it seemed like a whole new room. I'd been grateful, and still was.

Once Julian clopped back up the stairs, Marla and I divided the omelet, which was creamy, tangy, and utterly delicious. Then we portioned out the tasks. We would call Patsie together. She had been a great help when Holly collapsed. And we both felt sorry for her for marrying Womanizing Warren. So we would put my phone on speaker, we decided, then judge if our reactions to what she said were in sync.

When I phoned the Boatfields' place, Warren Broome answered, and I was very glad I'd put the phone on speaker. After I identified myself he barked, "What do *you* want?"

"I just, well"—should I call him Warren or Dr. Broome?—"your wife called me."

"Why did she do that?" he asked, suddenly suspicious.

"You live in the same house as she does," I said, suddenly fatigued by how cantankerous everyone was this morning. "Why don't you ask her?"

He hung up.

"Weird," said Marla. "Okay, let's give Patsie some time. Maybe she'll phone you back. If she doesn't,

THE WHOLE ENCHILADA · 173

I'll try to call her." She eyed the wall of file cabinets. "Please tell me you have this organized."

"More or less," I said, trying not to sound lame.

"I'll take our dishes to the kitchen," she offered. "While I'm there, I'll go into your dining room, to call a couple of people to see if anyone knows anything about this supposed affair between Warren and Holly. You see if you can find what we're looking for in the money department."

So I did. I kept the file for Amour Anonymous next to one with the curriculum for teaching Sunday School with Holly. We'd hardly ever needed the church school curriculum, and as Tom had kindly pointed out, I'd kept both files for close to ten years. But I was adamant. I might need my meeting notes someday. This morning, I had not commented to Tom that we were now seeing proof of this philosophy.

I extracted the file, and remembered why the Amour Anonymous members had started the whole note-taking enterprise in the first place. Even though we were anonymous to the outside world, we recognized early on that some of us were having great insights. We wanted to keep track of them. Since no one else had wanted to be secretary, I volunteered. At the end of each year, we had a big party where we celebrated each other's progress, and I read out our best insights.

I was dismayed to see that the edges of the pages of the spiral notebooks were now brown and curling, and was glad I'd labeled the notebooks by year. Luckily, I'd also written down who was present at each meeting. Holly had only been a member for two years. But as I looked at my notes, it seemed as if I'd spilled coffee or that my ink had run on at least half the pages. Even I had trouble making out what I'd written.

When Marla returned, she said gloomily that all of her regular sources said yes, they'd heard Holly and Warren had had something going, but they all thought it had ended a long time ago.

"Give me something to do," she said.

I gave her one year's worth of notes. She flipped through the pages and made a face. "What am I looking for in this run-together chicken scratch, Sherlock?"

I felt embarrassed that I hadn't at least typed up the notes when the group had ended, but back then, there hadn't seemed to be any point. "What we should search for at this point is Holly's settlement with George."

Marla shook her head. "All right, I'll try to look for numbers."

Half an hour later, neither one of us had been able to find the details of Holly's financial situation. But I was *sure* they'd been in the notes. Marla, convinced I might have written out the numbers in longhand, was taking longer to read my handwriting than I was. I offered to make coffee.

"It better not be Frank's finest," Marla said, peering close at a page, "or I'm going to have a fit."

When I brought iced lattes downstairs a few minutes later, she was puzzling over another page. "Now I know why lawyers make so much money." Marla was an expert on the law, at least when it pertained to money.

"There's something in there about attorneys?" I asked.

"Not yet. But they have to go through boxes and boxes of documents. They want to be paid for being forced to concentrate on what is excruciatingly boring, like details of divorces, wills, trusts, taxes, and lots of parties of the first part and parties of the second part."

"So, no lawyers yet."

"Nope. But I'll tell you this: I've never seen so many visits to doctors in my life."

"We were keeping tabs on each other!" I said defensively. "Wasn't that worth mentioning? Also, we're trying to find out if Holly mentioned having any medical problems, especially with her heart."

"I suppose," she mumbled. "I had no idea investigative work was so tedious." She sipped her latte and seemed to revive. "Let's try calling the Boatfields again."

But when she punched in the number, we got Warren once more. Marla shook her head and pointed at me. I cursed silently, because I hadn't thought of what to say if he answered. "Um, is Patsie there?" I asked, trying to sound innocent.

If possible, he was even ruder than he'd been the first time. "Why do you keep calling?" he said, his voice impatient. "I'll tell her to call you when she gets back. Who is this, anyway?"

"Goldy the caterer," I reminded him. I thought fleetingly of Kathie Beliar, but didn't figure the distinction was worth noting to Warren, who didn't seem to give a fig salad about who I was. Anyway, it was Patsie who had called me.

"Yes, yes, all *right*," Warren barked. Marla shook her head and pantomimed a corkscrew-next-to-the-ear motion.

"Actually," I hazarded, "there's something else you can help me with, Warren. It has to do with Holly Ingleby. She, Holly . . . gave me a piece of information," I added, "for you."

There was a long pause. "What was it?" he asked, his voice suddenly soft.

I said, "Uh, uh," while Marla scribbled rapidly on a piece of paper: *Not over the phone! Tell him you want to give it to him in person!*

"This phone is not secure," I lied breezily. "And anyway, I was only supposed to give this information to you face-to-face," I said. And then, in what I thought was a stroke of brilliance, I said, "You'll be at the church fund-raiser tomorrow night?"

"Yes, yes, Patsie insisted we should go," he said. "Although I think Father Pete is . . ."

"What?" I said, genuinely surprised. *Everyone* liked Father Pete.

"I'll tell you when you give me this information," he said smugly, like we were doing a drug deal.

This time it was my turn to hang up. Fifteen minutes later, we found some information *we'd* been looking for.

"Two hundred fifty thousand dollars as a settlement," I crowed to Marla. "And an additional two hundred twenty-four thou a year, with cost-of-living increases, for child support. And nine years ago, too! George also was on the hook to pay private school and college tuition, wherever Drew got in. Holy moly! The Jerk was a doctor, and I didn't get close to that kind of money. I *had* to work."

"The Jerk didn't have access to inherited funds," Marla said matter-of-factly. "*George* did."

"I see your point," I replied as the phone rang. I peered at the caller ID. *Boatfield.*

"Apparently, Warren can't wait until tomorrow night to get his gossip fix," Marla said. But it was not Warren. It was Patsie Boatfield, who sounded out of breath. I dutifully put the phone on speaker.

We exchanged mournful greetings. We both said how awful the previous evening had been, and how terrible it had been that Holly died. I thanked her for being so kind and helpful.

After a moment, she asked, "Has anyone reported to you that they were sick after the birthday party last night?"

"Well," I said, "not exactly sick. Why?"

"Oh, I just had horrific nightmares," she replied. "The worst I've had in my life. I thought it was because of Holly dying, but then I thought, 'This just isn't normal.'"

"I'm sorry." I grabbed a clean piece of paper. "What did you have to eat and drink?"

"Let's see. Chips and guac, arroz con pollo, salad, the torta, and cake. Plus a beer. It seems to go so well with Mexican food. Do you think there was something in the food? Did other people have problems?"

"Yes, some guests had nightmares," I said. I finished scribbling the list, tore off the sheet, and stuffed it into my pocket. "Um, what about Warren?"

"What about him?"

"Did he . . . have nightmares?"

"Not that he told me."

"He sounded upset when I called you back. Did he . . . know Holly?" I asked, while Marla made slashing motions across her throat. She was writing furiously on a new piece of paper.

"Well, I think he *did,* but that was a long time ago."

"How long ago, do you know? We're trying to piece together her medical history."

"I honestly don't know. The way I heard it, they were at a convention together over in Boulder. Some doctor thing."

"Some doctor thing?" I repeated. I was trying to get her to say more, but Marla was flapping the paper in front of me. I finally read what she thrust under my nose: *No! No! We want WARREN to tell us what was going on! Patsie won't know anything, and this will just give him advance warning that we're onto him, so he'll shut* was all she had written.

"So Warren and Holly were at a doctor thing in Boulder," I said. I wondered if it was the same conference that the Jerk and I had attended. Holly and George had been there, too. Since I'd never seen Holly at a subsequent conference, it sounded as if Warren might also have been there. "But you don't know exactly when this conference was. Can you ask him?"

"I would," said Patsie, sounding perplexed, "but he's in the bathroom and won't come out."

"Is he . . . sick?"

She paused so long I thought she might have hung up. I peered down at the phone. We were still connected.

"No," Patsie Boatfield said. "He's crying."

12

"I'm really sorry," I said again. "Everyone is just so upset about what happened last night."

"That's true."

There was a long silence between us while I tried to think of what to say in the present moment while I endeavored to call up the past. *A doctors' meeting in Boulder.* Eighteen years ago, Holly and I had accompanied our spouses to a doctors' conference in Boulder. We hadn't actually met each other there, though, which we'd always found to be funny. Our first meeting had been the one where we were cooing to our sons outside the hospital nursery, months later. Holly hadn't been very interested in the medical convention, no surprise.

Patsie couldn't mean the same one from all those years ago, could she?

"I suppose I should go knock on the bathroom door," Patsie said.

I said, "Wait, Patsie. Apart from meeting Holly at a doctors' conference, did Warren, you know, have any medical knowledge about Holly Ingleby?"

"I don't *think* so. I mean, he never mentioned her apart from that one encounter. Should I ask him?"

"I have no idea," I said truthfully. "I mean, do you know if she was . . . a patient of his? I mean," I rushed on, "I know there's doctor-patient confidentiality, even after death. But the department is desperate to learn Holly's medical history, and her physician is in Hawaii, out of cell-phone range. And I was providing most of the food last night, so I'm trying to see if she had a medical problem that may have caused what happened to her." I tried to say this casually, sympathetically even. I did not want to appear to be asking, *Was she one of the female clients that he was having sex with?* Which, of course, was precisely what I was getting at.

"I don't know if she was a patient of his," Patsie replied. "I do know that she was *not* the one who reported him to the Colorado Board of Medical Examiners. She is *not* the reason he lost his license for six months."

"Sorry, Patsie, I was just trying to come up with a theory for why Holly collapsed."

"I'm sorry, Goldy. People have such prurient interests," Patsie said, her tone apologetic.

"I don't," I said.

"All right, okay, I'm just sensitive. You wouldn't believe the number of people who want *all* the ghastly details about Warren and *all* of his supposed indiscretions. He told me, and I believe him, that he made *one* mistake, with a very needy woman. You know, I want to say to these nosy people, 'If you're so interested, go to the library and read the newspaper accounts!'"

"I am not one of those people," I replied. I did not add, *Lena Ingleby said they were having an affair. I just want information that will help me figure out what happened to my friend.*

"See you tomorrow night, then," she said, again apologetic. "It's just that your question hit a nerve."

"I didn't mean to."

"You know, I mentioned to a friend that we were thinking about having a midsummer's eve party? And yesterday, Kathie Beliar called me. Do you know her?"

I bit the inside of my cheeks and tried not to imagine steam coming out of my ears. "I know her," I said stiffly.

"Well, she wanted to cater it! She said if I hired her, she would only charge half of what you were asking."

"And what did you say?"

Patsie laughed. "I told her I was just thinking of doing hamburgers and hot dogs, and I would be doing all the cooking myself! But I thought you should know."

"Thanks. And again, I'm grateful you were so helpful last night." When we signed off, Marla and I exchanged a rueful look.

She said, "I heard."

"Damn Kathie Beliar."

"Indeed."

"Plus, I do feel sorry for Patsie. Being married to Warren, I mean."

"So do I. What she had to say was not what you'd call illuminating," Marla said. "Adding to our problems, you may have shut Warren up forever."

I waved this away. "Trust me. These things progress in stages."

"Stages? Like the first act and the second act? And by the way, you're looking piqued."

I shook my head. Talk about *hitting a nerve*.

"What have you decided to do about Kathie Beliar and Goldy's Catering?"

I felt myself flush with anger. "I don't know."

An hour later, I said I had to take a break.

"A cooking break," Marla replied, "if I know you."

"Is that so terrible?"

"No, go."

In the kitchen, I noticed that Julian had thawed and drained some frozen chopped spinach. I decided that even though I'd told Tom I wouldn't be cooking for the business that day, I would feel better if I did a little experimentation. Say with a hot spinach dip? Marla could deal with a few carbs, couldn't she? After Julian said he'd thawed the spinach to make a dip recipe he'd found for me on the Internet, I stared at what he'd printed out and decided to make a few changes. First I minced garlic and grated fontina and Parmigiano-Reggiano. Once the garlic was sizzling slowly in melted butter, I snagged cream cheese and Alfredo sauce from the walk-in. This was not going to be a low-fat recipe, but clients never liked those, anyway.

"Looks good," said Julian. "May I have a taste?"

"Sure." I handed him a cracker loaded with the hot dip, and he nodded his approval. "Think you've got a winner here, Goldy. What are you going to call it?"

I reflected for a moment. "Not-So-Skinny Spinach Dip."

"Good idea. Now why don't you let me take some dip plus a sandwich out to Boyd, and then I'll bring you all high-protein salad lunches?"

"Sounds great. Thanks."

To my great satisfaction, Marla cooed happily over the dip. Julian brought us Niçoise salads a short time later. After we reluctantly put our dishes away, we started in again on the notes, looking for medical information. My eyes were beginning to cross when we were interrupted by Arch, of all people.

"Mom?" he called down the stairs. "Are you here?"

"Yes, and I even remembered you were bringing Gus over."

"Mom? It's . . . something else." He clomped down the stairs. His face was sweaty, and his toast-colored eyebrows hooked with worry as he regarded me anxiously.

Fear raced down my spine. "Is everything all right?"

"I don't know." He swallowed.

"What's up? You're scaring me."

"When I drove Gus back here?" Arch continued in the typical teenager's interrogatory. "Past the church? Your van was there. I mean, it *looked* like your van. I thought the painting on the side said, you know, 'Goldy's Catering.' But those aren't the exact words on your van, are they?" When I muttered in the negative, Arch rushed on. "Well anyway, I didn't really think about it. I just figured you must have gone down to St. Luke's to set up for the dinner tomorrow night. But then I got home, and Julian said your van was in the garage. He said when you came back from being out with Marla, you'd stayed *here*. So, what's going on? Did you buy another van and have it painted . . . ?"

"No, I did not." When I enunciated each word, Arch stepped back as if stung. "It's not you, hon. Kathie Beliar is what's going on. Let's check it out," I said to Marla.

So the straw had officially broken the camel's back. Adrenaline fueled my somewhat faster limp back up the stairs. In the deep recesses of my brain, I knew you weren't supposed to act on anger. I was aware that reacting to irritation by becoming aggressive was not the answer. All this zipped through my mind as I hobbled across the newly emerging grass. Technically Boyd could have taken me, but Marla was revving her Mercedes. Julian followed me out the door and helped me into the passenger seat.

"Why is Boyd still here?" he asked.

"Just tell him we're going to St. Luke's, will you? Kathie Beliar is there, trying to manipulate Father Pete."

But Boyd was already beside Marla's window. She told him we had to go to the church.

Julian begged, "Please don't get into what's going to be a fruitless argument."

"I thought fruitless was a type of salad," I said.

Julian shook his head and said he would keep the boys inside. Boyd told him to set the security system. I gripped the armrest while Marla, her face locked, raced toward the church. When Boyd flashed his lights at us, she slowed down a bit.

"What do you think is going on?" Marla asked.

"I don't have a clue. But it's about time I found out."

In the lot, a van that looked almost precisely like mine, with the words GOLDY'S CATERING on the side, was parked outside St. Luke's. Father Pete's battered old green Chevy was also there. I found this odd, as he had not answered the church line when Marla called. If Audrey Millard, Father Pete's devoted secretary, had gone home—which would be normal for a Saturday— and Father Pete was the only one at the church, our dear rector *always* picked up the phone. Father Pete tried to expect the best, and usually got the worst. Had he deemed his meeting with Kathie Beliar too important to answer the phone? *That just isn't like him*, I thought stubbornly. *That damn Kathie Beliar.*

Marla heaved open one of the unlocked solid wood doors. Right behind her, Boyd said, "Wait. I'm going in front of you."

It took a moment for our eyes to adjust to the darkness of the sanctuary. Light from the sacramental candle shuddered. The air felt disturbed.

"I hear something," I said. We listened. After a moment, a faint groan coiled down the hallway to our left.

"Dammit," said Marla. "Let's get—"

"Stop," Boyd ordered, pulling out his weapon. "Let me go first."

But Marla ignored him and ran down the hall toward Father Pete's office. Slowed by my injured leg, I shambled behind a hustling Boyd, past the locked doors to the Sunday School rooms.

Marla screamed. When I hobbled up beside Boyd and her, my stomach turned over.

There were two bodies sprawled on the stone floor. Kathie Beliar, whom I recognized from her website photo, lay next to Father Pete. Blood slowly swirled out of both of them. An explosion of paper, hundreds of documents, along with scattered gray church files, lay littered on the floor. Some of them were sopping up blood. The back door to the church stood open.

"Call 911," Boyd ordered Marla. He held up his weapon. "Get behind me, both of you. Hey!" he called. "Police! Anyone here?"

When there was no response, I dropped painfully to my knees. Marla was on her cell with emergency services. I asked Boyd if I could touch Kathie Beliar.

He said sharply, "Wrist only."

Kathie Beliar had no pulse. If she was breathing, I couldn't tell. Father Pete was alive, but barely. His eyelids fluttered. Another weak groan issued from his lips.

Both of them had been stabbed. Whoever did this, I thought slowly, also broke into Audrey's office and found the key to the file cabinets. The drawers had been dumped out; the contents lay strewn everywhere. Whoever had attacked Kathie and Father Pete had then stepped around, and partially through, the pools of blood, in order to get out the back door.

I averted my eyes to keep from being sick. There were scarlet smears on the wall. If there was a weapon nearby, I couldn't see it.

Kathie's wounds were so deep, and there was so much blood, I could not tell exactly where she had been cut. I asked Boyd if I could check on Father Pete. When he nodded, I pulled up Father Pete's black clerical shirt, wiped away blood, and located two stab wounds on his abdomen. Without thinking, I tore off my sweater and pressed it into the cuts to stop the bleeding.

Marla, when she wasn't giving details to the emergency operator, could not stop saying, "I've never seen so much blood," alternating with, "Do you think Father Pete's going to make it? Oh, please, Goldy, tell me he's going to be all right," and "Yes, operator, I'm still here, yes, St. Luke's Episcopal Church in Aspen Meadow . . . yes, two people. Sergeant Boyd is here."

We'd learned a lot of things in Med Wives 101, but whether someone was going to make it after so much blood loss was not one of them.

It wasn't long before two pairs of EMTs raced into the church. Then, although there was no fire, came engines from the Aspen Meadow Volunteer Fire Department. The four EMTs told us to back off and let them do their job. Boyd moved efficiently out of the way, but Marla and I had a harder time allowing our priest to be out of our sight. The two techs assigned to Kathie were quickly able to tell she was dead. But I also knew their protocol was to keep working on her until they sent telemetry down to Denver to have their diagnosis confirmed.

I couldn't see what the two medics ministering to Father Pete were doing, because they'd told us to go back down the hall and stay out of the way. Marla and I retreated to the church kitchen. Eventually the two techs who'd been working on Father Pete raced past us, with our priest on a stretcher.

Finally, Tom came, along with more sheriff's department cars. He conferred quickly with Boyd. Then he gave me that look of his, a mixture of relief and worry. "While our crime-scene guys are working on this, we're going outside. You, me, Marla. You're going to tell me exactly why you came here, and what you were doing."

As we walked back through the vestibule, Marla insisted on telling the story, from Father Pete's message to me, to her calling him back, to Arch relaying the news that some other van with the name Goldy's Catering was parked at the church. We'd come down to St. Luke's, Marla said, to, to, to . . .

"To?" Tom prompted. We'd arrived in front of the church and were standing beside one of the tall, shaggy hemlocks.

Marla slumped against the exposed rock of the church's exterior wall. "I suppose," she whispered, "we wanted to confront her. Kathie, I mean."

"And you two and Boyd found this scene."

"I'm sorry, Tom," I said.

"Don't be," he replied, as he turned to a new page in his notebook. He looked me over carefully, and I was aware for the first time that I had Kathie Beliar's and Father Pete's blood on my clothes and skin. "You probably saved Pete's life. All right, now, tell me why you think someone might attack this woman and our priest."

Without prompting, Marla went through the story again with Tom. This time he wrote down everything.

I glanced at my watch: almost three. Without warning, I began to cry. I'd loved Holly. I hadn't known Kathie Beliar, and now that she was dead, I felt guilty and small. But I adored Father Pete. He couldn't, *couldn't* die.

"Goldy, in just a little bit here, you're going to go home, shower, and rest," Tom said, pocketing his notebook and pulling out tissues.

"Right." This actually made me laugh. I pressed my hands onto my closed eyes. I thought ruefully back to the doctor last night telling me I should take a week to recuperate.

A team of victim advocates showed up in a van. They cleaned off our skin and gave us fresh sweat suits to change into in their van. Then they wrapped us in handmade quilts. Our relief at receiving comfort in the form of a quilt was tempered by the sight of the coroner's van pulling up to the church.

It was for Kathie Beliar.

"I'm sorry, Miss G.," Tom said. "I want you to be able to leave, but I need your story while it's fresh." He pulled his notebook back out and lifted his chin in my direction. "Start with when I left this morning. I know Boyd went a couple of places with you. But I want to hear the whole thing from you."

"Okay." I told him about Marla coming over, that she'd had terrible nightmares, just like the Smythes and Patsie Boatfield. I remembered I'd stuck the piece of paper into my pocket that had the list of what everyone who'd had nightmares had eaten. I handed it over to Tom. "Have you found anything in Holly's bloodstream?" I asked.

"I'll get to that. Keep going."

I told him about our trip to the country club, where muscle-bound Bob had been training an uninterested but very studious Ophelia. She'd appeared bored with us, but intent on her book. Tom wanted to know what she'd been reading, and I told him.

"*Architectural Planning*?" Tom repeated incredulously. "Not exactly bedside-table reading material."

"Not exactly. What do you suppose it means?"

"I don't know. Why did you want to go to the club in the first place?"

I told him that Holly's having financial problems had made us wonder when, exactly, she had quit the club. We also wanted to find out if Bob knew something about Holly's medical history. Bob told us, as he had the sheriff's department, that yes, Holly had been a member of the club, and she had worked out in the new fitness facility. But she kept her own progress charts, which had been tossed by the club when they cleaned out the lockers. Tom nodded, but wrote nothing. Also, I added hastily, to show I was not a complete buffoon in helping figure out what had happened to my friend, Neil Unger said he had known Holly.

"He knew her?" Tom prompted.

"He didn't offer any details. The main thing was, he wanted to find out if Holly's dying would upset his party plans."

"After the country club, where did you go?"

"To Edith Ingleby's house," Marla said. "What a *bitch!*"

"The Inglebys' house?" Tom asked me. "We did question them, Miss G."

"I know." I stopped. "I took Edith some muffins that I remembered she liked. And Boyd was with us the whole time. Remember, you told me we could go out and talk to people. That's why you put Boyd with us in the first place."

"I know, I know," he said, his tone softer. "I just worry about you."

"We were still trying to find out more about Holly's financial situation, why she moved Drew from EPP to CBHS, why she lost her house, why she didn't seem to have any—"

"You thought the Inglebys would share that information?" Tom asked.

"Well, they didn't," I said flatly, and left Marla to tell the tale of Mustang Sally the maid, of Edith's cheap mugs and even cheaper coffee, and her inability to get along with anyone. She also told him about George appearing overcome with despair, and Lena acting alternately protective and angry.

"But you didn't get any information on Holly," Tom concluded.

"Oh, but we did," Marla said, her eyes lighting up. "Lena virtually spat out the news that Holly had an affair with Warren Broome. She didn't say when this happened. But back at your place, I called my pals who might know. They said that indeed, they'd heard that Holly and Warren had had, you know, a *moment.* But they thought it was long over and done with."

Tom said, "Anything else?"

I started sobbing again when I told him about the recorded call from Father Pete. Tom calmly asked what it was about, and I told him that once again, Kathie Beliar was pressuring our priest to let her help cater the dinner the following night. Marla called him back and left a message saying no deal. At this, Tom pulled aside one of his team and said to go to our house, to see if anyone there had actually talked to Father Pete.

"Good idea," I said. But wouldn't Julian have mentioned it if he had? Tom nodded to me to continue. "The second message on our machine," I went on, "was the one from Patsie."

"Warren Broome's new wife," Tom said. "To tell you about her nightmares? You called her, or vice versa?"

"She called me. But I got Warren twice, before Patsie called me back." I told him about Warren crying in the bathroom.

"Any other details?" Tom asked.

My brain seemed to fill with fog. I fought to clear it. "Remember, Patsie called *me*. We had the information from Lena, which we didn't trust, and some second- and third-hand gossip from Marla's pals. So after Patsie told me about Warren sobbing in the bathroom, I asked if she thought whether Warren actually knew Holly."

"You might have let us do that. But I know, I know, I *told* you you could talk to people." He inhaled. "So what did Patsie say?"

"She said Warren met Holly at a doctors' meeting in Boulder."

Tom noted this. "When?"

"Don't know, but I figured it was the one from eighteen years ago."

"You said you talked to Warren Broome twice?"

"When I was trying to return Patsie's call, I phoned their house. Warren answered, and he was awful. He . . . he . . . doesn't like Father Pete," I blurted out.

"He doesn't?" Tom's voice was sharp. "Why not?"

"He wouldn't say," I replied.

Again Tom motioned to a team member, and talked to him in a low voice. "All right," Tom said to me. "Was that the first call to Warren, or the second?"

"The second. He was so rude! But remember, we had that tidbit from Lena Ingleby, which nobody had confirmed yet," I replied. "And . . . I wanted to get more information out of him, so I told him Holly had left a piece of news for him, that I was supposed to relate to him, and that I would do so at the fund-raiser tomorrow night."

"*What* news?" Tom said, his voice disbelieving.

"Oh, well," I said, feeling foolish, "there wasn't any. Isn't any. I just wanted to know why he was gaping at Holly at the party, and if what Lena said was true. I thought I should sort of, you know, question him in person."

Tom shook his head. "Okay, Miss G., that was going too far. We are dealing with a murderer here. Even if Boyd accompanies you all over the Rocky Mountains, you *do not* set up meetings with people who were at the party, especially by using misinformation."

"*Okay.* But I was only trying to call Patsie back!"

"When was all this?"

"Oh, about an hour before Arch came home with the news that a van looking like mine was down at the church."

Tom pressed his lips together, thinking. "Miss G. I do appreciate your insights. I know you like to talk to people who are friends, or acquaintances, or former clients, or parishioners, or . . . whatever. And it's helpful when you and Marla get folks to volunteer information to you. That's different from interrogating people the way a cop does, okay? It certainly differs from telling someone you have information about his relationship to a crime victim that you really don't have."

"Okay," I said. "You're right. Sorry."

"Now there's something I'm sorry to tell you." Tom took my hands in his. "Since the van Kathie was driving looked like yours, and since she'd made her appearance like yours, we have to consider that someone was trying to harm, or kill, you."

The bristle of activity around us momentarily dulled. I was left with the questions: *Who would want to kill Father Pete? What could possibly be in the church files that a killer would want?*

Was someone after me, too? If so, why?

13

Even though Tom had said we could leave soon, he wanted me to take him through our entire morning yet again. My bruised leg was beginning to throb, and I desperately wanted to rest it. I asked if we could sit beside the stand of blue spruce that had been planted around a statue of Saint Francis, just above the church parking lot. The flow of cops and crime-scene techs in and out of the church continued unabated. I wanted to put my back to that.

"Sorry, Miss G. Of course. I should have thought."

When we'd settled by the evergreens, I pulled the quilt around the much-washed sweat suit I had just been given and willed myself to relax. As I did so, I remembered to tell Tom what we'd learned from the Amour Anonymous notes: that Holly had received a quarter of a million dollars as a settlement from George when they divorced, and she was supposed to get two hundred thousand-plus bucks in child support, in addition to private school and college tuition. He whistled. I asked if his team had managed to dig up anything on her financial situation.

"Yes," Tom said. He eyed Marla warily. She folded her legs beneath her and shrugged.

"Tell Goldy what you want," she said, tossing her head and raking her tawny hair with bejeweled fingers. "Leave me out of it, go ahead. But there's that driving thing. Julian has a license; so does Arch. What the heck, Boyd can drive her. *Maybe.* But while you're working on this case, you want to be *sure* somebody can chauffeur your wife around, right? Even if Boyd is with us on our way to Timbuktu? You also need to be confident of *my* help, yes? I, a longtime friend, fellow country-club member, and shopping pal of Holly's, am also a parishioner at St. Luke's, and know Father Pete well. And I'll bet I can get you more good scoop on Kathie Beliar and Warren Broome than your department can find in a week. So you'd better not give me that chilly shoulder of yours, Tom Schulz."

Tom sighed. "Holly stowed her financial files in her desk, but they were only for December to now. She'd only made six deposits in her bank account since the beginning of December. Nothing from George. The deposits were for amounts between four and six thousand bucks, for a total of thirty-one thou. The deposits matched receipts for collages she'd delivered. We talked to the buyers of the collages, and the amounts matched. CBHS allowed her to pay tuition on a monthly plan. Now get this. *Some* of that she paid in cash."

I said, "Cash?"

Tom nodded. "She filed for an extension on her taxes, and we have no idea what her income was for last year. We figured the rest of the income from this year went for rent, groceries, gas, and so on."

"If you're getting two hundred thousand-plus a year, thirty-one thousand on top of that is still pretty darn good—" I began.

Tom held up a hand. "As I said, we saw no trace of any two hundred-plus thousand. And she had credit-card debt in the thousands. But more interestingly, the people she did collages for provided clothing, toys, photographs, and so on. Holly told them it had to be stuff they were willing to part with and not see again." Intrigued, I didn't interrupt him this time. "They all said this. But we couldn't find a trace of clothing, toys, or photographs. There was no studio in her rental. There were no receipts anywhere in Holly's desk for studio rental or framing. Drew told you—and our guys, too, when we questioned him—that Holly rented studio space in Cherry Creek. But no, he said, he had never been there. And no, our guy thought to ask him, he had no idea what happened to all the *stuff* Holly got from clients to make the collages. Drew just said when a big cardboard container came, Holly said it was from the framers."

"And the twenty-five-K typed note inside the box with the collage?" I asked. "What was that about?"

Tom shook his head. "We have no idea."

I said, "Anything else?"

Tom took a deep breath. "Holly had sold the Audis belonging to her and her son in the past six months. We found the receipts. She used the money to hire a lawyer. She was suing George for back child support."

"I knew it," Marla said.

"Marla," Tom said, "I swear to God, if I hear one inkling of any of this from any source whatsoever, I'm going to—"

"Bash in the roof of my Mercedes? With me in it?" Marla said, opening her eyes wide. "How would that look? And just where do you get off threatening a civilian?"

Tom exhaled, then apologized. "All right, back to Holly's death. The crime lab is backed up, so we won't have the full toxicology report for a couple of weeks.

The medical examiner can't start on the autopsy until Tuesday. So I asked the lab to do a preliminary screen on Holly's blood. Something weird popped." He lowered his voice, although there was no one near us. "They called me when I was on my way up here. Loquin, heard of it?"

"It's an antibiotic," I said automatically. "I thought the FDA pulled that sucker from the market."

"Loquin got a black-box warning." Marla's voice was authoritative. "It can cause vivid nightmares, hallucinations, tendon tears, and God knows what else."

Tom shifted his weight on the grass, then looked first at me, then at Marla. "Neither one of you is still married to a doctor, but you're still current on Med Wives 101? I'm impressed. Anyway, Loquin doesn't come in liquid form. It's in pills only. And it was in Holly's system. From the reports we're getting about nightmares, it was probably in everyone else's system, too."

I asked, "So . . . if it doesn't come in liquid form, are you thinking Loquin was in the *food* from last night? Could an antibiotic kill Holly?"

"No idea," said Tom. "I don't suppose we have any of the leftovers that we could test."

Marla shook her head. "People took their own serving dishes home. There wasn't much food left, really.

I put a lot down the disposal. Patsie Boatfield and I washed the plates and flatware, and tossed the plastic cups. Even doing all that took forever. I mean, you all could check my trash . . ."

"We will." Tom gave me a questioning look.

I said, "I didn't pack up any leftovers, remember? I was falling through Holly's deck."

Tom pressed his fingers into his temples. "Goldy, do you have a list of who was supposed to bring what last night?"

"In my computer," I said. "But you know everyone, and I do mean *everyone*, was in and out of Marla's kitchen, including that weird artist guy nobody seemed to know. I don't suppose anything about *him* popped, as in a cell-phone photo?"

Tom said, "Nope. Anybody else around the food? Someone who wasn't at the party?"

I thought back. "Neil Unger made an unannounced visit Thursday, when Julian and I were working on the party prep. He sent Julian out to give his driver something to eat, while he insisted my computer had a virus, and I had to check it that minute."

"Was there food out? Food you weren't watching while you did a virus scan?"

I closed my eyes. "Yes. Julian had made the second batch of chile relleno tortas, but hadn't put them in the oven. Neil was ranging around the kitchen, opening and shutting cabinets. I just thought he was nervous." I shook my head.

"Nothing came up concerning that message on Holly's phone, either. Even though it was from an untraceable cell, our guys are working with the phone company now, trying to pinpoint where the call came from. They should be able to tell within a two-block area."

"Oh, technology," I said. "I don't suppose George or anyone else mentioned sending a text?"

Tom shook his head. "We're still working on the carton the collage came in. So far, we've only established that it was mailed from a nonchain shipping store in Capitol Hill. Our guys got the owner out of bed in the wee hours. The place doesn't have a security camera. We showed the owner the box with his mailing tag. He checked in his computer, and he said he had no idea who had sent it, because the customer paid in cash."

"Did you get a description of the customer? Male? Female?"

Tom said, "Nope. We don't know anything about who shipped the carton."

"Where is this place?"

"Clarkson Shipping, down near the cathedral. We talked to the owner *at length*. He has ten temporary employees. Our team is trying to locate any of them who would have seen someone mail an oversize box. So far, nothing." He eyed me knowingly. "Miss G., Marla needs to take you home so you can get some rest. And by that I mean *rest, in bed,* without going anywhere outside the house. Boyd will follow."

"But what about Father Pete?" I asked.

"I promise I'll call you once we know something." When I pursed my lips, he said, "I swear."

Tom took my hands and helped get me upright. I didn't want to leave St. Luke's. But under the circumstances, I didn't want to stay, either.

At home, Arch and Gus rushed down the stairs when Marla and I walked through the front door. Julian, who'd been working in the kitchen, came out to greet us.

"Father Pete, Father Pete," Arch said in a rush. "How is he?"

"One of Tom's people came to the house, asking questions," Gus supplied. With toast-brown hair, dark brown eyes, and the ghost of freckles, Gus looked so much like Arch—or at least, like Arch before he'd shaved his head—it always made me do a double take.

"He told us Father Pete had been hurt," Julian explained. "Hurt *badly*. But he didn't say what happened. He just wanted to know if any of us had talked to

Father Pete when he called this morning, if it sounded as if he was with anybody, if his voice showed stress, that kind of thing." Julian shook his head. "But when I saw the call was from the church, I didn't pick up."

"Hurt badly *how*?" Arch asked breathlessly. "Is he going to make it?"

Marla raced to the first-floor bathroom, slammed the door, and began crying. The boys gaped at me, stricken. I said, "Somebody attacked Father Pete. We think he's going to make it. We hope."

"*Attacked* him?" Julian pressed. "Father Pete was a boxer—"

I made my voice very quiet. "Listen, you cannot tell anyone this." When all three of them nodded, I said, "Somebody stabbed him. He was breathing when we got there, but just barely. Whoever knifed him also killed Kathie Beliar. She was the one driving the van that looked like mine."

For a moment, we stood in the hallway. We were trying to take it in. Marla, snuffling, came out of the bathroom.

"Boss," Julian said gently, "you look as if you're in a lot of pain. Please go lie down." When I hesitated, he said, "I'm making vegetarian lasagna for us tonight. Plus salad and bread. There's going to be plenty for all of us." He cocked his head. "Please go up."

So I went. Marla joined Julian in the kitchen, while Gus and Arch said they would be in Arch's room. They promised not to get onto the Internet. I knew they would want to talk about who could have been able to get the drop on Father Pete. I was so tired, and in such exquisite pain, that I couldn't run my mind back over Marla's and my discovery and make much out of it.

I didn't think I'd fall asleep, but I did. When I awoke, the luscious scent of cooking food was wafting up the stairs. But what all the psychologists say about insights coming when you're relaxed had happened. I'd thought of something. Or rather, I'd realized it.

The man at the party, the uninvited guest. The artist in the odd clothes. When I'd started out in catering, I'd done a party for him, or rather, I'd done an event where he'd been present. I remembered him now, standing in the corner, looking forlorn.

The party had been at a gallery, and very few people had shown up. The artist whose work was being exhibited had been such a severe introvert, he hadn't been out chatting with patrons, or with anyone, for that matter. Whatever the opposite of charismatic was, that man was *it*.

I'd realized something else. That man, that artist, did work sort of similar to Holly's. Where her portrait-collages were intimate, comprehensible, and commercial, this man had decorated his pieces with slashes and drips of paint, as well as scribbles of calligraphy. At his own show, he'd looked miserable.

And I knew his name: Yurbin.

I put in a call to Tom's cell and left a message. I felt frustrated that there wasn't more I could do, but I'd been warned to do nothing, at least for now. I sighed.

In the kitchen, I asked if anyone had heard anything about Father Pete. He was in a coma, Marla said. The sheriff's department was keeping a tight lid on all other information about his condition. We would know more later. I called up to Arch and Gus that if they wanted to shower, now was the time. I couldn't stand around doing nothing, so I laid the table. Marla poured Cabernet Sauvignon for Julian, me, and herself. Maybe the wine would take the edge off my pain, both physical and psychological.

I hadn't had a chance to ask Marla about Yurbin, had barely had a chance to sip the wine, when the phone rang. It was a woman from the diocese, saying she'd been called about Father Pete. She'd talked to our senior warden, and the diocese was sending a supply priest for the next day's service. She was calling me because the warden had said that I was catering and organizing some kind of fund-raiser for St. Luke's that night. The diocesan calendar said that even though we were slated to be grilling outside, the main part of the dinner was supposed to take place *inside* the church. Shouldn't the whole thing be canceled?

"It should *not* be canceled," I said firmly.

"I'm sorry," she said politely, "but the sheriff's department has said we cannot plan anything to be held inside St. Luke's itself until they have finished with their investigation. The service is going to be held outside, in the meadow near the church. But that won't work for the dinner. We simply cannot defy—"

"We won't defy anything. We can have the event at my conference center. I'll send out a mass e-mail to the congregation, announcing the change in venue." News embargo or no news embargo, the way information raced around Aspen Meadow, the fact that Father Pete had been stabbed would probably reach numerous parishioners before they even logged onto their computers. "But we need to have this dinner. Father Pete would have wanted us to."

"Should the supply priest stay for the dinner at your conference center, then?" she asked.

"Yes, please," I said, and gave the time for the dinner, as well as directions to the center. As soon as I got off the phone, I sent out a carefully worded e-mail to the St. Luke's congregation. I said that Father Pete was in the hospital, and owing to unforeseen circumstances, the fund-raiser for the columbarium would be at my conference center. Directions and my cell-phone number were attached.

I stared at my computer, thinking. Apart from a few special events, the center was closed for most of the winter. I had opened back up at the beginning of June, when a cleaning crew had come in. Since then, we'd had two weddings and another visit from the cleaners. I'd wanted to have the boys' birthday party there, but Marla had insisted on throwing the shindig at her new place. She'd thought the kids would want to swim in the pool, play volleyball, and pitch horseshoes, that all those activities would put them in a great mood for the beginning of summer vacation. And the guests had done all those things. But the conclusion of the party had put a horrid end to that whole good-mood thing.

When Arch and Gus, freshly showered and changed, burst into the kitchen, they demanded to be a part of whatever was going on. Well, what was going on?

I knew one thing: I needed to get away from the house. We all did. I had that major in psychology, didn't I? I felt a twinge of guilt, as I'd promised Tom I would rest and take it easy. But staying at home meant I would, as we say in our business, *stew*. On the other hand, if we went over to the center, and everyone worked, cleaning, setting tables, doing prep for the dinner the next night, and having dinner there, we would feel as if we were working to help Father Pete.

So I told Julian, Marla, and the boys that we were going to have to take the fixings for our dinner that night, and the church meal the next, to the center.

Marla cast a longing glance at the lasagna Julian was now covering with foil. "After I was up late last night, please don't tell me you want me to do more cleaning."

"You had Patsie Boatfield right there in your kitchen, and she helped you wash those seemingly endless piles of dishes," I replied cheerfully. "And anyway, what do you think this catering biz is all about? But no, there will be very little cleaning, just dusting and mopping and—" I stopped when she looked stricken. "I'm kidding. But listen," I said, to soften the idea. "What we're doing is what Father Pete would have wanted. Would want," I corrected myself.

Julian went out to Boyd's car, which had attached itself to our driveway like a shadow, to tell him where we were off to next.

Before long we had my van, which Marla was going to drive, filled with the foodstuffs for the church's fund-raiser, which was supposed to have been a prime steak cookout—with veggie burgers available. Having lots of people standing around a grill is always very sociable, and feels festive, Father Pete and I had agreed.

Everyone was then supposed to have gone into the church to hear about planning their funeral and donating to the columbarium.

I sighed. The best-laid plans, and all that.

Julian was taking his Rover and the lasagna for that night; Arch and Gus followed in the Passat; Boyd was behind them. I left word with Tom's voice mail of our plan. Each one of us had a charged cell phone, I concluded, so please call if he heard anything about Father Pete.

"Have you ever heard of an artist named Yurbin?" I asked, once it was just Marla and me.

"Yurbin? No, should I have?" Marla asked. "Is he an artist I needed to start collecting fifteen years ago, if only I'd known?"

"I catered a reception for a show of his at a gallery once. When I was just starting out in the catering business."

"And this is important because? I'm sorry, I can't think on an empty stomach, especially one that's been traumatized."

"I'm pretty sure Yurbin was the uninvited guest who showed up at your place last night. He's an artist. A *collage* artist."

"Oh, yeah? Picasso was a collage artist, too. So what?"

"When did Holly go to art school, *exactly*?" I asked. "Do you remember?"

"After she got divorced from George. It would be in the Amour notes, wouldn't it?"

"Maybe. I'm just wondering how close they were. Or weren't."

The six of us spilled out of our vehicles in the conference-center parking lot. Julian and Boyd said I was not allowed to carry anything. They and the boys took boxes, as did Marla—without grumbling, for once—and marched inside. I limped. Since we were so close to the solstice, the late afternoon light was still bright gold. The mountains, enveloped in a thick veil of pine pollen, appeared very far away. If I hadn't been in so much pain of every kind, I would have enjoyed it.

"We'll eat first," said Julian, smoothly taking over as chief executive, once we had all the food for the next night stored in my conference kitchen's huge refrigerators. He shimmied the lasagna out of the oven. The salad lunches he'd made for us were a memory, and the six of us fell on the rich layers of melted mozzarella, fontina, ricotta, tomatoes, onions, and mushrooms, as if starved.

Julian commissioned Boyd and the boys to help him with the dishes, to give Marla a break. She was so effusively grateful that I laughed.

"Don't worry, I'll be busy," she said indignantly, and pulled out her cell. She then began working her lines of communication, asking friends if they knew anything about Kathie Beliar. Also, had they ever heard of an artist named Yurbin? If not, could they please call their friends, and so on. Marla didn't say *why* she wanted information about Kathie and Yurbin, but her pals knew if she was calling, something was up.

I couldn't bear not to be doing *something*. I stared at the tables in the dining area, trying to figure out how I was going to make the twelve people who'd made reservations for the fund-raiser feel comfortable in the vast space.

But then something odd happened. Maybe people had read the e-mail from me, and were responding to that. But I didn't think so. What was more likely was this: the sheriff's department had by that time made several hours' worth of inquiries of parishioners. I could imagine the drill: "Your priest, Father Pete, has been attacked. Do you know anyone with a grudge against him? Who, exactly?"

So St. Luke's parishioners began calling my cell. They weren't phoning because they knew Marla and I had discovered Father Pete and Kathie Beliar. Nor, bless them, did they want the inside scoop on what had happened to Father Pete. No: they wanted to make reservations for the dinner. By the time I got off the phone an hour later, I had reservations for an additional ninety-eight people, putting us at one hundred ten. No one wanted veggie burgers, either.

Marla shook her head. "Now that our priest has been stabbed, parishioners suddenly care about what he's been begging them to do for a couple of months. There's Catholic guilt and Jewish guilt and now there's such a thing as Episcopal guilt. Go figure."

I took a deep breath, balanced on my good leg, and looked around the dining room. "Unless you know something about manna that I don't, you're going to have to tell me where I'm going to get eighty-some prime steaks on short notice. And don't ask: I know Tom will veto a potluck."

"Probably even a buffet," said Marla, unhelpfully.

14

"One hundred ten people?" Tom asked in disbelief when he came in at midnight. "You're kidding." He searched my expression in the pale aura from the maroon-and-yellow lamp he'd given me for my birthday. "You're not." His look turned tender. "Miss G., you still look exhausted. Call the dinner off, won't you?"

I swallowed. "I can't. Father Pete wouldn't want us to. Listen, we donated all the steaks and veggie burgers we were going to use to the freezers of Aspen Meadow Outreach. We'll figure something out. It'll be fine. Julian has been his usual amazing self. Plus, Boyd, Arch, and Gus have been great. So, do you have any news on Father Pete?" My throat began to close. I managed to say, "Is he . . . awake?"

"They did surgery to repair both lungs. He woke up briefly, but lapsed back into unconsciousness before our guys could question him." Tom's shoulders slumped. When he said he was taking a shower, I followed him into the bathroom.

"What about your team?" I asked from outside the shower stall. "Did they find out anything?"

"Why don't you take off your clothes and come in here? Then I'll tell you everything. I'll be careful of your leg."

I smiled in spite of all that had happened. Grief had temporarily emptied me of joy. Now I longed to be close to Tom. I unwrapped the bandages on my leg and slipped into the steamy stall.

"Oh, I like what I see," Tom said.

I laughed as he pulled me to him. I clasped his middle. We made love slowly, carefully, because of my leg. I almost collapsed when I shook. But Tom caught me.

"That was very nice." He carefully toweled my back. "Let me put some ointment on your leg and rewrap it."

I allowed myself to be tended to, then pulled on pajamas and slid between the sheets. "Seems to me," I murmured, when I was next to him, "that you were going to tell me what your team had found."

Tom sighed and tucked our quilt around my shoulders. "Kathie Beliar is pretty much a blank. Thirty-five years old, divorced a decade ago, moved up here from Aurora, according to the few friends we could find in her address book. She claimed she wanted to start over. She didn't seem to have any enemies, at least that we could find. No one with a grudge. Even the ex-husband didn't hate her. He just said she didn't want to be a housewife. She moved into a little place up here, then was a substitute teacher for a while. But she didn't like how hard it was to control kids. So the *Mountain Journal* hired her to sell ads. She took on office work for a couple of real estate companies. One of the real estate agents sold a piece of women's fiction, and that lady got so much attention—again, according to these same friends—that Kathie suddenly announced to anyone who would listen that *she* was going to be a *poet*. But as far as we can tell, she never got anything published. There was a slender file of . . . I suppose you would call it verse . . . in her house. We're talking twenty-some poems, mostly along the lines of the breeze in the trees making her knees freeze, then she sneezes."

"Walt Whitman's reputation will remain intact, then."

Tom chewed the side of his mouth. "Kathie's friends? They seemed to feel sorry for her. They said she used to talk incessantly about becoming a published poet. But the only file thicker than the poetry one was the one containing rejection letters from literary magazines."

All the hostility I'd had for Kathie Beliar evaporated. In place of the anger I felt sadness . . . and again, distress with myself, that I'd been so angry and judgmental.

Tom said, "When the poetry thing didn't work out, according to her pals, she was going to open a stable and raise show horses. Apparently she got the idea from a home buyer who came into the agency. He bought a huge, classy place, with a lot of acreage. Kathie volunteered to help out in his stable. 'Until,' she told her buddies, 'I can get established.' She mucked out stalls, cleaned tack, and bugged the owner incessantly to allow her to show his horses. I mean, like in horse shows."

"I'm from New Jersey, remember. I know from horse shows. But I wasn't aware Kathie was into equestrianism."

Tom's damp hair touched my cheek. "She wasn't. We asked the stable owner about her. He hemmed and hawed and said he didn't want to speak ill of the dead. Finally he confessed that he'd told her she couldn't ride, because, well, she was terrible at it. She quit in a huff, and he said he felt bad about it. But he simply could not allow her to be the one riding his mounts in shows. Kathie gave up on the stable-owning pipe dream and went back to working for a real estate agency.

Apparently some of the clients there talked about how great your parties were, how you were just the *best* caterer, but, wait for it now. Don't get angry. They said you were *not cheap*."

"Oh, for God's sake," I said hotly. "Anyone who goes into catering for the money should have his or her head examined. Sometimes I think that means me, frankly."

"Miss G., I'm telling you what Kathie's friends said. And here's the interesting bit. Kathie also told her friends she thought Holly was the most gorgeous, glamorous person around. Working for the real estate company, *Kathie* was the one who set up the rental for Holly. Holly had told her you were her friend. It was as if Kathie became convinced she'd make a mint catering, and become glamorous and gorgeous at the same time, if she could undercut you. She took a weekend cooking class in Denver, but never worked in a restaurant or for a catering company, as far as we can tell. She just decided, boom, to be a caterer, just the way she was going to be a glamorous poet or a glamorous owner of show horses. So she didn't need the breeze to freeze her knees as she carried her poems to the post office, or get stuck on a truck when she had stables to muck—"

"*Tom.*"

"Sorry. Kathie had taken notes on the parties she'd heard you were catering. Marla had talked about giving the boys' birthday bash at her fabulous new house. The St. Luke's fund-raiser had been opened to the Aspen Meadow community. So our theory is, she thought if she copied you but charged less, she'd become Holly's glamorous new best friend, and have a built-in clientele."

"That is just too bizarre."

Tom shrugged. "Those same friends we tracked down? They said she talked about nothing except becoming a caterer *like Goldy Schulz.*"

I thought of one of those Zen-type sayings I'd learned from my mentor, André: *Talking is not doing. The more you talk, the less you do.*

"But," Tom was saying, "since Kathie had also been energized about being a poet, and then about training show horses, they pretty much ignored her. That might explain why she was so eager to take over the birthday party at Marla's, as well as the church dinner. She wanted to *prove* that she was serious."

"But she's not . . . she wasn't . . . even a parishioner at St. Luke's." I took a deep breath. "What about Father Pete? Any idea why *he* was attacked? I mean, do you even know who was stabbed first?"

"Our blood-spatter guys have already developed a theory. The perp attacked Father Pete first. The hit punctured his right lung. He spun around, staggered into a wall, then slipped on his own blood and fell." I shuddered, and Tom stopped talking. "You sure you want to hear this?" I nodded. "Near as we can tell, Kathie tried to run away. The killer caught her by the hair, reached around and stabbed her in the heart. Father Pete had recovered a bit by then, we think. He stood up and tried to fight the attacker. So the perp knifed him in the other lung. How Father Pete avoided drowning in his own blood, we don't know. But after the second assault, he passed out. We figure that's when the guy, or very strong woman, broke into the secretary's locked desk, got the key to the church files, and rummaged through them."

I had a brief vision of poor, dear Audrey Millard, the church secretary. Lovely as a mountain bluebird, older, single, she was devoted to Father Pete and would be devastated by the attack. I made a mental note to call her, if Tom would allow it. "What was the attacker looking for?"

"Miss G., if we knew that, then we'd have a better idea of who, or what, exactly, we're dealing with here. Our guys are trying to reach the church secretary now." He stopped talking again. "Audrey Millard?"

"Yes. One of your guys should stay with her, I think. She . . . may come across as fragile. And she may *be* fragile. But she has a good memory. She'll probably be able to help you regarding any questions you have about Father Pete." I took a deep breath. "I know it's late," I said apologetically. "But did you hear my message to you about Yurbin?"

He said he had, but the investigation at the church had taken priority. So I began to tell him about Yurbin, collage artist. Tom turned the light back on, and scribbled in his notebook. When I was done, he called the department about Audrey. Also, the night crew still working on the Holly Ingleby case should be told about Yurbin, who might know something about Holly.

"Think your guys will be able to find Yurbin?" I asked, once Tom was back beside me.

"The guy shows up at a party Marla hosts . . . that's followed by a homicide? If he's listed somewhere, anywhere, we'll find him." He added, "Audrey Millard? She fell apart when she heard about Father Pete."

Julian beat us into the kitchen the next morning. He was reading my computer screen, but offered to make us both coffee. Tom said he would do it, then gazed around in sudden amazement at a dozen-plus loaves of frozen homemade oatmeal bread now thawing on our counters.

"Oh," said Julian, blushing. "I just took them out to thaw, because I thought we would need them tonight."

He looked at me, puzzled. "Dad's Bread, Goldy? I thought your father had passed away."

"A while ago," I said, then explained that the loaves were from a recipe of my father's. Unfortunately, Dad hadn't written down how he'd actually made the bread. He'd only taped the recipe he used—as a jumping-off point, he'd proudly told me, as he kneaded and slapped the dough—onto an index card. The now-crinkled bit of newsprint was almost illegible, as the tape, brown and curling at this juncture, had pulled off several apparently crucial words in the recipe. I'd made numerous guesses as to what the missing words were. As many times as I'd made the bread, I not only had ended up with a dough that was much too sticky, I also hadn't quite hit the taste or texture that my father had produced, seemingly without effort, in his own lovingly tended loaves. I concluded by telling Julian that it wasn't until Tom had stood beside me and pressed down on the tape, then guessed correctly at the missing words—*add two additional cups flour*—that the right combination of ingredients had revealed themselves.

Tom smiled. "Goldy was almost there."

"Super," Julian said. His face turned serious. "Now. Do we know what's going on with Father Pete? Nobody's called."

Tom put a cappuccino in front of me, swiftly texted the department, and moved outside to care for our animals. When he returned, his cell pinged. " 'Priest stable. Still unconscious,' " he read aloud. "Okay. Let's talk about this dinner tonight. Nobody brings anything. No buffet, no grill, no food standing out anywhere where people can mess with it. We think it's possible Holly Ingleby and all the birthday guests were given tainted food, but we don't know how or by whom."

Julian said he'd made lists of what we could cook on short notice . . . for dinner for one hundred ten. Tom listened to Julian run through possibilities. Maybe people could bring salads? Julian asked. Tom shook his head, as I knew he would. "Whatever the two of you decide to cook for tonight has to be plated up in the conference-center kitchen and brought out to the tables. Also. Tonight? I'm posting Boyd plus Sergeant Jones at your conference center, Miss G. Not only are Holly and Kathie Beliar dead, but Father Pete is teetering on the edge, and we don't have a clue as to who booby-trapped Holly's deck. We don't even know if any of this is connected. The *only* thing Holly, Kathie, Father Pete, and you have in common?"

I looked at him and waited.

Tom said, "St. Luke's."

"Pretty tenuous connection," I said.

Tom was adamant. "Our two sergeants will watch you at all times. I don't want *any* volunteers helping. No one will have the chance to doctor the food."

"But you don't even know—" I began.

Tom's expression was severe. "You either do it my way or you cancel this fund-raiser."

Julian intervened, ever the peacemaker. "Not to worry! How about this? We do a vichyssoise first. You have a dozen containers of frozen stock, and enough leeks, potatoes, and whipping cream to outfit the French armed forces, who would no doubt appreciate that we're making a French soup. The only challenge will be getting it thoroughly chilled by tonight. This bread will be thawed soon, so it'll work. Plus, you've got another dozen loaves in there." He gave me a quizzical expression. "Your freezer also has a mountain of zipped plastic bags of chocolate cookies. Where did *those* come from?"

I sighed. "Christian Brothers High School Bake Sale. They told me to bring a few loaves of bread and a dozen cookies. I thought I'd doubled my father's bread recipe, but it ended up making quadruple the number of loaves I was aiming for. And the cookies? CBHS had asked for so few, I was sure they must have said a *dozen dozen*. They didn't. But it was fun. I was experimenting with extra-bittersweet chocolate and had a whole lot left over."

Tom raised an eyebrow at me, as if to say, *A dozen dozen?* I ignored him. Math skills had never been my long suit. Not only that, but Tom had been asking me for a while to get my hearing checked.

"Okay," Julian continued. "It's going to be warm this evening until sunset, so the guests probably won't mind having all cold food. We'll start with vichyssoise, then move on to poached and chilled shrimp— you've still got lots of jumbo shrimp in the walk-in, remember, and instead of making something weird, I'll put together a sauce with zing that contrasts with the creaminess of the soup. And for those people with shellfish allergies, of which we have four? You have Cornish hens in there that we can roast. We can artfully arrange the shrimp or hens on the dishes, next to a salad of romaine lettuce with fresh tomatoes, scallions, and hearts of palm. We'll lightly dress those with sherry vinaigrette. Your supplier left you with lots of packages of early haricots verts. I can cook those quickly and chill them, then use a different dressing for them, for contrast."

I had forgotten that my supplier had left perfect packages of those long, thin string beans so favored by the French. I had no idea where she'd found them this time of year. So now we were up to vichyssoise, poached shrimp or Cornish hens, romaine salads with tomatoes, steamed haricots verts vinaigrette, bread, and . . . what were we missing? Something slightly sweet. To Julian, I said, "My head's reeling."

"It's all going to work out. But you're probably thinking we should have something slightly fruity. You've got lots and lots of strawberries and bananas. Do you have a recipe for molded fruit salad, to balance with the savory stuff?" I nodded. Julian said anxiously, "How does it sound so far?"

I swallowed. "Perfect."

Julian went on, "We'll have butter on all the tables—"

Tom said, "No. The butter comes out with the rest of the food. You slice the bread in the kitchen, and it gets served by you all with tongs."

Julian rolled his eyes, but said, "Okay, that'll give us a chance to warm up the bread. Then we'll bring out the plated-up food when we serve the bread and butter. We'll follow this with vanilla ice cream and your chocolate cookies. You or I can make a dark fudge sauce to go on the ice cream, if you think we need it. What do you think?"

"It sounds great." I smiled and did not say, *It actually sounds like a ton of work.*

"Yeah, super," Tom echoed. "Now you two, I have to take off. Sorry to be so difficult about the food." I told him not to worry. He nodded to Julian and kissed my cheek. "Boyd's coming with you to church this morning," he added. "He and his partner—and before you ask, yes, it's still Armstrong—are going to be here around half past seven. They'll be with you at church and while you set up. Then Armstrong goes off duty. Boyd and Jones will be with you tonight at the conference center. Just like yesterday, except you'll have a double escort. You're not going anywhere without at least one of them. Got it?"

"Yes," I said. When Tom gave me a warning look, I added "*Yes!* I heard you. We have so much work to do, I couldn't go running around asking questions, even if I wanted to."

"And you?" Tom pointed at Julian. "You shop? You take Armstrong. You work in the kitchen? Armstrong is at your side."

"Yes, boss's husband!" Julian said with enthusiasm.

I sighed and checked in with myself. My leg still hurt, but it did feel better. I looked around the kitchen. Summer mornings in the mountains brought early light the color of nickel. So although it felt like eight o'clock, I was unsurprised that it was not quite half past six. There had been no rumblings from Arch and

Gus, but when they did get up, they'd be hungry. Since
St. Luke's had gone over to its summer schedule, the
service in the meadow wouldn't begin until nine. I
chugged the last of my cappuccino and typed up a plan
for the cooking into my computer. Julian brought the
containers of stock out to the counter to begin thawing,
then started in on the long task of peeling potatoes for
the soup.

Thinking the boys would drive us batty if they had to
wait long for breakfast, I buttered a large pan and lined
it with thick slices of thawed bread. Then I beat eggs
with cream, added vanilla and nutmeg, and poured this
mixture over the bread, to make a baked French toast.
Once Arch and Gus were up, I would slide the dish into
the oven.

I checked my favorite recipe for molded strawberry
salad, and as it turned out, not only did we have plenty of
fresh bananas and strawberries, but our pantry yielded
up numerous cans of crushed pineapple. I got to work
straining the pineapple and then measuring the juice to
mix with the gelatin. But as I stared into the pot and
waited for the juice to boil, I thought that even if the
meal was going to be plated up individually, I did *not*
want to put cafeteria-style squares of molded salad on
each dish. Besides that, getting large sheet pans filled
with gelatin to actually *gel* was a lot more difficult than

getting small molds to do the same work. No doubt this had to do with some esoteric law of chemistry that I did not care about. What I *did* care about was the question of where we could get one hundred ten molds.

I shared my dilemma with Julian, who said he was sure he had that many individual china cups out in his boxes in our garage.

"You have china cups in your storage cartons?" I repeated.

"They're mismatched, but it doesn't matter. People think they're getting something special if it's in a china cup. *Any* china cup. Trust me."

"I do trust you." If I poured a judicious amount of the concoction into individual portions, all I would have to do was find space in the walk-in to put them all. I knew that would not be a problem. The molded salads would all gel, and best of all, there would be no need to unmold anything. We could just place one china-cup-filled salad on each plate, next to the shrimp or hens, dressed beans, and romaine salad. *Et voilà!* They would even look pretty.

Mindful of Tom's warning, I called Boyd on my cell. He was waiting out in his prowler, and promised to help us retrieve what we needed from the garage.

I watched Boyd lumber heavily up the driveway, and my heart constricted. He rubbed his crew cut, which was going from black to gray. After the trying events of the past twenty-four hours, he looked exhausted. But he was, as ever, stoic.

Although it was clear neither Boyd nor I relished the prospect of digging through Julian's storage containers—and early in the morning, no less—it wasn't a hassle. Julian had done an excellent job labeling each box. It took the three of us only ten minutes, first, to find and move the huge box containing Julian's cookbooks, and second, to lay our hands on the carton underneath, labeled only *Serving Dishes and Other Bits of China*. Boyd and Julian hoisted that box into our kitchen.

As we carefully unwrapped the mismatched pieces, I checked the bottoms of the cups and saucers, as Tom had taught me to do. They were all either French porcelain or English bone china. I asked, "How in the world did you find all this?"

"You know Maplewood?" he asked in return.

"Yes." To Boyd, I said, "It's an area of old homes in Boulder—"

"I know it," Boyd said.

Julian smiled. "I think the woman who died was a hoarder. Her heirs didn't like old stuff, and there were *crates* of dishes at the sale. Man." He held up a gilt-edged cup to the light. "They sure don't make dishes the way they used to. But one thing you taught me, Goldy? People think they're getting something special if it's plated up on the real deal. Which this definitely is."

I shook my head at Julian's memory of tricks of the trade. Once we'd counted out a hundred and fourteen cups—adding four for good measure—Boyd offered to wash his hands *and* all the cups. I thanked him, cleaned myself up, and went back to the fruit salad itself. I finished slicing the juicy strawberries and firm bananas, and folded it all into the liquid gelatin. Up to his elbows in suds, Boyd said he would rinse and dry the cups, then ladle out the mixture before placing everything into the walk-in. Julian and I thanked him again. Boyd hated culinary duties, so our profusely expressed gratitude actually made him grin.

I went back to Julian's recipe for vichyssoise. For one-hundred-ten-plus-four-for-good-measure people, we were going to need many piles of chopped leeks and onions. I retrieved one of my professional knives and got to work.

Just before seven, I started melting unsalted butter into golden pools in my stockpots. Julian tossed in the leeks and onions, and told me to go rest my leg. He would stir everything and make the fudge sauce at the same time.

"Better to have just one person standing in front of the stove," he said. "Fix yourself another espresso and put your feet up." He glanced at the ceiling. "When I hear the boys, I'll shoot the French toast into the oven."

I agreed, then offered espresso to Boyd.

He said, "Thanks, but I only drink real coffee."

"I can make that for you," I said quickly.

"I'm good."

I knew he meant that he was doing all right. He was also good. I sloshed whipping cream into a chilled glass, then pulled two shots of regular espresso and two of decaf on top.

I sat down, grateful for the rest. Try as I might, though, my mind would not stay still. I thought of Audrey Millard, the church secretary. Was it too early to call her, to make sure she was okay? What if she'd been up all night worrying, or been upset by the police-woman at her house? What if she'd only gotten to sleep this morning? In good conscience, I could not bother her. I also knew she would come to the service in the meadow, no matter how tired she was. She would need her community around her.

I wondered if there was any connection to St. Luke's that I was missing, apart from the fact that two homi-cides, Holly and Kathie, and an attempted homicide—Father Pete—had occurred so close in time. This was a small town, and Holly had only been coming back to St. Luke's for a while. Plus, she just hadn't seemed that involved, not the way she had been before, anyway.

I imagined the aftermath of someone attacking Father Pete and killing Kathie Beliar. That same someone had broken into Audrey's office and gone through the files. Why? What could possibly be in the church files that someone would want so badly? I wondered what files had been taken, if any.

As if in answer to my questions, a text from Tom buzzed through. *Church sec'y says only file missing is Counseling.*

I stared at this missive. Father Pete was the essence of discretion. Wasn't he? There really was no way he would have kept the names, dates, and particulars of problems, much less sins, preying on parishioners' minds. Would he?

Episcopalians weren't that big on confession. But they *loved* counseling. People were always saying they needed to talk to Father Pete "about a pastoral issue." Was it possible there had been details in some counseling files? I texted Tom back: *How does Audrey know that?*

I had almost finished my iced latte when Tom replied: *Counseling drawer contents gone. AM didn't know what notes Fr P kept.*

238 · DIANE MOTT DAVIDSON

Would Father Pete have disguised people's names? I wondered if Audrey would even be aware of *who* Father Pete was counseling. No doubt, Tom and his team were trying to find that out right now.

Anybody around church see anything suspicious? I typed.

No, Tom texted right back. *Back entry shielded by trees.*

I shook my head. My thigh began to throb. Worse, my heart felt as if it were in a vise. Unbidden, my mind conjured up Holly's happy face. *We'll get together soon, and talk . . .*

I felt sorry for Kathie Beliar, but I hadn't known her. I had faith that Father Pete would get better. But Holly, dear Holly, had been my friend. Someone had killed her. I was willing to bet that same someone had booby-trapped her deck, maybe to hurt her, maybe to hurt Drew.

It also seemed clear—to me, anyway—that George and Holly had been struggling over child support. But why?

I texted Tom, *Did Drew say anything about Holly's $ issues?*

I didn't hear back from him right away, which told me he'd gone into a meeting. Unfortunately, this meant my mind started spinning again.

Holly was barely making enough on the collages to keep herself and Drew going. Was that why she had turned to asking someone for money? Who could have sent that text back to her?

A collage client?

George, Edith, or Lena Ingleby? They were among the only people who knew Holly whom I could think of who actually *had* big money. Edith had not been present at the birthday party, but George and Lena had. Lena hated Holly . . . Was this normal aversion-to-the-first-wife, or was there something else going on?

Plus, if Holly needed money and was asking someone for it, why not take the cash Marla had offered her? Because she'd been too proud.

Did Warren Broome have access to big money? Would he tell me about his liaison with Holly? Somehow, I doubted it.

Had there been a connection none of us had uncovered between Holly and Neil Unger? He certainly had lots of money, and his showing up so unexpectedly the day before the party—and having access to the food while I ran a virus scan—made me nervous.

And how in the world did a reclusive artist named Yurbin fit into this?

I shook my head. Despite Tom's and my delightful lovemaking in the shower the previous night, I felt my mood sinking. Okay, I trusted Father Pete would be all right—he was a fighter in every sense—but I wished someone would call me and say he'd come out of his coma. I wished I could figure out what had happened to Holly.

Most of all, I wished Holly were still alive.

Boyd answered the door when Sergeant Armstrong arrived. I knew Tom was being extra protective. He'd been right, of course: Kathie Beliar had painted her van to look like mine, and had altered her appearance to look like mine . . . so perhaps he thought I was the target. But what made me the target? I'd *unwittingly* fallen through Holly's deck. And I didn't know anything. Did I?

When I greeted Armstrong, I noted his wispy reddish hair had thinned. Boyd and Armstrong seemed to have accepted the assignment of guarding their superior's wife with aplomb. I thanked Armstrong for coming, then carefully offered them both *regular coffee.* I knew I had my old drip machine in the basement.

Once I'd located the machine, I traipsed back upstairs, where the two cops were sitting, looking uncomfortable, while Julian set the table. I noted that he'd finished simmering the leeks, onions, and potatoes for the soup. He'd cooked and drained the haricots verts, which were cooling. So was the fudge sauce.

Never one to claim credit, Julian proudly announced that Boyd had finished *all* the molded salads.

Armstrong smirked at Boyd. Boyd quickly said, "Okay, smart guy. Next time you do it."

Sensing he'd said something amiss, Julian asked Boyd and Armstrong if they would like cheese omelets with salsa. The two cops were so pathetically grateful that I wished I'd thought of offering them eggs myself. Instead, I assembled the drip coffee machine, dropped in fresh grounds, and pressed the buttons. As there was still no sound from Arch and Gus, I wondered once more if what would help me out of my funk was trying to figure out what had happened to Holly. So I again descended to the basement.

It was time to renew my struggle with the Amour Anonymous notes. Marla and I had barely had time to go through the first few notebooks. I wanted to take a detailed look at what I had. I didn't know if it would do any good, but just sitting around with my banged-up leg elevated while Julian cooked for Boyd and Armstrong wasn't going to do a thing for my mood.

I got out a fresh pad of paper. I wanted to make a time line of Holly's relationship to the rest of us, plus take any notes that seemed significant.

Our sons had been born on the same day, in Lutheran Hospital. I wrote that down. Who had her doctor been? I did not know. Marla said there were all kinds of mentions of doctor visits in the Amour notes. But that was because we were a support group, emphasis on the *support*. Divorced women were not only at risk from their former partners, they had a heightened susceptibility to disease, accidents, and all manner of untoward events. So we made it a habit to check in with each other on our current stress levels. We held each other accountable for going to the doctor when we were ill, making sure we were current with physicals, and generally checking in on each other's health.

Tom had said it looked as if Holly had had a fatal heart attack. She and apparently all the other guests had ingested Loquin, which had only given the other guests at the party nightmares. Why? Was the Loquin related or unrelated? I clicked on Tom's basement computer and searched the Internet for side effects of Loquin. Of course, there were the usual warnings, which I doubted anyone read: *May cause nausea, vomiting, dizziness, hallucinations, vivid dreams, and, in rare cases, cardiac arrest leading to death.*

In rare cases, cardiac arrest leading to death?

Okay, what were the *rare cases*? I clicked through to see what those infrequent interactions might be, but could find nothing. Probably some advanced piece of medical software, not available to members of Med Wives 101, would have it. I resolved to tell Tom about what I'd found anyway. Law enforcement wasn't sure Holly had died from a heart attack. But they suspected it. For the investigators, it would be better to ferret out the interactions from an actual medical doctor, preferably one who knew Holly. For the fortieth time, I wished I knew more about Holly's medical situation at the time of her death.

But still . . . even if a killer had that information, how could he be sure he was giving enough Loquin to someone so that he or she would definitely die?

Maybe you couldn't be sure. In that case, you'd have to booby-trap her deck.

I went back to my time line. Holly and I had both attended a doctors-and-spouses conference in Boulder. She was a former Roman Catholic who embraced astrology and joined St. Luke's. I wrote down all the basics that I could recall about Montessori, about Drew at Elk Park Prep, about their move to Denver and Holly returning to art school.

She and Drew moved back to Aspen Meadow, where she joined Amour Anonymous, and kept us all laughing. Somewhere along the way—according to Lena Ingleby and some of Marla's pals—Warren Broome had been her lover.

She worked out religiously, was a member of the country club, and engaged in other sports, with unnamed guys usually accompanying her.

In the last year, something, I knew not what yet, had caused her finances to go south. She lost her house, withdrew Drew from Elk Park Prep and put him into the Christian Brothers High School. She quit the club, sold their cars, and was suing George for back child support.

She'd wanted to talk to me at the joint birthday party for Drew and Arch about a "relationship mess."

She'd died, despite being the picture of health, of what had appeared to be cardiac arrest, from what may or may not have been a big dose of Loquin.

I shook my head. After a few minutes, I went back to the set of notes I'd been reading. I wasn't expecting to have my heart squeeze when I read about how I'd told the group a story from when I was married to the Jerk: I'd made a tomato aspic to go with a *poulet bonne femme*. He'd taken the aspic, glazed ceramic mold and all, and violently tossed it into the trash, where it had shattered. He'd slapped me hard across the face. He asked if next time, could I remember that he was allergic to tomatoes? I'd cried, but then believed him when he apologized.

Silly me.

Holly countered that on one of her few forays into cooking, she'd used a newly purchased vegetarian cookbook to try to make an aspic for George and Edith. It had taken her all day to make the vegetarian consommé from scratch. While it simmered, she'd hard-cooked eggs, then chopped them before chopping celery, boiled potatoes, poached carrots, artichoke hearts—at this point, Marla had been doubled over with laughter, I'd noted, because Holly hated to cook.

"Then," Holly had dramatically told us, "I folded the five tons of chopped ingredients into the broth and gelatin. I refrigerated the thing for six hours." But when she'd served it, *Edith* had picked up the mold, dumped the salad into the sink, and ground every last bit of it in the disposal. That was when Holly decided George could take his vegetarianism and stick it where the sun didn't shine.

Julian called down, "The guys are awake. I'm putting the French toast in the oven. You coming up?"

"Be right there!"

My cell phone buzzed with a text from Tom. *Neighbor says Drew & Holly not fighting.*

Puzzled, I tapped back, *With attack on Fr Pete, Drew still a suspect?*

No. Just following up.

What about anonymous message?

Tom wrote, *I called Drew. He said H had been arguing with someone on phone. Not him.*

I pecked out, *Are you sure?*

No. But I believe Drew. He says Holly shouted, "You bastard! I've got you! People know! There's a record!"

I stared at this and typed, *Don't understand.*

Tom wrote, *According to D, H yelled, "It's in the notes!" H got off the phone, but wouldn't explain herself.*

I thought about this for a moment, then typed, *Loquin can cause deadly interaction, including heart attack. Possible Holly had condition or was on meds we don't know about? Your medical people checking this?*

Don't know; will ask. Don't know what we're dealing with yet.

I stared at that last message for a long time.

I thought about deadly interactions.

I reflected on Kathie Beliar, who'd gotten in the way. And of course there was Father Pete, who'd had a counseling file, which had been stolen. The file, presumably, had had notes in it. Had something incriminating been in them?

Drew had said that Holly was taking out an insurance policy. Yet she had not taken one out, or at least, not one that the cops had been able to find. She had unpacked some boxes. Was *that* where the incriminating notes were?

Once again, I cast my mind back over what I knew about Holly, but from more recently.

She and George were fighting over child support. Probably in retaliation, Holly had not invited George and Lena to the birthday party. This had upset George and Lena, and not a little bit, either. I wondered if the financial motive was enough to make you want to kill someone by sabotaging their deck. But if George had wanted Holly to have an accident, why label that envelope on the deck for Drew, who might have been caught in the trap instead? Could George have other secrets which had caused the dispute over child support, secrets that Father Pete had also known about? Holly was asking someone for money, which she received. But then she wanted more, and had received an angry *no more* in a text message. Had the message come from George? Why would George use an untraceable cell phone, though, to talk to the mother of his child?

Holly's art materials had not surfaced, and she was avoiding Yurbin, an odd artist who had shown up at Marla's place the night of the party. Holly had no studio that anyone knew about. This didn't mean it didn't exist, it only meant no one knew where it was, and she'd lied to Drew by telling him it was in Cherry Creek.

Holly had said she was "in a relationship mess." With whom?

She slept at least once with Warren Broome, maybe more than once. He'd been staring at her at Marla's, even though he was now married to Patsie. Why?

Tom had just found out that Holly had been arguing, loudly, with someone on the phone. She'd said, *You bastard! I've got you! There's a record! It's in the notes!* And then her house had been broken into, and a file cabinet destroyed.

I took a deep breath. Was it possible that kind, generous Holly wasn't just asking someone for money . . . but demanding it? Could she have been blackmailing someone? If so, about what?

Was it possible there was a connection between Father Pete and Holly that I had not known—specifically, that he had been counseling Holly?

Had she told him she had been blackmailing someone?

I wondered.

15

There were no more texts from Tom. I was startled when Julian called me again, so I stumbled up the stairs too quickly, then squawked as I tripped and my injured leg hit a step. When I finally arrived in the kitchen, Julian looked at me with concern. He apologized for summoning me and asked if I was okay.

"I'm fine. Just clumsy."

"The boys are showering," he said.

"Again?"

"Teenagers," he said, as if this explained everything. "Maybe they're figuring there will be girls at church. Anyway, I didn't think you would want to miss seeing them."

"I don't. Thanks for hollering."

Boyd and Armstrong were at the sink washing their dishes. They lauded Julian's omelets and said they didn't know you could make your own picante sauce.

Julian, embarrassed by the praise, interrupted them. "Boss? Why do you keep going to the basement? What's down there? Or, I mean," he quickly amended, "can you say?"

"Sure. I'm just checking to see if Holly told the group that she had medical problems."

"You look awful," Julian said. "Really tired. Please. Sit down."

A sudden, unwanted memory of Kathie Beliar and Father Pete's bodies gushing blood onto the church floor made me dizzy. I followed Julian's direction.

The perp had broken into Audrey's office and stolen the counseling file. If your main target was the priest and the counseling file, why go after Kathie Beliar, and kill her?

Because she'd seen his face.

Boyd and Armstrong had finished washing and drying. While Julian stowed the dishes and pans, the two cops sat at our kitchen table. Their eyes hooded, they watched me.

"Something wrong, Goldy?" Boyd finally ventured.

"I'm just . . . thinking." Father Pete had been stabbed in the heat of the moment.

"About what?" Armstrong asked.

Kathie Beliar had to have been knifed less than a minute later. More heat-of-the-moment stuff. I said, "Nothing, really." I certainly didn't want to share what I was pondering. But I wanted desperately to know what in the world Holly had meant when she'd said, *You bastard!* Which bastard would that be? *I've got you! People know.* Who knew? *There's a record.* A record where? *It's in the notes. What* notes?

Okay, I needed to clear my head and think. Usually what worked best for that was cooking. Unfortunately, at the moment I didn't have time to prepare anything challenging. As it was, Julian and I would have plenty of culinary work to do this afternoon. I groaned inwardly at the prospect of prepping all the lettuce, or worse, the shrimp. Better now just to content myself with laying out strips of bacon and zapping them in the microwave for Gus and Arch. No insights about bastards, people who knew, a record, or notes, presented themselves, with one possible exception: in general, people didn't call women bastards. Unless I'd missed the memo, they called *men* bastards. If they didn't like a woman, they called her a bitch. Holly hadn't said, *You bitch! I've got you!* She'd said, *You bastard!*

Plus, the person who'd sabotaged the deck had looked like a man, according to people who saw that person from far away.

If Holly had been blackmailing a man, what had it been about?

Gus and Arch pounded downstairs. Gus's freshly shampooed hair was wet and tousled. Arch's scalp gleamed. Their clothes were wrinkled but clean. I longed to gather them both in for a hug. But if I did that, Arch would blow worse than Vesuvius.

"You guys look great," said Julian, flashing them his cool smile.

I didn't say anything flattering, because when dealing with teenage boys, whatever words flitted toward my mouth were invariably the wrong ones. I only invited the guys to the table, then put out the butter and maple syrup. When the French toast emerged, puffed and golden, Julian invited Boyd and Armstrong to have some. The two cops exchanged a glance and allowed as how maybe they did have a bit of room in their stomachs for a second breakfast.

I found myself smiling, for the first time in a while.

The June beauty of the church meadow startled me. My throat clogged up when I thought of how much Father Pete would have loved to have been there.

Shimmering-white wild daisies speckled the banks of Cottonwood Creek. Volunteers, obviously called by the senior warden, were setting out folding chairs on a flat area of just-mown grass. The supply priest, a thin, bald fellow I did not know, was already in his long robes. He moved jerkily around the makeshift altar. He seemed disoriented. Welcome to the club.

The priest glanced uneasily among the parishioners arriving in the parking lot, and the teams of investigators and crime-scene techs still traipsing in and out of the church building. At one point, the priest stood still, immobilized. I even thought I could see his Adam's apple bobbing up and down.

I whispered to Boyd that it might be a good idea to let the priest know he should perhaps acknowledge law enforcement in the prayers, then ignore them. Boyd said Sergeant Jones would be there, too, since she was helping with the investigation.

"All the more reason to let the priest know what's going on," I said.

Boyd gave me a knowing look and moved off. The priest flinched when Boyd began talking. But Boyd must have reassured him, because after a brief chat, the cleric seemed to ease into his tasks. He talked in low tones to members of the altar guild, gave directions to the ushers, and marked the places in the Bible for the readings.

Although June, July, and August were prime months for people to take a holiday from church, the rows of chairs quickly filled to overflowing. Numerous parishioners seated themselves on the grass as someone rang a small bell. When everyone was quiet, the senior warden announced that Father Pete was still in a coma. He was sure our rector would appreciate our prayers. We also needed to pray for law enforcement to do its job.

Many in the crowd of about a hundred quietly wept. Even Brewster Motley, a criminal attorney who'd moved to Aspen Meadow a couple of years ago, had come. Brewster didn't often make it to church, because the Furman County Jail had longer visiting hours on Sunday. Yet this morning he'd come to St. Luke's, and now pressed a handkerchief to his eyes.

Marla scooted in next to me and quickly squeezed my hand. At the Intercessions, the whole congregation fervently prayed for Father Pete. Some people began sobbing. This was so unlike Episcopalians that I just blinked. Next to me, Marla shook, and I hugged her. The supply priest also prayed for the souls of Kathie Beliar and Holly.

I scanned the crowd. I noted with surprise that Patsie Boatfield and Warren Broome were not in attendance. But then I remembered that Patsie and Warren had both told me they would see me that night, not in the morning.

Then I saw Audrey Millard. Fortyish and pretty, the church secretary had thick gray-blond hair and a petite, slender figure. I motioned to her questioningly: *May I talk to you?* She held up her hand to indicate five minutes, or at least I thought that was what she was saying. Like math, sign language was not one of my long suits.

Boyd, Armstrong, and Sergeant Jones remained behind when the service ended. Why? I wondered. Did they think Kathie's killer, the person who had attacked Father Pete, might be there? I had no idea. I only knew the three sergeants were taking in every move made by those still in the meadow. I wondered how many years in the sheriff's department it would take to become so unobtrusively watchful.

"Think I should stay?" Marla asked. "You probably want to speak to Audrey alone. I might frighten her off." Marla was aware of how intimidating her presence could be.

I said, "Better hop, then. If she says anything of interest, I'll let you know."

People filed away to their cars. Audrey Millard was still visiting with people, hugging them, reassuring them. The altar guild was helping the priest pack up.

To my surprise, Ophelia Unger approached me. She was not a member of our church. Also to my surprise, she was alone. There was no Bob Rushwood brushing his dreads out of his face, telling her how to lift weights. There was no overbearing father. My heart raced. Had Ophelia heard about her surprise party, as her father had feared? All the food had already been delivered to our house. I pressed my fingers into my temples.

"Goldy?" Ophelia asked. "May we talk for a minute? Just the two of us." Her voice was so low I could barely make it out. Or maybe I did need that hearing test Tom had urged me to have.

I said, "Sure."

We moved in the direction of the creek bank. Boyd gave me a questioning look. I nodded: *Everything's okay.*

"First of all," Ophelia began, "I want to say how sorry I am that your friend died. I'm afraid I was rude at the club. Bob was driving me crazy, but that's no excuse. I apologize."

"Thanks."

She shook her head. "He'd been ranting and raving the night before, how the cops were bothering him with their questions. Bob can be *such* a pill."

That was exactly the description I would have used to describe *Ophelia's* behavior, but never mind. She was set to marry Bob the Pill. Yet she'd never seemed really to like him. I suppressed the desire to scream, *Get out while you can!* Instead, I followed her to the stack of folded chairs.

"I'm looking for a lawyer," Ophelia said, once we were sitting between the chairs and the tall daisies in the unmowed area of field grass. Well, maybe *Get out while you can* was what she had in mind. Still, one didn't need a lawyer to break an engagement. The breeze made a swishing sound as it moved around us and bent the grass. I watched Ophelia carefully. Why did I have the feeling she wanted the chairs, the flowers, and the grass for cover?

"A lawyer," I repeated. Again my mind returned to the Unger wealth. If you had money, why ask your friendly neighborhood caterer for a legal referral? But I continued, without missing a beat: "You want *me* to find *you* a lawyer."

Ophelia's deep blue eyes held me. "Look, I know about my so-called surprise party tomorrow night. You don't need to worry about that."

"I'm not. But you need legal help because . . . ?" I prompted.

Ophelia lowered her voice still more. "I think my mother left me some money before she died of cancer. She tried to tell me about my own special piggy bank.

But I was so upset by her illness, I screamed at her that she could never die. I was eight when she got sick and nine when she passed away. I was devastated. It took me years to recover." Ophelia's expression was suddenly dejected. Speech eluded her, and I wondered if she really had dealt with her loss.

"I'm sorry."

"It's all right." She resolutely shook off the memory. "Unfortunately, my mother's lawyer had a stroke, and his practice dissolved a while ago. He has mild dementia, and now is in a residential facility. My father remarried. A few years after my mother passed away, I thought to ask about my special piggy bank. My father said that my mother had been hallucinating toward the end of her illness, and there was no special fund." She pressed her lips together. "My mother was *not* hallucinating, Goldy. But every time I ask about the money, my father and my endlessly critical stepmother say I'm wrong. Still, one thing happened. Three years ago." Her sapphire eyes turned fierce. "It was my eighteenth birthday. We were at the country club. The step-monster had too much to drink, and said, 'I don't know why your mother ever thought you could go to a university, and—' My father interrupted her, and quickly shut her up. He later told me I wasn't college material. So he wasn't going to pay for me to go." Ophelia again appeared to be struggling for emotional control. "Over the past three years, since that terrible birthday, all my father has given me is an allowance for clothes shopping."

I took a deep breath, but did not say, *And we see how well that's worked out, don't we?*

"My father said he wasn't even going to discuss my education. He said he'd paid for me to go to an expensive prep school, and I was *finished*. I think he sent me to that place because he thought I'd find a nice husband, preferably one who belonged to the country club. I swear, the man's mind is stuck in the Eisenhower era. But you know what? I started taking advanced courses when I was in ninth grade. And I had twelve hours of AP credit! But Dad said I was *done*, and needed to get married, as my own mother had."

I shook my head in sympathy.

Ophelia's face, framed by the ragged dark hair, turned solemn. She said, "I've been studying trusts online. Not only do I think the money my mother left me exists, I think I might actually be able to get it when I turn twenty-one. But I don't know where some of the important papers are. After the birthday-party fiasco, I went to see my mother's old lawyer. He was coherent enough to point me toward some files in his old house, where his wife still lives." She hesitated. "I *do not* want my father, or Bob, or anyone else, to know about this, okay?"

"But," I said, still confused, "doesn't your father already know about this money?"

Ophelia sighed and glanced down at the rushing water. "Of course he knows. He just doesn't think *I* have suspicions. And remember, my father doesn't think I'm very smart. I've done all I can on my own. I have some documents, just not *all* of them. So I'm at the point where I need a lawyer to help me. I'll use *any* kind of lawyer who isn't associated with my father. And don't worry, I won't tell my father or the step-monster that you gave me a name, if you do give me one. I just thought, with your reputation and contacts . . ."

I took a deep breath. In fact, one of the few lawyers I knew was less than twenty yards away. Brewster Motley had helped me out of a jam once. Had Ophelia only come to our church service because she wanted to talk to me about a lawyer? Apparently so.

I looked around. Brewster, his blond hair brushed back, was talking to Armstrong. He was wearing khaki pants, a pink oxford-cloth shirt, and tassel loafers with no socks. Unlike Ophelia, Brewster was an actual style maven. To most folks in Aspen Meadow, "dressing casually" usually involved torn jeans, T-shirts or tank tops, and—invariably—cowboy boots. Brewster had his hands in his pockets, and was telling a long story that was making Armstrong chuckle. He occasionally glanced at the water rushing downstream, as if he longed to ride it on a white-water raft.

I asked Ophelia if she knew Brewster, and she said she didn't know anyone in our parish. "My father expects me to go to his megachurch. I hate it. The pastor there said it was absolutely right for my former fiancé to be in prison. My father said he wouldn't allow *his little girl* to be married to a man with low morals. Then we went to that stupid shrink, Warren Broome, who echoed what the pastor had said." She snorted. "Do you know what my former fiancé did? He offered to sell some of my mother's jewelry for me, to pay for my education. At least, that's what he told me. He took the jewels, which, again, I am sure had been left to *me*, to a fence. The fence turned in my former fiancé as part of a plea deal. My father insisted to the D.A. that the jewelry was his, and that *his little girl* had been duped by a con artist."

"Are you trying to get justice for him?"

Ophelia firmly shook her head. "He had quite a few shady dealings going on, which is how he knew the fence." She laughed harshly. "I guess I'm not a very good judge of character. Anyway, the D.A. charged my former fiancé with fifteen counts of armed robbery.

After a plea deal, he was sent to prison, and wrote me a long letter of apology. He wanted me to wait for him to get out. He said I should try to get a scholarship, though. Like he knows about that kind of thing! I wrote back wishing him well, and that was that."

I couldn't tell Ophelia yet again that I was sorry, but it seemed that this particular poor little rich girl had had her share of troubles in her first twenty years. "I don't know the D.A., but Tom—"

"No, don't worry about it. I've told myself a thousand times that I don't care. The worst part was, my father said I never should have had the jewelry in the first place. My mother had only let me 'play' with it. He said my mother left it to *him*. So when he got it back from the cops, he gave it to the woman who became my stepmother. Okay, end of sad story. Can you introduce me to your friend?"

"He's a criminal attorney," I warned, as we walked over.

"I don't care if he does tax law," Ophelia replied. "I just want someone who can help me find out if I have my own money, and if so, where it is."

So I introduced Ophelia Unger to Brewster Motley. I said Ophelia was a potential client who needed to speak to him in confidence. I did not say that she was a cipher to me, but Brewster was a big boy, and he could size people up pretty well. His face relaxed, he said it would be better if he and Ophelia talked in his car. She dutifully followed him to his BMW. I was curious about that conversation. But there were limits even to *my* nosiness.

I turned and walked over to Audrey Millard, the church secretary. Standing alone, having comforted everyone who'd come up to her, she now looked bereft. Audrey seemed to shrink into her navy dress with its rows of white buttons. This morning, her gray-blond hair was parted on the side and pulled into tight curls around her forehead and ears. She had once told me she thought hair dye was strictly for movie stars, or for people who wanted to be thought of as movie stars. But today her face held none of that staunch rectitude. Her face looked gray with grief.

"Oh, Goldy, I'm so glad you came—" She stopped, clutched a handkerchief, and pressed her lips together. Her cool hand grasped my forearm, and I pulled her into an embrace. Some people lingering by their cars stopped to watch us, but Marla, who stood about twenty feet away, marched up to the parking lot and fiercely ordered the Nosy Nellies to mind their own beeswax.

"Tell me Father Pete is going to be all right," Audrey said, once she had pulled away from me. She sniffed. Her voice wavered and caught. "Please. Tell me."

"He'll . . . he'll be fine."

Her eyebrows knit in sudden fury. "I *wanted* him to start locking both entrances to the church. I *told* him it would keep the wrong element from coming into the building. But he said, 'Absolutely not. The people who make up the wrong element are the ones who need the church.'" Audrey's imitation of Father Pete was dead-on. She shook her head. "Then he said I should not use phrases like 'the wrong element.' And now just *look* at what's happened—"

"He is going to be fine," I said, assuming as reassuring a tone as I could fake. "You know how strong he is."

"But . . . but . . . he's in a *coma*." She used the handkerchief to dab her eyes. "What if he doesn't wake up?"

"He will."

"Do you have any updates? I mean besides the vague one we got from the senior warden."

"No, sorry." Something occurred to me. Would Audrey know what *the wrong element* was looking for? "Yesterday. You talked to the sheriff's department?"

"Yes." She cleared her throat and took a deep breath. "First I talked to two investigators, then a policewoman spent the night at my house, a Sergeant Xavier. 'What was in the counseling file?' the investigators wanted to know. I told them I didn't know the contents of that file, that's why the drawer was kept *locked*. 'What people was he counseling?' they asked. Couples? Individuals? Well, I didn't know everyone. The sheriff's department took the church calendar, so they could look up Father Pete's appointments. But sometimes people would just drop in, you know, when they had a problem. And with the church being unlocked—"

"Audrey," I said, more sharply than I intended. "It's okay." I looked at her intently. "Did you have more visitors than usual this week? Any weird folks dropping in?"

She looked surprised. "No. I don't know about Saturday, when that poor woman, Kathie, was meeting with Father Pete. I do know that Holly Ingleby came to the church on Friday. The investigators didn't ask that, but I told them anyway. She had appointments. For confession. Father Pete never kept notes on confessions, of course, which I *also* told the investigators." Audrey's tone betrayed a bit of impatience. "She made her confession once a quarter—"

"Once a quarter?" I asked. "Why once a quarter?"

Audrey drew in her chin. My every question seemed to mystify her. "It's just what she did."

"But why?" If Episcopalians made confession at all, it was usually during Lent, and we were way past that.

Audrey exhaled. "Well, I don't know. I think it was a hangover from when she was a Catholic." Her thin-skinned forehead crinkled. "You were her friend. Did you not know she used to be a Roman Catholic? I mean, before she became an Episcopalian?"

"Yes, yes, I knew."

"Her confession . . . it was her habit, is what she told me. You know, Holly always made me laugh. She said, 'You know what a habit is, Audrey?' And when I said it had to do with customary behavior, she said, 'I have some new habits and some old habits, but you'll never get me into a nun's habit!' " Audrey's eyes searched my face. "You knew she was a jokester? You knew she was an artist? You knew she also believed in all that astrology mumbo jumbo?" She was questioning me as if I hadn't really known Holly.

"I knew she had her chart done. But that was a long time ago."

Audrey sighed. "I think that might have been what she was confessing. That she naughtily kept track of all that."

"Audrey, it doesn't matter now." My heart squeezed again. But then I had a thought. "When she transferred to St. Luke's, where did she come from? I mean, what Catholic parish, do you remember?"

Audrey pressed her lips together as she thought. "My memory is pretty good, unlike poor Father

Pete, having to keep those counseling notes." She said crisply, "Holly's previous parish was called Our Lady of Perpetual Grace." Her face turned even more pale. "I feel so bad about Holly. And to think poor Drew . . ."

"To think poor Drew what?"

"Well, I don't know. That he will be left motherless."

Audrey seemed to grow even more fragile. I had the feeling that this conversation was draining her. I looked away. Cars were moving slowly out of the church parking lot. Brewster's BMW sat alone near the law enforcement vehicles. I glanced at Boyd and Armstrong, who still stood at the edge of the meadow. With no one around them, their attempt to look nonchalant was fading. Once a semblance of silence enveloped Audrey and me, I asked, "When Holly moved down to Denver after she divorced George, did she go back to Our Lady of . . . what was it called?"

Audrey shook her head sadly. "Perpetual Grace. No. I mean, she told me she tried. But it's a very conservative parish. They said she was a divorced person, and she couldn't receive Communion. So she still came up to see Father Pete, even though she didn't attend the services. She did *not* want to run into George. I told her, 'George never shows his face here.' I mean, he didn't attend services after the divorce. Faithfully, though, for all those years, Father Pete did the sacrament of confession with Holly. He knew why she didn't come to the Eucharist, I mean, he knew she didn't want to see George. So he would give her some of the reserve sacrament." Audrey suddenly looked embarrassed. "That may not be . . . allowed. Don't tell the bishop."

"Not a word," I promised, as if the bishop and I were good buds, which of course we weren't.

"Sometimes I would have to warn Holly, you know. I mean, if there was going to be a committee meeting at the church. She didn't even want to *see* . . . Edith." She fairly spat out the name of Holly's ex-mother-in-law.

"George and Edith didn't come today," I noted.

"Oh, no, of course not." Audrey fluttered a hand. "Edith says having Communion in the meadow is barbaric. She gets too hot in the sun. And her heels sink down in the mud. And she can't hear the priest. And, and, and. I don't know how Father Pete puts, put— oh, dear—*puts* up with her. I shouldn't be talking like this." She touched her hair and searched my face. "I suppose Edith will be at the dinner tonight. No way around it."

"Don't worry." I reassured her the way I used to do Holly. "I won't let her near you."

Audrey looked away nervously. What was she not telling me?

"Audrey? What is it?"

"There's something I've never told anyone, except for Father Pete. I'm afraid it's what got him stabbed."

I waited a moment, then said, "Do you want to tell me? Do you want to tell Tom, or someone else from the sheriff's department?"

"I don't want it in the newspapers," she said, this time fluttering both hands.

I didn't dare signal Boyd and Armstrong, because it had taken this entire conversation for Audrey to get to this point. I stood motionless, not encouraging, not discouraging. When she finally looked at me again, she pressed her lips together, then rushed forward. "I'm another woman."

"Another woman?" I prompted, thoroughly confused.

She gave me a determined look. "I was a victim of Warren Broome, M.D., I was in therapy with him. He said he'd fallen in love with me. He said we should have sex. I thought *I* was in love. Silly me. He used his position of power and trust. He used *me.* His first victim went public, and got called a whore and who knew what all. So I just kept my mouth firmly closed—"

"Oh, dear God, Audrey, you have to tell law enforcement. I mean, you say Father Pete knew. Maybe Warren thought Father Pete might turn him in. Did Warren and Father Pete talk? Did they argue? Do you know?"

When Audrey just shook her head, I thought back to the events, the conversations, of the previous day. Warren Broome had been angry on the phone. He did not like Father Pete. He'd hung up on me. When Patsie had called me back, Warren had been sobbing in the bathroom. Then at least an hour had gone by, while Marla and I went through the Amour notes and had lunch. Arch had come home and told me about the van that had been at the church, the one that looked like mine. An hour would be plenty of time to race down to the church, stab Father Pete and Kathie Beliar, and break into the church office to get the counseling file.

I said, "Was there anything in the church files about you and Warren Broome?"

Her shoulders slumped. "I don't know." She exhaled. "Father Pete gave me a second chance in life. He gave me a job. He gave me confidence. I was a wreck. Afraid to go out, afraid to be seen. *That's* why I wanted the doors of the church locked. And now I'm so afraid he's going to die—" Audrey collapsed against me, sobbing.

I raised one hand toward Armstrong, beckoning him over. I murmured to Audrey that I was turning her over to one of Tom's most trusted associates, and please, *please*, could she tell him what she'd just told me. Audrey clutched Armstrong's elbow, and allowed herself to be led away.

I saw Arch standing, dejected, farther up the creek bank, near the parking lot. I walked toward him. He'd been hurt by the events of the last couple of days as much as anyone else. What could I do to help him, without being a Helicopter Mom?

"Arch, hon," I said, when I was beside him. "Is there anything I can do?"

"I wish Drew were here," he said, staring at the water.

"Well," I said cautiously, "could you and Gus do something *for* Drew?"

"Mom, don't. I don't have his address, and it's not like I'm going to buy him, you know, a sympathy card. Just . . . let me—"

At that point, Gus came up. To Arch, he said simply, "Didn't Drew do that trail building last summer?"

Arch turned to him. "Yeah. I suppose."

"Well," said Gus, "we signed up for it, didn't we? We could build a special trail and put a sign up, if Bob would let us. 'Drew's Trail,' we could call it."

"Or 'Holly's Trail,'" said Arch.

"We could hike up there today," said Gus. "Up into the Aspen Meadow. See where they're working."

I swallowed. I had wanted Arch to do something, but now that Gus had hit on an idea, I was worried. After all that had happened, I didn't want him out of my sight.

Audrey Millard had gone off with Armstrong. Would Sergeant Jones be available for a bit of distance babysitting?

"Will you take Sergeant Jones with you?" I asked Arch.

"Oh, Mom, don't."

"It's what Tom would want. And besides, Gus is right. You hike the trails up there, it'll get your mind off all the awful stuff that's been going on."

When he reluctantly agreed to the escort, we walked over to Sergeant Jones, who nodded once in agreement. She seemed to sense Arch's displeasure. So she said casually that she knew the wildlife preserve well, and that once they parked out there, she bet him five bucks she could beat Gus and him up to the trailhead.

"Wait," I said, as Arch began to bolt for his car. "Please don't forget the church dinner tonight."

"Do I have to come?"

"No, Arch. You do not have to come."

Arch heaved a sigh, checked with Gus and Sergeant Jones, and said they would arrive together. Yes, he and Gus would help with the serving. What would have happened if I'd said he *had* to attend? Arch and Gus trotted off to the Passat. Since the weather was glorious but cool, I called after them to have a good time, and I bit my tongue trying not to remind him to take a rain jacket.

At home, I called Tom and left a message about Warren Broome, and how he'd taken advantage of Audrey Millard, church secretary. Audrey had told Father Pete, who may or may not have kept notes about her problems in the church files. I didn't have the dates, I added, and wasn't aware of any of the particulars.

But I did want to know more about Warren Broome, M.D. I looked him up on Google, and found the name of the previous woman who'd gone public about his exploits. Mary Zwingen went not only to the Colorado Board of Medical Examiners with her story, along with supporting evidence that Broome could not refute, but also to the Denver papers. Broome had had his license suspended for six months and had had to undergo remediation through therapy and classes; he also denied having sex with other female clients. Mary had been adamant that there were other victims, but had not been forthcoming with details. Broome had threatened a libel suit, and she had shut up. Unfortunately, Mary had died of breast cancer the year before, so there was no way anyone could question her.

I offered Boyd more coffee, which he politely declined. I fixed myself an espresso with cream— damn the doctor, anyway—and whisked together a vinaigrette for another lunch salad. It was summer, after all. Julian announced he was going to hard-cook some eggs. Between chopping up leftover bacon—to be omitted from Julian's plate—and tomatoes, celery, and scallions, I tried to make sense of what I knew. I looked up the website for Our Lady of Perpetual Grace.

According to the map that popped up, the church was not far from our own Episcopal cathedral, St. John's. Hmm.

I stared at the map. If I was going down to Denver to talk to the people at Clarkson Shipping—and I was, never mind that Tom's people had already been there— then I could visit Holly's former parish. I made a mental note to run the expedition past Tom. He would probably okay it, but would insist that Boyd come with me.

Poor Boyd.

I doubted that any official person at Our Lady of P.G. would talk to me about Holly. But the website said the church gift shop was next door. The elderly women who ran those shops might talk to me about a former parishioner. Emphasis on the *might*.

Beside me, Julian sautéed some wild mushrooms and efficiently laid out beds of arugula, which he dotted with slices of mushroom, egg, two kinds of cheese, and all the vegetables I'd chopped. For the first time since getting up much too early, I realized that my stomach was growling. We were facing an exhausting evening, I told myself, so better to put lots of goodies on the salads for myself, Boyd, and Armstrong. Better yet, I thought, we needed thick slices of homemade bread spread with unsalted butter—yum!—otherwise we might get hungry later.

The ringing phone ticked me off. I was ravenous, finally able to indulge my appetite, and now somebody wanted something. The interruption was more than I could bear, so I took a big bite of my slice of bread.

"Better let the machine get it," Julian advised, grinning.

But I peeked at the caller ID anyway. Audrey Millard? After what she'd told me this morning, there was no way I was going to refuse to take her call.

I picked up the receiver, but only managed to say, "Mmf," before being relieved of the phone by Julian.

"This is Goldilocks' Catering," he said. He gave me a wary glance and then said, "No, she's eating lunch right now—" But I'd already swallowed and grabbed the receiver.

"Hello there, Audrey. Did you tell the sheriff's department what you told me?"

"I did. They asked me if, besides Father Pete, Holly knew about it, about *him*. But I really couldn't say. I certainly didn't tell Holly. Now I'm scared to death that the department will go pick . . . him . . . up, and then he'll come after me."

"Sergeant Xavier?" I asked. "Is she with you?"

"Yes." She did not sound reassured.

"Audrey, you'll be okay. The department will have someone stay with you for as long as you need it."

"Yes," she said again. Then she didn't speak for such a long time that I checked the receiver to make sure we were still connected. "I remembered something," she went on, her voice cautious. "When the investigators were here about Father Pete, I was so upset I forgot to tell them. Sergeant Xavier said I should call the sheriff's department to tell them, and an investigator is on his way up now."

Another long silence. "Audrey?" I said.

"It may not be important. But my birthday was the sixth of June. D-Day. Anyway, I'd been asking Holly for years if I could buy one of her homemade jigsaw puzzles for my nephew. But she never seemed to have time to make one. I thought with all she'd gone through with the divorce, with Drew, with trying to establish a new career, well . . . I'd always thought she'd forgotten. So I stopped bugging her about it. You know, she was becoming famous for her collages. Who cared about the jigsaw puzzles? But I thought they were charming. Then, when she came for her confession on Friday, she surprised me with a belated birthday gift. She said because I was a Gemini, I wouldn't mind. Which made no sense to me, as usual. But then I opened it and it was a jigsaw puzzle."

I waited through all this, wondering why such a present should occasion a call to me, or to the sheriff's department. I remembered the unfinished jigsaw puzzle on the table in Holly's living room. "And . . . what was the puzzle of?"

"It's a map. I don't know why Holly thought my nephew would enjoy a map of Asia, but it *is* pretty, I suppose."

"A map of Asia?" I repeated dumbly. "Is your nephew . . . interested in Asia?"

"Not in the least. But here's the part I thought was bizarre. She asked if I had a security system. I said I did . . . I mean, you know, I'm a woman living alone. She seemed relieved. *Then* she said I needed to open the box at my house. After that, I absolutely had to keep what was inside at home. I could not leave it at the church."

My heart rate quickened. "Did she say why?"

"She did not. She also said I should keep its existence to myself. The puzzle, I mean. I said, 'Well, I guess my nephew won't be getting it, then.' And she said, 'No, Audrey, I want this *just to be for you*.' She really emphasized those words." Audrey hesitated. "I still don't know what's going on."

"I don't get it."

"Neither did I. I said to Holly, 'Why is it just for me? Why can't I show it to anyone?' And she laughed. But then she got serious again. 'Okay, Audrey, listen carefully. If something happens to me, please give it to Father Pete.'"

"*What?*"

Audrey was crying. "And now I can't. Oh, the police-woman says the investigator is here. I'm going to give him the puzzle from Holly. Do you want to talk anymore? You made me feel so much better this morning."

"Could you photocopy the puzzle and bring it to the dinner tonight?"

"Yes, I'll bring you a copy of this map puzzle. I hate to give it up, but Holly was so odd about it, I thought you all should know. I . . . just don't understand why any of this is happening."

16

I closed my eyes. All my energy and ability to think were draining out of me. A map. Of Asia. And if something happened to Holly, Audrey was supposed to give the puzzle to Father Pete. But Father Pete lay in a coma. Maybe Holly had told him what all this was supposed to mean: the notes, the jigsaw puzzle, somebody who knew. "Thanks, Audrey."

"You will find out what happened?" The anxious tone made her voice rise. "I mean, to Father Pete? And . . . and . . . to Holly? You'll figure out what this important puzzle means?"

"I'm trying," was all I could manage to say. *Maybe it means nothing,* my mind unhelpfully supplied.

Marla rang our doorbell—she didn't bang, for which I was thankful—just as Julian, Boyd, Armstrong, and

I were once more trying to sit down to lunch. Still, relief washed through me. Maybe she would be able to figure out what had happened to our friend, and why.

"You look like hell," Marla said.

"Thanks. You look great." She had changed into a hot-pink blouse and lime-green pants, with a pink-and-green-paisley sweater to match. She wore twinkly diamond-and-gold earrings, with a necklace and bracelet set. I said, "Come have some lunch."

As I walked down our hall, my leg began to ache again. I resolved to put the mysteries of Holly, Father Pete, Kathie Beliar, and Audrey Millard out of my overstimulated brain. I was thankful when the chef salads plus homemade bread revived all of us.

As we did the dishes, Marla insisted that she was still helping out with the fund-raising dinner. She dutifully washed her hands while I told Boyd, Armstrong, Julian, and her about Holly's giving Audrey Millard a gift for her eyes only, apparently—a jigsaw puzzle that was a map of Asia.

Boyd and Armstrong exchanged a glance. Despite the fact that a sheriff's department investigator was on his way to Audrey's house to hear this story at that very moment, Boyd took out a notebook and wrote. Marla dried her hands and shook her head.

"Goldy? That makes no sense whatsoever. Holly's parents were of British and French extraction. I never even heard Holly *mention* Asia." She sighed. "Maybe it's a really *pretty* map of Asia? I mean, since she was an artist?"

I said, "Holly gave a puzzle of a really pretty map of Asia to Audrey, so close to when Holly died? And Audrey was supposed to give it to Father Pete if something happened to her, that is, Holly?"

Marla's brow crinkled. "What does Father Pete care about Asia? Was he a missionary there or something?"

"I don't think so." I didn't say, *If and when he wakes up, we'll have to ask him.*

Julian said, "You know, sometimes when we cook, you get ideas, Goldy. No matter what, we need to get started. Sorry."

So we got down to the prep. Marla followed Julian's instructions for washing and spinning dry the heads of romaine, which then had to be separated into leaves, rinsed, spun, and dried again. It was my bet that Marla had never cleaned a head of lettuce in her life, but on this subject I stayed mum. To their credit, Boyd and Armstrong offered to assist us. Julian and I assured them we were doing fine. The two cops gratefully headed for the living room. A moment later, I heard Boyd on his cell phone.

Julian, meanwhile, laboriously pureed the vichyssoise and stored it in the walk-in in small covered containers. Storing the soup in one big vat never would have gotten the concoction cold. I sliced loaf after loaf of Dad's Bread. Colorado's weather was so dry, in elementary school Arch had actually done a science experiment that involved leaving corn chips out overnight, to see if they became *more* crisp by morning. Unfortunately, he'd left the plate of chips on our back deck, where they'd proven to be too much temptation for the neighborhood squirrels, and maybe even a bear, because I found the empty metal pie plate halfway across the backyard. I remembered how furious Arch had been. "What am I supposed to say?" he demanded. "The wildlife ate my homework?" Then, as if guilty, he'd added, "I suppose those animals were really hungry."

"I suppose so," I whispered, as I had then. To keep the bread slices moist, I carefully stored them in zipped plastic bags.

Marla startled me out of my reverie. "Didn't you say Holly had installed a security system in her rental because she claimed to have lots of *valuable antiques*? On which she had an insurance policy that nobody seems to be able to find?"

"That's what Drew told us." I put the bags of bread into one of the boxes we were taking. "But then they had that break-in."

"When was that again?"

"June sixth," I said. "Which was also Audrey's birthday. This past Friday, Holly gave Audrey a jigsaw puzzle, which she said was a belated gift. Think those two events are related?"

"I don't know. On that day, though, the sixth, nothing was stolen from the house except files," said Marla.

"Nothing that she told Drew or the cops. A file cabinet was broken into."

"No antiques missing," said Marla, working hard at the logic, as was I.

"None that we know of." I tried to recall the interior of Holly's cluttered living room. There had been all that statuary, all those crosses. The collage of Drew had hung on one wall. Three oil paintings of landscapes, which even my untrained eye dismissed as copies, also graced the walls. There were the threadbare love seat and wingback chairs, along with the cherry furniture that Holly had inherited from her parents. This included the hutch containing lots of dishes, including her grandmother's Limoges . . . and plates with yet more religious symbols.

A square mahogany table sat in the corner, with the unfinished jigsaw puzzle on top. Maybe *it* was a map of South America.

"Nothing that looked to be of value jumped out at me," I said finally. "Then again, I didn't go upstairs, where there might have been valuable stuff. Still, Tom's the expert on antiques. We should ask him."

"Still." Marla frowned at the first bag of lettuce leaves nestled in paper towels. "The sheriff's department hasn't mentioned finding anything worth a lot of money, right?" When I said they had not, she went on: "Forget the break-in for a minute. If you were having severe money problems, and you had so-called *valuable antiques,* so costly that you had an insurance policy on them, so precious that you installed a fancy security system, why would you even hold on to your stuff? Why not *sell* the damned antiques?"

"That's what Julian thought." I recalled my assistant's pride when he'd shown me the mismatched cups and saucers he'd bought at the yard sale in Maplewood. That owner had been a hoarder, though, which I didn't think Holly had been, in spite of her desire to collect religious figurines. I pulled the butter out of the walk-in, unwrapped it, and carefully began slicing the stick into tablespoons. "I'm no expert, but it didn't look to me as if there was anything of extraordinary value in that house."

Marla tucked the last lettuce leaves into a plastic bag before turning to me. "Then why take out an insurance policy that the department cannot find? Why install a security system?" She paused. "And here's what bugs me most of all. If our friend, who was generous in every way, was having money problems, why wouldn't she accept financial aid from me? Call it a bridge loan, or whatever you want. That's what really sticks in my craw. *She* would have helped *us*. Yet for whatever reason, she wanted to keep her money problems secret. Why?"

I shook my head, and posed a few questions of my own. "Why schedule a quarterly confession with Father Pete, and never tell us when she was up here to visit? Why give Audrey Millard a birthday puzzle, which was a map of Asia? Why say you had a studio in Cherry Creek, when you didn't?" Marla groaned at the obvious implication, but I soldiered onward. "How much did we not know about Holly? How much did her own son not know about her?"

"Maybe it's not really a map of Asia," Marla said hopefully. "Maybe it's a map to where her stuff is."

"Then why not tell Drew about it?"

Marla shrugged.

Julian, meanwhile, was heating stockpots of water and herbs, for poaching all the shrimp. He gave us worried glances, as he quickly brought out the bags of jumbo raw shrimp. "Why don't you two go back downstairs and read some more of your notes? I mean, from your meetings. Maybe that will help you figure out . . . whatever. Here," he said, handing a bag of brownies to

Marla, "take some low-carb treats. I thawed these this morning. It says on the label that my boss here used almond flour and sweetener that isn't sugar for them."

"Low-carb brownies?" Marla asked as she clomped ahead of me down the stairs, clutching the bag and plates Julian had given her. "You made these and didn't tell me?"

"They were an experiment that didn't turn out very well. I was also making Spicy Brownies, with crystallized ginger and ground ginger. Those came out pretty well. I wasn't crazy about another attempt at adding spice to brownies—chipotle chile powder. Those burned out the inside of my mouth."

"But I'll bet Arch loved them," said Marla.

"You got that right."

"Why did you discard the low-carb ones?" Marla wanted to know as we settled ourselves at the long table with the Amour Anonymous notebooks.

"I didn't discard them. I tasted them. They didn't seem like the kind of thing that adults at a catered dinner would enjoy."

"Mmm," said Marla, once she'd taken the first bite. "When you don't eat sugar, you don't mind the fake stuff so much. Okay, before we start, have you figured out what you're going to say to Warren Broome tonight?"

The despondent expression on Warren Broome's face floated in front of me. He had not been at church, but he and Patsie were supposed to attend the fund-raising dinner tonight. I'd tried to lure Warren into telling me something about Holly before I'd found out that Audrey was the second woman he'd victimized. Had Holly, who supposedly had had an affair with Broome, possessed that tidbit of knowledge? Had she been blackmailing Warren Broome?

Presumably, Tom and his crew now knew all about Warren Broome and Audrey. I wondered what the fall-out from that would be.

"I very much doubt Warren will talk to me now, even if he's at the dinner tonight."

"All right," Marla said resignedly. "Let the department handle him." She shook her head at our spill of papers. "Where were we?"

I told her about my attempt to make a time line of my relationship with Holly. Marla's enthusiasm bounced back. She eagerly took the legal pad I handed to her.

"*So* glad I don't have to do this on a computer," she said, munching a second brownie. "I tend to kill them." I sat across from her and tried to concentrate on the notebooks. But my mind kept wandering back to my odd conversation with Audrey Millard. Just to satisfy my own curiosity, I got up and pulled down an atlas from our long shelf of books.

"Now what?" Marla demanded, without looking up.

"I'm going to make my own map of Asia, and compare it to the one Holly used for Audrey's puzzle."

As our copy machine was whirring away—like Audrey, I would have to do this in sections—I sent a text to Tom: *H's house broken into 6/6. Audrey M birthday = 6/6. A says H gave her jigsaw puzzle as belated gift. Is map of Asia. Meaning in any of this?*

Don't know. Deputy bringing puzzle from AM, Tom replied. *Asia doesn't compute in any way with investigation. No Asian suspects, etc.*

Unfinished jigsaw puzzle on table in Holly's living room, I tapped back.

Have it, Tom texted back. *Also Asia. Hunan Province. No hidden code.*

I wrote, *Tonight, AM going to bring me copy of one H made for her. OK?*

See no relevance to investigation. But OK. See you at 6.

"Whoa!" Marla cried, and I jumped. "Here's Holly saying she went to see her cardiologist! *What* cardiologist?"

I laid aside the map of Asia I had taped together and bent over the notebook in front of Marla. *Holly visited her cardiologist,* it said. *He gave her a clean bill of health.*

"She had heart problems?" I asked. "Did we know this?"

"No, definitely not," Marla said. "Or if the group did know, it didn't stick in my memory. I'm the one who went through cardiac arrest a few years ago, and I would have remembered. I think," she added uncertainly.

I tapped out this news to Tom.

He phoned me almost immediately. "She had an issue with her heart? We did not know that. Okay, look. George Ingleby is a cardiologist. He *must* know about this. Whether he'll tell us is another matter."

"You can't get around privacy regulations, even for someone who's dead?"

"Don't know. Before I go see George, I'll call Drew in Alaska, ask him again if his mother had a condition he forgot to tell us about. We didn't find any medications in the rental. But I'll tell the deputy—the one bringing down the jigsaw puzzle from Audrey?—to detour over to Holly's rental and look through all the cabinets again. Hold on a sec." I waited while Tom talked to someone. "I need to go," he said, his voice low. "But a guy just told me we tracked Holly's cell phone, and figured out how someone could have spent a couple of hours planting a note on her deck, then sawing out the beams underneath, without anyone *in the house* noticing. Near as we can figure, no one was *in* the house."

"No one was in it all day?" I said incredulously.

"Not for a couple of hours in the morning. The day of the birthday party, Drew was out with friends. Audrey Millard told us Holly was due to come to the church."

I said doubtfully, "You'd still be taking a big chance that someone outside the house would see you."

"Not really, Miss G. Unless you drive up a long road, then a steep driveway, the only way you can reach that house is by ascending from the lake, and that involves several staircases anyone *could* see, or else some serious rock climbing behind boulders that *would* conceal you. Anyone looking at that place from a distance—say from a boat out on the lake?—would see a person in a uniform, doing what looked like window washing. The end."

I exhaled. "Any news on Father Pete?"

"Still in a coma. Gotta run."

I felt guilty that Tom was taking time out to talk to me. But he knew how much I'd treasured Holly, how much I valued Father Pete, and how desperately I wanted to figure this out. After he signed off, I turned to Marla. I told her about Friday's time frame, which had provided a couple of hours for the saboteur to screw up Holly's deck.

"So . . . is Tom thinking someone was watching Holly's house, and saw her and Drew leave?" Marla asked.

"Either that or somebody knew Holly was going to be at St. Luke's on Friday morning. Maybe he saw her calendar when he broke into her house."

Incredibly, it was getting on to four o'clock. We had to go back to working on the dinner. Overhead, heavy footsteps indicated that Julian had put Boyd and Armstrong to work. I wondered how they felt about that, and figured they'd probably have preferred to be doing anything else: interviewing witnesses, canvassing neighborhoods, or putting time in at the crime lab, anything besides culinary work.

But they were hard at it. Armstrong was packing up a freezer box with containers of vichyssoise while Boyd was laboriously peeling the shrimp. Next to him were a mound of firm pink shellfish bodies and another, bigger pile of shells. Boyd's face was unreadable. Julian, meanwhile, was whirring the sherry vinaigrette in the blender. I felt guilty about our time in the basement. But Julian only looked at us and nodded.

"Everything okay?"

"I wouldn't go that far," said Marla. "When we find out what happened to Holly and Father Pete, we'll give ourselves permission to feel okay."

Once my van, Marla's Mercedes, and Julian's Range Rover were packed up, we took off for the conference center. Boyd accompanied me; Armstrong followed Marla in the prowler. When the cops said Julian had to stay where they could see him, he sighed, but agreed.

Marla called my cell. "Tom doesn't want to take any chances," she observed. "That's sweet."

Tom didn't want *me* to take any chances, I thought sourly, as our little procession made its way up Main Street.

The sun was beginning to slide toward the western mountains, but it would be another four hours before it set. Fishermen ringed Aspen Meadow Lake. A fresh breeze was splintering the afternoon light on the water's surface. Boaters paddled furiously toward the boathouse, where rentals were due at five. Gaggles of geese and flocks of duck swarmed the center of the lake, the better to keep away from humans.

My cell phone buzzed again. This time, Boyd took it and read the caller ID.

"Yeah, Chief?" he said. We were almost to the conference center. "She's here. Will do." He handed the phone to me.

"I'm going to see you in an hour," I said, but I could feel the warmth in my voice. I'd just seen him that morning, but I missed him. "Please tell me you're not calling to cancel."

"No way. But I wanted to warn you to get your investigative antennae up."

"They *are* up."

"I mean tonight, and I mean *way* up. With the Inglebys." I sighed, but Tom went on, "First of all, you should know we talked to Drew. No cardiological condition that he knew of. Our deputy went through Holly's rental *again*. No meds, no suspicious notes or files. And still no insurance policy stashed somewhere. So, being as how George Ingleby is a cardiologist, I drove over there, to see if I could find anything else out."

"And?"

"Mustang Sally, the maid? She opened the door and looked frightened. Wanted to know if some of the neighbors had called us about the noise."

"The Inglebys don't have any close neighbors. What noise?"

"George and Lena were fighting in the kitchen. I mean, screaming at each other. Mustang Sally let me in, and raced toward the kitchen to announce me. Then there was sudden silence."

I managed to say, "What were they fighting about?"

"Oh, Miss G., I wish I knew. Lena stormed out of the kitchen and toward me. She was like a cartoon character with steam blowing out of her ears. She saw me, and hollered, 'Wanna have sex?'"

"*What?*"

"Exactly. Well, not exactly. She didn't say 'have sex.' She used the F-word. You'd think churchgoing people would know better."

"Tom! What did you say to her?"

"Miss G., I have a job to do. I said, 'Are you offering?'"

"What job is it," I said, biting each word, "that would involve having sex with Lena Ingleby?"

Tom laughed. "Aw, love your jealousy, Miss G. I wanted to know what had led her to say such a thing to me."

"Did you find out?"

"I did not. She stomped off, marched through the front door, and slammed it behind her."

"And George?"

"Well, he was all red-faced, out in the kitchen, drinking a glass of water. That man certainly does seem to favor overbearing, demanding women."

"Holly was neither overbearing nor demanding."

"According to George, she was. But I'd already heard that bit from him. So I just asked if Holly had a heart condition. He hemmed and hawed and finally said, yes, she did."

"What kind of heart condition?"

"You know how the heartbeat is divided into sections? Q, R, S, T?"

"I was a member of Med Wives 101," I said impatiently. "What does that have to do with Holly?"

"According to George, she had a prolonged S-T interval. That's why she died. The antibiotics. Loquin, to be exact. I just got the side effects from the doc we consulted. With a prolonged S-T interval, if she'd been given enough Loquin, her heart would have stopped—"

"Oh, my God," I interrupted.

"Yes," Tom said, his voice so infinitely sad that I had no reply. "And somebody knew. George did. And maybe other people, too."

I thought back to the visit from Neil Unger on Thursday. On Friday night, there was all the back-and-forth movement in Marla's kitchen. There were numerous people who could have stirred crushed Loquin into the glasses of wine, or even into the chile relleno torta, a few bites of which Holly had eaten several minutes before she walked out of Marla's house.

But I could not bring back a mental image of someone standing over the casseroles. All my mind's eye tossed up was Holly's smiling face at Marla's door.

We'll get together soon, and talk.

17

True to his word, Tom pulled into the conference-center parking lot just before six. Armstrong peeled off as Arch and Gus, with Sergeant Jones following in her prowler, pulled up in a pale cloud of dust. I knew better than to run out and hug or even greet Tom, much less Arch and Gus. I did watch Tom, though. I was happy to see my family, no question. But the thought of both Boyd and Jones, not to mention Tom, being armed at a church dinner made me swallow hard.

The three cops took their duties in stride. While Gus and Arch ruefully informed me that Sergeant Jones had, indeed, beaten them to the trailhead, Tom briefed Boyd and Jones on their duties. Jones stationed herself at the French doors, with a clipboard of guests' names, to be checked off when they arrived. Boyd greeted me when he came into the dining room. He walked all around, checking the shelves and under the tables. I should have reassured myself, thinking we were now more secure. Instead, the cops' presence made me feel more vulnerable.

I raced back to my work while Gus and Arch washed up. Tom pushed through the swinging kitchen doors and nodded to Boyd. He then strictly ordered us not to use the exit to the Dumpster until the dinner was over, the guests had left, and one of the three of them had accompanied us outside with the trash.

"Also," Tom added, "there's been no change in Pete's condition. Still unconscious." His voice did not betray the emotion that suffused his green eyes. I wanted to hug him, but, again, couldn't.

Marla said she did not want to be out schmoozing with the diners. It would make her think of Father Pete. She wanted to be with us, serving. I told her that would be fine.

While Tom conferred with Boyd, our five-member crew—Julian, Marla, and I, along with the newly deputized Arch and Gus—worked an assembly line. We had enough sense to begin by pouring vichyssoise, of which we had an abundance, into a pair of paper cups, for Boyd and Jones. Arch and Gus reported back that the cops gladly took the offerings. The boys then moved on to filling water pitchers with ice and either water or iced tea. That task finished, they hustled back into the kitchen and asked for the first trash bag. They wanted to get the sergeants' cups stowed, because the arriving guests were lining up to be checked in.

Marla and Julian began with laying out chilled bowls in rows. They then brought more cold soup out of the conference-center walk-in, while Arch, Gus, and I readied the trays for drinks.

Marla, madly ladling soup, said, "I know I wanted to be here with you. And I know I shouldn't be nervous, but I am." She slopped soup outside one of the bowls and shrieked, which made Boyd bolt into the kitchen.

"Just take your time," Julian told her, once Boyd had been assured there was no calamity. Julian showed Marla how to wipe each bowl with a clean kitchen towel. "Just make it a routine. And remember, the guests want this food. They have paid, and they're hungry. They need you more than you need them. Okay, Auntie?"

Marla nodded and went back to her task. When Julian wasn't looking, I could see her smiling.

Through the swinging doors, the muffled voice of the supply priest said grace. When the expected *Amen!* did not arrive, Arch gave me a confused look, while Gus pushed the door open a crack. The priest had launched into a lengthy prayer for Father Pete's continued healing. Tom muttered under his breath. Even after the *Amen!* finally arrived, the supply priest found it incumbent upon himself to reassure the guests that Father Pete, who had conceived of this dinner and to whom it was dedicated, was getting better.

The expected murmur rising from the crowd—Father Pete was improving?—became so disruptive that Tom shook his head. "You shouldn't give people hope when you don't have any news."

I momentarily stopped searching for the plastic bag of chopped chives that I knew was in one of our boxes. "Father Pete would say there's no such thing as false hope."

Tom grunted.

The supply priest began to talk about how gratified Father Pete would be when he heard how many of them had signed up for the dinner. St. Luke's had surpassed the goal set for tonight's fund-raiser, and if all went well, the columbarium should be built within two years. An appreciative murmur went up from the crowd. But because of the . . . problems Father Pete was having, the priest added delicately, and because of the recent deaths of Holly Ingleby and Kathie Beliar, he would not be outlining ideas for funerals that night. There would be handouts about memorial services, and some ideas for music to be played at those rites, by the entrance. Any guest would be welcome to take home those materials.

I thought this sounded like a good plan. Raise money tonight; take literature home; wait for Father Pete to recover. Then regroup.

From out in the dining room, however, the audio system squawked with static. I peered through the round window in the kitchen door. To my dismay, Edith Ingleby had wrestled the microphone away from the supply priest. I swallowed hard.

Edith's thin high voice squealed, "Now listen, people! Father Pete would want all of you to write *extra* checks tonight toward the building of the columbarium . . ."

An angry buzz arose from the hungry parishioners, who'd already sprung a hundred bucks a pop for their reservations. The supply priest had just told them that things were going well, that money from this dinner was putting us ahead of our goal for the columbarium. So what gave?

"What ails that woman?" Marla asked. She'd finished ladling the soup and was standing next to me.

I whipped around and looked for something to do. I seized on the bag of chopped chives. "I don't know."

"Well!" Marla exclaimed. "Since *I* am paying for this dinner, and, I might add, I'm also *serving* it, and, I might *also* add, since our rector's life is hanging by the thinnest of threads at Southwest Hospital, is it really appropriate for Edith Ingleby to sabotage this fundraiser with one of her narcissistic power plays?" She tapped her foot. "You know what?" Her voice rose perilously. "I've got half a mind to go out there and grab that microphone from her, right now. I don't care what people think—"

"You care what people think, and you're not going anywhere," Tom's low voice rumbled.

"Honestly," said Marla, turning her attention and argument to Tom. "This is too much. Remember that saying from . . . who was it? Max Planck? Let me think. 'Science advances, funeral by funeral.' Actually, we're not talking about science here. We're talking about church finances, and she—"

"Marla," I interrupted. "Please calm down. I don't want you to have another coronary."

Swathed in a white apron, one hand clutching a ladle, the other on her hip, Marla looked like a furious chef about to paddle an ungrateful guest. "Calm? You want me to calm down? Get that damn woman back to her seat!"

Another, deeper voice barked into the microphone. Someone was endeavoring to silence Edith Ingleby. I was glad it wasn't Marla, and I was especially glad to be in the kitchen.

"Who's that talking?" I asked Arch, who was now squinting through the swinging door's window. "Carl, the music director," he said. He stood listening. "He's saying he moved the printed material that the supply priest had put by the entrance. He's telling people to look at the pamphlets in the center of each table, where they will find lists of hymns they can pick out for their memorial services." Arch shook his head. "Now Carl says he brought a portable keyboard, and he can practice some of those hymns with the guests in just a few minutes. Mom! Can't *we* play some music or something?"

I shook my head. Whoever paid for events in the center usually brought their own music, either in the form of a small band or a disc jockey.

"Well then," Arch continued, "maybe somebody could go out there and tell jokes? Something needs to happen, 'cuz the mood needs to change. Big-time."

"Ah, mood rings!" Marla trilled, looking over the boxes we'd brought. "I knew we'd forgotten something."

"Happily," said Tom unexpectedly, "we don't need mood rings. We have just the guy." He swung through the door and returned with Boyd. "Sergeant Boyd, you've been wanting to try out some of your stand-up material. Now's the time."

"Uh, I don't—" said Boyd. Boyd's fair skin blushed scarlet to the roots of his salt-and-pepper hair.

"That's an order," said Tom, as he snapped on some latex gloves, picked up a ladle, and began spooning vichyssoise into the second group of chilled bowls Julian had laid out on the counter.

Julian grinned. Maybe all that time in Boulder had taught my young assistant to go with the flow. Sad to say, this didn't feel like a flow. It felt like paddling a canoe in very shallow water, with submerged rocks about to make dinner run aground.

Boyd pushed through the swinging door. Clearly curious but with jobs to do, Julian and Marla helped Tom scoop the rest of the creamy cold soup into bowls. I moved along the line and sprinkled dark green chopped chives on top. It was the old rule of garnishing: light on dark, and in this case, dark on light. Out in the dining room, I was hoping things were going from dark *to* light. We were interrupted in our feverish work by guffaws from Gus and Arch, whose job, refilling people's water glasses, then taking the guests coffee or tea, had not yet begun.

"What's so funny?" I asked, but the boys waved away my question so they could listen to the rest of Boyd's monologue.

I picked up the first tray of soup bowls and walked to the door. Marla, holding her own tray, crashed into me, but gave only a mini-shriek. I said to my son, "Could you open the door for us? Please?" But he was brushing tears from his eyes. Tom quickly pushed the door ajar so we could pass through.

"Don't worry," Tom said. "I've heard all of Boyd's material."

"Arch! Gus," I hissed over my shoulder. "Please pick up the trays of water and iced-tea pitchers and start checking on the tables!"

Out in the dining room, Boyd was saying, "So she pointed at me, and said, 'I know what you're thinking!' And I said, 'Oh, yeah? What am I thinking?' And she said, 'You wish I would shut up.' And I said, 'No, I just wanted to ask your husband if he knew how fast he was driving.' And she said, '*I* can tell you that. He always drives too fast when he's been drinking.'"

The diners howled. Or at least most of them did. I took care to lower the bowls of soup at the table where the Inglebys sat. Edith, having lost the microphone, scowled. George Ingleby, worried about his mother but amused by Boyd, tried to suppress a smile. Lena Ingleby, clearly there under protest, yawned. Carl, the music director, looking lost, sat with empty chairs on each side. He clutched his portable keyboard under his arm and wasn't eating. The dinner had not gone the way he or anyone else had planned.

Boyd continued his "Traffic Stops I Have Known" routine while we quietly finished serving the soup. Unfortunately, he was winding down when we cleared the bowls. By the time we schlepped out the prepared entrée plates, complete with their slices of bread and china cups of molded salad, a mournful quiet had dropped over the dining room. I gave the supply priest an expectant look. He seemed to know what I was asking, but just shrugged. Really, where was his stand-up routine about Clinical Pastoral Education? Best not to ask.

I arrived behind Edith Ingleby and lowered her plate. She was talking indignantly in not so sotto a voce. Really, she was saying, she should march right back up there and try once again to get people to give extra money to the columbarium project. I steeled my nerve. This was my catered affair, and there was no way I was going to allow Edith to take charge of the audio system again.

Audrey Millard, meanwhile, was seated at a table as far away as possible from the one containing Warren Broome and Patsie Boatfield. She nodded to me when I lowered her plate, then handed me the photocopy of the puzzle Holly had given her.

Back in the kitchen, I posed the question about entertainment to the crew. Did anybody have *any* lighthearted music we could play for the guests? Arch, bless him, remembered an old boom box he'd stored in the trunk of his car. Boyd, done with his routine, accompanied us as we walked quickly through the dining room, where everyone was silently digging into their entrées. Out in the lot, Arch popped the trunk to his VW—and revealed, in addition to the boom box, an *unopened* CD I'd bought him for Christmas: *The Best of Kenny G.*

I said, "I see my ability to give you inappropriate gifts has not changed."

"Mom, you wanted my help and I gave it."

"True. Thanks."

At the entrance, Warren Broome stood smoking a cigarette. I thought, *Doctors!* Boyd and Arch were a few steps ahead of me, chatting happily about Boyd's stand-up routine as they ambled back into the dining room. Warren Broome suddenly tossed his smoke and grabbed my forearm. The compact disc slid out of my hand and down the wooden steps. I turned to Warren, who held my arm in a death grip. His dark eyes were furious, his face cold with anger.

"Let. Go. Of. Me," I enunciated loudly.

"Where's this information you say Holly left for me? What are you doing calling my wife and asking all sorts of questions? Where is the collage of my wife? I should throw you—" was all he was able to get out of his mouth before Sergeant Jones burst through the door and wrenched Broome's hand off my arm.

"Go inside, Goldy," Jones ordered, her voice arctic cold.

I picked up the CD, scooted into the dining room, and rushed over to Boyd and Arch. Pairs of curious eyes ignored me and watched the drama outside: a tall, muscular black woman giving a tall, muscular white man hell. Sergeant Jones gripped Warren Broome's wrist with one of her powerful hands. As she spoke—I imagined a scathing *How do you think this feels?*—he seemed to crumple. Whispers rose. Marla sidled over to where I was scanning the wall, the errant disc in one hand and the cord to the boom box in the other. I was desperately trying to remember where the electrical outlet was located.

"What was that about?" Marla demanded, in true sotto voce.

Arch sighed. "Mom? Just give me the cord." He plugged in the boom box.

I exhaled. "Clearly, I shouldn't have promised Warren Broome information I didn't have." I ripped through the various plastic barriers that makers of compact discs seem to think are necessary. "Can you glance casually over at Patsie Boatfield and see if she's looking this way?"

"I don't do anything casually," said Marla. "But I'll try. Yup, she's giving you a puzzled stare."

"Arch?" I said, after he had taken the CD from me, unwrapped it, and slotted the disc into the player. "Could you go ask Patsie Boatfield to come into the kitchen?"

"Sure," my son solemnly replied, and marched to the other side of the dining room. Outside the French doors, Warren Broome was arguing with Sergeant Jones. Everyone strained to hear what was being said. Nobody was having any success.

Finally, *finally*, the upbeat strains of alto saxophone music threaded through the air. Arch had convinced Patsie to follow him, so I joined the rest of the team in the kitchen. Julian was oh-so-quietly rinsing out the soup bowls. We would wash them thoroughly once everyone left.

"Goldy?" whispered Patsie Boatfield, once she was through the swinging doors. She wore a shimmery silver dress that set off her blue eyes and pale complexion. "Where's this thing that you told my husband Holly had left for him?"

"Actually," I lied effortlessly, "the cops have it."

"But what was it?"

"I'm not at liberty to say."

"Is that why my husband is such an emotional mess?"

"I was hoping you could tell me that."

"Why did that policewoman drag him off?" Patsie asked, growing agitated.

"Because your husband grabbed me and demanded information."

All the air seemed to go out of her. "Oh, God. Please forgive him. I don't know what you had for him from Holly. But he's a real sack of nerves. He's just gotten his license back, and he was all set to start practicing again. He should be happy, but since the birthday party at Marla's house Friday night he's done nothing but fidget, cry, get angry, give me the silent treatment, or race off in his car without telling me where he's going. The only thing I told him was that you had asked about him, and if he had ever known Holly."

I said, "Then what?"

"He—"

We were interrupted by the door suddenly swinging open. Warren Broome pushed inside, his face livid. Sergeant Jones was at his side.

"We're leaving," Warren announced curtly to Patsie. He did not look at me. "We're *leaving*," he said, more authoritatively this time.

Patsie, now confused in addition to being dejected, meekly followed her new husband out of the kitchen. I'd give that marriage a year, tops.

"What happened?" I asked Jones.

"Nothing," she said. "Sergeant Boyd and I were assigned to protect you, your crew, and the guests at this event. He grabbed you and threatened you, so I talked to him." Her expression gave away nothing. "He'll probably be making a complaint to the department. But his own previous misbehavior is a matter of public record, so I don't think anyone will pay any attention."

"Goldy?" asked Julian, startling me. "We need to clear."

Which we did. Because of the china cups, picking up the entrée plates proved more challenging than dealing with the soup bowls. Marla decided to place all of the cups on one side of her tray, then pile the plates on the other. The resulting imbalance caused the tray to teeter in her hands, first one way, then the other, until it finally crashed to the floor.

"Sorry, so sorry," Marla cried meekly, as I rushed to her side.

"Don't say anything," I ordered her. "We'll have this cleaned up in two minutes." Which we did. The less fuss you make over something going wrong at a catered event, the less likely it is that people will remember it. But so far we'd had the supply priest addressing the crowd adequately, while Edith Ingleby and the music director had made a hash of things. Boyd had done his routine, which had turned the mood around somewhat. Then we'd suffered through the imbroglio with Warren Broome and Sergeant Jones.

And now we had twenty broken cups and dishes.

I told myself to put it out of my head. Once I'd shoved all the shards into a heavy-duty paper bag—not plastic, as broken china can tear right through it—Arch appeared with a wet mop. He knew the drill.

In the kitchen, Julian waved away Marla's apologies. "I have *plenty* more cups. Don't even think about it."

After Marla scooped ice cream into bowls, Tom ladled fudge sauce judiciously over each sundae. Arch and Gus tucked cookies beside the ice cream, and Julian sprinkled berries on top. I started to clear the last tray of entrée dishes, from the Inglebys' table. Edith hadn't eaten a single shrimp. George hadn't touched his molded salad.

Lena said in a high, shrill voice, "That entire meal was disgusting."

I kept a straight face and removed her plate. Fundraising dinners weren't supposed to be gourmet meals. Every single one I'd attended in my predivorce years had featured a salad, very dry baked chicken, lukewarm rice, and a cookie. Compared to those dinners and lunches, this meal was Escoffier.

I said none of this, of course, but merely attempted a brave smile. "Thank you for supporting the church."

At that point, everyone but Carl at the Ingleby table made a great clattering noise as they unceremoniously stood and began a loud exit.

In the kitchen, though, I felt the full sting of Warren Broome's fury and Lena Ingleby's denigrating remark. Sometimes just one cruel comment can ruin an evening; in this case, virtually the entire night had been a disaster. I knew how to deal with broken plates. But in my years as a caterer, I'd had less luck learning how to deal with snarky people. I took a deep breath and told myself to buckle down and get through the cleanup.

Which I did. While Julian and I were washing the dishes, Marla eagerly counted the checks. "Well, maybe it was a good thing that Edith asked for extra contributions," she announced triumphantly. "The meal plus extra checks brought in five thou, so that puts us at fifteen thousand bucks for Father Pete's columbarium. Pretty darn good. And now," she went on, rummaging in her purse, "we have the tips for the staff."

"Marla," I protested, "you've already done enough. The gratuity is part of the contract, as I am sure you know—"

"Hush," she said gravely, and proceeded to give Julian, Arch, and Gus crisp one-hundred-dollar bills. Still clutching her wallet, she called to Boyd and Jones, "Hey, law enforcement! What can I—"

"Nothing," Tom said firmly, as he snatched her wallet away from her. "You want to write out a check to our widows' and widowers' fund, you can. It's a bona fide 501(c)(3) organization, with an A from CharityNavigator.org. Your gift is tax deductible." He handed her a card. She sighed dramatically and tucked the card into the wallet he handed back to her.

The guests all pulled out of the parking lot, leaving only the two police cars. Julian packed up the leftovers and put them in a cooler for Gus's grandparents. The dishes done, we swabbed the kitchen and dining room floors. Boyd, Arch, and Gus took out the trash. Then the boys announced they were taking off for Gus's house. Sergeant Jones agreed to accompany them, bless her. Gus and Arch were eagerly chatting about what they were going to do with their hundred-dollar bills.

"Boyd?" said Tom. "Can you walk Marla to her car?"

"I am perfectly capable—" Marla began huffily.

Julian put his arm around Marla's shoulders. "Go with Boyd, Auntie. I've found it's better not to argue with Tom."

Once Tom, Boyd, Julian, and I had all finally arrived home, Tom said Boyd wanted to have a shower before he settled down for the night. Would that be okay? Tom asked. He knew I was exhausted and would be desperate to kick back. I told him to tell Boyd to go home.

"He wants to stay," Tom said. "He feels guilty that he didn't sense Broome was about to grab you. He's doing this on his own time, not the department's. Says he owes it to you."

I, too, knew when it was better not to argue. I said sure, he could go ahead. Julian should shower, too, if he wanted to. Then Tom could see if there was any hot water left. I'd go last, I said, and no doubt have a quick, cold shower.

"You sure?" Tom asked.

"You know how I'm always wound up after a dinner. Especially a dinner that didn't go particularly well."

Tom gathered me into his arms. "It went great. The food was delicious, and at least Boyd and Jones told me how much they appreciated the soup. Don't be so hard on yourself."

"This feels good," I murmured into his shoulder. "I feel myself getting the Dreaded Second Wind. Think I'll take half an hour to go through some more of the Amour Anonymous notes. I really want to try to remember as much as I can about Holly. We did find that cardiologist tidbit in there. Plus, there might be more about Warren Broome. Something we haven't found yet."

"I'll wait for you, but please don't stay up late. You've got that dinner for Ophelia tomorrow night."

"I promise not to be later than eleven. And maybe I'll come join you getting washed up."

"I'll tell the guys to take extremely short showers," he said, chuckling.

First I made myself some decaf espresso. Then I headed to the basement, where I tried to remember where I'd been when Marla and I had last looked at the notes. Once I found that spot, I would have to check carefully to see if Holly had ever mentioned going to a psychiatrist, Warren Broome in particular. Maybe she hadn't just had a fling with Warren Broome. Maybe it had been something more serious. If that was the case, her heart problems could have been part of their pillow talk. I didn't remember ever seeing or hearing Warren's name before reading about him in the papers. But if Holly had been arguing with someone, and said, *It's in the notes,* then by damn, I was going to check *our* notes, to see if anything was there.

Say Holly had *not* had a fling with Warren. What if she'd been another female client he'd victimized? Say, then, that her financial predicament had erupted, and she'd started blackmailing him, that she'd shouted that the information was in the notes, notes he took of their sessions that she'd gotten hold of, maybe during their affair. Or perhaps Holly had acquired information about other female patients Warren slept with, like Audrey. He could have paid her for a while. But maybe he saw no end in sight. Then he got his license back, broke into her rental, and rifled through her files, but found nothing. If Holly had kept up her threats, maybe Warren tried to figure out another way to deal with her. Hence the text on Holly's phone. Then, maybe Holly issued a final threat: *Pay up, or I'm going to the Colorado Board of Medical Examiners.* He could just imagine his license being handed back to him, only to see the entire grievance/possible-suspension drama starting all over again. He could have seen killing Holly as a quick way out of his troubles. And then perhaps he'd felt remorse, hence all the weeping in the bathroom.

I *had* seen Holly staring into Marla's backyard the night of the birthday party. I hadn't seen the person she'd been glaring at. But I *had* caught Warren watching Holly with . . . what? His eyes had not looked as if they were filled with unbridled hatred, I reflected.

No. He'd looked like he was in love. With Holly. I wondered if there was any chance that she'd been a client, he'd fallen in love with her, they'd had a fling, and then . . . and then *what*? I had no idea.

But there was one other bit to this hypothesis: Warren Broome had gratuitously given me his opinion of Father Pete, and it was negative. Marla had said she'd heard Father Pete had refused to perform the marriage ceremony for Patsie and Warren. If true, could this be the source of his bitterness? More seriously, could Holly have confessed the affair to Father Pete, and Broome had sensed yet more disapproval coming from our rector? Priests were now legally bound to report people in positions of authority and trust who'd exploited their position. Maybe Father Pete had done that.

This theory would explain why Father Pete had acted so strangely—drinking too much, not being like his usual pastoral self—after Holly died.

I slugged down the espresso and began reading the notes again. After a few minutes, it was clear my body was having a second wind, but my mind was not. The words danced around on the page, and the only thing I gleaned from this reading was that when she was at a dinner with others present, Holly did not like to eat when others did. Instead, she would have a few bites just as everyone was finishing up. That was precisely what had happened at the birthday party, but I didn't know if it was important.

The air in the basement was stuffy. Upstairs, Jake was whining to be let out. Scout the cat, meanwhile, had disappeared. Since I'd been in the cellar, I had no idea if the cat was inside or out. "Okay, okay," I said aloud to Jake. I took my cup to the kitchen and placed it in the dishwasher.

I opened our kitchen's back door, and Jake shot out, barking madly. Since it was almost midnight, I ordered him to be quiet. As usual, he paid me no heed.

Our backyard runs along an alley. To prevent Jake from getting out, Tom had erected a stockade fence along it. So far, the fence had not prevented the elk from hopping through and depositing their usual waste products. This summer, we hadn't seen the usual number of elk, but we'd certainly had our share of bears, whose scat Arch had identified for us. The bears, likewise, were not deterred by the fence. They'd even figured out a way to push open the gate, to be spared the trouble of climbing over the fence. Tom had promised to fix the latch, but had been so swamped with work that he hadn't had a chance.

I peered into the backyard. I couldn't see Jake, who was still barking madly. Oh, no, I thought as I scanned our garden for our bloodhound. The gate was open. A bear had undoubtedly once again pushed through, looking for garbage. Well, if it was a she-bear with cubs, I didn't hold out much hope for Jake.

I shoved open the kitchen door and called Jake again. The night air was cool, and provided a welcome break from the basement. And then someone pulled me out the door and spun me around.

An arm wrapped across my neck from behind, pressed hard against my windpipe, bending my body backward while my attacker pinned my arms with his other hand. He seemed to be wearing a mask and had on gloves and a heavy jacket.

"Who knows?" a harsh, low voice growled in my ear. His arm choked my throat tighter. Even if I'd had a clue what he was talking about, I couldn't have said anything. I tried to wrench an elbow free so I could shove it into his stomach, but he shifted his stance. He slammed my hip and the side of my face against the house, scraping my cheek with stinging pain as the shock emptied me of breath again. My bruised leg started to buckle and I half sank to the deck. I gasped when he tried to jerk me upright.

"Where are Holly's notes?" he demanded. Black patches appeared in front of my eyes as I grew dizzy. I gargled something unintelligible. I felt the thump of Jake jumping onto the deck, snarling and barking in a ringing bellow I'd never heard him use before. I struggled to break free as my burning leg twisted awkwardly. *Help me*, I thought. *Doesn't anybody hear Jake?*

At this point, Julian must have looked out the kitchen's back windows. His muffled voice yelled, "Hey! *Hey!*"

As quickly as my attacker had appeared, he disappeared. The back alley that ran behind our house, with trees lining it, afforded anyone, man or beast, a quick exit. Jake chased after him, but I managed to croak out our canine's name. This time, he listened to me and turned back. I didn't know if my attacker had a weapon and I didn't want Jake finding out.

Julian, Tom, and Boyd spilled out the door. Tom, his hair wet, was clad only in his undies. He was carrying his .45. Boyd helped me up while Tom shouted, "Why in *the hell* did you come out here alone?"

"I didn't! Jake was barking, and I saw the gate was open—"

"All right," Tom said, "come inside. Everybody. Now."

I felt frustrated. And stupid. I meekly followed my husband into the kitchen, where he and Boyd wanted every detail of the attack: Did I recognize the person? The voice? Anything, even a smell? No, no, no, I said. The guy wore a mask, gloves, and a jacket. I hadn't even been able to scratch him. I was so upset at not being able to get any DNA or other evidence from whoever it was, I almost started crying.

Julian made me some more decaf espresso and silently placed it in front of me.

At length, Tom said he wanted me to see a doctor. I said I was *fine*, that there was no way I was going back to the hospital. In fact, I didn't want to see anyone at all, except for him.

He shook his head, checked my cheek, and said I could go have a shower. He was going to call the department to get a crime-scene unit up to the house, just in case the guy had dropped anything at all. He was also going to request extra police cars for both front and back.

Upstairs, I allowed scalding water to surge over my body. I didn't care. I gasped at the heat. I rubbed my cheeks, my still-throbbing leg, and every other inch of my skin so hard it turned red. I was trying to get that touch, that brutal questioning, off me.

When I finally climbed into bed, I reflected on the evening: the dinner, the food, the guests. The attack. Except for the money we'd raised for Father Pete's pet project, it had been a catastrophe.

It was only much later that I realized that after the dinner, when we were cleaning up in my center's kitchen, I'd held the solution to the puzzle of who had killed Holly in my hands. I just hadn't known it, seen it, or understood it.

18

That night, I dreamed I was blind. Arch, Tom, Marla, Julian—none of them were in the nightmare. But Holly was. She was calling, "Why can't you see it?"

"See what?" my voiceless scream had called back.

Tom woke me. My yelling hadn't been so silent after all. I was shivering, drenched with sweat. "It's all right," he told me, over and over, as he held me. "You're okay."

With Tom's arms around me, I finally went back to sleep. I told the Holly-in-my-head that if she wanted me to discover something, she should have been clearer.

Her faint reply was, "I couldn't."

Well. Clearly.

Very early Monday morning, Tom told me again, patiently, that I absolutely, positively could not make a

THE WHOLE ENCHILADA · 323

step—outside the house, outside the car, anywhere—without Boyd physically by my side.

"You're going to make me a prisoner here?"

"You'll have protection from Boyd."

I said stubbornly, "The only reason I opened the back door—"

Tom's green eyes regarded me solemnly. "Miss G.?" he interrupted. "Two people have died in this town in the course of a weekend. One of the victims looked like you. Father Pete has been stabbed, and Holly's killer might have been trying to murder or injure Drew as well. Maybe the cases are connected, maybe they aren't. But they have a lot of people in common, including you. You're the one who fell literally into the trap that was Holly's sabotaged deck. You're the one who found Kathie Beliar and Father Pete. So even if we're dealing with people from outside our community, you're a witness and a target." He paused. "Not only that, but someone, very likely Holly's killer, clearly thinks you know *something* about these notes we can't find. Maybe you have some knowledge we haven't unearthed yet. Yet here you are, giving me reasons why you should be able to go out. Talking to me about our gate being open—"

"I only had the door open for a second—"

"Which is longer than it takes to kill somebody."

I said, "I'm sorry," and meant it.

Tom said that the crime-scene techs had set up lights to work out back through the night. They'd been trying to get foot- and fingerprint samples from our yard and the alley. They had packed up the lights at dawn; another team was on its way up and would continue the grid search this morning. Meanwhile, he was headed down to the department. Yes, he said, before I could ask, he'd checked with the hospital. Father Pete had not regained consciousness. I asked if the doctors could tell whether our priest had sustained any serious, as in permanent, injury to his brain.

"As long as blood is getting *to* the brain," Tom said, "there shouldn't be permanent damage. But the doc told me that Pete's blood is still not sufficiently oxygenated to allow him to regain consciousness."

And why wasn't the blood sufficiently oxygenated? my own mind asked. Because Father Pete's lungs still weren't bringing in enough oxygen. Sometimes I hated that I had just enough medical knowledge to make me worry over every physical setback.

The only thing Tom had found out during the night was that even though Kathie Beliar had run away from her attacker, Father Pete had apparently been able to dig his short fingernails into the skin of the person who had stabbed him. DNA analysis usually took several weeks, but they were going to put a rush on it. Tom hugged me silently, pointed to the iced latte he'd put on our bedside table for me, and left.

I tried to move through my yoga routine. My breath, rapid and agitated, refused to cooperate. I ordered myself to breathe in acceptance, then exhale forgiveness.

Yeah, fat chance.

Sitting on our bed once I'd finished, I noticed that my neck hurt. A look in the mirror confirmed bruises from where my attacker had choked me. My hip, where the attacker had pushed me into the house, ached, as did my arms and shoulders from having them pinned behind me. I slugged down the latte and mentally reviewed the assault from the night before. Apparently, my attacker was worried about two things: *Who knows?* and *Where are Holly's notes?*

Tom was right. Whoever this person was, he was worried about me, or someone else, or several other people, having knowledge of something. But what was that piece of knowledge? And why be worried about it?

Holly's voice in my dream: *Why can't you see it?*

I was pretty sure my attacker had broken into Holly's rental, occasioning the need for the security system. It was very possible that the person or persons who had attacked Father Pete and Kathie Beliar were connected to Holly's death, and stole the church file because he or they thought the desired data were in there. But whatever the information was, it hadn't been in that file either.

My mind returned to a familiar rut: Was the secret that Holly had over the person she wanted money from, the secret that could be found in the notes, from her distant past, or from her more recent past? If it was from her distant past, could Marla and I find some clue in my notes from the Amour Anonymous meetings? Could there be a reference in there to something that had happened in the past, but was only now related to what had been going on with Holly more recently? If so, Marla and I weren't making much headway in discovering it. Yet my attacker must have believed that Holly had told me about the notes she had, whatever they were and wherever she had hidden them. Would she have confided her secret to Father Pete? I didn't really see our priest agreeing to be a party to blackmail. Then again, maybe he hadn't really known exactly what Holly had been up to. He'd said nothing to me at her house after her death, when we were helping Drew. But perhaps he didn't feel he could divulge information Holly had given him in confidence. I certainly couldn't ask him now.

So I called Marla, always my default option.

"Lord God in heaven," she said when she answered the phone. It took her a moment to find and read the caller ID. "Goldy? Do you have any idea what time it is?"

I glanced at our bedside clock. "Ten to seven?"

"Right," she said. "Ten to seven in the evening. In Tokyo. Where I wish I were at this very minute, about to get a long, deep massage, before drinking an entire bottle of sake. What could you possibly want at ten to seven in the morning?" Before I could say anything, she rushed on: "Friday night and all the dishwashing was bad enough. But last night! You never told me that catering was so exhausting. Every muscle in my body is screaming."

I smiled. "Sorry."

"You don't *sound* sorry. You *sound* as if you're grinning."

"I *am* sorry. But listen, I need to tell you about something." I gave her the briefest possible account of what had happened in our backyard the night before, and added that the crime-scene techs had been working on trying to find some evidence concerning the identity of my attacker.

She was immediately awake. "Wow. Okay if I come over? I want all the details. Plus, we could keep going through the Amour notes."

"Yes, absolutely. Thanks."

"I'm going to need a quintuple espresso with cream when I get there. And none of your decaf stuff."

"How about a sextuple-shot latte with whipping cream?"

She groaned. "If only it were as romantic as it sounds."

I assessed myself in the bathroom mirror, and tried to ignore the blackness still blooming around my neck. Somebody tries to choke you, you're going to show it. Of course, I knew this well enough from my years with the Jerk. I smoothed concealing makeup over it, which didn't help much.

In the kitchen, Julian had pulled up the menu for that night, the twenty-first-birthday party for Ophelia Unger. Since Ophelia's deceased mother had been Greek, Neil Unger had thought it would be "fun" to have a menu featuring Greek food. Julian and I had offered a menu of Greek lemon soup, aka *avgolemono*, filo dough filled with spinach and cheese, aka *spanako-pita*, marinated lamb-and-vegetable skewers, aka *shish kebabs*, a Greek walnut cake, aka *karadopita*, and saffron rice and Greek salad, neither of which, as far as I knew, had an aka.

We'd made the cake the previous week and frozen it. Julian had thawed the lovely creation, and now was spooning a luxurious homemade honey syrup over the top. The cake would bathe in the glaze until we took it to the Ungers' place that night.

"Ready to start on the spanakopita," Julian announced as he put the pan in the sink and headed for the walk-in. He pulled out bunches of fresh spinach. As he came out, I went in for the lamb roasts. My job was to trim and marinate the meat. I wondered if I could get it done before Marla arrived, then knew that I probably could, since Marla would want to shower, try on several outfits before deciding on one, then sashay over in her own time.

I set the lamb aside and began heating dry red wine with garlic and herbs for the marinade. Since I always believed you could learn new aspects of cooking, I'd been open-minded recently when I'd discovered that the way I'd been marinating meat and chicken all these years was incorrect. The new thinking was that alcohol should be cooked out of a marinade before it was poured over meat. All this time I'd thought that it was the wine itself that imparted flavor to meat. Well, it did, according to the book I'd read. But the alcohol in the wine did not. It just made the meat mushy.

"Goldy," said Julian.

"Yes?" I'd been leaning in too close to the steaming wine mixture.

330 · DIANE MOTT DAVIDSON

"You're not looking too good. Is that bruise where the guy—"

"Indeed it is." I stood up straight and decided my doctor might kill me for not calling him the previous night when I'd been injured, but he wouldn't, after all, if I had a second espresso. "That's better," I said, after dousing the espresso with cream and taking an exploratory sip. I began to sharpen one of my knives.

"I should have come outside earlier," Julian said suddenly. "I should have heard Jake barking and—"

"Will you stop?" I asked. "You didn't know someone was out there. Obviously, I didn't know someone was out there, or I never would have opened the door in the first place."

"But still," he insisted, "I should have figured it out." His sneakers squeaked across the kitchen floor as he transferred all the washed spinach to several large pots. "I should have—"

"Woulda, shoulda, coulda," I interrupted as I began trimming fat from the first of several lamb roasts. "Stop putting yourself on a guilt trip."

Julian sighed loudly as the front doorbell rang. Quarter past seven? No way it was Marla yet. And then I heard Boyd talking to men he seemed to know. Ah, the second team of crime-scene guys. Boyd went outside to direct them toward the alley.

Holly had had Catholic guilt, I reflected as I cut the lamb into cubes. She'd had so much of it that she'd come up to see Father Pete *once a quarter* for her confession. Once a quarter? Had she done one thing that was hounding her conscience, or was she committing lots of sins? If so, had she resolved to do better, been absolved, and then done more bad deeds?

Had Holly indeed been blackmailing someone? Did it have anything to do with her fighting with George over child support for Drew? Did she tell Father Pete about that?

And what was the relationship mess she'd wanted to talk to me about? Was she talking about Warren Broome? Had Holly been a patient of his? Maybe all this mess was connected to Womanizing Warren's tendency to seduce his patients. Yet I'd also learned that Holly had met Warren many years ago at that doctors' conference in Boulder. Would Tom's team be able to find out the nature of their relationship? I doubted they had enough to secure a warrant to search his house or his office.

I set aside the first pile of cubes.

Holly had said that the artist I now suspected was Yurbin was trying to manipulate her into giving him money. Did he think she'd cheated him out of a client? She'd seemed frightened at first, then just annoyed.

Had he threatened her? Did it have to do with her art career, or something else?

Had anything happened when Holly went to the church, the morning of the birthday party?

Why did Holly give Audrey the puzzle with the strange instruction about "if something happened to her"?

Why would Holly's killer set a deadly trap for Drew, the one I walked into? Had it actually *been* for Drew?

And were Holly's death, the assault on Father Pete and Kathie Beliar, and the attack on me truly connected?

Round and round my mind went, with no answers appearing.

Once I had the lamb all cut up, I threw the stainless-steel knife into the sink. It clattered so loudly that Julian jumped.

"Sorry," I said.

"What's wrong now?"

"I feel like I should be able to figure this out."

"Shoulda," said Julian as he turned down the flame under the pots of spinach.

"Well, I do."

I removed the marinade from the heat, set it aside to cool, then started washing mountains of vegetables. We would be threading skewers with cherry tomatoes,

THE WHOLE ENCHILADA · 333

squares of green pepper, and quartered onions. We'd do the lamb separately. Despite all those women's-magazine photographs of grill-marked kebabs featuring juicy chunks of meat, cubes of tomato, crisp pepper squares, and tangy onion slices, there was one thing I'd learned the hard way. When it came to making shish kebabs, cooking the meat on the same skewers as the vegetables meant digging charred, petrified, unrecognizable-except-to-an-archaeologist   produce off the floor of your grill—for the next six months.

"Sorry I said that about the *shoulda*," Julian said.

"Don't worry about it." I stopped peeling onions, blinked madly, and turned to him.

He gave me that surprised-expression look. "You're crying."

"I'm prepping onions."

Julian sighed. "First, Tom told me about the antibiotic that the killer used at Arch and Drew's party. He thinks it was likely that it was put in the tortas, which they know for certain that Holly and everybody who had weird symptoms ate. I made those tortas special so Holly would eat some. They were one of the main dishes at the party, so it makes sense that the killer would have gone for that, or maybe knew Holly liked them. If I hadn't brought them, maybe she wouldn't have gotten poisoned. A few people had nightmares, but Holly *died*. That's guilt trip number one for me. Number two, or maybe it should be three, is you falling through the deck, and me not—"

"What?" I demanded, savagely quartering the onions, just so I could finish them. "Throwing out a net to snag me? You were inside. And anyway, the department is pretty sure that trap was meant for Drew or Holly. Remember, it was your swimming that *saved* me." When Julian said nothing, I went on, "What else?"

"Boss."

"What?" I washed my hands and cut plastic wrap to cover the onions. "Just tell me, and I'll absolve you, even though I'm not technically able to do that."

"I should have heard Jake!" He held his arms out in a gesture of helplessness. "I should have protected you from that guy who attacked you right outside the back door!"

"My son," I said, "your sins are forgiven." I didn't make the sign of the cross. Some blasphemy was beyond even me.

"I'm not your son," Julian pointed out, but he was grinning. He moved the first pot of spinach over to a giant colander in the sink, where he pushed down on the steaming green mass to extract as much water as possible.

"Speaking of Arch, when is he due home?"

"He and Gus have that trail-building project today, so it'll probably be late." Julian's brow wrinkled, as if he were trying to remember something. "Wait, I forgot something. Arch sent me a text saying Gus had forgotten he had a physical this morning, so he, Arch, is going out to the project with Sergeant Jones. He'll be hungry when he gets home, so we should leave him some dinner, because we'll be at the Ungers' place. Do you think the sergeant will be with him?"

I sighed. "I have no idea. I'll call Tom later about it."

Julian and I worked side by side without talking for the next ten minutes. Out back, the second squad of crime-scene guys was checking for any usable footprints, bits of clothing snagged on bushes, or fingerprints on the gate, garage, or back wall of our house—anything the team from the previous night might have missed. I didn't hold out much hope.

Without warning, Julian asked me, "Why do you do this?"

"Catering?" I replied. "Same reason you do. I love to work with food. Most people don't. That translates into money."

"I'm not talking about catering. Here, let me fix you another espresso."

"Uh-oh. More caffeine. I might just explode." But I'd finished prepping the vegetables. I bagged the peppers, onions, and tomatoes separately, then washed my hands again, and plopped into one of our kitchen table chairs.

"I'm talking about getting involved with these crimes," Julian said as he put two cups of espresso onto the table. I closed my eyes while he dumped sugar into his. "Nobody pays you for it, and for crying out loud, it's dangerous."

We'll get together soon, and talk. Holly's last words to me made a fist around my heart and squeezed. "I do it," I said quietly, "because I care about these people. The Jerk ripped my sense of self to shreds. Helping victims, people I know, helps me recover that self."

Julian didn't have time to respond, because Marla was banging on our front door. When I heard her arguing with Boyd—"Goldy didn't tell you she invited me over?"—I quickstepped down the front hall.

Boyd gave me a tired look. "You need to inform me when you ask people to come to the house."

"It's just Marla," I said.

"You need to inform me—" he began again.

I interrupted him. "Okay. Sorry!"

Boyd pulled the door ajar, and Marla marched through, staring daggers at Boyd. Neither one of them spoke.

Thank goodness Julian had had the good sense to fix Marla that multiple-shot drink I'd promised her. The oversize china cup sat, steaming, on a gold linen place mat. When Marla, who wore a red-spangled black top and matching pants, stormed into the kitchen, Julian was busily slicing Gruyère onto a plate. On any diet, people need to eat. If they don't eat, their blood sugar slips down around their ankles. They get cranky. It was my bet that this was what had led Marla to shout at Boyd.

"Boyd was just doing his job, Marla," I murmured.

She had already sat down and was sipping gratefully from her cup. She shut her eyes, waiting for the combination of caffeine and cream to hit. When she opened them again, she inspected my face.

"You look even worse than you did yesterday."

"That's what everybody keeps telling me."

"I want all the details of this attack on you last night."

I told her. Fatigue threaded through my voice when I finally said, "Let's talk about something else."

She took a bite of cheese and then regarded her cup. "This is gorgeous."

"The cappuccino?"

"The cup, silly."

I smiled, and told her that it was from a set that Tom had given me for our most recent anniversary. A drug dealer had shot a police officer, and was on his way to prison. His assets—undoubtedly bought with drug money, since the criminal had no income—had been seized. At the forfeiture auction, Tom had picked up a dozen place settings of French porcelain decorated with an intricate blue-and-gold design. It wasn't the kind of thing you pictured a drug dealer going for, but apparently, this one had.

Marla picked up the saucer and turned it over. "It's by Bernardaud," she said appreciatively. "The pattern is called Grâce."

"I know that." When Tom had given it to me, he said the china reminded him of me, that I was a slice of capital-*G* Grace in his life. I was suddenly glad that Julian had pulled the cup out for Marla.

"Gruyère, boss?" Julian asked me.

"Sure. Thanks. But no more coffee."

"Boyd knows me," Marla was complaining. "I'm here before eight in the morning, and he thinks I'm going to attack you?"

"Eat your cheese, will you?" I told her, then put one of the slices Julian had set before me into my mouth. It was salty and creamy at the same time, and tasted sharply of smoke. I always tried to picture the caves in France where they aged Gruyère, and usually only got as far as seeing the cheeses hanging upside down from dark ceilings, like bats.

"All right," said Marla. She sighed. She'd eaten; she felt better. "Should I go apologize to Boyd?"

"If you want," I said. "It's just that he has to keep track of who visits, and let the department know."

Julian offered to wash the cups, saucers, and dishes by hand, but I told him I would do it. While I rinsed the china Julian said we were done until tonight, except for the saffron rice. So should he start on it? I said yes, and thanked him.

"Act of contrition complete," said Marla as she reentered the kitchen. "I suppose we're off to the basement again?"

"Don't you *want* to keep looking through the notes?" I asked anxiously, as I felt an unexpected jolt of guilt myself.

"Of course I do," said Marla, although she didn't sound convinced. "I'm just tired from doing that dinner last night. I'll revive."

We descended to our lair. Marla started in with six months' worth of notes from later meetings; I took earlier ones. My handwriting, or at least the ink from my cheap ballpoints, had faded on one side of each sheet, and then, perversely, bled over from the other side. Sometimes even I couldn't make out what I'd written.

It was hard to concentrate. I was tired and in pain. But that wasn't entirely it. I had realized something that morning, while we were cooking. It had been important. But the insight had flashed by like a dark shadow. It reminded me of a mouse you see out of the corner of your eye. In Aspen Meadow, the little buggers come inside in October, when we're enveloped in our first chill.

Holly's words in my nightmare: *Why can't you see it?* See *what?*

My brain had seized up, and nothing was forthcoming.

So I went back to reading that Holly and I had realized that we'd probably become pregnant at the same time, at that conference over in Boulder.

I sat back in my chair, remembering. Holly and George and the Jerk and I had attended the same three-day meeting eighteen years ago, with the gloriously interesting name Setting Up a Medical Practice. What I recalled about the conference was that the sessions had been so stultifyingly boring, I'd had a hard time focusing, just as I was now. In order to keep my attention sharp, I'd forced myself to make up acronyms: BAD, for *Billing, Affiliation* with insurance companies, and *Documentation,* and UHIT, for *Uniforms, Hiring* a staff, *Insurance* files, and *Training* a staff to protect privacy.

Bad U Hit, indeed. The Jerk and I had had a furious fight before we arrived, and I was all set to file for divorce once I'd pulled together a little money. But at the conference, the Jerk had been at great pains to convince me that the argument was my fault. To keep the peace, I'd agreed. We made up. During the day, to show my devotion, I'd sat through the sessions and taken notes, as the Jerk requested. One of the nights, I'd become pregnant with Arch. And that was that. There would be no divorce, I told myself. I would stick it out, "for the baby." I could do it. At that point, I thought I could do anything. At that point, I was twenty years old.

I'd never seen Holly at the conference, she'd laughingly told me later, because she'd gone off to hike the Flatirons, a set of peaks that erupt at a steep angle west of the flat plain of Boulder. She, too, had become pregnant at the conference, she'd said, blushing. But she and George had made love because she'd felt so guilty about not going to a single presentation. George, studious and dedicated, had gone to all of them.

And then the dark shadow flashed again. I had knowledge from Med Wives 101. *That* was where the insight had come from. I knew, or suspected, something.

Yet even a suspicion had to be confirmed. Telling Marla I had to stretch my legs, I walked over to the computer Tom used for the Internet.

From the notes I'd already taken, I remembered that Holly and I had talked about how our first attempts at cooking had met with disgust. The Jerk had tossed the tomato aspic I'd made into the trash. Why hadn't he told me before then that he was allergic to tomatoes? He said that he had, and I'd forgotten.

Edith Ingleby had ground up a molded salad that Holly had made, one with hard-cooked eggs and homemade vegetable stock. I'd kept trying to perfect my cooking for the Jerk. Holly, on the other hand, had thrown in the kitchen towel, the spatula, and every pan she owned.

Then, last night, at the conference center, when I'd cleared the dishes, I'd noticed that George hadn't even touched the strawberry molded salad. It didn't have vegetable stock or hard-cooked eggs. Yet he hadn't even tasted it. Why?

I tapped into a medical search engine that Tom used from time to time. *Allergy to gelatin,* I wrote, and soon was rewarded. *An allergy to gelatin usually reveals itself when a child has the first shot for measles, mumps, and rubella. The mumps vaccine is made with gelatin, so a child with an allergy to gelatin should not have the booster shot for mumps.*

Okay, so far, so good. Then I typed in *Boys who contract mumps.*

Boys who contract mumps, the search engine spit out, *will sometimes become irreversibly sterile.*

Even though I'd known what I was looking for, I sat back from the computer, stunned.

Who knows? my attacker had demanded.

I picked up my cell phone and tapped out a text to Tom: *Ask George Ingleby if he is sterile.*

Tom texted back: *Why?*

I wrote: *Because I think he is. Based on scientific evidence.*

Tom: *What evidence?*

Think he's allergic to gelatin, I typed. *Ask if he contracted mumps when he was young.* After a moment, I reflected on Lena's rage, which had seemed so out of place. I recalled Edith saying "my daily miracle" when we visited the Inglebys on Saturday. She'd nodded when Marla asked her if she meant the muffins I gave her, but she hadn't been paying much attention to us . . . and right before that, she'd complained about Tom sending Drew away.

Tom had found out Holly was suing George for back child support. Lena had made a crude suggestion about having sex with Tom.

I typed, *Ask when he found out he was sterile.*

Tom's text said: *Will do. Remember: reveal nothing to anyone but Boyd & Marla, no matter how much you trust that person.* A moment later, he texted, *We talked to Broome again. He's not happy.*

He didn't say anything else, so I had time to think. Marla stopped reading and said, "Okay, I'm over here busting my butt trying to read your squiggles, and you're secretly doing something, checking the computer, sending texts. So what in the world is going on that you're not telling me?" When I turned to her, she said, "Uh-oh. You found something out."

"Let me ask you something," I countered. "Say two parents have a child. The parents get divorced. The father, who's helped raise the child, finds out when the child is a teenager that he did not actually, I'm talking biologically here, *father* the child. Does he still owe child support payments?"

"He does," replied Marla, the maven of all things not only medical but also financial and legal. "The child was born into an existing marriage. Once the marital knot is tied, all bets are off in the sperm department. The guy doesn't pay, he's going to get hauled into court."

"Which Holly was trying to do to George—"

"But it usually takes a while—" She stopped talking and gazed at me. "Are you saying that George Ingleby is not the biological father of Drew?"

"He's his *father,*" I said immediately. "That man helped raise Drew, and is devoted to him. But Edith calls Drew her 'daily miracle,' and won't explain herself. George and Holly only had the one child." I went on: "What we should have seen is that Drew is tall and lithe, and looks nothing like George, whose shape resembles Stalin's. I'd always thought that those height genes came from Holly."

"But you're thinking differently now."

I stared hard at Marla. "Maybe Edith finally got around to telling George that she'd been told he was sterile. She thought Drew's birth was a miracle. Or maybe it came up in a medical test, and that's how George found out. So then imagine Lena saying, 'Either you cut off funds to that slut, or I'm going public with this story. All of Colorado will know you're sterile.' "

"That sounds like Lena, actually," Marla said thoughtfully. "But if what you're thinking is true, then why would they show up at the birthday party, and pitch a fit about not being invited? Why protest about being escorted out?"

"I don't know."

"Well, when will you know for sure about the fertility thing?"

"I texted Tom. He'd go Chernobyl if we went over to the Inglebys' place again, escorted by Boyd or not escorted by Boyd."

"So wait," Marla said at length. "Do you think George and/or Lena are after you? That you 'know'? Was Holly threatening to expose the truth if George didn't go back to paying child support? Maybe she just pointed out that he'd still have to pay the support because they'd been married when Drew was born, and George and/or Lena didn't like that prospect. But would they crash the party, just to drop the antibiotic into the tortas, to murder Holly? And who is Drew's *biological* father? Do you think he's even aware he fathered a son?"

"I don't have a clue. Drew's biological father might not even live in the state. It could be that Holly never told him. Or he might not care. Then again, Holly might not have known for sure that George wasn't Drew's biological father, since she probably didn't know his being sterile was a possibility."

Marla said, "There's another question lurking here. With Drew in school up in Aspen Meadow, why exactly did Holly buy a house in Denver nine years ago? Okay, she went to art school. Do you think that's related?"

"Good question." I walked over to the file cabinets. "Do we know where she lived, so we could ask the neighbors?"

"From a decade ago?" Marla scoffed. "You must be joking. I think she rented first, before she bought the house. And anyway, we never visited her down there."

"Let me look at one of my files."

"If it's addresses for Holly," Marla insisted, "I think you're wasting your time."

"That's not what I'm looking for. Can you keep going through the notes? We still haven't found any mention of Holly being in therapy. It might be in there somewhere."

"I can't wait," Marla said sourly.

I searched the file cabinets until I found the medical-meeting notes from eighteen years ago. Tom's accusation was correct: I kept everything. I leafed through the pages until I found a printed list of the attendees.

"Whoa, wait a minute." I swallowed. "You'll never guess who was there, giving a talk on getting cut-rate uniforms for medical office staffs."

"Not Neil Unger."

"The same. Looks like he wasn't yet smitten with the idea of cleaning up America."

Marla shook her head. "How old was he back then?"

"Early forties. Athena would have still been alive. Ophelia would have been three-ish. But maybe Neil was on the prowl."

"Gosh," said Marla. "Do you think he and Holly could have hooked up?"

"I don't know. I suppose anything is possible." I went back to the list of M.D.s who'd attended the Flatirons conference. Ingleby, George, Cardiology, was there, as was Korman, John, Obstetrics and Gynecology. As was Broome, Warren, Psychiatry. So. He had been there, too.

I said, "Well now, isn't that interesting?"

"What is?"

"Warren Broome was indeed at the Flatirons conference eighteen years ago."

"Are you saying he was her lover," Marla asked carefully, "or she was his patient, and they had sex that way?"

"I'm not sure what I'm saying, because I don't know."

19

I exhaled and tried to think. What else did Holly and Warren Broome have in common?

Audrey Millard, I remembered suddenly. *The other jigsaw puzzle map.* I raced up the steps, with Marla calling behind me, wanting to know where I was going. I didn't answer. In Tom's and my bedroom, I dumped out the contents of our hamper. I pulled out the pants I'd worn the night before, then retrieved the folded map from deep in the right pocket.

I opened it, smoothed it out, then held it carefully as I descended to the basement.

"Goldy," Marla said in a singsong tone, without looking up, "you're beginning to scare me."

"I'm trying to find out how Holly and Warren could have been connected."

"And?"

"Okay, check this out," I said as I pressed the map down, right next to the one I'd photocopied from the atlas.

"Hunan Province," Marla read aloud. "Both of them. If Holly meant for us to distill meaning from either of these maps, that meaning is eluding me."

Frustrated, I flopped into one of the basement's metal chairs. Whatever it was Holly wanted all of us to see, it just *was not visible*—not to Marla, not to me, not to Tom, nor to any other member of the sheriff's department investigative team.

I couldn't face the Amour notes anymore just then. We hadn't found any mention of Holly being in therapy. I knew we should be looking, but the chicken scratch of my notes was giving me a headache. I asked myself if there was anything else I hadn't yet followed up on.

As I tortured my poor brain with questions, Julian clattered down the basement steps. He clutched a large tray with plates of much-welcome field greens topped with poached eggs and pan-grilled asparagus. He poured sparkling water into frosted glasses. "Hate to mention this while you're doing your note taking, ladies." He looked over at us nervously as he set place mats and napkins on the one long worktable that wasn't papered with our notes. "In about an hour, we need to shove off for the Ungers' place. Also, Arch called the house line. The Passat had a flat."

"You must be kidding," I said in disbelief. "Those tires were new this past winter."

"Boss, it's okay." Julian straightened. "He thinks he picked up a nail. Anyway, Sergeant Jones and Bob Rushwood helped him change it. They're all on their way back here. Bob is following Arch and Sergeant Jones, in case the *spare* goes flat."

My mind felt far away. "When did this happen?"

"This morning," said Julian. He shook his head. "Bob e-mailed the kids doing trail digging today, canceling it. Since it's Ophelia's birthday, he was going to take her out to lunch. But each of the kids was supposed to e-mail him back, saying they'd gotten his message. Arch and a couple of other kids did *not* e-mail him back. So Bob had gone out to the trailhead in the Aspen Meadow Wildlife Preserve, in case anyone showed up. Which only Arch and Sergeant Jones did. When Arch turned around, one of his tires went flat." Julian shrugged. "Arch said Bob was already late to meet Ophelia, to take her out for a birthday lunch. So when Arch arrives, he and Sergeant Jones are going to eat quickly, then she's going to follow Arch to the tire place. She left her prowler out front."

"*Dios mío*," Marla murmured. "I feel as if I'm in the middle of an FBI operation."

Julian gave her a sympathetic look. "I told Sergeant Boyd what was going on. Boyd doesn't trust anyone, I suppose, even tire guys. Sergeant Jones is going to stay with Arch at Goodyear, while the flat's being patched. Then you and Boyd and I have to go over to the Ungers' house to set up—"

Marla rolled her eyes. "I can't follow this without having something to eat."

I held up my hand. "Thanks, Julian. The salads look great."

Julian's sneakers squeaked as he trod carefully back up the wooden stairs. We set aside our pens and papers and dug into the eggs and sumptuous piles of sweet, crunchy grilled asparagus. I made a mental note to ask Julian how he'd done the latter.

"Divine," said Marla. She put down her fork and appeared thoughtful. "So, getting back to Warren Broome, psychiatrist extraordinaire. Or maybe not so extraordinary. We *still don't know* if Holly was ever in therapy. It's not mentioned in the notes. I mean, if she'd been seeing a shrink, don't you think she would have mentioned it?"

"Maybe not, if it was Warren Broome, and they were having an affair. She might have been ashamed."

"But we were her friends," Marla protested. "She could have told *us*."

"You mean, the way she told us about the other guys she was having affairs with? Which she didn't? The way she told us that she was having money problems?"

"Okay, point taken. The woman kept secrets."

"Perhaps she told Father Pete everything. There was that quarterly confession."

Marla shook her head. "I don't think so." She looked down at her notes. "I have lots of stuff in here about her playing in a tennis tournament with this boyfriend, hiking Mount Evans with that one, then skiing Beaver Creek with somebody else. I mean, after she moved back to Aspen Meadow, the woman did nothing but shop, get her hair and nails done, and then engage in sports with an unending stream of guys. And you're right, there are no names. She certainly didn't seem unhappy to be divorced from George. In fact, she seemed ecstatic. And this was all before her collages began to get lots of attention and bring in big bucks. So what gives?"

"I don't know," I said, for what felt like the fortieth time since we'd started this expedition into the past. "Maybe she *wasn't* ecstatic. She had a lot of secrets, Marla. It looks as if she was trying to extort money from someone, which I never would have expected from Holly. And it looks as if she had more conflict in her life than we knew about. Somewhere she stashed some kind of evidence. 'Notes,' she called it. 'A record.' Whoever attacked me last night thought I had that evidence. And maybe that same person was the one who attacked Father Pete and stole the church file. Perhaps the attacker knew Holly went to see Father Pete on a regular basis. The answers to our questions may be *in those notes.*"

"And you still think something in your notebooks from our old meetings might give us a clue as to what was going on in Holly's life?"

"What else do we have to go on? We haven't even developed any long shots. Right?"

Marla nodded solemnly.

"Holly shared much of her journey with us in those meetings. Maybe she let something slip about the parts of her life she was hiding. Or she could have said anything that might lead us to a clear connection to what got her killed."

"So," Marla concluded, "I suppose we have to finish going through these."

We reluctantly set aside our empty plates and went back to reading.

"Whoa, here's something," Marla said. She squinted at the page. "Do you recall a session you and Holly did on something you called 'merciful lying'? It was in December, and there was a blizzard. I wasn't there yet, because of the snow. Holly was over here, because the two of you were doing some planning for Arch and Drew's Sunday School class."

" 'Merciful lying.' " I closed my eyes and tried to remember. "I vaguely recall it."

"You'll know in a minute, because the evening, if not the meeting, was memorable. According to what you wrote," Marla said, "you said lying was okay sometimes, if it was merciful. You wanted the group to discuss the idea."

I frowned. "I did? Just Holly and I were going to discuss that?"

Marla peered down at the notebook in front of her. "Yes. It all started when you saw someone in town, an elderly woman. It made you pose the question to Holly: if it's an act of mercy, is it okay not to tell the truth? This elderly woman was someone you had waited on in that southwestern accessories store where you worked, before you went down to André's restaurant and started cooking. An infinitely better choice, I might add. Turquoise-and-silver jewelry is so seventies."

I thought back. "Yes. That woman's got to be dead now. I mean, she was in her late eighties back then."

"Right," said Marla. She took a moment, reading. "You say here that the woman and her husband had come into the store on their sixtieth wedding anniversary. He had picked out a necklace for her."

"Navajo," I said, the memory of the lie suddenly clarifying.

"But you didn't actually wait on her the first time they came into the store. On the anniversary visit, the *owner* waited on them. The customer told her husband the necklace was too expensive. He was very disappointed, because he'd really wanted to buy it for her. The next week, he died of a heart attack. Every week thereafter, for months, according to the store owner, the widow came in, usually with her elderly female friends in tow. She was looking for the necklace."

I said, "I do remember. The owner told me they'd sold the necklace the day after the woman and her husband came in. Not long afterward, I started working there, but I'd never waited on the widow."

"Until one day . . ." Marla prompted.

"Yes. One day, the store owner was working with me. When she saw the widow and her coterie of friends walking across the parking lot, she quickly told me the story. Then she said she couldn't face the widow one more time. As she ducked into our storage area, she called over her shoulder that *I* needed to deal with the situation. The lady came into the store with her pals, and started to tell me about the anniversary visit and the necklace. I stopped her in the middle of her story. I said that *I* was the one who had waited on her and her husband—"

"You note here that that was a lie," Marla interrupted.

"Yup. Then I pointed to *another* Navajo necklace and said, 'I recall when you and your husband picked this out for your anniversary. But you didn't buy it.' She didn't remember the necklace I showed her. She didn't remember me. But she was overjoyed, bought the necklace, and went on her way with her friends. And before you ask, I did *not* work on commission."

"No, you worked on heart," whispered Marla. She cleared her throat. "But listen, according to your notes, Holly then said, 'I've been lying mercifully for years. To George, and to Drew.'"

"Oh, my Lord. Really? Did I write down what she meant?"

"No, you didn't, because at that point I arrived out front with a bang. My brand-new gold Jaguar slid through the unplowed snow into your next-door neighbor's pickup truck. The Jag then ricocheted into somebody's Jeep across the street, then back across the street into another pickup, and it was bumper cars all the way down."

"Right. How could I forget?" The fierce *crack* and *bam* and *crunch* of Marla's rear-wheel-drive Jaguar careening into first one vehicle, then another, had sent Holly and me catapulting out the front door. Since the hour had been late and the snow was deepening, we told Arch and Drew to stay in the living room. They were already staring out the front window, trying to see what was going on.

"My ego never recovered," Marla said wistfully. "Nor did the Jaguar, sad to say. The highway patrol guy said, 'Lady? How many cars did you hit, exactly? Is this what they mean by a slippery slope?'"

I remembered Boyd's routine: "Traffic Stops I Have Known." "Come on, Marla. Everyone was just glad you were all right. But your bumper-car routine aside, what follows in the notes?"

"Nothing," Marla said. "You wrote down what Holly had said, that she'd been mercifully lying to George and Drew for years. Because of my accident, the meeting was suspended. Next week it was my turn to pick the topic. I said, 'How about the cost of car insurance?'"

"But what did we actually talk about the next week?" I asked.

THE WHOLE ENCHILADA · 359

"You told me to get serious," Marla went on, "and then I said, 'How about when someone insults you? Doesn't that tell you something?' At a friends-of-the-library meeting, someone had sneered and called me 'an armchair liberal.' Actually," she said, surprise still in her voice, "I don't have any political beliefs, and I don't have armchairs—just wingbacks. But then the man came up to me after the meeting and asked for a check for his charity, which was called Clothes Horse. He said they raised money to buy kids from poor areas of Denver new clothes and shoes for school. I told him I'd think about it. Then I came home and called the people who regulate that type of thing. *Regulated.* There was no Internet back then. In any event, the regulator told me the charity was bogus. That guy was a crook. Thought he could insult his way into my good graces! What a jerk."

"And did we talk about that?" I asked.

Marla peered at the notes. "No, because I was the only one who had inherited money that I wanted to give away. Which this crook no doubt knew. But I've been on the lookout for people who hurl insults ever since. My experience has been, they're trying to put you down so they can hit you up for something. And they're usually hiding a thing or two."

Arch clomping in overhead shook us out of the memories. Voices, deep and high, agitated and composed, threaded through the air.

"What's going on up there?" Marla asked.

"Sergeant Jones may be trying to calm Arch down after the flat-tire mess."

We went up. In the kitchen, Boyd stood in a corner, watchfully listening to Arch, Julian, Bob Rushwood, and Sergeant Jones. Sergeant Jones was indeed trying to soothe Arch, saying things like, "It could have been worse. Much worse."

Boyd gave me a hooded look of warning that I did not think Marla caught. But I remembered Tom's warning: *reveal nothing to anyone but Boyd & Marla, no matter how much you trust him or her.* So neither Sergeant Jones nor Bob Rushwood would hear about the merciful lying and responses to insults. I wondered if Marla had seen Boyd's expression, and would know to keep her mouth shut.

"Bob?" said Marla as she stared at the enormous sandwiches Julian was placing in front of Arch, Bob, and Sergeant Jones. "What about your lunch with Ophelia? The birthday girl?"

Bob Rushwood brushed back his dark dreads. He gave Marla a look of such dejection that I was immediately aware that something had gone terribly wrong.

I certainly hoped that helping Arch hadn't meant Ophelia had canceled on him.

"Mom!" Arch cried. "What happened to your neck?"

"Oh, I . . ." I stammered. *Reveal nothing.* I trusted Arch, of course, but I knew better than to talk about being attacked the previous evening. Still, I was aware of the fact that I presented quite a sight: a caterer who looks as if she's survived an angry client trying to choke her to death. "I was trying on a shirt for tonight—"

"Tom was trying to show her how to do a four-square knot for a tie she was going to wear," Julian lied smoothly. "You know, the way some caterers wear? Anyway, he feels terrible."

"I never should have asked him in the first place," I said. Apparently, my gift for lying on short notice had not dimmed over the years. "Arch?" I asked. "Are you all right?"

"I'm fine," said my son. He sat at the kitchen table, his legs thrust out in front of him. "I'm just ticked off that I went to help build trails, then got a flat, and now have to waste the rest of the day at a tire place."

I bit back words saying it was a good thing he'd had Sergeant Jones and Bob Rushwood there to bail him out. But Arch would not want to be corrected in front of others.

"I'm glad you had enough turkey in the walk-in for sandwiches *for everybody*," Julian said, too cheerily. He raised his eyebrows. If there was something else I wasn't supposed to talk about, I didn't know what it was. So I looked at Bob to get a clue.

Bob Rushwood's face was set in a scowl, which I hadn't seen on him before. It appeared he'd washed the dreads, which couldn't be that easy, in preparation either for his lunch with Ophelia, or the dinner that night. Not only that, but the effort he had used to help change Arch's tire had made him sweat. Large circles of perspiration showed dark under the armpits and down the chest of his yellow sports shirt. It was not flattering.

Since we'd just been talking about being careful not to insult people, Marla and I said nothing—not about why Bob was there, or about what had happened to his lunch with Ophelia. An uncomfortable silence fell over the kitchen. Bob picked up half of his sandwich, then peered around Julian.

"Why is there crime-scene tape in your backyard?" Bob asked.

"We had a bear," I said quickly, glancing through the windows. Thank God the crime-scene techs had left already. "It made a lot of noise and broke some stuff on our deck. At first we thought it was a vandal.

So Tom called an investigative team, but by the time they got here, we'd figured out it was a bear, and he was gone."

"What a relief!" said Marla.

"A bear?" said Arch. "Again?"

But Bob had lost interest. He put down his sandwich, bunched his hands into fists, and pushed them into his eyes. Marla and I exchanged another glance, but kept mum.

"Ophelia's seeing somebody else!" Bob cried. He tried to make his sob sound like a cough. Then he turned his wet, red face to us. "Before I went out to the Preserve—to make sure the kids who hadn't answered my e-mail didn't show up?—I drove over to her house to give her some roses. She wouldn't see me. And there was some *other* guy there. I could see him through the front door glass. He'd parked his stupid BMW in the driveway. It has surfboard and snowboard stickers on it! Like he has to announce that he's *so cool.* So now we all know he's a jock. Duh! Pretty soon I was pleading into the intercom, 'Ophelia, you already have a jock! And I'm it!' But she wouldn't listen, wouldn't even come out. She finally announced through the speaker that she didn't want to have lunch, that she would see me tonight, and that I should just go away. Go away? Is that the way you talk to someone you're going to spend the rest of your life with?"

I pressed my lips together, ignored Marla, and tried to look sympathetically at Bob. He was at least ten years older than Ophelia, so maybe the age difference was bothering her. Afraid he could read my mind, I turned away. While Julian carefully placed chips on Bob's plate, Arch loudly cleared his throat. He knew that Brewster drove a BMW with Hobie and Burton stickers on it; we all did. I shook my head, trying to telegraph to Arch: *Don't let on that the guy at Ophelia's place is Brewster.* Arch opened his eyes wide at me, as in, *What's going on?* But I ignored him. Bob, meanwhile, picked up the sandwich half he'd put down and demolished most of it in a single bite.

"*Mom,*" Arch began, but we were interrupted by a horrendous banging on the front door.

"Goldy Schulz!" a male voice cried. "Get out here!"

Sergeant Jones immediately called for backup.

"Mr. Rushwood? Everybody?" said Boyd, drawing his weapon. "I'm going to have to ask you to stay put."

"For how long?" asked Bob. "My life's falling apart. I have to see Ophelia again."

The banging continued on the front door.

"All right," said Boyd. "Go through the back door. Go now. This minute."

Bob clutched the other half of his sandwich in midair and gave it a look of longing, even as his frown deepened. Julian, meanwhile, hastily pulled out some waxed paper. He deftly removed the half sandwich, wrapped it along with the chips, and handed the package to Bob.

"We'll get back to trail building tomorrow, Arch," Bob said hastily. He looked confused, but took the proffered food and hustled out the kitchen door and across the deck. There, if he'd have cared to notice, no furniture or anything else was broken, by either bear or human.

"Goldy Schulz!" the male voice was hollering. "Answer this door!"

"Who *is* that?" Arch demanded, looking around the kitchen. "Why is everything around here so weird? You had a bear last night, so there's crime-scene tape in our backyard? Brewster Motley is sneaking around with Ophelia? You won't tell Bob what's going on? *Mom?*"

"Goldy Schulz!" the shrill voice called again. "Get your fat ass out here!"

"I'm going to kill whoever—" Marla began, starting for the front door.

"You are going to do nothing except stay right here," Sergeant Jones said calmly. She'd moved quickly to the back door to lock it, then nodded at Boyd.

"Goldy Schulz!" screamed the man. He banged on the front door.

Boyd, his weapon drawn, moved down the hall's right side. Sergeant Jones also had her gun out, and was moving down the left side of the hall. Marla, Arch, Julian, and I clustered around the kitchen door. In the distance, a siren wailed.

"Who's there?" Boyd barked through the door.

"It's Warren Broome. Who the hell are you? Send that damned meddling bitch out here. I have some questions for her. She talked to my wife and now Patsie thinks I'm keeping secrets from her, which I'm *not*. I'm putting my life back together, and now Goldy Schulz is tearing it apart!"

The siren was squawling. *Boop boop boop.* The prowler stopped in front of our house.

"Let me talk to him," I said.

Sergeant Jones warned me with a look. "Forget it."

Boyd was speaking into a walkie-talkie. A harsh, low male shout greeted Broome, who had the temerity to yell back, "Oh yeah? Why don't you come up here and make me?"

A moment later, Boyd holstered his weapon and nodded to Jones, then to us. Marla, Arch, Julian, and I raced down the hall and into the living room. We made it just in time to see Warren Broome, M.D., being led down our sidewalk in handcuffs, accompanied by a policeman. When they got to his prowler, the cop put one hand up on the doctor's blond scalp and gently guided him into the backseat.

"Aw," said Marla, "you should have jammed that big old head into the roof of the car. I mean, after last night, doesn't the guy ever learn?"

I wondered. But there was something else bothering me. Warren Broome had insulted me. *Fat ass* and *bitch* I could probably handle. But I was left wondering.

Like other people who insulted people, did Broome fit Marla's pop-psych analysis and have something to hide? Did he, in fact, have secrets? Say he had a piece of information that I did not yet know. It could be along the lines of *You caused a fight between Patsie and me. I attacked you last night, and watch me try to attack you today.* In the middle of the day, with neighbors who could hear? Maybe. How about this: *I had sex with Holly Ingleby at the doctors' conference in Boulder and am the biological father of Drew; Holly was blackmailing me and I killed her.*

Setting aside the attack on me and what we still didn't know about Holly's secrets . . . what questions did this psychiatrist, who disliked Father Pete and had known Holly, perhaps intimately, have for me? Did they start with Audrey Millard and end with Holly

Ingleby? Maybe, maybe not. I'd told him I had a message from Holly for him, and I hadn't delivered it. Oh, dear, I felt guilty for that lie. And now the shrink was losing it.

"Okay, crisis over," Boyd announced. He nodded in my direction. "Just do what you would normally do now."

"What did Broome want?" I asked.

Boyd lifted his chin. "I didn't wait to find out. He's on his way down to the department, where he'll sit and wait a bit. Maybe our guys will throw some charges at him, like disorderly conduct or threatening and intimidation. See what he has to say." He turned a kindly eye to my son. "Arch, Sergeant Jones is going to accompany you to the tire place now."

Arch gave me a concerned look. "Mom? Are you okay?" When I said I was fine, he said, "Gus has invited me to spend another night. Is that all right? Sergeant Jones can come again. I think Gus's grandparents liked her. We'll go together to the trail-building site tomorrow."

"If it's okay with Sergeant Jones," I replied, "it's fine with me."

"I'll go get some clean clothes." Arch regarded Marla and me with skepticism. "I hope there aren't any bears at Gus's place."

"There won't be," Marla assured him. "And just look at it this way, Arch. At least you don't have to help cater Ophelia's birthday party tonight. We could see a fistfight between Bob Rushwood the trainer and Brewster Motley the attorney."

"That might actually be kind of cool," said Arch.

I packed up the Julian-made sandwiches for Arch and Sergeant Jones. After seeing the two of them off, I put the marinating kebab ingredients into the box, then stared inside. What was I forgetting? The skewers! I placed them in doubled plastic bags and packed them. Julian, meanwhile, fluffed the cooled saffron rice and spooned the cucumber-and-yogurt salad into a plastic container. Marla gently wrapped the birthday cake.

While snapping on lids, Julian said, "Did I ever tell you what happened that one time I worked for Neil Unger?"

"Remind me," I said. "How was it?"

"Awful. Guy is a control freak and a cheapskate. I was ready to strangle him by the time I skedaddled out of there."

Everyone thought Julian was just cute and easygoing. But like most caterers, he missed nothing. "What was the problem?" I asked.

"Neil and his wife, Francie—Ophelia's stepmother— stayed out in the kitchen the entire time I was trying to work. At first I thought they were afraid I was going to steal their stuff. Let me tell you, by the time I finished, I was ready to pull out a cleaver and break all their damn stuff."

"Easy there, boy," Marla said.

But Julian was having none of it. "Neil asked me a bunch of leading questions about politics. In my apron, do I *look* political? I answered his questions as mildly as I could, but forget it. Neil disagreed with me, point by point. Meanwhile, I was trying to manage a dinner for eight, using two ovens, heating twice-baked potatoes and making lemon vinaigrette for the salads, flipping fillets, and trying to figure out when to put in the baked Alaska. The whole time, Neil's giving me his views. I mean, the guy's a bully. Acts like he knows everything about running any type of business—"

"That's rich," said Marla as she placed the cake and candles into their own box. "Neil inherited his uniform-making business from his father. He doesn't know the first thing about business, except how to send jobs overseas."

I said, "Does he only make medical uniforms, like for the conference in Boulder all those years ago?"

"No, they make any kind of uniform," said Marla as she rolled out plastic wrap for the candles and matches. "Maids' uniforms, mechanics' uniforms, you name it. The only thing Neil Unger has ever done is go to Mexico and the Philippines to build sweatshops where underpaid workers make uniforms day and night. Do you not know this? It was all over the country club."

"I rely on you for country-club news."

"All right, then, I'll tell you," Marla said, taping up the box. "Neil Unger was indicted for bribing foreign officials."

"Indicted?" I asked dumbly.

"Charges dismissed," Marla said with an exaggerated shrug. She was relishing her role as deliverer of bad news. "And of course then everyone was wondering what U.S. official he'd bribed to make *that* happen."

I said, "He can't outsource catering."

"What a relief," Marla said. "Now, what else do we need?"

Neil Unger's maid had told me the Ungers had their own silverware, china, and crystal. The maid had also told me that Mr. Unger had ordered all the floral arrangements for "his little girl." Like Julian, I picked up on vibes. The maid didn't like Neil Unger any more than Julian had. And Ophelia believed her father was hiding money that belonged to her . . . and she was having Brewster help her find it.

Marla asked if my leg was healed enough for me to drive my van. I told her it was, and she said she would keep me company. "The better to figure out a strategy for when the you-know-what hits the fan tonight," she said lightheartedly, once we'd shoved the last box into Julian's Range Rover.

"Just give me a minute," I replied. A quick phone call to Arch confirmed that he and Sergeant Jones had arrived at Goodyear. The cop was waiting patiently with him, and would accompany him to Gus's place.

"Does Sergeant Jones *have* to be with me tomorrow?" Arch whispered. "I've been thinking about it, and I'm afraid the other kids will laugh at me."

"Tom says yes. Sorry. She knows how to be unobtrusive."

Arch had not yet started AP English, but I was sure he knew the meaning of *unobtrusive*, especially since he had a mother who was decidedly the opposite.

Before Marla and I could chat, the cell rang: Tom.

"Are you all right?" he wanted to know. I assured him that I was fine. Boyd was with us on our way to the Unger mansion. Tom's tone turned resigned. "Our crime-scene guys are reporting to me in a little while."

"We'll be okay," I said. "Anything on George Ingleby?"

"He was in surgery. Then he lawyered up. I'm trying to think of a way to get his medical records, to see about this sterility business." Frustration made Tom sound uncharacteristically anxious. "I'm just worried about you, Miss G."

"I keep telling you, we'll be fine. Boyd's with us. And remember, Neil Unger is the fiercest gun-rights advocate in the county. He probably has a conceal-carry permit. If anybody tries to hurt someone at the party for *his little girl,* I'm sure he'll pull out a twenty-two. Maybe something bigger."

Tom said, "That does not make me feel better."

"I'm trying," I said, and we signed off.

20

On the winding, seven-mile drive to the home where Ophelia lived with her father and step-mother, Marla gave me the background on the house, which I had visited only once, to see how we would set things up. The Unger place had been built fifteen years before. Craning her neck as we began our climb, she said the expansive stucco manse, from the Taco Bell School of Architecture, was only occasionally visible from the road. But it wasn't long before I could afford no glimpses upward; I was just trying to manage the dirt road.

"So," Marla said, "you've seen the place already?"

"Just briefly, because Ophelia was due home from one of her clothes-shopping expeditions. We signed the contract. Neil gave me a check and ushered me out.

Remember, this is, or was, supposed to be a surprise, so he didn't want me hanging around. But Neil thought she found out about the party, then figured it was still a go. Nevertheless, Ophelia told me at church that she knew the party was happening. She didn't seem to care much."

"So you've never had to deal with Neil Unger before?"

"Just once, but not at his house. He paid me well, but didn't want to tip, which was what Julian discovered."

Marla whistled. "He is a cheapskate. When I called to say I was helping you tonight, instead of being a guest, I made sure to say that I was *volunteering*."

The switchbacks became acute. We were climbing an extra two thousand feet above Aspen Meadow to arrive at what old-timers simply dubbed The Peak. Tourist operators in the forties had christened the mountain Sunset Peak, because of the three-hundred-sixty-degree vista from the summit. Since the blazing sunsets were reputedly spectacular, busloads of tourists had started trekking up from Denver. But the mountainous road was perilous. No guardrails bordered its sides.

A bus was lost over the mountainside in the sixties, with thirty-two lives lost. The road was closed for years. There had been only muted local opposition to

Neil Unger's acquisition of the top third of the mountain. The purchase had coincided with the death by
cancer of Ophelia's mother and perhaps with Neil
Unger making a killing in foreign-made uniforms.
And—maybe with a bribe or two in place, I now sur-
mised as the van's tires threw dust each time we made
a hairpin turn—Neil had convinced some government
department that it was much too dangerous for buses
ever again to mount the road to the peak. With the
advent of gambling in two historic Colorado towns, the
tourists had taken their shekels elsewhere. Sunset Peak
was renamed The Peak.

We finally arrived in a cloud of sun-glittered dust
at a carved wooden sign, its background painted red,
the letters white. It read PRIVATE ROAD NO ENTRY.
The switchbacks had been emotionally draining, so
I stopped to rest, then looked toward the Continental
Divide. The sun slid toward the mountains between
pink layers of cloud. I could just make out Aspen
Meadow Lake, a tiny patch of silver far away. My cell
phone buzzed: Julian.

"You all right, Goldy?" Boyd's voice.

"Fine. Traumatized by that drive, but fine."

"Julian wants to know if you're aware of how to get
to the service entrance."

"Uh, no."

"Let him take the lead, then. The Ungers' paved driveway starts a little ways up, and you can follow him to where we need to be."

Julian overtook me. We wended our way carefully upward until we landed on pavement. I found myself breathing a bit easier. Eventually we came to the beige stucco residence, which looked more like a hotel than a house. It boasted a three-story, windowed main section flanked by two-story wings. Red-tile roofs and ornately carved double doors completed the imposing sight.

Two vehicles were parked in front. Brewster Motley's silver-gray BMW I knew. The other car was a silver Mercedes convertible. When we were ten yards from the Mercedes, Bob Rushwood got out, leaned against the hood, and crossed his arms. He'd showered and changed into a somber gray suit. Unfortunately he looked completely ticked off. He held out an arm. Julian ignored him and kept on driving. I stopped and buzzed my window down.

"Yes, Bob?"

"She still won't see me."

Marla leaned across the space between the seats. "Do we look like advice columnists?"

"Could you take me around back and let me in through the kitchen?"

"No," said Marla. "Do you have any idea how much trouble we would get into if we—"

"All right, never mind." He shook his head. "I've already called Ophelia's father. He's on his way. I was supposed to keep Ophelia away from the house until the party, but I guess her father will have to convince her to come out."

"Bob," Marla said sagely, "if you're already relying on the father of your prospective bride to bring her into line, it might be a good time to rethink the whole marriage thing." Before he could reply, she said to me, "Step on it, Goldy."

Which I did, a bit too forcefully. We lurched forward and eventually came around to the back of the house, where Julian and Boyd were standing by a plain red door. Julian was speaking into an intercom. He shook his head at me, exasperated. Whoever was inside wanted our driver's licenses slid through a mail slot. I hadn't met the maid, only talked to her on the phone. Apparently, she was being very careful with the caterers her boss had hired.

Boyd, Julian, Marla, and I all extracted licenses and pushed them through. It must have been Boyd's sheriff's department ID that got the door quickly opened.

The gray-haired maid waiting for us was unsmiling. "I'm Violet. Mr. Unger is not going to be happy," she warned.

"About what?" I shot back. "Us showing up on time? Us showing up at all?"

"He wanted the party to be a surprise," she replied.

"*I* didn't spill the beans," I replied. After that drive up the mountain to get here, I was *not* going to be intimidated.

Talk about being surprised, though: Ophelia Unger, dressed in a dazzling, bead-embroidered, lime silk dress that actually fit her perfectly, shimmied down the hall. She apologized for the delay. "Don't be upset with us. I just don't want to see Bob yet."

"Good plan," said Marla as she slid past Ophelia. "Have you thought about not seeing him ever?"

"Actually—" Ophelia began, but then she stopped. By this time our team had arrived in a large kitchen where gleaming white-and-blue tiles covered the counters and backsplash beneath maple cabinets. Ophelia glanced nervously into one corner of this vast space. Brewster Motley stood leaning against the counter. He was totally relaxed, as usual. Dressed in a pink oxford-cloth shirt, madras cut-offs, and boat shoes, he shook his head at Ophelia.

"Wait until your father gets here," he said calmly.

"Nice dress," I said to Ophelia. "It looks new."

"I just bought it." Ophelia beamed. Then I noticed that her usually straggly dark hair had been fashionably highlighted and cut. Her face was impeccably made up. Tiny diamonds glittered in her ears.

"Turning twenty-one suits you," I said. Maybe Ophelia was happy because Brewster had found her money. But she was glowing, and in my vast experience of catering to wealthy people, money usually didn't make you *glow*. I briefly wondered if what Bob had worried about was true: that Ophelia had taken up with Brewster Motley. Wasn't sleeping with clients what had gotten Warren Broome into such trouble?

Ophelia giggled nervously and put a shy hand over her mouth. I realized it was the first time I'd ever seen her smile, or, for that matter, express happiness of any kind. The metamorphosis was astonishing.

"Okay, Brewster, spill it," Marla ordered as she whacked the cake box onto the center island, next to a neat pile of gold-edged plates. "What are you doing for our dear Ophelia here? I mean, now that she's reached her majority, are you taking advantage, and making her happy, in the process?"

Brewster allowed a small Cheshire-cat grin. "You know I would never do that. And aren't you supposed to be a guest at this party, not a caterer?"

"Light is both wave and particle," Marla replied serenely. "I can be both guest and server. But I already called Neil and told him I was just helping Goldy."

Ophelia giggled *again*. Violet cleared her throat.

"Uh, everybody?" Julian interrupted. "As cool and teen-slumber-partyish as this all feels? We have to know which refrigerators to use, and to see the table, the grill, the wine, the crystal, and everything else. Please," he added.

"Yes, yes, of course," said Ophelia, back to her usual solemn self. "We just have the one refrigerator." The maid opened the door to it, and we got busy.

Over the next half hour, we were periodically interrupted by the sound of Bob ringing the doorbell or talking through the intercom. "Please, dear Ophelia," he said. It was clear he was trying to sound calm and cool. "Please let me take you out for a drink. One drink. Then we can come back. This is supposed to be a *surprise* party."

Ophelia lifted her chin in defiance and disappeared with Brewster to "iron out last-minute details," whatever that meant. Violet seemed to smile. Or was I imagining it? Bob continued calling into the intercom, but no one answered. Violet shook her head, and offered no explanation.

Violet showed us the long table that she had set, on a glassed-in porch that overlooked the Continental Divide. I noted that one entire wall was constructed of moss rock, with a fireplace and TV built in. The grill was actually part of the massive countertop stove in the kitchen itself.

Julian had barely said, "Okay, we're ready," when a low rumbling sound indicated a mechanized garage door being opened. "Uh-oh," Julian said. "Beware the ogre."

"Why?" asked Boyd, his first words in a while.

"The man is a terror," Julian replied. Violet nodded in silent, but vigorous, agreement.

"Then it'll be interesting," Boyd said mildly.

We could hear Neil Unger storming up a distant set of stairs. He was bellowing for Ophelia, who made no sign of responding. I wondered where the birthday girl and Brewster had concealed themselves.

Francie Unger, whom I knew only by sight, wandered into the kitchen, looking bewildered. Fortyish, with heavy blond hair and a slender build, she was well known in the gossipy, fund-raising, country-club set. She wore a tweed skirt, a pullover, and golf shoes, which she wrenched off. She asked, "Will somebody please tell me what is going on?" When none of us answered, she narrowed her eyes at our team. "Marla? Aren't you early?"

"I'm helping Goldy." Marla's arm swept out in a courtly gesture. "Your caterer."

Francie looked genuinely perplexed. "But why are you here *now*?"

"Uh, because Goldy's my friend and needed me? Didn't Neil tell you I was serving, and not eating?"

Francie still wore a mask of puzzlement. When Bob Rushwood began talking into the intercom again, she disappeared to let him in. Meanwhile, Ophelia hustled Brewster out the back door with a whispered warning that he should avoid Bob, drive down the hill, and wait. She would text him when she needed him. A moment later, she whisked back into the kitchen and winked at us, just as Bob came in and took in her dazzling appearance.

"Oh, my God," he said, thunderstruck. "What . . . happened to you? Is this because of that . . . BMW guy?"

"That BMW guy was my fashion and beauty consultant," Ophelia lied, smiling broadly. "Do you like what he picked out for me?"

"I do," said Bob. He showed no remorse for his earlier ill temper, only bewilderment mixed with suspicion. "So . . . that's what you've been up to with him?"

"Of course," said Ophelia. "I wanted to surprise you. Now, can you wait in the library while I go talk to Dad and Francie?"

"There aren't any books on fitness in there," Bob complained. He recovered some of his usual smoothness, though, and warned Ophelia in a conspirational murmur, "Remember to tell them it wasn't my fault you figured out about the surprise party." Ophelia nodded, and Violet led Bob away.

There was some thumping and door slamming in the far reaches of the house, and then, apparently, either reconciliation or acceptance of defeat. Ophelia had probably sold the fashion-and-beauty-consultant story to her father. When the noises of acrimony were replaced by the sounds of water gushing through pipes, I took it as a good sign. An even better one was the fact that nobody reappeared in the kitchen.

The doorbell rang at six, and Violet scurried off to answer it. Julian readied the iced champagne bucket and drinks tray. Boyd and I removed the appetizers from the refrigerator, something Julian had thought at the last minute that we would need: deviled eggs topped with halved Greek olives. Marla washed her hands and carefully placed the starters on a platter rimmed with the egg-and-dart pattern.

"Should I start passing these out?" she asked nervously.

"Sure," I said.

And so the evening got going. The guests, who, I assumed, were friends of Neil and Francie's, hid in the living room and burst out with "Surprise!" when Ophelia appeared. She thanked them quickly, then walked purposefully to the porch. It was there that Neil held court, giving everyone a lecture about politics, whether they wanted to hear it or not. Ophelia did not reappear in the kitchen. Bob hovered around her on the porch, and I wondered if he'd bought her "fashion and beauty consultant" story.

There was no sign of Brewster.

When I went back to the porch to begin clearing the hors d'oeuvre plates, I saw Francie down the second half of what I sensed was not her first glass of wine. I overheard her murmur to Ophelia, "You look so nice, dear. And that is a welcome change. Did you finally use the clothing money your father has been giving you?"

"Yes," said Ophelia.

Francie put on a simpering expression. "Couldn't you have acted happier when our guests surprised you?"

Ophelia did not turn to her stepmother when she said, in a low, fierce whisper, "Leave me alone for once, will you?"

"Ex-cuse me," said Francie, too loudly.

Ophelia sat almost motionless. She had not touched the egg I'd put in front of her. I wondered how far down the hill Brewster had driven. After half an hour, Ophelia began to act agitated. Her hands fluttered about and she dropped her glass, which shattered on the floor. Bob Rushwood's protective stance at her side was clearly making her nervous. I wondered if he was afraid she was going to bolt—from her own party.

"Julian," I said mildly, once I'd cleaned up the broken glass and we were back in the kitchen, "could you please check to see if Brewster's BMW is where you can see it?"

He took off, then returned a moment later. "Nope."

We had, as we say in food service, bigger fish to fry. Julian lit the gas grill burners. Marla, Boyd, and I served the Greek lemon soup. Although the porch conversation felt a bit stilted, it did seem as if some of the folks were genuinely concerned with asking Ophelia polite questions: What was she going to do now that she was twenty-one? Did she have plans? Was she going to travel before she and Bob got married? Where were they going on their honeymoon? She blushed and fielded the questions by saying she hadn't made up her mind.

I, meanwhile, kept a covert eye on Neil Unger as he alternately charmed and lectured the guests. He could have been Holly Ingleby's lover in the distant, and maybe even the recent, past. Could he be Drew's biological father? I tried to concentrate on his facial features: did Drew look like him? Hard to tell.

Would Neil have submitted to being blackmailed by Holly?

Could Neil have put the Loquin in the tortas when they were on the counter in our kitchen?

I stared at his big hands. Could he have attacked me on my own back porch the night before?

Nothing was clear, and I shook my head to rid it of the buzz of questions. Soon the hiss of shish kebabs hitting the grill, and the resulting heavenly scent, got me focused on the dinner.

We placed the luscious kebabs onto the steaming rice and sprinkled chopped fresh herbs over it all. Everyone seemed grateful. I was still keeping a close eye on Neil Unger. What was I hoping to learn? I didn't know, but after a while my observation seemed to be making him wary, and I could see that he was watching me out of the corner of his eye. I cleared my throat and went back to smiling and serving, lowering dishes from the left and raising them from the right.

The guests, meanwhile, continued to interrogate Ophelia, and my heart bled for this shy, studious young woman.

When people complimented her on her new look, she self-consciously touched the ends of her gorgeous new hairstyle and thanked them. When women asked her where she'd gotten her "new do" done, she answered

388 · DIANE MOTT DAVIDSON

simply, "In Denver." When they asked where she'd bought the dress, she said, "In Denver." She'd always faded into the background before, and wasn't used to being the center of attention.

"What in the hell is going on?" Marla demanded. "We have to go through a security nightmare to get in, Brewster sneaks out, Bob comes in, Ophelia is all beaming and gorgeous when we arrive, and now she looks like she's afraid of her own party."

"You never know with catering clients," I said. "Let's just clear the dinner dishes and light the candles."

It was when we were poking the candles into the cake that Ophelia rushed into the kitchen. She pressed buttons on her cell phone, then retrieved what were clearly two heavy suitcases from the pantry. Julian offered to help. She gave him a small smile, but said she was fine. All that time working out with Bob had clearly made her biceps and triceps strong. She did ask nervously for Violet to go to the front door and let Brewster in.

The maid disappeared, and it wasn't long before Brewster Motley sashayed into the kitchen, toting his own briefcase. He looked even more like the canary-swallowing cat than he had earlier.

"Why, Brewster," said Marla, "you never told me you were a fashion consultant."

He flicked her a glance. "I'd lose the apron, Marla. It's not you."

"Hungry, Brewster?" Julian asked, his tone teasing. "We could have saved you some food."

"I'm good," said Brewster. He snapped open his briefcase and turned to Ophelia. "Ready?"

"No," she said, her voice shaking. "But I want to get this over with."

I asked, "Does that mean I should or should not light the candles on the cake?"

"*Not*," Ophelia and Brewster answered in unison.

A shiver ran down my back. Did this have to happen *right now*? I couldn't bear the thought of another party being ruined by tragedy, conflict, or some other untoward event.

"Goldy," said Ophelia, "could you please ask my father to come in here?"

"To the kitchen?" I asked, dumbfounded.

"I want to spare him the embarrassment of having this confrontation in front of his guests."

His guests, I noted. Not hers.

So I went and got Neil, who responded by looking confused. Bob Rushwood followed us into the kitchen. Neil's complexion was more florid than I'd ever seen it, either from the wine served during the evening or because he was ticked off.

"What is the meaning of this?" he said as he took in his daughter and her suitcases. "Who are you?" he demanded of Brewster.

Bob, who had turned stone-faced and cold, said, "He's supposedly Ophelia's fashion consultant. He's been spending an awful lot of time with her."

At the moment, Brewster was leafing through papers in his briefcase. Neil said to him, "You don't *look* like you have anything to do with fashion."

Ophelia stood resolute. She stared at the cake and the neat pile of gold-edged plates beside it. Finally she said, "He has nothing to do with fashion. He's my attorney."

"Your *what?*" Neil exploded.

Brewster Motley introduced himself and offered his hand to Neil Unger, who refused it. So did Bob Rushwood. Well, well. So much for civility and all those values you say you care about, Neil. As if he were used to dealing with difficult people, Brewster said smoothly, "Your former wife, Athena Unger, inherited a fortune that she wanted passed down to her daughter. It was left in a trust for her. Thirty million dollars."

I felt my mouth drop open. Had *Holly* been aware of this? The voice of my attacker grated in my ear. *Who knows?*

"Why, you ungrateful—" Neil Unger turned to address his daughter, but Brewster held up his hand, interrupting him.

"Since Ophelia was so young when her mother died," Brewster continued, "she did not know about this money. Nor, of course, did she know about the provisions of the trust. And Quentin Laird, the cotrustee along with you, the other cotrustee, never told her. But Laird, Athena's attorney, has an excuse. He had a stroke ten years ago, has mild dementia, and had to give up practicing law. He's been in a nursing home for the past decade." Brewster paused. "When Ophelia turned eighteen, you were duty bound to tell her about the trust, its provisions, and its management. Last time I looked, that was breach of trust by a trustee. Not to mention failure as a parent."

Neil hurtled toward Brewster, but Boyd got between them. "Sir," he said respectfully, "I am a sergeant with the Furman County Sheriff's Department. You will not touch anyone, do you understand?"

"It's. My. House," said Neil.

"I. Don't. Care," replied Boyd.

Chastened, Neil stepped back. Violet, the maid, came back into the kitchen. She took in everyone's expressions and scooted over to a bank of cabinets. She stood very still there, as if to make herself invisible.

Bob Rushwood was glancing from Brewster to Ophelia to Neil and back again. I put my gaze back on Neil Unger. If Holly had known about this trust, couldn't that have made Neil a tempting blackmail target?

I wondered.

Brewster was saying, "Something your current wife said to Ophelia a while ago tipped her off. Along the lines of her not being college material? The fact that you hushed your wife made Ophelia suspicious, as well she should have been. So she hired me. We went to see Quentin Laird, who was lucid enough to tell us which files to check from the boxes in his basement." Brewster took a deep breath and pulled a packet of clipped papers out of his case. He read, " 'The trust shall terminate and be distributed, free of any trust or other restrictions, to Ophelia when she turns twenty-one and has completed a college degree.' " He handed a document of numerous pages into Neil Unger's hands. "As you can see, she just finished her bachelor's."

"You never—" Neil Unger began again.

"But I did," Ophelia declared, defiant. "All that shopping money you gave me? It was used for tuition at the University of Colorado. With my AP credits from high school, I was able to complete a degree in architecture in two years." She eagerly reached into Brewster's case and pulled out what looked like a transcript and a diploma. "You see, Dad? I'm not so dumb after all."

With a look of barely controlled fury, Neil Unger grabbed both the diploma and the transcript and tore them in half.

"Those were copies," Brewster said mildly.

"I don't care, and I don't care about her having gone to college."

"Obviously you do care," Brewster countered, "since you forbade her from getting a college education and fulfilling the terms of the trust." When Neil said nothing, Brewster went on: "Now, the only thing that would prevent Ophelia from assuming control of her own money was if she had a child. Because of her large fortune, she would have to support the child, and probably its father, too."

"She's pregnant," Bob announced triumphantly. "With my child."

"Ophelia!" Neil Unger looked apoplectic.

Ophelia stood her ground. "I am not pregnant. Sorry, Bob. I know you thought I was hormonal when I stopped sleeping with you."

"I thought you loved me." Bob's voice had turned plaintive.

Ophelia shook her head. "I liked you when we first met. Being with you was fun, and made me forget my former fiancé being in prison, and my father refusing to pay for my education." She narrowed her eyes at him. "But then I learned that you'd been trying to find things out about me. Did I have money of my own? you asked Francie. She told you I did, but that the only way *you* would get any of it was if you and I got married and I had a child. Once I got wind of that conversation, our relationship was over. But I only needed a few more weeks to finish my degree, so I agreed to marry you, to keep my father off my back until I could graduate from CU." Ophelia glanced at her father, but Neil was clearly so choked with rage that he could not talk. "Engagement's off, Bob," the young woman continued calmly.

"You little shit," Bob said, his voice low and flat.

"Here's your ring," said Ophelia, retrieving the item from her elegant dress's pocket. "I know my father bought it for you to give to me, just like he bought you that Mercedes. See, one thing I learned in my college finance class was how to read the bills." She shook her head sorrowfully at her father. "And checkbooks. And the investment reports that you locked up in your files in your office—"

Neil suddenly whirled on Violet. "You helped her! You . . . you . . . you're fired!"

"Okay," the maid replied calmly, and winked at Ophelia. "I'm working for somebody else now. Who do you think overheard Bob asking Francie about Ophelia having money? And who do you think told Ophelia? Just because I am a maid doesn't mean I am invisible—or deaf."

At this point, Brewster again took over. "The great thing about this trust is that before Quentin had a stroke, he filed paperwork with the state. I spent the entire day tracking down those documents . . . so Ophelia could claim her money." He waggled a reproving finger in Neil's direction. "I'll bet the only reason you didn't drain the trust yourself is that the Bank of Aspen Meadow is named as an alternate trustee, in case either you or Quentin died. If you'd tried any worse funny business, the bank would have discovered it in an audit and had you prosecuted faster than you could cry 'thief.' Unfortunately, you did get Quentin to sign over management of the trust to you. So you were able to appropriate one percent of Ophelia's trust every year. Hmm, arithmetic. That's three hundred thou a year. Lucky for Ophelia the stock market has done well recently, so her trust has grown." He tried to hand another paper to Neil, who let it flutter to the floor. "That is a notarized copy of Ophelia's intention to manage her own trust from now on."

"Okay," said Ophelia, who seemed suddenly exhausted by the proceedings. "Let's get this over with."

"Here are your copies of the trust papers, Mr. Unger," Brewster said, laying them on the counter. He paused. "You can tear them up, too. I have copies. But the bottom line is that Ophelia now controls her own fortune."

"But . . . but . . ." Neil blustered, "the money was always being held *for* her. Quentin and I worked it out—"

Boyd interjected quietly, "It doesn't sound to me like you worked anything out."

Neil spun around slowly. I had a sudden vision of him banging around my kitchen the day before Arch and Drew's party, rifling through drawers and cabinets, as he claimed I'd been hacked. "You know nothing," he said now. "I am the head of The Guild. I know exactly how the money was invested. You do not. None of you do." He turned back to Ophelia. Once again we all stood in tense silence, although I noted that Boyd had ever so nonchalantly placed his hand on his weapon.

Marla looked around. "Uh, are we done here?"

Neil Unger turned on Bob Rushwood. "You knew she had done this, that she hired an attorney."

Bob snapped, "I did not. All I knew was she'd been acting strange lately. I thought she was, you know, expecting. And then this guy"—he waved a hand at Brewster—"showed up at the house. That's why I called you. I figured maybe she was seeing him behind my back, ever since I saw Goldy here bring the two of them together yesterday." He glanced toward me. "But then Ophelia told us he was just a fashion consultant, and you wanted us to get ready for this idiotic party. Your daughter has been lying to both of us all this time, so there's no point in getting mad at me about it. Lying seems to run in your family."

Neil jabbed a finger at my face. "You did this!"

"*Me?*" I asked.

"*Goldy?*" Julian and Marla echoed.

"You were behind this," Neil said, his voice suddenly sounding assured. "You're always meddling in other people's business. Everyone knows that."

Chills ran down my arms. Meddling, huh? Had Holly meddled in Neil's attempt to trick his daughter out of her inheritance, and then used her knowledge to blackmail him? Had Neil decided that I was involved in Holly's scheme and attacked me the previous night? He was certainly strong enough to have done it.

"Bob saw you." He kept pointing, and it reminded me of the Jerk's old pattern of point, accuse, slap. "He saw you with Ophelia and this . . . this . . ."—he faltered, wagging his spare hand at Brewster—" . . . this lawyer. It's all your fault!"

"Easy, now," said Boyd, his voice barely audible.

Probably wondering where her family had disappeared to, Francie entered the kitchen at that moment. She took in the enraged faces of our little tableau and, for once, said nothing.

Bob turned his attention back to Ophelia. "After all I did for you, after all the opportunities I gave you, after all the people I introduced you to—"

"I learned you only do things for yourself," Ophelia stated calmly. "My life doesn't have anything to do with you now, so you might as well shut up."

"I will not shut up," he said. "I've wasted a year of my life trying to help you. I've tried to take care of you—"

"By being possessive?" Ophelia interrupted. "Obsessing over whether I was pregnant? That's not love. Keep the Mercedes, Bob, it'll be ample pay for services rendered. I just thank God I don't have to finance a life of leisure for you." She nodded in her father's direction. "Or for you."

"How dare you—" Neil Unger now lunged at his daughter.

But she was too quick for him. Picking up one of the gold-edged dessert plates, she held it in front of her father's face. He charged head-on; the plate broke. Neil staggered backward, clutching his suddenly blood-streaked forehead.

"This ends now," Boyd said, his tone authoritative. He planted his substantial body between Ophelia and her father.

"She attacked me!" Neil cried.

"She acted in self-defense," Boyd replied, "to which I will testify. Mrs. Unger?"

Ophelia's stepmother, looking dazed, didn't seem to realize that Boyd was addressing her. She recovered long enough to say, "Yes?"

"Please make Ophelia's excuses to your guests. Brewster? Ophelia? It's time for you to leave."

Brewster said, "Mr. Unger, my firm will be drawing up papers to file a civil suit against you."

"For *what?*" Neil Unger was pressing a kitchen towel onto his bleeding face.

"We'll start with breach of trust by a trustee and go from there."

Brewster snapped his case shut while Ophelia allowed Julian to hand her the suitcases. She thanked him and me, and over her shoulder said that Brewster was going to drive her to a car dealership so she could buy one of her own.

And then they were gone. Boyd put a restraining hand on Bob's shoulder and told him he had to wait until we all heard Brewster's car leave. Bob sulked, but obeyed. As soon as the BMW roared away, he bolted for the front door.

Francie fled back to the porch. Neil stood next to me and snarled, "I've paid you for this party, and you are going to wrap up that cake for us by God, or I'll take you to court. As soon as my guests leave, pack up your team and your stuff and get out."

When he left the kitchen, Marla quipped, "Dang. If only I'd used my cell-phone camera! I could have filmed the goings-on here to use as the pilot for a new reality show: *Killer Catering Careers.*"

"I *knew* I recognized Ophelia from someplace," Julian mused. "She's a regular at the Boulder Goodwill Thrift Store! That's where she got her out-dated clothes and saved money for CU tuition. Pretty smart."

I nodded, too exhausted to speak. Marla disappeared to the porch, ostensibly to start picking up the entrée plates. Really, I suspected, it was to hear the way the contretemps in the kitchen was being reported to the rest of the guests.

Julian whisked around the kitchen, first wrapping the birthday cake for the Ungers. Somehow, I doubted they would be enthusiastic about consuming it. Boyd and I began packing up boxes.

I worked as if by rote, my mind teeming with unanswered questions. I wondered just how far Neil Unger might have been willing to go to conceal the truth about his daughter's money. I wondered if knowledge about him had been one of Holly's secrets. In an evening of surprises, though, one stood out most.

Bob Rushwood could only have seen me introduce Brewster to Ophelia if he'd been watching the meadow below St. Luke's on Sunday morning. Had he been following Ophelia then, spying on her for her father? I hadn't caught sight of him, nor, apparently, had the squad processing the crime scene of the attacks on Kathie Beliar and Father Pete. If he was spying, why didn't he tell Neil earlier about what Ophelia was doing?

What else had Bob Rushwood seen that he hadn't told anyone?

21

"I'm going to have to give up a cherished pastime," Marla lamented on the way back to our house.

Following in Ophelia and Brewster's cloud of dust, Violet and the guests had hastily departed. Julian, Boyd, Marla, and I packed the boxes into our vehicles.

"Give up a cherished pastime?" I said to Marla. "Is this more reality-show stuff?"

Marla tapped her hand on the dashboard. "I don't really watch those. But I used to love scary movies. Still, why *should* I watch them, when catering is the real deal?" I felt her eyes on me. "No *wonder* you insist on being paid in full before the party even starts."

"I did not expect all that to happen tonight."

"How could you? One thing's for sure, though." Marla sighed. "You won't be doing any more catering for Neil Unger."

I drove with grim determination. As I navigated the hairpin turns on the route back from the Ungers' place, Brewster called. He was at a Lexus place in Denver, waiting for Ophelia to finish up buying a vehicle.

He said, "I forgot to tell you all one provision of the trust. If anything happened to Ophelia before she inherited her mother's money, the funds would go to the Shakespeare Festival at the University of Colorado."

"Makes me think Athena didn't exactly trust Neil."

"I had the same thought," said Brewster. "Don't worry; I told Boyd. The very best thing for Neil would have been if Ophelia married Bob, never got an education, then had a kid. That way he could keep collecting his fees for managing the trust as long as he lived."

"Or until Quentin Laird died. And as long as Ophelia never found anything out."

"Exactly."

He signed off. I speculated about the idea of Neil being the one who had poisoned Holly, stabbed Father Pete and Kathie Beliar, and attacked me—all to keep his management fees. I wondered, too, if Brewster would actually act on his threat to file a civil suit against Neil

404 • DIANE MOTT DAVIDSON

Unger. I had no idea what kind of evidence you would need to justify such a suit, much less win a case. Still, I bet Brewster could and would help in any way he could legally do so.

Onward and upward. The following day we had no catered events. I sent up a brief silent prayer of gratitude. But Marla and I, with Boyd, were going to visit the gift shop at Holly's former Roman Catholic parish in Denver. After that, I wanted to stop at Clarkson Shipping, to see if the owner or his help remembered any details about the person who'd sent the box to Holly's house.

I felt as if I were grasping at the thinnest of straws. Still, I had to persevere. Holly and Kathie Beliar had been killed. Father Pete had been stabbed. And someone had sabotaged Holly's deck, probably in an attempt to kill Drew.

That last part bothered me deeply. If Holly had been blackmailing someone, like Neil or Warren Broome, why would that person also want to kill Drew? Because they thought he knew the information Holly was using to extort money? George certainly wouldn't have wanted Drew dead, even if he was chafing at having to pay child support for a son who was not biologically his own. He loved Drew. Lena clearly had wanted to hurt Holly, but she seemed devoted to George, and going into cahoots with someone to kill Drew would have hurt George too much.

Then there was this artist, Yurbin, with whom Holly had been fighting. She'd shrugged off the idea of his being her current romantic partner. But what if he'd been one in the past? He wasn't her usual type, but he was attractive in a bullish sort of way, and he was, after all, an artist. Could *he* be Drew's biological father? And even if their dispute had nothing to do with her son, why would Yurbin target Drew? To frighten Holly? Then why try to kill her first with the antibiotic at the party? That envelope on the deck with Drew's name on it was like a puzzle piece that had been cut wrong, and wouldn't fit into the puzzle.

In front of our house, Marla wished me good night. When she got back to her place, she said cheerily, she would make some phone calls to her country-club pals, to relate the story of the blowup at Ophelia's. It wasn't, after all, confidential, and the phone lines of the guests who'd been witnesses were probably already buzzing as they called everyone they knew. Marla also wanted to see if any of her friends had any inkling about this money of Ophelia's.

"You can rely on one thing," she said, before climbing into her Mercedes, "the top priority in discussions at Aspen Meadow Country Club is money."

"What's the second priority?" I asked, smiling. "Golf?"

"Oh, hell no," she said, and winked. "That would be sex."

Tom was eating a sandwich in the kitchen when Julian, Boyd, and I traipsed in. I suddenly regretted not being able to bring him any leftovers. Come to think of it, *I* hadn't had any dinner.

"Sit down, the three of you," Tom ordered. We did. Tom's miss-nothing eyes moved from one of us to the other. "You're home early. And you all look like hell."

"Somebody make this man an investigator," Julian observed drily.

Tom's mouth turned in a half grin. "I'm assuming the party at Ophelia's was not, after all, a surprise?"

"Oh, it was a surprise, all right," I replied. "Ophelia made it one."

"Everybody stay seated," said Tom. "I want to hear this."

Julian, Boyd, and I took turns telling him about the fiasco. Meanwhile, Tom carefully sliced a loaf of Dad's Bread, a bunch of fresh tomatoes, most of a boiled Danish ham, and large chunks of roast turkey and Havarti cheese. He filled an enormous bowl with baby field greens, and smaller ones with mayonnaise, Dijon mustard, and chutney. My mouth watered.

Tom tilted his head thoughtfully as he placed his offerings before us. "It wasn't a total failure. Ophelia is lucky to be rich, now, and away from her controlling father and fiancé. And Brewster's people might be able to sting Neil with a huge civil lawsuit."

"Okay," I said. But something was bothering me. "Look, I'm just going to say what I'm thinking."

Tom shrugged. "Have I ever stopped you?"

"Holly knew Neil Unger. I don't know how well. But he was at the medical conference in Boulder, and could be Drew's father. Holly was blackmailing somebody, right? And Neil showed up here at the house when Julian and I were cooking the meal for the boys' birthday party. A pair of tortas, uncooked, were on the counter. He sent Julian outside on a fool's errand, then insisted that I check to see if my computer had been hacked. Which I did, while he moved all around the kitchen. If Holly knew about Neil's finagling with the trust, if he knew about her S-T interval problem, that could have given him a motive to sprinkle crushed Loquin into the tortas to kill her."

"It's a long shot, Goldy. We think they were just the barest of acquaintances. But we can keep an eye out as we follow leads."

"Also, Bob was spying on Ophelia when she asked me for help with a lawyer. He saw me introduce her

408 · DIANE MOTT DAVIDSON

to Brewster. He might know something else, maybe something about Neil or Holly."

"That's another very long shot. And we certainly don't have enough to pull Bob in for questioning. We've already talked to him about the boys' birthday party, how he knew Holly, that kind of thing. After the party tonight, I very much doubt that he would talk to us without being fully lawyered up. Not only that, but since you helped Ophelia get her hands on her money, I think you should steer clear of Bob Rushwood for a while. He's big and he's strong and he's pissed."

"Okay." I smiled at him. "I just wanted to think aloud."

"And I appreciate it, as ever."

Somewhat cheered, we put together our sandwiches and dug into them. While we ate, Tom told us that unfortunately, the crime-scene techs had not come up with anything usable from our backyard. Whoever had come through our gate—and made it look as if a bear had broken in—had worn gloves, had stayed on the gravel, the grass, or the deck, and had not had his clothing snagged on a helpful nail. With our recent dry weather, there were no footprints conveniently etched into mud.

"That's the second trap we've dealt with in the past four days," he concluded gloomily.

"Second?" I echoed.

"The first was the deck at Holly's house."

I shook my head and had almost finished my turkey-and-Havarti sandwich when Tom said the department had finally been able to find Kathie Beliar's one living relative, an uncle. He would be flying in the following week, and was taking over the arrangements with the funeral home and our local Methodist church.

I put down the unfinished bit of sandwich and asked Tom if they'd gotten any other leads on who could have killed Holly and Kathie. The attacker's DNA, from the skin Father Pete had managed to snag under his fingernails, had yet to be analyzed, despite the effort to speed things up. Even if the analysis had been done, the attacker might not be in the state's DNA database.

Gloomily, he said the department wasn't even sure of a motive for the attacks. They thought they might be tied to this paternity-of-Drew situation, but were by no means sure. Warren Broome had refused to take a DNA test to determine if he was Drew's biological father. The only thing they'd been able to find out about Yurbin was that he was actually named Andrei Yurbin, and he'd been Holly's teacher when she went back to art school after her divorce. The one bit of personal information they'd been able to extract was actually a slip on the part of the art school secretary, who said he was diabetic.

"Diabetic?" I said. "Why in the world would she tell you that?"

"The man loves sweets," Tom announced. "When she saw us, she thought, and I quote, that 'he'd been naughty again,' and was in diabetic shock. She seemed disappointed that we weren't there to tell her he was sick. And by the way? He hasn't taught there for six years. But at least we got an address. And then Yurbin lawyered up."

"May I have Yurbin's address?" I asked.

"Miss G. The man has hired an attorney. I don't want you to track him down and harass him. Then he could sue the department."

"Did you ask him if he was doing the collages Holly was selling?"

Tom gave me a look. "Is that what you think?"

I said, "It makes sense. The styles of their work are eerily similar. Holly has no studio that we can find. She lied to her own son about having one in Cherry Creek. You can't find scraps from the collages. And unless you're using solid gold, no one charges twenty-five-thousand dollars for framing." I paused. "My bet is that they were fighting over money. Say she got the commission, and provided the basic outline of what she wanted. He charged a few thousand for a work, she marked it up, and made just enough to get by. Then he wanted more, so he showed up at the boys' party. Did you ask him any of this?"

"Goldy, he wouldn't answer any of our questions."

I exhaled. "If I find Yurbin on my own, and Boyd comes with me, may Marla and I just have a teensy-weensy visit with him? On the q.t.?"

Tom said, "Teensy-weensy. And I'll talk to Boyd about staying with you the whole time. And you know I'll have to disavow knowledge of you going down there. I'm telling you, it's a long shot."

"I know."

Discouraged, I asked if there had been any word on Father Pete's condition. Tom shook his head grimly. There was no good cause for optimism in that situation, except to hope that our priest didn't die.

The following day, Tuesday, dawned clear, bright, and cool. A cloud of pollen still hung in the air above the mountains. Even with the windows closed, I sneezed as I sat up in bed. Tom had already departed, but he'd left a note with an iced cappuccino on my night table, and included the term *teensy-weensy.* I sipped the luscious coffee and prayed for Father Pete, then moved through my yoga routine. My thigh still ached, and my shoulder tingled with pain. The bathroom mirror revealed that the bruises on my neck had diminished only slightly. I didn't bother with concealing makeup but I *did* allow myself an extra shot of caffeine to compensate.

Arch called the house line early. He, Gus, and Sergeant Jones were on their way out to the Pails for Trails site, but he'd forgotten to tell me that Bob Rushwood was going to take pictures of the guys— the trail builders—that day, to make into the annual school-year calendar the charity sold. Was that okay? He was supposed to get a permission slip signed, but had forgotten about it. He was wondering if Gus's grandparents could sign his.

"Could you put Sergeant Jones on the line, please?"

"Mom." But he handed the phone over.

"Jones," came the clipped voice.

"Sergeant," I said carefully, "I don't want my son to know what we're actually talking about."

"Should I call you from my car?"

"Don't think that's necessary. Just act as if I'm giving you permission to sign that slip Arch has."

"Go ahead."

"Last night, I catered a party where Bob Rushwood was a guest. It didn't end well."

"I'm listening," she said, her voice deadpan.

I gave her a quick rundown on Bob and Ophelia's breakup. I told her about Bob's spying on Ophelia and his seeing me introduce her to Brewster Motley.

"The main thing I'm worried about," I concluded, "is that Bob was apoplectic with rage last night, and so I was hoping you would keep Arch as close to you as possible today. This is just in case Bob does indeed blame me, and he extends that blame to my son."

"Done," she said. "Anything else?"

"That's plenty. Thank you."

I sat at the kitchen table and stared at the note Tom had left for me, sweetly warning me again not to harass Yurbin. If I had Boyd and Marla with me, though, how dangerous could Yurbin be? It didn't matter that he had a lawyer. Did it?

I didn't have answers to those questions, but the diabetic issue had given me an idea. Yurbin loved sweets but couldn't have them. So I would make him a rich, creamy, sugar-free gelato. I separated eggs, covered and refrigerated the whites, and whisked the yolks along with milk, cream, and sugar substitute in a saucepan. Once the custard was smooth, thick, and shiny, I removed it from the heat, added Mexican vanilla, and set it aside to cool. Luckily, I kept the inner container of my ice-cream maker frozen. When I was packing up the other components, Marla's horn sounded from our street. I grinned.

Once Marla was up on our front porch, she called through the window that she was only wanting to announce her arrival to Boyd. I tried not to think about our neighbors and their children being awakened on a summer morning. Boyd opened the door and merely shook his head as Marla swept past him.

"I'm starving," she said as she peered into the walk-in. She wore a black-and-white-checked top and white pants, along with jaunty red earrings, barrettes, and shoes. "Have any protein in here? Ah, cheese," she answered her own question. She pulled out a wrapped chunk of Gruyère. I handed her a knife and plate. Before she could even ask, I pressed the buttons on the espresso maker to pull her shots.

"Where is everybody?" she asked, suddenly realizing that neither Tom, Arch, nor Julian was in the kitchen. Even Boyd had disappeared.

"Boyd's in the living room, I think. Arch is at Gus's. Tom, work. Julian, sleeping, I hope, although I don't know how he could after your horn blast that I'm sure woke everyone in a three-block radius."

She waved this away. "So," she began around a mouthful of cheese, "I talked to a number of friends. The Athena Line. Heard of it?"

I closed the cooler with the custard, taped it shut, then did the same with the cardboard box. It took me a moment to shift mental gears. "The Athena Line?"

"Oh, Goldy, what we don't know about international business! That's one topic we didn't discuss in Amour Anonymous."

"Marla, I don't—"

"So," she interrupted, "fifty years ago, the Greek shipping magnate Alexander Alexandropolous, named his freight line after his only daughter and heir, Athena. Ring any bells?" When I shook my head, she continued, "Have to say, it was vague for me, too. Well before my time. Anyway, in school—a Greek school, let us remember—forget Homer, Socrates, and all those fellows, young Athena Alexandropolous fell in love with Shakespeare. No word on whether she tried to make it to England for her university years. Maybe she heard about the weather."

"Marla . . ." I placed an iced four-shot latte at her place.

Marla held up a hand. "I'm getting there. Athena got a bachelor's, a master's, and a doctorate, in English literature, in California. She shunned her father's fortune at first, insisting she would make her own way in the world. Unfortunately, she could only manage to find adjunct teaching gigs. In the summer, she worked as a volunteer for the Colorado Shakespeare Festival. So that's where you get her partiality to *them*. Along the way, she met our dashing Mr. Neil Unger. Maybe he used to be dashing, anyway. She was thirty-two. He was twenty-nine and—wait for it—*acting onstage* as a lark. I mean, he had the uniform business he'd inherited from his father, but he was able to take time off for the occasional play. He had a bit part in *Measure for Measure*. Now, remember that dashing thing. Athena already had the cancer that would kill her at forty-one. Neither she nor Neil knew this, of course. But when he found out she was worth very, very big bucks, he married her, and they settled in Boulder. And Athena became pregnant. Before she delivered, her father sold the shipping business, then died. Athena didn't reject her inheritance. She left most of the fortune, thirty-plus million smackers, in a trust for her only child, whom she named Ophelia, after—"

"Thanks. I know my *Hamlet*."

Marla sipped her latte and shot me a grateful look. "In their years together, Athena must have figured out that Neil was actually a jerk. Okay, he had the uniform business, but he was aghast when his wife left him a paltry two million. She didn't have many friends in Colorado, and no relatives, so she made Neil and her

THE WHOLE ENCHILADA · 417

lawyer, Quentin Laird, trustees for her estate, which she left to Ophelia. As we heard last night, Neil could— and did—charge the trust an annual percentage of the value of its portfolio. For management fees. So he got his best role ever: acting like a manager."

"Who in the world informed you of all this?"

"I told you, friends." She shrugged. "Before Neil married Francie, Ophelia's stepmother, he got drunk one night and told her most of the details. The uniform business wasn't doing so great, and he was tired of overseeing the day-to-day operations, dealing with factories abroad, the whole shebang. He could make a lot of money every year doing practically nothing, but only if his daughter never got her college degree, which was one of the provisions of the trust that you and I found out about last night. Neil needed to keep managing his daughter's trust, and more important, managing his *daughter*, if he was going to hold on to those big fees."

I sat down. "Neil is a jerk."

Marla licked her fingers. "He is indeed."

I lifted the cooler onto the kitchen table. "But getting back to Ophelia. She jumped from a guy convicted of being a thief to Bob Rushwood. That's a big change. When do you think Bob started spying on her for Neil?"

Marla gave me one of those you've-got-to-be-kidding-me looks. "From the beginning, probably. According to my sources, Neil apparently promised Bob that he'd invest in a chain of fitness clubs Bob wanted to start up once Bob and Ophelia got married. All Bob had to do was help keep Ophelia in line and report what he saw of her movements to her father. I mean, you got a look at that Mercedes convertible. You can't afford that vehicle on a trainer's salary."

"If he was spying on her, how in the world did she finish her degree?"

Marla laughed. "Late last night? I was able to talk to a friend of Ophelia's from CU. She's the daughter of a club pal. Anyway, this friend told me that Ophelia scheduled all her classes in the mornings when her father would be at work. That's also when Bob usually had most of his training sessions at the club gym. Plus, he was always schlepping around to pick up the buckets for Pails for Trails. I mean, those buckets are all over the county, and probably beyond. That's a lot of collecting. Ophelia didn't know Bob followed her sometimes. She just felt that he was clingy and wanted to spend a lot of time with her. When she found out that he was after her money and taking dough from her father to get engaged to her, she had only two months until she graduated. At that point, Ophelia apparently told Bob that she thought they shouldn't have sex while they were engaged, because of her father's family values shtick with The Guild. But Bob would keep pestering her, saying it would be great if they had a kid. He thought her putting the brakes on sex meant that she might be pregnant, you know, and hormonal. Ophelia didn't tell him that she was on the pill and knew she wasn't expecting. Until yesterday, that is."

"That young woman is smart."

Marla sighed. "If you had a father and fiancé like that, and you were ambitious, you'd have to be wickedly intelligent."

"And capable of being devious."

"Well, that, too." She tapped the table with her fingers. "This is all nice gossip, but it doesn't really figure into our narrative with Holly—"

"But it could," I insisted, as I had to Tom. "If Neil and Holly had a fling, and he got plastered with *her* and told *her* the details of the trust, then he could have been the one she was blackmailing."

"True," said Marla. "Is Tom going to talk to him?"

"The department is going to see if any leads develop regarding Neil. But getting back to Bob. If he was spying on Ophelia, do you think he could have seen something else—something recent, involving Neil and Holly, say—that would help solve the case?"

"I don't know," Marla admitted. "Holly never said anything to me about Neil, but she didn't really name names, as you know. Still, no one I checked with knew of a connection between them. Bob's task was only to watch Ophelia."

"And Tom has told me absolutely to stay away from Bob."

"What a spoilsport."

Boyd said he would follow us to Denver. I gave him the addresses of Our Lady of Perpetual Grace and Clarkson Shipping, and told him what Tom had warned me about Yurbin: that we were not allowed to harass him. So, even if we found him, it could be a pointless journey. Marla promised Boyd a lovely lunch for being so accommodating.

"You know I can't accept lunch from you," he said. "It would be classified as a bribe."

"It would be classified as *lunch*," said Marla, with fire in her eyes. "And if you don't come with us, we'll give you the slip and—"

"Okay, okay." Boyd held up his palms in a gesture of defeat. "Church, shipping place, lunch, crazy artist, if you can find him. Sounds like a plan."

Our Lady of Perpetual Grace, located on Downing Street in Denver, was a Gothic-style building featuring large blocks of sparkling silver granite. The imposing façade was composed of three carved arches. Stained-glass windows soared two stories high. I wished we could have seen the church from the inside, but I didn't want to alert any stray clergyman to our presence, much less to the questions we were hoping to pose about a former parishioner. Instead, we walked on a stone path beside the flying buttresses toward a separate wooden building with a painted sign that said PARISH GIFT SHOP.

I'd checked the gift shop's website, and the place was supposed to be open. When we pushed into the cluttered space, though, no one was in evidence. About the size of the Ungers' kitchen—big for a kitchen, small for a shop—the place smelled pleasantly of incense. Two long tables took up most of the floor space. They were stacked with the kinds of statues we'd seen at Holly's, plus bookends, kitchen tiles, and other odds and ends. Bookshelves lined the walls. An elderly woman with her gray hair pulled back in a neat bun appeared just as I was perusing one shelf, which was given over entirely to the work of Henri Nouwen.

"Ah, Nouwen," she said lovingly. "Do you admire his work?"

"I do," I said. "Very much."

She pulled down a copy of *Life of the Beloved* and put it in my hands. "This is my favorite," she said, and looked at me sincerely from watery blue eyes.

"I'll take it," I said, even though I had my own copy, and the audio, to boot—read by Nouwen himself.

She walked over to the cash register—the old-fashioned kind, on which you pushed down on keys—and put the book next to it. "Would you like to look around a bit before buying?"

"Sure," I said. Boyd and Marla were eyeing the stat-uettes of the Holy Family. I looked down into a case of rosaries and tried to think how to broach the subject of Holly. *Maybe you knew my friend who used to be a parishioner here, but now she's been murdered?* Could I say that?

"We're having a special on those," the elderly woman, whose name tag announced she was *Nan*, said. She pointed at the rosaries.

"Well," I said, waiting, hoping, that Marla would jump in. No such luck. I said, "Um, how about a Jerusalem Bible?" Nan thumped a paperback copy on the counter next to my Nouwen, and I blithely asked, "How about a CD of Taizé chants?"

From behind me, Marla said, "Goldy, for God's sake, get to the point."

Nan said with a smile, "Do you know which one you would like?"

"The most popular one," I replied.

She brought me a CD of Taizé chants and asked if there was anything else I wanted or needed. I stared at my small pile of purchases, and again tried to think how to bring up the subject of Holly.

"You've been so helpful," I said. "Really, I've never had anyone in a church gift shop be as . . . perfect as you."

Her smile was genuine. "Thank you."

I inhaled and quickly said, "We had a friend. Holly Ingleby. Did you know her?"

Nan was only momentarily taken aback. "Yes. She was a parishioner here."

I nodded, hoping she would continue.

Nan shook her head. "Dear Holly, she used to say that I had good business acumen and I was helpful to others. She guessed I had been born in the north node of Cancer, and she was right."

Now it was my turn to be taken aback. "Holly talked to you about astrology?"

"Oh, it's not really heretical." Thinking I was questioning her orthodoxy, Nan made a dismissive gesture. "Well, I suppose technically it *is* heretical." She sighed. "Not that it mattered. Well, anyway.

She was a parishioner here, but then she got married and moved to Aspen Meadow. She became an Episcopalian. But she obtained a divorce and moved back. She tried to return to Our Lady of Perpetual Grace. They wouldn't let her receive Communion, though."

"We were fellow parishioners of Holly's up in Aspen Meadow."

"Yes, the church beside the creek. St. Luke's." Her brow furrowed. "With Father Pete. How is he?"

I did not know how much information about the attack on Father Pete had been in the paper. I said simply, "He's in the hospital. He needs some tests, and should be out soon." Before we could detour into a discussion of his condition, I said, "So. When Holly was a parishioner here, you . . . were well acquainted with her?"

"Well enough acquainted to talk about astrology, I suppose," she said sadly. "We met when she first attended, and then after her divorce, she did come back from time to time to visit me. I was so angry about her excommunication, I told her she could sell her jigsaw puzzles here in the shop. No reason why the priest should know about that."

My heart jumped. "What kind of puzzles did she bring you?"

"They weren't really religious. But they were very popular choices among the young parents. The children loved them."

"I know," I said. "Holly's son, Drew, and my own son were in preschool together. She made them for the kids. They all loved Holly."

"Well, that wasn't hard to do." Nan hesitated. "I did feel sorry for Holly. She and Drew just broke my heart."

"Broke your heart? You mean, because of the excommunication?"

"No, no." Nan made the same dismissive gesture that I was becoming accustomed to. "When she moved back to Denver, she said she was in love, really in love this time. That was what she said."

"Really in love?" Marla had sidled up beside me. "Sorry"—she read the name tag—"Nan. Holly was my friend, too. Who was she in love with? I mean, it seemed to us, after she divorced George, that she had one relationship after another. She never mentioned *love*. Who was the lucky guy?"

"I don't know," Nan said defensively. "I wasn't going to ask. But I think he was the *reason* she had moved down here. To be near him."

Marla asked, "Was he a doctor? An artist?"

"I don't know. He never came into the shop with her."

"She didn't describe him?" Marla persisted.

"Good Lord," said Nan, putting her hand on her chest. "No, she didn't *describe* him. You two are making me nervous."

"Welcome to my world," said Boyd, from the back of the shop.

"Please." I focused on Nan's lovely face. "My name is Goldy Schulz, and my husband, Tom, works for the Furman County Sheriff's Department. He's leading the investigation into Holly's death—"

"Investigation?" Nan asked softly. "Into what?" Boyd groaned so loudly I thought the statues in the shop quaked. Nan's voice trembled. "I . . . thought Holly died of cardiac arrest. What is being investigated? Why would—"

"I'm sorry to have upset you," I interrupted, cursing myself silently for not checking what had been released to the media. "Tom—"

"Your husband," said Nan, her blue eyes turning steely.

"He's trying to cover all the bases."

"So the sheriff's department sent *you* down here?"

"No, sorry. Because we were Holly's friends, we're asking some informal questions of people who might have known her. Our problem is that, you know, with Holly caring so much about her body, we're . . .

mystified that she would have a coronary. We thought maybe some of the parishioners here, at her former church, might remember her as you seem to."

Nan exhaled. "Of the people who are left here, she knew me the best."

Marla said, "I'll buy that genuine Swarovski crystal rosary if you can give us any details about Holly that we—"

Nan drew herself up. "Are you trying to bribe me? Will you buy me an ice-cream cone if I give you the name of Holly's boyfriend?"

"Marla." I turned to her and opened my eyes wide. "Could you please go stand next to Boyd?"

"I'd like to see some identification, please," Nan said crisply. "I have no idea who you are. I've never seen you before, and now you're spinning some tale about a young woman whom I held dear."

Finally, finally, Boyd shuffled forward. He pulled out his wallet and offered his sheriff's department ID card, which Nan read with rapt attention. Boyd refused to meet my eyes. In a low voice, he said, "Ma'am, Miss . . . Nan, we would appreciate anything you could tell us about Holly. The name of any special male friend would be of particular interest."

"I'm sorry," said Nan. She turned away from him and began purposefully ringing up my purchases. "I don't know any details. Holly seemed like the kind of person who kept a lot of secrets. All I know is that, years ago, she came in one time, and she'd been crying. She always looked so pretty, and she took such good care of herself. Not on this occasion. Her eyes were bloodshot and her skin was splotched, as if she'd been sobbing not just for hours but for days. I comforted her, held her, tried to say encouraging words. But it was all for naught."

"How long ago was this?" asked Boyd.

"Somewhere around eight years ago?" said Nan. "I'm not sure of the time frame. All I am certain of is that she said the man she'd adored, the man she was going to marry, the love of her life . . ." She stopped talking and swallowed. "He had dumped her."

Nan seemed on the verge of tears, and resolutely shook her head when I asked if she remembered anything else. I didn't want to upset her further, so I paid for my purchases and thanked her. Then the three of us left the shop.

"Dumped her?" said Marla, once we were back in the car. "Who would dump Holly?"

"I don't know," I said as I accelerated toward our next stop, Clarkson Shipping. "But at least we have confirmation of one of our theories as to why she moved to Denver after the divorce. It wasn't *just* to go back to art school."

22

I wanted to go find out where Yurbin lived, to see if he would answer some questions. But first, I wanted to check if I could establish whether he was indeed the one who'd sent the box with the collage in it to Holly. Tom had already told me that this could be a fruitless errand. But sometimes people will talk to a couple of civilian women, when the presence of cops intimidates them. At least, that was the slender theory I was working on.

The short young woman working at Clarkson Shipping wore no name tag. She had glossy red curls and when she tilted her head and smiled at us, she revealed crooked teeth. Her freckled brow furrowed as she tried to answer Marla's questions. I looked around. Not only had the owner not spent money on surveillance cameras, he hadn't wasted any dough on decorators. The spare, dirty-white, linoleum-floored space, with a mini-mum of racks displaying packing envelopes and bubble wrap, was meant to discourage lingering.

The redhead searched through computer screens to check on a delivery to Holly's rental address. Yes, she said triumphantly, there it was, a cash transaction. A line began forming behind us; I tried to ignore it. No, the redhead said when we pressed, she was not aware of a tall, buff, forlorn, balding man bringing in that particular package. They sent out big boxes every day, all over the country. In fact, she could think of no tall, muscled guy, between forty and fifty, *ever* coming in.

Belatedly, she asked, "Don't you need a warrant or something?"

"No," said Boyd, proffering his ID. In a low voice, he said, "We're investigating a homicide, and need help. We're trying to identify someone, and we'd appreciate anything you could tell us." He turned to me and lifted one eyebrow, indicating that, of course, the sheriff's department had already been here, and had procured exactly the same information. But they knew where Yurbin lived. We didn't.

No, the redhead went on, the sender did not have an account with them. No, they did not keep track of senders. And of course, what we already knew: no, they did not have a surveillance camera.

We must have looked extremely frustrated. Marla had her hand on her purse, as if to signal that she would try to bribe the redhead, too, if she thought it would get us anywhere. Boyd had thought this expedition was pointless, but now even his shoulders were slumped in defeat.

Marla let out a particularly loud sigh. The line of package-sending hopefuls behind us was lengthening. The redhead groaned. Either she was relenting or just wanted to get rid of us. "Look," she said finally, pointing out the dingy front window. "Try over there. Try Chris. He does a lot of errands for people in the neighborhood, and he's in here all the time. He might be able to help you."

"Over where?" Marla demanded.

"Cathedral Grocery," said the redhead. "Ask for Chris." She called out, "Next!"

Dismissed, we spilled out of Clarkson Shipping and attempted to see what the redhead had been talking about. And there it was, right across the street: a corner store. A dusty sign with gold lettering emblazoned on a dark blue background read CATHEDRAL GROCERY. A newer notice put up next to that one declared AND CAFÉ!

"That remnant of yesteryear," Marla said under her breath. "The neighborhood grocery store. Ah, and there are even tables and chairs out on the sidewalk. I'm suddenly starving. Who wants lunch?"

The three of us sprinted across Clarkson, a one-way street that could bring sudden streams of traffic. The Cathedral Grocery, run by an Asian family of father, mother, teenage son, and teenage daughter, had not only the standard-issue shelves of canned goods and ramen noodles, but also bins of fresh produce: tomatoes, lettuce, string beans, bok choy, mushrooms, and three varieties of onions.

"Your mouth is hanging open," Marla said to me. "Come on, let's sit, order, and find this Chris character."

"Okay."

In typical cop fashion, Boyd had picked out a table in the corner, facing the door. When we joined him, the Asian boy stepped up quickly and handed us menus.

I said, "What do you recommend?"

"*Bánh mì*," he replied without hesitation.

"Great," said Marla. "Beer, Boyd?"

He shook his head. "On duty."

We settled on three iced coffees. Marla thanked our server and he whisked away.

"Tell me what we're having for lunch," said Boyd, his tone resigned. He reluctantly set aside his menu. He had the look of a man who'd really wanted a BLT.

"Vietnamese-style sandwich," I replied. "You're going to love it."

It wasn't long before the daughter of the shop's family brought us small, crispy baguettes bulging with thin slices of grilled lemongrass pork and English cucumber, plus piles of pickled carrot, daikon, and onion, all smeared with a sauce of mayonnaise zipped up with soy sauce and chopped jalapeño. It only took Boyd one tentative bite before he proclaimed it delicious.

I thanked the young woman and looked up at her thoughtfully. "Do you have someone who works here named Chris?"

She nodded and said he was in the back, taking inventory. Did we want to talk to him?

"Very much," I replied.

"Is there something wrong?" she asked anxiously.

"Not at all," I said, pointing to Marla and Boyd, who had their mouths full. "We just need to talk to Chris for a few minutes. About a delivery."

We ate our sandwiches, drank our coffee, and waited.

The shop owner himself came over for our plates. "Chris is almost finished," he assured us. "He can't stop something when he's in the middle. When he's done, he has a couple of deliveries. Is that all right?"

"May we see him before the deliveries?" Marla asked, with a sweet smile.

"Absolutely."

It wasn't long before a short, portly fellow, maybe in his early twenties, stepped up to our table. His complexion was splotched. The sides of his scalp were shaved, with a profusion of blond curls on top. He said, "Do I know you?" His tone was polite, but puzzled.

I asked him if he could sit down. He said he was sorry, but he had work to do. I took a deep breath and asked if he ever picked up parcels for folks in the neighborhood, and shipped them. He gave us a long look. Then he shifted his glance away and said he did, sometimes. Marla, sensing an opportunity to trade money for information with a person who might be willing to accept it, leaned over and snagged her wallet.

"We want to talk to an artist named Yurbin," she said. "We think he might live around here. Chris? Let me see your palm."

When Chris held out his callused paw, Marla put a pile of twenties into it. Boyd closed his eyes and rubbed his forehead. "Holy cow, lady!" Chris exclaimed. "What's all this for?"

"Information," I said quietly, as I didn't want Marla plunging ahead. "A friend of ours died. It's a . . . suspicious death. The day she unexpectedly passed away, a large cardboard box arrived on her front porch." I pointed across the street. "It came from Clarkson Shipping. The object inside the box was a collage that *might* resemble the work of an artist named Yurbin. Do you know him?"

Despite his earlier refusal, Chris now flopped into the one empty chair at our table. He blushed furiously and groaned. "Yeah, I know him. I deliver his groceries and take him lunch three days a week. I also do the occasional odd job for him." He hesitated. "Am I in trouble?"

"Depends," Boyd said quietly. "Did you do something illegal?"

"No." Chris vehemently shook his head. "But I'm the one who takes Yurbin's monthly packages to Clarkson Shipping. They go to a lady in Aspen Meadow." He exhaled. "Yurbin told me I couldn't tell anybody. But then I saw the Furman County Sheriff's Department cars outside his house a few days ago. So I checked the news online. The boxes went to that Holly lady who they said had died. Are you saying she was murdered?" Chris's voice cracked. "Is Yurbin a suspect?"

Boyd pulled out his sheriff's department ID and laid it on the table. Chris looked at it, then moaned. "We don't know if he had anything to do with anything," Boyd said. "But you could help us."

"I will," said Chris. "But *he* won't. I mean, I don't think he would actually hurt somebody. He eats in his house and he makes his art in his house. He's sort of like a hermit."

A hermit who took the trouble to show up uninvited at a birthday party, after which Holly died. A hermit who lawyered up, my brain supplied.

Boyd pulled out a small notebook and pen. "Does Yurbin own a car?"

Chris mulled this over. "Yeah, an old VW. I used to take him where he needed to go, because he doesn't like to drive. So I was surprised to see him go by Friday morning. Yurbin was all hunched over the wheel, like he wasn't sure he remembered how to pilot a vehicle."

Friday had been the day of the party, the day I'd seen someone whom I now suspected was Yurbin in Marla's neighborhood. The day someone had cut off the supports from underneath Holly's deck.

"Did he say why he hadn't had you take him wherever he wanted to go?" I asked, too sharply.

"Nope. He called and canceled his Saturday lunch order, though. I took him lunch on Monday. He didn't mention his little excursion. I don't know where he went or when he got back. He did seem depressed, though. On Monday."

Boyd held his hand up for me to be quiet. "Did you do other errands for Yurbin? Like, say, pick up prescriptions for him?"

Chris thought about that. "Yeah. I used to go to the drugstore, Downing Drugs, for him, but they went out of business a few months ago. I think he orders his meds online now. Mostly, I just take him his meals and I ship boxes for him."

"What sort of medications was Yurbin taking? Does he have an illness?"

Chris looked uncomfortable. "I'm not sure I should be talking about someone else's health stuff, even if you are a cop. I feel like it's invading his privacy. And he's a nut about privacy."

"Someone else told us he was a diabetic. I'm just trying to confirm that information. So you're not breaking any confidences."

Chris shrugged. "Yeah, he's on regular meds for diabetes. And last winter, when we got that big snowstorm and the power went off, Yurbin got pneumonia. I had to go back to the drugstore twice for him then, because he said the antibiotic he'd been given was making him feel sick. So he got a prescription from his doctor for a different one."

Boyd wrote in his notebook. "Do you by any chance remember the name of Yurbin's doctor? That might help us."

Chris shook his head. "Sorry."

"Unbelievable," Marla said under her breath. We were all quiet for a few moments.

"Okay," I said. "So. Yurbin is a diabetic who doesn't like to leave the house. And he loves sweets."

Chris's brow furrowed. "He always wants candy. He said his doctor told him to stick to sugarless sweets. But I'm telling you, unless you've got a Snickers bar for him, he won't let you in. He doesn't like strangers."

"But we're not strangers to *you*," I said cheerfully. "We're Goldy the caterer, her friend Marla, and Sergeant Boyd of the Furman County Sheriff's Department. All you have to do is introduce us as the catering team that makes fresh homemade gelato, right in your home, no charge."

Chris looked dubious, agreed to give it a try, then looked at his watch. "He works out in the afternoons," he added.

Aha, I thought. He had looked muscular. "He doesn't dress as if he cares about his appearance."

Chris held up his right index finger. "He doesn't. But I'm telling you, the man's a beast. After he's done his artwork for the morning, he has lunch. Then he lifts weights. He says it gets his mind off sweets. And even if he lets you in, don't expect hospitality." He arched an eyebrow at Marla and me. Behind us, Boyd chuckled.

Boyd insisted on helping Chris schlep his boxes up to the door of Yurbin's house: a dilapidated two-story, gray-shingled affair. Chris rapped out what sounded like a code on the door.

"Mr. Yurbin?" he called. "You have some visitors who are going to make you some . . ." Chris gave me a puzzled look. "What is it again?"

"Genuine gelato," I supplied.

There was some shuffling and scraping behind the door, but no voice. Then Yurbin's voice said, "No, they can't come in."

"I told you," Chris said noncommittally to Boyd. "And don't think you can shoot your way through. Yurbin had a metal door installed."

"What is he," Marla asked, "a drug dealer?"

Boyd said, "We don't actually shoot our way into houses so much anymore."

When Chris grinned, two dimples like commas appeared in his cheeks.

"Tell him about the gelato," I urged Chris.

"This lady out here?" Chris called. "She's a caterer? She makes this killer gelato that's okay for your diet! Don't you want to try some?"

There was a long pause. Then, "You can bring it in. Tell her and the other two people to go away."

"Whoa," said Marla. "How does he know we're out here?"

Boyd pointed at what looked like a mirror set behind a grate in the metal door. Then he turned away from the mirror and said in a low voice to Marla and me,

"This guy is a hermit who has no social graces. What's more, you know I can't question him, because he's already asked for a lawyer."

"You're not going to question him," I replied. "We are."

"Whatever you get out of him won't be admissible in court."

"I'd rather have you here, and feel safe. Besides, do you think he's going to cop to a murder during this visit?"

Boyd shook his head. "You never know."

The metal door, meanwhile, squeaked open a few inches. "All right," came Yurbin's raspy voice. "Wait!" he exclaimed when he saw me. "You're the one who gave that party Friday night, the party I was kicked out of! Is this a trick?"

"No, no," I said. "We're here to apologize."

"Apologize?" He gripped the edge of the partially open door.

"Look," I said patiently, "Holly Ingleby was our friend. She . . . she felt bad for getting you ejected from the party. She told us what a great collage artist and teacher you were—"

"I simply don't believe she said that to you," Yurbin said, his tone bitter.

Marla trilled over me, "Did you know she had a heart attack and died after the party?" When he didn't answer, she said, "If you'll just let us in for a few minutes, we'll all feel much better. I've always wanted to visit the home of a famous artist."

"The gelato is to make things up to you," I continued. "Chris doesn't know how to make it, so I need to do it. It won't take long."

Finally, finally, he opened the door, but the narrow-eyed skeptical look he gave Marla, Boyd, and me told me he didn't entirely trust us. Which he shouldn't have.

"Since when does it take three people to make gelato?" he asked sarcastically, to which none of us wisely gave an answer.

I followed Boyd, Chris, and Marla through the spare, neat living room. A set of weights lay racked in one corner. We entered the spare, neat kitchen. Despite their reputation for being slobs, most artists I'd encountered were actually quite well organized, and lived in pristine spaces.

I said, "I catered a gallery reception many years ago, where you were the featured artist. So I'm not a stranger either to you or your work. Okay, let's find an electrical outlet."

Yurbin followed us into the kitchen. His plain white T-shirt, black sweatpants, and ancient sneakers spoke precisely of what Chris had told us: Yurbin's artwork might be good, but the man definitely lacked a sense of style.

I plugged in the ice-cream maker, removed the frozen inner container from my cooler, poured in the custard mixture, and let 'er rip. "Okay!" I announced. "Now, that will take about half an hour. Mr. Yurbin?" I said, as if I'd just thought of something. "I still remember those gorgeous collages you made for that gallery showing all those years ago. You began teaching, too, right? But then I heard that you quit that. Did you also stop having shows?"

Yurbin crossed his arms, lifted his chin, and stared at the wall.

"Actually," Marla gushed, "I own a collage of yours from fifteen years ago! I'll bet that piece is worth megabucks now!" She smiled brightly to reinforce her lie.

Yurbin exhaled but did not look at her. "It *should* be worth megabucks."

"But," said Marla, with exaggerated puzzlement, "why wouldn't it be? You're *so* talented."

That did it. The other thing I'd learned about artists in my years of catering was not only were they neatniks, they had ultrasensitive egos.

"Well," Yurbin said, relenting. "Thank you."

"Oh," I said, feigning excitement. "I knew it! Would you show us your studio?"

Yurbin's gaze traveled from Chris, who said, "Aw, go ahead," to Boyd, who managed a shy, well-acted grin, to Marla and me, who were nodding enthusiastically.

"I suppose," he said finally, then blushed. "Since you're fans."

"We're definitely fans," I said emphatically. "Why do you think I'm making you gelato?"

"I'll stay here and hunt up bowls and spoons," Chris volunteered.

Yurbin pretend-grumbled under his breath, but then led the way up a flight of wooden, uncarpeted stairs. Boyd followed directly behind him in the narrow space. As we all turned a corner and climbed another flight, I wondered when the last time I'd worked out was.

"Do you think it's possible this guy is the father of Drew?" Marla whispered, right next to me.

I stopped, panting. "I have no idea."

Yurbin led the way into the airy space of what must have once been an attic. Skylights had been installed in the ceiling to allow studio-quality light. The floors and walls had been painted a pale blue. A long worktable was set against one wall, underneath which sat neatly stored plastic bins. An oversize corkboard hung above the table, with several newspaper articles tacked to it. An easel was set up, but empty.

Yurbin walked with uncharacteristic quickness over to the corkboard, ripped off the articles, and stuffed them in a pocket of his sweatpants.

"Oh, you're so humble," said Marla. "I'll bet those were articles about you and your work!"

"No," he replied, then looked up at a skylight.

"You won't show them to me?" asked Marla, acting dejected.

"Maybe this was a bad idea. I think it's time you left," Yurbin said, as he moved his gaze to the floor.

I said, "But your gelato will be ready soon. It's creamy, and sweet, and absolutely luscious."

Marla walked up to the easel and stared at it. "I thought we could see one of your collages in progress. Are you not working on anything now?" she asked, acting hugely disappointed. "Oh, that's *such* a shame."

"Well . . ." Yurbin began, but then clamped his mouth shut. He reflected for a moment, then said, "I could show you a few raw pieces, but nothing really worked out. I'll be starting on a big project again very soon."

I asked, "What sort of project?"

He lifted his chin in what appeared to be defiance. "I'll be giving a one-man show in the near future. Maybe . . . Christmas."

And then. And then. I spied something in one of those plastic boxes. "Is that Chris calling from downstairs? Maybe he can't find the spoons," I said. Yurbin moved toward the staircase, while Boyd placed himself casually between the muscled artist and me. I raced over to the worktable and pulled out the bin I'd noticed, popped the top, and pulled out pieces of Patsie Boatfield's blue-striped dress.

Yurbin heard the noise and whirled. "What do you think you're doing? That's my property. You had no right."

I held up the fabric in accusation. "I recognized this dress. It belonged to a friend of mine. She gave it to Holly to use in a collage for her. You weren't just Holly's former art teacher, were you? You were her business partner. She found the clients and obtained the materials, but you created the actual collages. That's why no one knew where her studio was located, because this"—I indicated the spacious loft—"was where the work was done."

"Did Holly tell you that?" demanded Yurbin.

"No," I admitted. "But she said you were trying to manipulate her. I'm guessing your partnership had gone sour and you wanted more money. Twenty-five thousand, to be exact. Was that what you expected from Holly? Was it why you showed up at her son's birthday party, the night she died?"

Yurbin said, "I want a lawyer."

I said, "You don't need a lawyer. I'm not a cop. Holly was my friend and I just want to know what happened to her. You may need a lawyer later, though, after I tell the cops what I saw here, and they get a warrant to search this workshop. You lied to them about your relationship with Holly and you may have been trying to blackmail her."

"I wasn't blackmailing her," Yurbin protested. "And you came here under false pretenses."

"No," I countered. "That sugar-free gelato is still churning away down in your kitchen. And I did want to talk about Holly. And about your art. Is that what those articles you put in your pocket are about? How successful Holly was with her collages? That must have made you kind of resentful, her getting all the glory."

Yurbin's face fell. "It's none of your business."

"I can just reach into your pocket and we can find out," Marla said, her tone menacing.

Yurbin spun around, fists clenched. His biceps bulged under his T-shirt, but then he stepped away from her. "Leave me alone!" he cried. "Go away."

"The truth is going to come out, Mr. Yurbin," I said, "one way or another. If you offer your side of it, you won't have to keep living a lie. Were you the talent behind Holly's success?"

He looked at the fragment of Patsie's dress still dangling from my hand and seemed to be calculating what to say. "Yes. Yes," Yurbin said. "All right? She had the beauty and the body and the ability to promote herself, to promote my work. She was making big bucks off *my* collages. I wanted to be fairly compensated."

"How much did she pay you for each piece?" I asked.

Yurbin gazed at the skylight. "Just two, sometimes three, thousand dollars each."

"And do you know how much she sold them for?"

"*Lots,*" he replied, his tone again enraged.

"Between four and six thousand dollars each," I said calmly. "*And* she came up with the ideas for the projects. She did the promotion and dealt with the clients. Remember, I saw your work at your opening." I didn't mean for my voice to sound as derisive as it came out. "Your work wasn't *popular*. Holly found a way to make it appealing to a wide audience." When Yurbin glared at me and crossed his arms, I went on: "But you wanted to confront her, and wanted far more than what had been the going rate for the collages." I tilted my head at him. "Maybe what you missed was the attention, the prestige that came to Holly, instead of you."

He flicked this remark away as if it had no bearing on the matter. "If Holly didn't tell you about me, how did you know I asked for twenty-five thousand dollars for this last piece?"

"You put a note with that amount typed on it in the box that held the last collage. It was delivered to Holly's porch the day she died. The police have it, and the collage with part of this dress in it, and they know that the box was mailed from Clarkson Shipping. And now we know for sure that Chris mailed that box and others to Holly for you."

"She promised me," he continued stubbornly, "that our arrangement would be a fair partnership. She assured me that she would help me promote other art projects under my own name. But she just kept taking all the credit for my work."

"Heads up, Yurbin," said Marla. "You and Holly were collaborators. She never cheated you. And now all you have are crappy collages no one else wants."

"You're wrong," he insisted. "I'm going to have a one-man show and give you all a lesson in what superb art really is."

I said, "Mr. Yurbin, you're going to have to talk to the police eventually. We know from Chris that you left Denver on Friday morning. He didn't see you again until Monday. I'm pretty sure I saw you near Marla's house on Friday. You darted out from behind a bush, and to avoid you, I steered my van into a boulder. You ran away, but we know you were at the party Friday night, because we saw you there."

"So? Holly and I had a business dispute and I was trying to resolve it. I never threatened her. She used to be my student, after all."

"Holly was your student," I said slowly. "At one time the two of you were close. Was there more between you than art? Maybe long ago? Before her divorce, even?"

Yurbin's brow furrowed. "I have absolutely no idea what you're talking about."

I said pleasantly, "I'm talking about you and Holly having an affair. Maybe when she was in art school the first time, say, eighteen years ago? Then she got married. Did you keep up a relationship?"

Yurbin said, "You're sick."

I persisted, "Perhaps you felt rejected in more ways than one. Seventeen years ago, Holly had a son, Drew. It was his birthday party you decided to crash. If you and Holly had a thing, there's a very real possibility that Drew is your son."

Yurbin's jaw dropped, but he gave away nothing. "I've lost my taste for gelato. And I'm done answering your questions."

Boyd, who'd been quiet through this entire exchange, said, "That's our cue."

Yurbin gestured to the narrow staircase. His tone was frigid when he said, "Take your ice cream and get out. Don't come back. Ever."

23

We took the gelato home. I wasn't going to leave it with a creep who hadn't cared about Holly, even if he was a diabetic. On our way back up the mountain, I called Tom and left a detailed voice mail summarizing our visits with Nan at the gift shop, Chris at the Cathedral Grocery, and Yurbin, that arrogant collaborator. Boyd was writing his own version of them in his notebook, so there would be two records of what we'd witnessed.

Plus, I'd kept the scrap of Patsie's dress. I knew it was probably not worth much as actual incriminating evidence. Still, I wanted Yurbin to think we had something on him.

On the way home, Marla and I speculated, yet again, as to who had killed Holly and why. She'd been trying to get money out of someone, that much was clear. Whether it was to pay Yurbin his newly hiked-up prices, we did not know. Nor were we any closer to figuring out who Drew's biological father was, or if this information was even relevant to the case. Boyd contributed nothing to the discussion. He was actually looking a bit haggard, which was the way I felt, too.

Once we were back in my kitchen, I heated Julian's leftover fudge sauce. Boyd declined a sweet fix, as did Julian. So I doled out large scoops of the creamy vanilla gelato for Marla and me. Julian cluck-clucked over our little detour from strict nutritional guidelines. Marla countered that we needed the dessert for emotional, not dietary, reasons. Julian smiled, said nothing, and whipped around the kitchen preparing our family dinner: fresh corn chowder and my signature chef salads, grilled chicken optional.

I felt a delightful shiver from eating the chocolate. Was my mind kicking back into gear, or was I imagining it? Who cared? I licked my spoon and set my empty bowl aside. "We know Holly studied with Yurbin after her divorce, when she was in art school. But she may also have studied with him before she married George, back before she had to drop out the first time."

"Could Tom check?" Marla asked.

"He can try. Let me send him a text." When I'd done this, I said, "We don't know if Yurbin and Holly were sexually involved. But for someone who says he's innocent, he's acting awfully guilty."

"Agreed," said Marla. "But he might be feeling a twinge of conscience for demanding more money for the collages." We left hanging the unspoken question, about whether poisoning Holly could be weighing on Yurbin's soul. If he had one, that is.

I said, "Let's go back. Holly *dropped out* of art school when she married George. We have no idea whether Yurbin was her teacher at that time, and we have no further idea whether she'd been sleeping with him—"

"So Yurbin may or may not be the father of Drew."

"Right. She got pregnant around the time of the medical conference in Boulder, which would mean Neil Unger or Warren Broome could still be the father—"

Marla said, "You're right. But let's not forget Yurbin. Say Holly studied with him and put him on a pedestal. So say their sexual relationship continued, after she divorced George and moved to Denver. If he was the man Nan was talking about, why would he dump Holly?"

"I don't know."

"The guy is arrogant but talented. He could have dumped Holly, and then, years later, had regrets. That could explain why he showed up at the party, or why he suddenly got all pissy about the prices for collages. But going back, Holly could have become pregnant anytime in July, eighteen years ago. You know how unpredictable this forty-weeks-of-pregnancy statistic is."

"True," I admitted. "What we need to find out is who Holly was seeing in July, eighteen years ago."

"Good luck with that," said Marla, setting aside her bowl.

"So segue to when Holly went back to art school, after she divorced George. None of her pieces had sold up to that point. It was in that time period that I catered the gallery show where I saw Yurbin's new work, the collages that reminded me of what Holly later started doing. At some point during that time, Holly *also* saw Yurbin's work. She started studying with him again. She realized Yurbin's work could be used for a new concept: the portrait-collage. She hired him, and because she was gorgeous and a good promoter, the work was a success, if not on the level of, you know, Rembrandt."

"Did Rembrandt even do collages?"

"Marla, please. No. Okay, so. Eventually, Yurbin wanted a bigger piece of what turned out to be a pretty small pie. Or maybe he just wanted Holly back in the sack."

Boyd rubbed his forehead. "You two are so much worse than men."

Marla and I ignored this while we washed and dried our bowls and spoons. We hadn't come up with any new ideas by the time Arch phoned and asked if Gus could come over for dinner. Julian heard the request, and nodded.

"Tell him it's cool," he said. "I can make more chowder and salad, maybe add some focaccia I have frozen. And this afternoon I baked two more kinds of brownies using extra-bittersweet chocolate. One is flavored with ginger, the other with chile."

I said, "Sounds fabulous. Between the two of us, we're going to come up with a great spicy brownie."

Julian just grinned.

I told Arch that we were having corn chowder, chef salads, focaccia, and spicy brownies. Would Gus go for that?

"Is Julian making it?" When I said he was, Arch said, "Oh, that'll be fine, then." It didn't occur to me to be offended, because Julian's cooking truly was amazing.

"May I stay, too?" Marla asked. "I've been wondering about this spicy chocolate phenomenon. I mean, if they can put salt in caramel and Parmesan cheese in ice cream, why not?"

"Of course we want you with us, Marla," I replied. "You, too," I said, motioning to Boyd.

Boyd said, "Thanks. I won't be able to stay for supper. Although I do think your food is great, Julian."

Julian smiled, nodded, and went back to shucking corn.

I tried to think while I was setting the table. At length, I asked Marla, "Do you think there could be *anything* else in the Amour Anonymous notes?"

She groaned. "Oh, *please.* We've gone through those notes. I mean, I want to figure this mess out as much as you do. We need to protect Drew. It's important to find out what happened to Holly and Father Pete and Kathie Beliar. But the Amour notes? Forget it."

"I just can't imagine where else to look." I turned this question over as we put out the dinner dishes. Finally, I said, "There might be a couple of long shots we haven't yet investigated. Got to warn you, though, I think the chances of finding anything in either spot are pretty remote."

"Please tell me we don't have to go back out today."

"Let me check my schedule, see what I have coming up." The kitchen computer was already booted, so I scrolled through screens. Julian and I didn't have

456 · DIANE MOTT DAVIDSON

anything planned until late Thursday afternoon, when we would take a food delivery. On Friday, we would prep for a wedding on Saturday, to be held at my conference center. I asked Marla, "How do you feel about tomorrow? Wednesday?" When she nodded, I said, "Let me call around, see if either of these ideas could pan out."

While Marla checked her own messages, I called the Shangri-la Spa in Cherry Creek. It was still in business. I could not remember the name of the colorist who had put the highlights in my hair all those years ago, when Holly had treated me to our day of pampering. My description of a short, thin, pale woman with curly blond hair did not sound familiar to the receptionist. When I asked if I could speak to the owner, she went and got him.

"Sure, I remember that stylist," said the owner, whose name was Phil. "Wendy Williams. A very talented woman." When I took a deep breath and asked if he knew where she was working now, Phil said, "I'm sure *we* could put in some *gorgeous* highlights for you."

"I know that. I just really need to speak to Wendy. It's on a personal matter." Phil, resigned, gave me the name of a hair place in Boulder: Mane Street. Cute. But I said only, "That's perfect."

"Perfect?"

I said hastily, "I have to go to Boulder tomorrow anyway."

Tom arrived home just after five. He looked as discouraged as I'd ever seen him. He said he was taking a shower and would be down shortly.

"Your husband doesn't look too good," Marla observed. "Do you have any decent wine we can open?"

"Just some of that Cabernet you gave us last time. It's in the pantry."

"Great news. Julian, find me a corkscrew."

When Tom came down to the kitchen, I handed him a glass of wine. We made a toast to Father Pete's recovery—Tom said the latest update was *no change*—and then Boyd, Marla, and I gave Tom a live blow-by-blow of our visit to the church gift shop, to Clarkson Shipping, to the Cathedral Grocery, and finally, to that ever-unhelpful artist Yurbin. I handed him the piece of fabric from Patsie's dress.

"Yurbin called the department to complain about you," said Tom, turning the material over in his hands. "He said you came into his house under false pretenses, and that nothing he said to you or showed you could be used against him. I mean, not that you would use the fact that he was making those portrait-collages against him."

"The heck you say," said Marla, refilling everyone's glasses. "I'm calling the *Denver Post*. 'What failed artist is abusing the reputation of the now-deceased Holly Ingleby—' "

Tom shook his head. "Don't even go there."

"Him wanting to take credit for the collages, and wanting more money for them than Holly could give, strengthens his motivation to kill her," I said stubbornly. "He wanted more cash and *all* the fame. Plus, he may have had leftover antibiotic that he could have used."

"Maybe." Tom skewed his mouth sideways. "A lot of people keep leftover antibiotic. If you're looking for the person who knew Holly's cardiac problems, had the easiest access to medicine, and was having some kind of conflict with her, that would be George Ingleby."

"But you've come up with little that would implicate him," I said.

"Right. In answer to the questions you texted me? We found out Holly was taking a course in design with Yurbin right before she married George. After she divorced George, when she moved to Denver? She took another course with Yurbin, this one in collage. Not long afterward, he quit the school. As far as anyone we talked to knows, he has no visible means of support. Our guys are going to pay him another visit tomorrow, try to put the fear of God in him. See if he owns up to anything more than making the artworks and working to extract more money from Holly."

"Yikes," said Marla. "With the golden goose dead, maybe he'll have to build another business. He could start one called Yurbin's Turbans."

"Anything else, Tom?" I asked.

Tom gave Marla a look, then went on: "We can't track down any credible source who can definitively tell us Holly had a thing going with Warren Broome. Lena Ingleby admitted to hearing gossip that they'd had an affair, but it was in the past. One person *was* willing to say Holly was flirting with Warren, in an outrageous manner, at that conference eighteen years ago."

"An outrageous manner?" I echoed. "Who's your source?"

"*George* Ingleby," Tom said. "When Holly told him she was going to hike the Flatirons with Warren, he admitted he was crazy with jealousy. He and Holly were newly married, and he felt the way she acted was inappropriate."

I shook my head, remembering how, after we were married, the Jerk had thrown his flirtations with other women in my face. I sympathized with George on this one. Still, I didn't think it was right, in the ethical department, for George to have cut off child support for Drew all these years later, once he found out Drew wasn't his biological son. In the choice between placating Lena and providing for Drew, he should have chosen the latter, I firmly believed.

"Problem is," Tom went on, "Warren Broome remembers Holly flirting with him, but he claims he never went hiking with her. That doesn't mean that she didn't hook up with him, at the conference or later. But Warren denies ever being with Holly, even after her divorce." He seemed to be turning a thought over in his head. Finally he said, "A number of people told us Holly had the reputation of being what we used to call *loose*, if we still talked like that."

"Oh, come on, Tom," Marla teased. "We still call someone a loose *cannon*, don't we?"

"Look, ladies, whatever Holly got up to in her sexual life, whoever the biological father of Drew is, these things may or may not have relevance to Holly's actual death, unless the truth about Drew's paternity was what she was using to blackmail someone. That could be Neil Unger. He was at that conference in Boulder, right? He's only fifty-something now—"

"And not bad-looking," Marla murmured.

"Warren Broome was there," said Tom.

"True," I said. "Also with money, also good-looking. And despite what he says, he seems a bit obsessed with

Holly." I took a sip of wine. "Maybe the reason he's had not one but two meltdowns, both directed at me, is that she had something on him."

Tom said, "I can tell you what he told us after we hauled him away from our front door here. He said you, Miss G., kept asking questions, and he wanted to know why you were harassing him and his wife about Holly Ingleby."

"Me?" I said. I tried to sound innocent.

"He lost his temper because people are coming out of the woodwork now, trying to accuse him of misconduct." I thought of Audrey, but nodded for Tom to go on. "He says when you told him you had some information for him from Holly, he was worried about what kind of lies Holly could have been spreading about him. Then he and Patsie had a big argument about it. And this was all right after his suspension was up. So he drove over here and had a meltdown, all because he saw his life going back down the tubes."

"*Lies?*" I asked, incredulous.

Tom shrugged. "Drew's paternity is just one issue. You have George and Lena. They were fighting with Holly. You have Yurbin in a conflict with her over money. You have Warren, sort of, and Neil Unger, maybe. Plenty of suspects to go around. We just don't have that missing piece, or several missing pieces, that would tell us more about Holly."

"How about Drew?" I asked quickly. "Arch and Gus are on their way back home for dinner. I want to hear what you know about him before they arrive."

"Drew has been great," Tom admitted. "He's answered all our questions. The trooper who's keeping an eye on him says Drew stays up after his aunt and uncle are in bed." He stopped. "Then the kid goes out on the back porch of the cabin, the one facing the water. And cries."

"Oh, Lord," I muttered.

Boyd asked if he could take off; Yolanda, his girl-friend, was waiting for him. Tom told him absolutely, that he hadn't even needed to spend the previous night with us. He tipped his head and said he'd wanted to be here for our family. We all thanked him for his help. He was so good-natured, not to mention long-suffering, that I wanted to give him some wine or food to take home. But he said that Yolanda and her aunt, Ferdinanda, were making *cubanos* for their supper. He'd promised to come home hungry.

Arch and Gus arrived not long after Boyd left. From their day building trails, they were both red from sun-burn, not to mention covered with dirt and dust. They promised to shower and change quickly. And yes, they'd use more sunscreen next time. Bob had been in a bad mood all day, Arch said. That might explain why he had forgotten the tube of sunscreen he usually brought.

"Huh," said Marla, with exaggerated innocence, "I wonder why Bob Rushwood could be in a bad mood."

Tom gave her another one of his hooded looks, and she didn't pursue it. The boys clomped upstairs.

Once everyone was showered and seated, we gave thanks for the food, and again prayed for Father Pete and for Drew. I added a silent request that we could figure out what had happened to Holly, as I'm sure Tom did, too. We dug into the rich, thick chowder, and swooned. Whoever thought fresh corn could impart such sweet, creamy loveliness to a soup? The chef salads were made with luscious, sweet tomatoes, sliced hard-cooked eggs, chopped celery, dollops of smooth chèvre, chopped pecans and dates, chunks of ripe avocado, and buttery homemade croutons, all arranged over plates of baby field greens. Julian said the dates gave the salads an exotic quality. The homemade lemon vinaigrette was perfect, and didn't clash with the wine. And as if all that weren't enough, there were platters of grilled chicken and focaccia in the middle of the table.

To my surprise, the mood of Arch and Gus was much more glum than it had been at the fund-raising dinner. I gently asked them what was going on. They said their work out in the Preserve had been fine, but they were tired. And sunburned. And . . .

"And what?" I prompted.

"And we're putting money together for Drew," Arch said. "Each kid on the fencing team has committed to putting in, or raising, a hundred dollars over the summer. We want to give him over a thousand bucks in the fall, in case he needs it for clothes, or whatever. I mean, okay, George Ingleby is rich, but who knows whether Lena will be nice to Drew? We're also making a card for him." He stared at the table. "It's just depressing. You know, Holly was such a happy person. She was always having fun, helping other people make stuff, you know. This is just . . . wrong."

"You got that right." I looked at my son. "I remember when Holly was your art teacher at Montessori. I'd be there sometimes, making the snacks, and I saw you all gathered in a circle around her." I hesitated. "Do you remember when Holly and I helped your class make papier-mâché breakfast foods?"

"Sort of," Arch said.

"Do you recall some of the other projects you did with her?"

"Mom, are you kidding? You want me to try to remember some stuff from, like, a million years ago?"

"If you can," I said mildly. "Sometimes recalling something good from the past helps a person deal with a loss in the present."

Arch exhaled loudly. *"Mom."*

Tom said, "Please, Arch? I'd like to hear it."

There was a long pause while Arch stared at the kitchen wall. "Okay," he said finally, "by the time we were five, it wasn't like she only did art projects with us."

Marla said, "It wasn't? What did she do with you?"

"She wanted us to be more creative, or to show us that being creative was fun. She had this big canvas bag that she called her Fun Sack."

"Oh, wait," I said. "I remember that bag."

Arch said, "She'd bring in things—"

"What kind of things?" Tom asked, endeavoring to sound only mildly interested.

Arch's brow wrinkled in frustration. "Okay," he said after a moment, "like a toy, say. Or a dish. I only remember a couple of these, you know."

Tom made his voice encouraging. "Just tell us what you recall."

Arch scratched the back of his head. "Every year, she brought in a dish with a picture of a horse on it. We guys in the class thought it was lame"—I pictured five-year-old boys pretending to gag—"but she said, 'This horse is trapped near a castle. Make a picture. Tell a story with what you paint.' So we'd do that. Then she would say, 'Okay, now I'm going to turn this exercise around. What else could "pony" mean?' And we were like, 'What?' And she said, 'You pony up money, or goods, like in a store. You can do a dance called the Pony.' And then she put on some music and did this dance that was called the Pony. We thought that was pretty cool, actually, and so kids did pictures of horses, and people dancing, and shoppers handing over money. Like that."

After a pause, I said, "Anything else you can think of from the Fun Sack?"

Arch pointed his chin to the ceiling as he thought. He was not enjoying this. But I wanted to know every single thing about Holly that was in anyone's memory, the better to reconstruct the case. And I really did think it would help Arch if he could fish up some pleasant recollections of Holly. What he was dealing with now, what we were all dealing with, was recalling her sprawled on the pavement outside Marla's house, all that life and energy gone out of her.

"No," said Arch. "Mom, these memories are *not* all great."

"Sorry," I said.

Arch reached out and squeezed my shoulder. "It's okay. I know you're trying to help. Gosh, Mom, *don't*."

It wasn't until then that I realized tears were streaming down my cheeks. Later, after we'd done the dishes, Marla had departed, and Gus and Arch had unrolled sleeping bags, I thought of Drew.

Arch was right: these memories were not all great.

Wednesday morning arrived very early, or rather the sunlight associated with the coming solstice did. Once again, Tom was up first, moving silently around the bedroom so as not to disturb me.

"How's your leg, Miss G.?" he whispered.

"Throbbing. But not as bad as the past few days."

"I made your iced coffee last night," he said. "Didn't want to wake up Arch and Gus with the espresso maker. I thought they were going to sleep in the living room. But Arch convinced Julian to sleep on one of his beds, and Gus curled up on the other. Arch slept on the floor of his room." Tom paused. "Arch told me last night that he felt really bad, making you cry."

"He didn't bring on my case of the weepies. The memory of Holly did that."

"I told him." He checked his watch. "So, where are you going today?"

I said we were off to the Flatirons Conference Center, to see if they had any records or photographs from the long-ago docs' convention archived, or if they had staff still there who would remember Holly. "Someone might remember her, recall who she'd been hanging out with. There could be notes there about what activities she did, and who she did them with, like, I don't know, who she hiked with, or played tennis with, or whatever."

"Oh, Miss G.," said Tom, resigned. "From eighteen years ago? That is such a long shot."

"Tom, being there might jog my own memory." When he groaned, I said, "But first, I'm going to try to visit with a woman named Wendy Williams. She's a hair colorist who works in Boulder now," I rushed on. "She used to do Holly's highlights. The day Holly took me down to Cherry Creek, Holly chatted away with her about her love life. As far as we all know, Holly still went to Wendy. She could have told her about issues we haven't fully uncovered, such as, who was the guy in Denver she loved so much? What were her past romances? She might even have told Wendy about the fight with George about child support."

Tom shook his head. "Goldy . . ."

"You always said you trusted my instincts."

"Yeah," he said. "I do. In fact, since I gave Boyd the day off, I'll come with you today."

"Really?"

"There's not much I can do until the medical examiner gets back to me with the full autopsy results."

"What else is going on?" I asked, unable to keep the suspicion out of my voice.

He reared back in mock astonishment. "What, am I not allowed to accompany you on your fact-finding missions?"

"No, no, of course you are," I said hastily. "Besides, you're right, poor Boyd needs a break."

He told me Sergeant Jones had volunteered to accompany Arch again that day, and would be at the house at half-past seven. I made mental notes to thank, and give baked goods and anything else I could think of, to both Sergeant Boyd and Sergeant Jones.

While Tom left to make phone calls, rearranging his schedule for that day, I moved through my yoga routine. My leg was doing a bit better, and had gone from being black-and-blue to being mostly purple. I supposed this was improvement. Then I showered, dressed, and sipped the coffee Tom had left for me, a chilled latte laced with whipping cream. I walked downstairs carefully, so as not to wake the boys. Tom, meanwhile, had disappeared into the dining room, where he was asking someone to check on something.

It was quarter to seven. Arch and Gus would be leaving at quarter to eight, and we were set to take off soon after that. But the boys would need breakfast. The walk-in revealed—miracle of miracles—a package of Arch's favorite Canadian bacon. That would do for the protein, but what else would the boys like?

Back in the dark ages—when I was a scholarship student at a Virginia boarding school—I'd fallen in love with a particular breakfast: cinnamon toast and applesauce. Just like the early evening gelato, the cinnamon toast wouldn't meet any of Julian's preferred nutritional guidelines. But I figured, what the heck.

"Cooking, boss?" Julian's voice from the kitchen doorway made me jump. "We don't have an event today."

"This is breakfast."

"A salty meat?" he said. "I knew I should have stayed in bed."

Tom entered the kitchen and pocketed his cell phone. He washed up and said he and Julian could set the table.

The cinnamon toast took some thought. It had not been the version people usually eat, which comes from toasting bread slices, spreading butter on them, then sprinkling cinnamon sugar on top. No, the southern kind I remembered had a crunchy, buttery texture, as if the cinnamon sugar had baked into a crust on top of the bread. How would I achieve that?

I stared at a loaf of plain white bread that we had thawed the night before, just in case there wasn't enough focaccia, which there had been. After some thought, I preheated the oven and sliced the bread. While a stick of unsalted butter slowly melted and swirled into a golden pool on the stove, I made the cinnamon sugar. I toasted the bread slices lightly on one side in the oven, flipped them, brushed them with melted butter, and sprinkled a thick layer of cinnamon sugar on top.

"Well," said Tom over my shoulder, "if the boys need a sugar rush to get started on their trail building, they'll have it."

"Can you check to see if we have applesauce in the pantry?"

"We do. I'll put some out in a bowl."

Arch and Gus's thrashing around upstairs was my signal to put the toast into the oven, along with the sliced Canadian bacon. Julian, Tom, and I quickly poured the juice. When the doorbell rang, Tom said, "Don't let anybody but Jones in."

It was indeed Sergeant Jones, who'd come in her own prowler. I made her regular drip coffee—I'd learned my lesson about coffee-for-cops—then pulled shots of espresso and poured cream on top for Marla, who arrived at half-past seven, complaining that it was too early for anyone to be up. She sported a bright green top, blue pants, sapphire barrettes in her hair, and green flats.

"I wanted to wake myself up with color," she said by way of explanation. I handed her her iced latte and noticed her eyes were twinkling. "But I didn't even need my outfit to cheer me up, because I checked my voice mail. A country-club friend left a message for me last night. You'll never guess." When I didn't, she went on, "Ophelia Unger has hired an attorney from Brewster's firm to go after her dear old dad for fraud."

Tom chuckled. I shook my head. I certainly hoped at least *one* financial criminal in this nation was going to be held accountable for his actions.

I said, "I wonder if somebody in law enforcement could demand a DNA sample from Neil. It's still possible he's Drew's biological father, and that Holly threatened him and tried to get money out of him, and that he tried to get rid of both her and Drew."

"Because," Marla said triumphantly, "that might really get him into boiling water with The Guild."

Tom sighed but said nothing.

The cinnamon toast emerged crusty and perfect, and everyone except Marla agreed it was the best. She held up her hand in a gesture of forbearance and said simply, "Carbs. No can do."

We finished eating around ten to eight. I looked at the detritus in the kitchen—the toast crusts, the few remaining slices of Canadian bacon, the puddle of applesauce—not to mention all the dishes and cups. I was worried about getting everything cleaned up before we left.

Julian, as usual, read my mind. "Boss? Let me do the dishes."

"No—"

"Wait." Julian waggled his eyebrows, Groucho Marx–style. "I'll do it in exchange for some information."

Intrigued, I leaned forward, as did Marla, nosy as ever. "What?"

"Do you know if Ophelia Unger and her first fiancé made a clean break?"

"Yeah," I said, "they did. But she was still broken up about it, and that led her into the arms of Bob Rushwood. And we all know how that ended up."

"All right, then," said Julian. "Ophelia seems like a together person who knows her own mind now. I have money and don't need any from her. So . . . can you find out if she would be willing to go out with me?"

24

Tom offered to drive my van, and I gladly accepted. Marla sat in back, nursing a second latte.

The cool morning boasted a crystalline blue sky, with snow visible on the far mountains. A breeze had swept away the pollen and now broke the light on the lake into shards. I twisted around to get a look at Holly's house above the water. The collapsed deck above the rocks had the appearance of a half-done construction project. The crash from the deck had also taken out part of the outdoor staircase to the lake. I sighed. We would have to go back into the place before the memorial service, to see if we could dig up photos to display . . .

I veered away from that thought as we descended the interstate. The meadow grass on both sides of the road went from barely emerging to neon green. That was the difference between eight thousand feet above sea level and six thousand. Late spring in the mountains was a long-arriving affair.

Tom turned onto the road between Golden and Boulder, which runs along a geographical formation called the Hogback. That's what it looks like: the razor-spined exoskeleton of a wild hog. Maybe other states had hogbacks, too, but this was *our* hogback, and it had two distinguishing features, aside from the aforementioned razoring. The first was, you could hardly get any cell-phone reception when you were driving along it. The second was that there was a great white *M* painted on one of the mountains rising above Golden, home to the Colorado School of Mines—hence the *M*. When Arch was five, he'd asked if the whole alphabet was written across the country. The Jerk had told him that it was a stupid question, and Arch had begun to suck his thumb.

"Now that just pisses me off," said Marla. Something hit my back, and I realized it was my friend flinging her cell phone. "Oops, sorry, Goldy. My aim isn't too good. I mean, I'm trying to hold my latte, too."

"Who were you trying to reach?" I asked.

"Ophelia Unger, to see if she would go out with Julian. But I couldn't get any stupid reception along this stupid hogback."

"Marla," I said, "she's been through a lot of trauma. She lost her first fiancé, had to deceive her father, then was stalked and spied on by Bob Rushwood. At the very least, she'll need a good therapist. Are you sure you want to do this?"

"I'm not saying they have to get married, for God's sake," Marla argued. "But she could help him with, you know, direction. He could give her loyalty and trustworthiness, both of which have been sorely lacking in her life."

"Loyalty and trustworthiness," I muttered, then closed my eyes.

Tom put his hand on my knee. "Are you all right?"

"Yeah, thanks. Fine."

"What's going on?" Marla asked, her voice suddenly threaded with concern.

"Oh, I was just remembering when the Jerk used to yell at Arch. I was thinking about fathers telling their offspring they're not good enough. The Jerk did it to Arch, and Neil Unger did it to Ophelia."

"Ophelia was older," Marla said authoritatively. "Neil probably didn't hurt Ophelia's confidence as much as the Jerk hurt Arch's. And of course," she added quickly, "Arch is doing great now."

"I keep thinking there should have been something I could have done."

"Miss G.," Tom murmured.

"You did do something," Marla said. "You kicked his ass to the curb. As did I."

"But apparently he didn't learn," I said.

"Neither did you," Marla replied tartly, "if you're going to replay this tape of 'Oh, there should have been something I could have done.'"

"All right, all right."

Marla's phone pinged, indicating reception. She had to scrabble around on the car floor to find it. I smiled as she asked one of her pals if she had Ophelia Unger's cell number.

Tom asked, "Where do you want to go first, ladies?"

"Mane Street," I said. "The salon. If we get there before clients start flocking in, we should have a better chance of seeing Wendy."

We took off for Mane Street, which was actually on Pearl Street.

Pearl was clogged with parked cars, so Tom searched for a place on Pine.

"Is this Wendy character even expecting us?" asked Marla. "Because I'm trying to figure out if we should come back over here for lunch. There are some good places to eat on Pearl."

"I left a message on the salon voice mail," I said.

"That does not reassure me," said Marla. "What if she doesn't get in until later?"

As we walked to Mane Street, Tom said he would wait outside. "It would be better if you all just chatted with her. If I come in, it adds a whole law enforcement dimension to this thing that I'm not sure you want."

"Just chat," I said, for clarification.

"Yup," said Tom.

"Okay, Marla. Here's our story: We're planning the memorial service for Holly—"

"Which we are," Marla said.

"We . . . can't find Holly's address book, let's say. The cops have it, but never mind that. We'll say we want *all* her friends to be notified of the service. And there was a certain someone she was going to tell us about, but died before she could. We were wondering if Wendy knows who that is. We'll also try to find out about other issues in Holly's life, like the child support thing."

"I tell my colorist everything," Marla said. "And she's the best source of gossip I have. So maybe this isn't such a long shot."

"Let us pray."

Inside, Wendy Williams was waiting for us beside the reception desk, where a Pails for Trails bucket was perched next to the sign-in sheet. One thing I had to hand to Bob Rushwood: the man had market penetration. Wendy was as petite and pretty as I remembered, with wide brown eyes, a smattering of freckles, and stray blond strands artfully spilling out of a ballerina-style topknot. She did not look a bit older than she had seven years ago, when Holly had dragged me out of my bed and my blues, so we could have a spa day. Wendy cocked her hip.

"I remember you," she said, pointing a purple-lacquered nail in my direction and smiling. "You were Holly's good friend. She brought you down to Cherry Creek right after a big snow. She always spoke so lovingly about you."

"Back then," I said, "you were her colorist—"

"I was her colorist until she died." Wendy inhaled, and her breath caught.

I introduced Marla, whom Wendy said she also knew from Holly's description.

There was an awkward pause until Wendy asked in a low voice, "How's Drew doing?"

"Not so hot," I said. "He's in Alaska now, with Holly's sister."

Marla pressed her lips together. This conversation was proving to be more difficult than I imagined. Finally Marla said, "We're putting together Holly's memorial service."

Wendy asked, "When is it? I'd love to come."

"Um, we're not sure yet." Marla faltered. "Our priest is in the hospital. We're . . . trying to compile a complete list of people who should be notified. After lunch, we'll be . . . looking for her address book at her rental . . . but we thought maybe *you* would know more than what we could find."

"Sure," said Wendy. "How can I help?"

"Well," Marla continued, "this past Friday, the day Holly died, she was at my house for a birthday party for Drew and Goldy's son, Arch."

Wendy shook her head. "I knew she was looking forward to that. I did her hair right beforehand. She wasn't going to invite George and Lena. Did they show up anyway?"

"They did," I said, surprised.

"She hated them."

"So we gathered," I said. "They had a bit of a blowup at the party."

"Poor Drew." Wendy crinkled her nose. "Holly didn't like George or Lena, or Edith either, for that matter. Well, can you blame her, after the way they treated her?"

I nodded regretfully. Wendy knew about the cutoff of child support? Holly, that keeper of secrets, had told her *that*? She hadn't even told *us*. Well, as Marla had said, Holly had been ashamed.

"Anyway," I said, "getting back to this memorial service. We really do want to include everyone who meant something to her. George and Lena and even Edith will probably come, but so what? Here's the thing. We found out that Holly had a boyfriend when she lived in Denver, a long time ago. We heard she adored him, and we'd like to include him. Do you know who the guy is?"

When Wendy shook her head, a few hairs flew free of the topknot. "Sorry. I didn't know she had a boyfriend when she lived in Denver. You mean, when she went back to art school?"

"Yes," Marla said, a bit too eagerly, I thought.

"She didn't mention anyone by name," Wendy said, and frowned.

"Well," said Marla, "can you think of any man she was . . . involved with . . . who would want to be invited to the service?"

Wendy held up fingers in a V sign. At first I thought she meant *victory*. But actually, she meant *two*. "Holly had a thing for two different guys over the years." She looked over her shoulder, as if another employee of the salon might be eavesdropping. "One of them has a company that supplies uniforms for the salon. Name's Neil Unger. Big shot. Wealthy. Know him?"

"We do," said Marla. Again I had the unwelcome memory of Neil Unger slamming around my kitchen Thursday morning. "I don't think he'd be inclined to come to the service," Marla went on, "but you never know."

"Why's that?" asked Wendy.

"He's just a jerk," I said. "Who's the other guy?"

"I can't remember his last name, but he was a shrink who slept with patients. Warren something."

"Oh, Lord," said Marla.

A couple of women came into the salon, chattering. Wendy said quietly, "I'm going to have to wrap this up. I can call you later, if you want."

"It's okay." But a feeling of desperation gripped me. "Right before she died, Holly told Marla and me that she was in a relationship mess. We have no idea who she was in the mess with, or if it was a big or a small mess. But we'd like to invite *that* guy, whoever he is, to the service."

Wendy shook her head. "Not a clue. Sorry."

We duly reported what Wendy had told us to Tom as the three of us strolled back up to the van.

"So the hairdresser thinks Holly was hooking up with both Neil Unger and Dr. Warren," he said.

"Unfortunately," I said.

Marla commented, "This detection work can be *such* a slog."

Tom did not say, *Do you think?* But I knew him well enough to know that it was going through his head.

When we parked in the conference-center lot, the wind whipping off the massive, steep Flatirons caused me to shudder. The center itself was a pale blue lacy Victorian structure whose steps creaked as the three of us ascended. A loose shutter banged against an exterior wall. Marla jumped.

"I love this building," said Tom, once we were inside. "A true antique."

"Are there no conferences today?" I asked a young blond woman, who gave us a bright, toothy smile as we approached the mammoth wooden desk of the beadboard-paneled lobby. One of the red Pails for Trails adorned the desktop, along with a pad of paper and a sign-in sheet. I concentrated my gaze on the young woman, whose name tag announced that she was *Kimberly.* I would have been willing to lay money on her being a summer school student at the University of Colorado.

"Our next conference doesn't start until tomorrow," she said, the bright smile still in place. "We were closed for a few days, to get everything ready for our summer season. I can get you a brochure—"

"No, thank you," I said, smiling to match Kimberly's sunny expression.

Marla exhaled. "We just need to talk to a person in charge."

"You can't talk to a person *in charge* unless you have an *appointment*," Kimberly cheerily replied, unoffended.

"Here's the thing," I said, "we've come over from Aspen Meadow to speak to the person who organizes the conferences."

"Organizes the conferences?"

"Whoever keeps the files," I said, "on past conferences. We need to know more than who attended. We need to know who all the vendors were, who your staff people were, what activities attendees enrolled in, that kind of thing. And if you all have any photos of the goings-on."

"Um, I don't understand," said Kimberly.

I turned to Marla and asked if I could speak to her for a second. Tom followed us to the blue-painted door, but said nothing. Marla began to whisper that Kimberly was incompetent.

Tom said, "I wouldn't go that far."

I said to Marla, "Now might be the time for you to break out some of that cash."

Tom said, "So *now* I see how you two work."

Marla turned on her heel and strutted back to the reception desk. Tom and I had to hurry to keep up with her. Kimberly wasn't smiling anymore.

"Kimberly!" said Marla, as she reached for her wallet. Kimberly eyed her warily. Maybe she was afraid Marla was going for a gun. But no. Instead, she pulled out an impressive wad of cash. "Here's about a hundred bucks, give or take. Who's the most senior person who's currently here?"

Kimberly took the proffered bills, and smiled again. "Thank you. That would be Mrs. Peterson. She's just dropped her kids off at child care and is in her office now."

"Great," said Marla, as she wrote on a handy pad of paper on the desk. "So while we're talking to her, could you get us those lists my friend was just mentioning? We need to know the staff people who worked here over the past twenty years, the activities they led, as well as the names of the attendees who signed up for those activities, plus all the vendors. And we'd love any photos."

"Twenty years?" Kimberly said faintly, as the smile evaporated once more.

Marla grinned. "You all have computers, don't you?"

"I can't do that without permission," Kimberly crisply replied.

"How about this," I said, attempting to be conciliatory. "Could you please show us to Mrs. Peterson's office?" I asked. Kimberly, who had pocketed Marla's cash but was no longer smiling, led us down a hallway to Mrs. Peterson's office, where she knocked. She said she would just be a moment, as she wanted to tell Mrs. Peterson why we were there. The dark wooden door had an old-fashioned piece of opaque glass in the upper section, and its hinges creaked when Kimberly swung it open.

Moments later, she came out and said in singsong fashion, "Good luck!"

Tom looked at me. "I may have to go official," he said, "on your long shot."

I said, "Thanks."

Mrs. Peterson, fiftyish and wiry, with a long nose and thin lips, had iron-gray hair pulled into a severe bun. She sat tall behind a desk that was a monument to organization: there were no stray papers in flyaway piles, no written reminders taped to the desk lamp, no mementos of trips anywhere. There was only a computer, which was turned off, and a closed gray file.

I looked at Mrs. Peterson, puzzled. This woman needed child care? I glanced around at the wall behind us: neat rows of photographs of two Asian children, from infancy to about age seven, were ranged across it. If Mr. Peterson existed, there was no photographic evidence of him.

THE WHOLE ENCHILADA · 487

I said, "Mrs. Peterson, thank you for seeing us." Did I sound charming? I wondered. "My name is Goldy Schulz, and I attended a three-day conference here eighteen years ago. It was called Setting Up a Medical Practice. Now . . . I've lost a friend who was here at the same time . . ." I faltered. Would the memorial-service bit work with her? I soldiered on. "Anyway, my husband, Tom, and my friend Marla"—I indicated them—"and I are setting up her memorial service, and we're looking for any photos from the conference or people who might have known our friend Holly Ingleby, so we can invite them to her memorial service."

"You don't have her address book?" Mrs. Peterson asked.

"We're going to look for that later," I assured her. "And I have program notes from the conference all those years ago. But we thought we'd come here first."

"For a memorial service, you need photos and records of all the activities and all the staff from eighteen years ago?"

I sighed and turned to Tom. He showed his ID to Mrs. Peterson, and began to speak in that convincing-but-authoritative way he had. He just had a few questions that had come up with regard to the suspicious death of Holly Ingleby. The Furman County

488 · DIANE MOTT DAVIDSON

488 · DIANE MOTT DAVIDSON

Sheriff's Department was pursuing all possible leads. He repeated our request for staff, activities, and any photographic records from a conference held eighteen years ago.

Mrs. Peterson stood. "I want to be helpful," she said. She lifted her chin and stared down her nose at the three of us. "But I simply can't violate our employees' privacy by handing over all our records. I don't suppose you brought a search warrant, Officer Schulz?"

"If you don't want to give us the information, that's fine," Tom said, in his endearing way that said, *You'd better give me what I came for, or I'll bring a warrant back here and make such a mess out of this place you won't know what hit it.* "We're *only* looking for a list of staff people from that conference. We need the lists of activities, and the staff and attendees who participated in them. And any photos. Please."

"Setting Up a Medical Practice," she said evenly. "I worked that conference. It was one of the largest we've ever done and quite successful. There were classes in billing, affiliation with insurance companies, documentation, hiring a staff, insurance files, training, and uniforms." She sighed. "You know our staff turnover is high. It is very unlikely that some of the same people are here. And we don't keep the photos. There are too many of them." She finally opened the gray file in front of her. We waited while she leafed through it. "There were excursions and unofficial presentations. Do you remember those, Mrs. Schulz?"

"Other presentations?" I said, confused.

"Being given by the doctors' spouses." She looked expressionlessly at Tom. "One woman led an exercise class. Another showed us how to paint pottery that you take to be fired. Still another gave a talk on making jigsaw puzzles for children."

"My friend Holly Ingleby probably gave that one," I said.

"Yes," Mrs. Peterson said, gracing us with the first genuine smile since we'd arrived. "A tall, pretty, athletic blond woman? She showed everyone how to make a two-sided jigsaw puzzle for their children that would be ready for Thanksgiving. On one side was Turkey, the country; on the other was a picture of a turkey. She was so enthusiastic, everyone wanted to learn." She came to a neat pile of papers, but hesitated once again. She'd had it all the time! Kimberly must have warned her of what we wanted. Mrs. Peterson had printed out the sheets in that meticulous office of hers, and now she was waiting for some magic words from us before she would hand it over. "I'm sorry," she said, "I simply must err on the side of protecting the privacy of our conference attendees." She closed the file.

This was all finally too much for Marla. She strode forward and slammed her hand down hard on the desk. The lamp, computer, and file all jumped slightly. Marla leaned into Mrs. Peterson's face.

"Marla," Tom said. "Don't."

But my friend was not to be deterred. "Listen to me, Mrs. Peterson. I understand you run a tight ship here. But I am involved with fourteen different charities in the state of Colorado and am on the board of three. If you don't give us what we want, I'll make sure that none of them—*none*—ever has a conference here at Flatirons."

Mrs. Peterson began to gasp, which proceeded into a choking noise, which proceeded into a shallow, heaving cough. Dammit, she was having an asthma attack. Tom whipped out his phone to call 911.

Marla turned to me, shaking her head. "Do you remember mouth-to-mouth, just in case?"

"Mrs. Peterson!" I called through her heaving and gasping. "Where is your inhaler?"

Mrs. Peterson pointed to the floor. I dove down and located a sensible black leather bag deep under the desk. I fumbled open the closure, found the inhaler, took off the cap, and handed her the apparatus. She gave herself a puff of the medication.

"Breathe it as slowly as you can," I ordered, my elbows on the desk. I stared deep into Mrs. Peterson's watery blue eyes. "Breathe it all the way in."

Tom was on the phone with the emergency operator, explaining Mrs. Peterson's symptoms. But within ten seconds, it appeared that the woman was recovering from her attack.

She removed the inhaler from her mouth and glared at Marla. "How dare you come in here and threaten me?"

"Easily," Marla said, straightening her shoulders. "I dare *all* the time. Next time, why don't you act more helpful to law enforcement?"

Mrs. Peterson ignored her, and turned to me. "I owe you an apology."

"Oh?" I said, confused.

"I initially doubted you were a doctor."

Come to think of it, I hadn't mentioned that I was at the conference with the Jerk. "Oh, I never—"

"You're very good at your job," said Mrs. Peterson warmly.

"Thank you," I said. Well, I was a good caterer.

She took a shallow breath. I leaned toward her, as if to help. But she picked up the pile of papers and handed them to Tom. Then she quietly asked us to leave.

"Today I learned some important lessons," Tom said as we walked back to my van. "In interrogation, that is. Try a bribe. If that doesn't work, threaten the person you're interrogating. Bring her to the brink of death. Then pretend you're a doctor who helps her back to life. Too bad the sheriff's department doesn't allow this stuff."

25

Tom asked if I could drive back to Aspen Meadow. When Marla complained that we hadn't had lunch yet, he said we could pick up something on the way back. She grumbled, but Tom said he wanted a few minutes to look through the sheets that Mrs. Peterson had given us. He shook his head. "Broome, check. Ingleby, check. Unger, check. 'Excursions and classes offered by Boulder Fitness,'" he read. He tried to call the department to see who was working there, but since we were once again driving along the Hogback, there was no cell reception. He went back to reading aloud. "Presentations by blah, blah, blah, nobody we've heard of, except for Holly Ingleby, who did her jigsaw puzzle shtick. 'With Thanksgiving puzzles for sale,' it says on here."

I was staring at the road, thinking about Mrs. Peterson. Then one of those dark bits flashed across my mind, and I gasped. "Oh, my God."

"What?" demanded Marla. "Did you see a deer? By the road?"

"No, no," I said, as we zoomed onto the interstate. "We have to go to Holly's. Right now."

"To Holly's?" Tom asked. "What, the rental?"

"Yes, yes," I said. "The puzzles she left? The one she gave Audrey and the one on her living room table?"

Tom said warily, "Yes, Hunan Province. So?"

"They're like the Turkey puzzle. The country is on one side. The bird is on the other. China is a place. It is also *dishes*. And Holly has plenty of them."

"So?" said Marla.

"I am willing to bet that some of those dishes we saw weren't just there for decoration."

"Goldy," said Tom, "you're reaching."

"But, Tom, she loved jokes and word games and puzzles, and she gave a puzzle, also of China, to Audrey the day she died. She wanted Audrey to give it to Father Pete if something happened to her. She had no idea that Father Pete would be stabbed, thus depriving us of the key to what she was trying to tell us."

"Why not leave us a message," Tom persisted, "saying, so-and-so is threatening me?"

"If she was blackmailing somebody," Marla said, "she couldn't be that obvious."

"Look," I said, "the China thing *might* be a message to us."

Tom said, "I was in that house, Goldy. I didn't see dishes that would contribute to solving a murder." His cell phone beeped, indicating a message. He looked down at it and began tapping out a reply.

Marla said, "The only dishes I ever saw in Holly's house in Aspen Meadow Country Club were her Limoges."

"Okay, but in the rental," I said, "there was china in her hutch that I didn't recognize. There was a collage of Drew on the wall. I want to look at it again. Plus there was a bunch of religious statuary and whatnot when Julian, Father Pete, and I took Drew home," I replied. "Drew said his mother had just put it out recently. Remember that break-in she had earlier in the month?" When Marla asked what that had to do with anything, I answered, "With all her valuable antiques around, the *only* thing the burglar took was files. She was probably afraid that if she left written information about who was threatening her, that person could just destroy it. So she left it for . . . Father Pete, or for us . . . or for whomever, in a way she thought we might unravel."

"If you have indeed unraveled it," Marla said, her voice dubious.

"Do you have any other ideas?"

Marla said she didn't, and we went back and forth, spouting theories. "Something's off," Tom said. "I just don't know what it is."

The wind had picked up even more when we arrived at Holly's rental at half-past one. Dust blew in great clouds across Aspen Meadow Lake, and a gray mantle of cloud rose above the Continental Divide. Marla was still complaining bitterly about not having any lunch, but she stopped when I said this simply could not wait. I had to find out if Holly had left something for us that would not be apparent to the casual observer. Tom did not even roll his eyes when he said he would indulge me.

The narrow road up to the house was nerve-shattering to drive. I was so frazzled by the time we arrived that I couldn't remember the code to the security system. Tom called the department, which sent it to him as a text: zero-nine-zero-four to get in; zero-four-one-five once we were inside.

When we arrived, Tom took all the necessary precautions. He told us to stay in the locked van while he entered both codes and went through the house. The steady wind lashed the yellow crime-scene tape over the busted deck and the boulders of the cliff. The broken staircase banged incessantly. The garbage had been picked up; the can lay on its side. Otherwise, the place looked forlorn.

After Tom had secured the house, he motioned for us to enter.

"The only thing I'm seeing that's actual china are some of these dishes, and these religious statues that you say are new," he said, doubt in his voice. "I can tell from looking at them that they're porcelain."

We stood at the entry to Holly's living room and took it all in: the religious statues, the crosses, the collage, the furniture, including the hutch.

"Hold on," I said. I pointed to a statue of a saint—I had no idea which one, Episcopalians aren't big on them—that was situated away from the other ones. He held out his arm in a blessing sort of way. Or a pointing one. "That saint is pointing toward the hutch."

So we all went over to the hutch and stared at the grooved rows where Holly had propped up a dozen plates.

Tom said, "Yes, these are all dishes. But you can't eat off of three of them. And they're not antiques. Nor are they Limoges."

"What do you mean, not Limoges?" Marla demanded hotly. Holly herself told me they belonged to her grandmother."

"She called it 'Granny's Haviland,'" I added. "The ones with the pink flowers, I mean. And I've eaten off of them."

Tom carefully removed the flowered plates from the grooved rows and placed them on the open shelf in front of us. He smiled. "True Limoges porcelain, ladies, is made from kaolin, a type of clay that can be fired at very high temperatures. True Limoges china, of which Haviland is one manufacturer, also has feldspar in it. When fired, feldspar gives the porcelain a shiny, almost transparent quality. That's why it always looks as if you're staring at the pattern through a layer of glass."

We all peered at the peculiar arrangement of the newer dishes that remained propped on the grooved rows. Each was painted with religious symbolism: a lamb, a fish, and an angel. I hadn't looked closely at them before, and Tom was the expert on china. But if Holly had deliberately displayed the plates with some of her grandmother's Haviland, that had to be significant.

I turned toward the collage of Drew that Yurbin must have done in the earlier days of his partnership with Holly. The portrait was full of bits of Drew's past, plus photos and playful painted images.

"Okay, wait," I said. I moved to the other side of the room and glared at the collage. "I'm seeing a painted margin around the photographs, the badge, and the toy car. It's a pattern that repeats: A pair of fish. A ram. An angel. Then the fish again, and so on."

Marla and Tom turned away from the china cabinet and crowded in next to me. They saw the same things I did: a pair of fish; a ram; an angel.

I said, "Let's go back to the china. We retraced our steps to the hutch with its trio of dishes.

Two of the three were on one row. Another was below those. All three dishes had gold rims, deep blue backgrounds, and symbols at their center. There was the angel, then the lamb, a symbol for Christ—only it wasn't, on closer inspection, a lamb—and a fish, another early sign for Christ. Problem was it wasn't actually one fish, but two.

Tom picked up the angel plate and turned it over. "The Morgan Library and Museum," he read. "Virgo." He screwed his mouth to one side. "The image is from a book of hours attributed to Venturino Mercati, from about 1473."

"Astrology," said Marla.

I said, "Oh, my God. Not Catholicism, after all. Are they all from the Morgan? By this Mercati fellow?"

Tom gazed at the other plates. "Looks like it. They're not valuable. The images from the book of hours have been transposed onto the plates, that's all."

"Then put it back," I said impatiently, "so we can try to see what she was telling us."

On the top row was the symbol for Pisces—the *two* fish. Holly's birthday was in February. Also on that row was Virgo, which I had thought was an angel. Well, Mercati had given her great big wings, what was I supposed to think? Plus, in my head I'd had the religious story, not the astrological one. In the middle, on the next grooved row down and directly between the two, was the ram, which in my sadness and stupor, I had glanced at too quickly and initially thought was a lamb. When I'd seen all the religious statuary, I'd just assumed the symbols on the plates were religious. I hadn't seen its horns. Silly me.

The animals and symbols were the ones Holly or Yurbin had painted in the margin of the collage of Drew.

"The ram is *Aries*," I said. I felt disgusted with myself for not seeing this sooner.

Tom's cell buzzed, but the reception in the house was fuzzy. He announced that he was going out on the front porch to take the call.

"That's Drew's birth sign, Aries, the one for April the fifteenth," I remarked to Marla. "And Holly is Pisces, the fish."

"So who is the third one supposed to represent, the Virgo sign? Drew's biological father? Or George?"

"George isn't a Virgo, if I'm remembering right. I'm guessing it's Drew's father. It's not any evidence that would hold up in court, but if we could figure out which one of our suspects is a Virgo, we might—"

Outside, a tree branch banged against the house. Did I hear someone grunting? I looked out onto the busted deck. No one was there.

"Did you hear something?" I asked Marla.

"Yeah, a branch. Or a ghost"

"All right, let me—"

"Let you nothing," Marla said. "I'm getting the heebie-jeebies. Let's go get Tom and skedaddle."

I stared at the plates and said, "It's the wind. We're fine."

Two jigsaw puzzles. China. There was *something* here. But what?

Holly: Pisces. Father: Virgo. Drew: Aries.

Holly had said, *I'm in a relationship mess.* She'd also said to someone, *I've got you, you bastard! There's a record!*

Holly was truly an artist. She thought in images and symbols: the puzzles that meant both China and china plates, the plates that meant astrological sun signs and the relationship of three people born under them, signs that she'd had Yurbin repeat on the collage of Drew, to symbolize where he'd come from. Drew had always been the center of Holly's world.

I picked up the Aries plate and turned it over. And there—taped to the back—was a piece of dotted cloth. It matched a piece of dotted cloth in the collage of Drew.

I said, "We have to open that collage of Drew."

Marla exhaled. But across the living room we went again, and this time we lifted the collage down from the wall. It actually had an easily removable back. Tucked into one corner, near the edge, was taped a sewn finger puppet. Everything else was flat, so I carefully pulled the tape off the puppet. There was something hard inside it. I slowly extracted a flash drive.

"Oh, Lord." I held the drive carefully. "Remember when Holly said there was a record? Well, it looks as if what we've been looking for—" What I was going to say was—"is right here," when a man in a mask erupted from the kitchen. He wore gloves and was holding a gun in one hand.

"Who the hell are *you?*" cried Marla, all heebie-jeebies gone. "How'd you get in here? What'd you do, climb up the cliff outside?"

"You . . ." I said, my voice meek. "You're the man who wanted Holly's notes." I raised my voice. "Did you kill Kathie Beliar and try to hurt Father Pete?"

The man put his free hand to his lips. Then he shook his head and held out the same hand for the flash drive. I put it in his gloved palm.

Marla cried, "Oh, wait, there's another flash drive!" She picked up one of the religious statues and sailed it in an arc not far from the man. His eyes followed it, just long enough for my brave friend to run at the man and tackle him. I raced forward, tried to grab the gun out of his hand, but managed only to send it flying under a chair. I yelled for Tom. Marla, who had once assaulted the Jerk right after he'd hit her, held down our would-be attacker. With a loud groan, he struggled on the floor. Marla jumped on his chest, then pulled the mask off Bob Rushwood.

Bob, agile and strong, managed to throw her off him. He then scooted under one of Holly's love seats, where he nabbed the gun.

I didn't know if I imagined Tom yelling "Get down!" at me, or if I fell to the floor on my back, just out of instinct. I only knew there was a loud bang, and then I couldn't hear anything. I also knew something very hot and painful had exploded through my ankle. I was screaming in agony, but couldn't hear my own voice.

Tom pulled out his gun and fired. He shot Bob Rushwood in the chest. Bob didn't die, but as he writhed on the floor next to where the collage of Drew had fallen in the melee, I saw something I had not expected—the physical resemblance between young Drew and his biological father, Bob Rushwood.

At the time, I just hurt. Later, I was sad.

Epilogue

W hen I was in the hospital recovering from the wound I'd received when the bullet went through my ankle, Tom came to visit. He said the flash drive Holly had left for us informed us of many things. I sighed and stared at my cast. I just wished I could have figured out those things earlier.

First, Bob Rushwood was the biological father of Drew. His birthday was September 4. I hadn't thought that zero-nine-zero-four, Holly's outdoor security code, could be anything but random numbers. But perhaps I should have deduced that puzzle from the interior security code: zero-four-one-five, Drew's birthday. The man is outside. The child is inside.

On the flash drive, Holly wrote the notes she'd been talking about: that she'd discovered too late that Bob was a narcissist who always wanted some new woman at his side. But he preferred a woman with money. That was what had attracted him to her, she concluded. She had acquired some wealth through her ex-husband, George. It just wasn't enough to satisfy Bob. Plus, she had a child. His child, but he didn't care about that.

I'm in a relationship mess.

Yes, she had been.

On the flash drive, Holly confessed that she had had sex with *Bob* when he took her hiking in the Flatirons. At the time—during the doctors' conference eighteen years before—he had been working for Boulder Fitness. He didn't show up as a staff member at the conference center, because he was working for one of the vendors at the conference—and seducing Holly on the side. When the fitness center fired him, for stealing from the cash drawer—*allegedly*, Bob's lawyer added—he went to work for a gym in Denver, from which he was also let go, for stealing athletic equipment to resell elsewhere. *Allegedly.*

When Tom laid this out for Wendy Williams, whom Holly had introduced to Bob, and who had dyed Bob's hair and put it into dreads, she said, "You just wouldn't believe the number of accusations that have been hurled at that man."

"No," Tom solemnly replied, "I probably wouldn't."

So . . . Bob Rushwood was the biological father of Drew. Holly had not known from the beginning. She hadn't known about George's allergy to gelatin, his mumps, or the sterility. But there were no more children, which George desperately wanted. And then . . . Drew had begun to look not like George, but like Bob.

This put Holly into something of a quandary. Edith kept calling Drew her "miracle." Holly knew Med Wives 101; she remembered when Edith had tossed the molded salad she had made. She looked up *allergy to gelatin*, just as I had later, and found what she needed to know.

I did not know if George Ingleby had truly loved Holly. He'd been captivated by her *beauty*, that was certain. But Holly had been deeply hurt by George's penny-pinching, and by the fact that he paid so little attention to her. She unburdened herself on the flash drive, writing, *I thought I needed to be married to George, that he would help me care for this child.* And she had needed it. That was why she'd been lying to George and Drew all those years, as she'd half confessed to me in Amour Anonymous.

Like me, Holly had said, *I'd thought we could make it work.*

But George had not loved Holly the way she needed to be loved. To be fair, Holly had married George for his money, and hadn't given him what he needed, either. Worse for Holly, after they broke up, she thought she could get the affection she wanted from Bob Rushwood.

And of course, Holly's chart had told her she would be a successful artist. I could hear her laughing through her words on the flash drive: *I thought I'd become rich and famous and ride into the sunset with the man I really loved.*

Yes, she went back to art school, studied with Yurbin, and figured out a way to make money commissioning portrait-collages from him. But the main reason she'd moved with Drew down to Denver was that she wanted to be with Bob.

Despite Holly's protestations of love, despite the gifts she'd showered on him, Bob had responded first with indifference, then with disdain. Worse, she was dependent on George for money. She did not have access to the Ingleby oil fortune. And she had an encumbrance: Bob's son, Drew.

Bob didn't care. He rejected her.

In the midst of the police processing what they'd learned from the contents of the flash drive, Father Pete woke up. We all praised and thanked the Almighty. Father Pete said Holly had told him, and *not* under the seal of confession, as we'd thought, about her conflict with George, and Bob being Drew's biological father, but not about the blackmail she had going. She had tried to put Bob behind her after the disaster in Denver, Father Pete told the police, but when Bob moved to Aspen Meadow and then took up with Ophelia, Holly suspected that he was running a scam. Moreover, Bob was the one who attacked him and killed Kathie Beliar.

Father Pete provided some more of the missing pieces. He said that when Drew began to look like Bob—sandy-colored hair, tall, athletic build—Bob had no doubt noticed, probably at the country club. Holly suspected that Wendy Williams had begun dying Bob's hair, and that she had put in the dreads. Holly knew this for certain, though, after she set up cell-phone video surveillance outside the Mane Event in Boulder. It hadn't taken long for Bob to show up, needing his roots done.

And Bob did all this, Holly had concluded, because he wanted a bigger payoff: a very wealthy woman without encumbrances.

Enter Ophelia Unger, stage right. She was young. She was pretty. But best of all was the trust that her father, Neil—who confessed as much to Tom later—dangled in front of Bob. Neil said Bob's one job was to marry Ophelia and make sure she had a baby as soon as possible, and never got a college degree. Bob was handsome; he was charming. At thirty-eight, he was

THE WHOLE ENCHILADA · 509

older than Ophelia, and could provide a steady hand, Neil felt. Neil was sure Bob could keep Ophelia close.

As the photos Holly had taken, and preserved on her flash drive, confirmed, Bob was two-timing Ophelia. Holly had told Father Pete that he had been two-timing Ophelia with Wendy. And Wendy, like so many other women, had fallen in love with Bob herself.

But there was that money thing, and the inconvenient kid thing. If sanctimonious Neil Unger, the head of The Guild, had discovered that Bob Rushwood had fathered a child by another woman out of wedlock, it would have meant bye-bye to Bob's gaining control of Ophelia's trust through marriage. Bob promised Wendy that soon they could be together, and that he would set her up in her own salon.

Holly and Bob had been exchanging e-mails; these were on the flash drive. She knew about Wendy and Ophelia; she knew about Neil's wealth. Now she needed money, and Bob needed a secret kept. He'd paid her, for a while.

And then he'd balked. They'd had the loud phone conversation: *I've got you, you bastard! There's a record!*

She had been convinced that Bob was the one who had broken into her rental to see if he could find some record of his biological connection to Drew. He'd found none. She'd put out all the clues for us to figure out what was going on, just in case . . .

And that deadly case had come.

Tom was convinced that Bob knew about Holly's heart issue from their pillow talk. Bob had taken Loquin for a sinus infection, and been stupid enough to keep the bottle. So Tom was pretty sure Bob had not taken the Loquin, but had kept it to make Holly's murder possible.

Bob had also tried to kill Drew—only I'd fallen into that trap. He'd attacked me in our backyard, hoping to find out what I knew. Then it seemed he'd left Arch out of an e-mail loop that canceled the trail building. Out by the Wildlife Preserve, we believed Bob had laid down a strip of tacks so the Passat would have a flat tire, and Bob would then have an excuse to come to our house—sit in our kitchen!—to look out back and ask what had happened. Did we know who had done all that damage? We said it was a bear, which Bob knew was a lie since he'd been the one who attacked me. But we hadn't acted suspicious of him at all. After Bob had given us his sob story about Ophelia, Warren Broome had shown up to handily distract the police, and Bob had made a quick exit out the back.

Holly had left a final puzzle for us, and she'd made it so challenging, and surrounded it with so much religious statuary, that the arrangement of astrological signs had slipped right past Bob—and Tom, and the rest of the sheriff's department.

And me.

When confronted, Wendy Williams said yes, she'd started sleeping with Bob after Holly introduced them. He'd told her that if anybody from Aspen Meadow showed up asking questions about Holly's past, she should point them in the direction of Warren Broome and Neil Unger, both of whom were from Aspen Meadow and had ties, however tenuous, to Holly. And Wendy had done just that: tried to point us in the wrong direction. But we'd said we were going over to Holly's to get her address book to plan for the memorial service. She'd called Bob and warned him: they're going to Holly's house to nose around.

We'd arrived at Holly's house first. But Bob was an athlete. Never mind the broken staircase. He'd climbed the rocks outside the deck he'd sabotaged. We'd found the *notes*, the *record*, that he'd been so worried about.

Bob had thought he'd had the whole child-out-of-wedlock thing knocked until George Ingleby found out he was sterile. When Lena insisted that George cut off child support for Drew, George told Tom that he had *known* that this would only be temporary. He *knew* the court would eventually force him to pay child support, per the initial agreement. He trusted that Holly and Drew would be okay until that happened. But in the meantime, Holly had to deal with a mountain of credit-card debt, and little income except the paltry amount she earned from the portrait-collages, a greater percentage of which Yurbin was now demanding. She had been forced to use the collage money, plus the funds she obtained from selling Drew's and her Audis, to hire an attorney to go after George.

Unfortunately for everybody, cases in family court take a long time to be decided. Holly fell behind on her house in the country club, then lost it entirely. She pulled Drew from his expensive prep school and put him into a large parochial one. She went from imported Gruyère to a block of supermarket cheddar.

The e-mails in which she attempted to blackmail Bob had begun in January: *Start getting money from Ophelia to help me with my expenses, or I'll expose your secret. I'll get a paternity test ordered. I'll wreck your dreams.*

Bob ponied up at first, but by June, he responded with a threatening text of his own. And then he hatched a murder plot he was sure would work, as long as he, like everyone else in the kitchen the day of Arch and Drew's party, could get to the Mexican food, and pretend to be stirring something in. Well, he was stirring something in—enough antibiotic to kill someone with an elongated S-T interval.

Tom speculated that Bob had been afraid of leaving loose ends. Father Pete had spoken with Bob and made thinly veiled remarks about parenthood and being responsible to your loved ones. Bob knew that Holly had gone to see Father Pete that morning, which had given Bob an opportunity to sabotage the deck at the rental house. He must have worried that Holly had told Father Pete about Drew being his son. Maybe the priest knew where Holly had stashed her evidence on him. So Bob had staked out the church office, hunting knife in hand, come in, stabbed Father Pete, and gone through the church files, looking for evidence that Holly had confessed her secrets to Father Pete. Kathie Beliar, who'd been meeting with our rector, had simply "gotten in the way." She had seen Bob's face, and so he couldn't allow her to escape.

But there was a second issue, beyond the paternity one, that Holly had fully documented on her flash drive. Bob had furiously told Holly about losing the two jobs where he'd been accused of theft. Long after he dumped her, she resolved to find out if he really *was* a thief. Bob Rushwood, Holly's flash drive revealed, was hedging his bets with the engagement to Ophelia. He was making about thirty thou a year as a trainer at the country club, and he couldn't get caught again stealing from employers. So he supplemented his income with the untraceable cash people dropped into the ubiquitous Pails for Trails buckets. Holly had taken pictures of him picking up the pails, of him putting the cash in a storage facility, of him taking money out of the facility when he needed it. The shovels and other pieces of trail-digging equipment, the sheriff's department discovered, were donated by half a dozen hardware stores.

In his Aspen Meadow apartment, Bob had posted an elaborate schedule for picking up the pails. According to workers in the establishments where the pails were posted, the pails were often filled to the brim with cash and coins. A rough estimate of the amount of money Bob was making from the hundred-plus pails in Aspen Meadow, Denver, and Boulder, ranged from fifty thousand dollars a year to over a hundred thousand. And of course he didn't pay taxes on any of that.

Holly, in addition to detailing the whole paternity situation on her flash drive, plus copies of her e-mail communication with Bob, had provided so many pictures of Bob engaging in his scam that his conviction on charges of grand larceny was a slam dunk. Bob might have survived the public revelation of Drew being his son and forced Neil Unger into sticking to their deal, rather than having to reveal the existence of the trust to Ophelia. But once Holly threatened to expose Bob's criminal doings to the cops, he must have decided that killing her, and anyone she'd confided in, was the safest option. He may have had some charm and cunning, but Bob had also panicked. Keeping the last of his Loquin, so it could be matched with what Holly had in her system, was pretty dumb.

Bob had to have surgery after Tom shot him. The bullet narrowly avoided his lung. Then he demanded to see a lawyer. But given that he was facing two charges of first-degree murder, two of attempted murder—Father Pete and me in my foray onto Holly's deck—and grand larceny, the district attorney told Tom there was no way she was doing a deal.

News of Bob's schemes began to be reported in media outlets. Neil Unger puffed himself up and told the papers, "I never trusted that young man." Of course, that was before one of Brewster's colleagues filed a civil suit against Neil claiming malfeasance in his handling of his daughter's trust.

Tom gave me updates as I lay in a hospital bed down in Denver. Tom had insisted I be admitted and checked over, with every possible test administered. He wanted to make sure I didn't have bits of flak in my system, so my blood was drawn, I peed into a cup, my foot was X-rayed, the whole nine yards, except I couldn't even walk an inch. I only hoped I didn't get the same medical staff that had treated me when I fell through Holly's deck. They hadn't seemed to like me.

After the shoot-out at Holly's house, an obliging sheriff's department deputy had taken Marla home. There, she picked up her own vehicle and used it to zip back down to the hospital.

So after all the obligatory tests, both Marla and Tom were present when Dr. Quartz—his real name, if you can believe it—whisked through the door to the private room Tom had arranged for me. I didn't even want to contemplate how much *that* was costing.

"Well, Mrs. Schulz," said Quartz, "I have good news and bad news."

I gave him my best stone face. "I don't want to hear it." I immediately imagined that one of the tests had shown I had cancer. Who would take care of Arch, if I was gone? Who would—

"The bad news is that I'm not going to be your doctor anymore. Still, there will be no catering until you're out of that cast, do you understand?"

"Yeah, yeah," I said. "What's the good news?"

Dr. Quartz smiled at me. "You're pregnant."

We had the memorial service for Holly Ingleby the following Tuesday, right after the one for Kathie

Beliar. Father Pete was a bit unsteady on his feet, but did a wonderful job.

There was one thing that Holly had asked for on the flash drive: *Please don't tell Drew about Bob. Drew and George adore each other.*

But Tom said we couldn't do that. If Bob contacted Drew from the prison where he would surely end up, it would be an even nastier shock than if Tom told Drew that his biological father was, as Tom put it, "deranged." George Ingleby was and is Drew's father, Tom said. My dear husband also promised to tell Drew that Holly's momentary lapse in judgment with Bob should not be held against her. Without Bob, Drew, who was wonderful in every way, would not even be here.

Drew Ingleby—accompanied by his aunt and uncle—came back from Alaska that Monday. Tom and I told him all that had happened. He cried.

Bob Rushwood, as it turned out, did not have a chance to talk to Drew. An infection set into his chest after his surgery. Ironically, no amount of any antibiotic was able to save him. He died before Holly's service.

We told George Ingleby the truth, right before he went down to meet Drew's plane. He said he didn't care; he was just happy he had Drew. Tom was right: George *was* and *is* Drew's father, even if he hadn't contributed the sperm for his creation. That was why he and Lena had crashed Drew's party; George loved Drew. George promised us—*swore to us*—that once Holly's sister and her husband packed up Holly's rental, Drew would have his own apartment in the Ingleby mansion. He would even have his own entrance. Edith was delighted to have her miracle back. And, George told us, Lena had promised to be kind. Her earlier unpleasantness was only owing to her devotion to George.

Neil Unger was charged in a civil suit, now pending. It doesn't look good for him.

Nor do things portend any better for Warren Broome. Audrey has brought her complaint to his supervisory board. Patsie heard the story first, and filed for divorce.

Yurbin had his one-man show—a flop. The most damning review came from the *Denver Post*: *Yurbin has clearly shown how much he is trying to copy the ideas made popular by his most famous student, Holly Ingleby. Yet he lacks both the vision and the ability to replicate Ingleby's stunning success.* Marla, giggling wildly, gave me the results of her gossip-gathering mission after the show closed, with no pieces sold. Yurbin had tried to get his old job back with the Denver Art Academy. They didn't want him. Nor did the University of Denver, the University of Colorado, or

THE WHOLE ENCHILADA · 519

any other local college or high school, private or public. The last Marla heard, Yurbin had been hired as a delivery boy for the Cathedral Grocery, where Chris is now the manager.

Julian began going out with Ophelia. They're both rich in love, in Shakespeare, and in fact. What more could you ask for? Julian bought his own small place in Aspen Meadow, and has promised to help me with the catering business "for as long as you want me, boss."

"That would be for the foreseeable future," I told him, once I was out of the hospital and learning to use crutches.

We got through the summer, with its many weddings, and the busy season, Halloween to Christmas. I grew big. In my eighth month, the doctor said Julian would have to take over the catering business. I acquiesced.

On the cold, snowy morning of March 22, I was having a small decaf espresso with cream and contemplating what I would fix for breakfast for Arch, who was on spring break. Without warning, I doubled over. Tom scooped me up before I hit the floor.

"Miss G.?" His handsome face was creased with worry. "What is it?"

"Tom." I gasped, as another cramp hit. "I'm in labor."

Tom, so full of anxiety and questions about how I was feeling that I had to remind this normally calm, unwavering cop to keep his eyes on the road, drove me down to Southwest Hospital. The labor came so fast that I was spared the hour-after-hour contractions of Arch's birth, almost eighteen years before.

Arch was too nervous to pilot his own car. So he called Julian to ask if he, Julian, could pick him up in the Rover. Julian said he could, but Ophelia wanted to come, too. Julian had also promised that when the baby-arriving drama began, he would swing by Marla's house to pick *her* up. Gus and Drew had said they wanted to come to the hospital, too. So Julian, Ophelia, Marla, Gus, Drew, and Arch all squeezed into my van, which Julian had commandeered. Either Marla or Arch called Tom every ten minutes to make sure I was okay. Tom finally said he couldn't concentrate on his driving if they didn't stop phoning. His reply was cut off when we passed through the Hogback and lost the signal.

Farther down the interstate, two prowlers met us. One police car pulled in front of us, the other fell in behind the van. They put on their lights. Cell service was restored, and we received another frantic call from Arch.

"What is *happening?*" he cried.

"We have an escort," said Tom. "Now please tell Julian to pay attention to his driving."

Finally, finally, we arrived in the hospital parking lot.

"Oh, God," Marla said, as she picked her way through the slush. "A convoy of cops and my best friend having a baby. I'm so nervous, I think I'm going to pass out."

"Don't do that," Julian warned, taking her by the elbow. "The doctors here can deal with only one crisis at a time."

"I'm quite confident they can deal with simultaneous crises," Marla assured him.

Tom, swathed in hospital garb, was allowed in the delivery room. Above the mask, the smile in his eyes was reassuring, even as the waves of pain rolled over me. He said, "Arch, Julian, Ophelia, Gus, Drew, and Marla are in the waiting room. Father Pete just arrived. All of them are more anxious than I am, so . . ."

"Yes, yes." I choked, as a contraction engulfed me. "I'm trying."

Grace Holly Schulz emerged with a throaty cry less than an hour later.

"Here's your daughter," said Dr. Marbury, my obstetrician, proudly placing long, pink, bawling Grace on my abdomen.

Tears slid down my face. There was no snow, no slush, no ice, no pain. There was only this lovely, new creature. Our creature. *Our baby.*

I had tried to help a lot of people along the way to this moment—Holly's son, Drew, among them—and in that helping, I had found a sense of belonging, of caring, of rebuilding my inner self after it was wrecked by the Jerk. I was, and am, thankful for that.

And now I had what I had always wanted—a loving husband, darling children, a tight community: *the whole enchilada.*

Once Grace was wrapped in a blanket and nestled in my arms in the hospital room, Arch, Julian, Ophelia, Marla, Gus, Drew, and Father Pete were all allowed in. They beamed.

"We're all here for you, baby," I murmured to my newborn.

She heard. She understood. That was the only way I could explain why Grace, with her tiny nest of blond curls, craned her little head around . . . to see her family.

Acknowledgments

The author gratefully acknowledges the assistance of the following people: Jim Davidson; Jeff, Rosa, Ryan, Nick, and Josh Davidson; J. Z. Davidson; Joey Davidson; Sandra Dijkstra, Elise Capron, Andrea Cavallaro, Thao Le, Elisabeth James, and the rest of the amazing team at the Sandra Dijkstra Literary Agency; Brian Murray, Michael Morrison, Carolyn Marino, Amanda Bergeron, Megan Swartz, Tavia Kowalchuk, Joseph Papa, and the entire brilliant team at Morrow; Richard Staller, D.O., for offering the idea for this book; Kathy Saideman, for her patient and helpful readings of the manuscript; Carol Alexander, for testing the recipes and making many valuable suggestions; Jasmine Cresswell and the rest of our brainstorming group: Connie Laux, Karen Young Stone, and Emilie

Richards McGee; Linda and David Ranz, M.D.; Dan Sheehy, Esq., expert in wills and trusts; Shirley Carnahan, Ph.D.; Carole Kornreich, M.D., for numerous clarifications; J.R. and John Suess; Julie Kaewert; Triena Harper; the Reverend Andi Suess Taylor and St. Boniface Episcopal Church in Sarasota, Florida, and the Reverend Nina Churchman and St. Laurence Episcopal Church in Conifer, Colorado; my far-flung family: Adam Mott, Janie Mott Fritz, Lucy Mott Faison, Sally Mott Freeman, and William C. Mott, Jr., plus all their wonderful spouses and dear children, with special acknowledgment of the passing of our beloved Tom Fritz; John William Schenk, who taught me how to cater; Marty O'Leary and the staff at Sur La Table in Sarasota, Florida, for numerous helpful suggestions; and as always, Sergeant Richard Millsapps, now retired from the Jefferson County Sheriff's Department, Golden, Colorado.

RECIPES FROM
THE WHOLE ENCHILADA

Enchiladas Suizas

Not-So-Skinny Spinach Dip

*Julian's Fudge with Sun-Dried Cherries and
Toasted Pecans*

Crunchy Cinnamon Toast

Chocolate Snowcap Cookies

Dad's Bread

Love-Me-Tenderloin Grilled Steaks

Goldy's Chef Salad

Sugar-Free Vanilla Gelato

Spicy Brownies

Enchiladas Suizas

12 corn tortillas

⅓ cup olive oil

Filling:

2 cups shredded rotisserie chicken, dark and light
meat, skin and bones removed

2¼ cups *crema* (homemade sour cream, also
known as crème fraîche, recipe follows) or
commercial sour cream

2 cups grated mild or medium cheddar cheese

1 teaspoon kosher salt

Sauce:

2 tablespoons olive oil

2 cups chopped onions

2 tablespoons minced garlic

14½ ounces diced Italian-style (with garlic, basil,
and oregano) tomatoes (Check contents of can.
You may need more than one can.)

9 ounces (contents of two 4½-ounce cans)
chopped fire-roasted mild chiles

1 teaspoon dried oregano

Additional *crema* or sour cream for topping

Crema (optional):

2 cups heavy whipping cream

¼ cup active-culture buttermilk

If you are making the optional *crema*, pour the cream into a glass container and stir in the buttermilk. Cover the container tightly with plastic wrap and leave at room temperature until thick (usually 24 to 48 hours). Covered *crema* can be kept in the refrigerator for a week.

When you are ready to make the enchiladas, pre-heat the oven to 350°F. Have ready a large plate and 13 absorbent paper towels. Fold the paper towels into quarters.

Overlap the tortillas in two large (9-by-13-inch or larger) pans so that as much of the surfaces of the tortillas is showing as possible. Drizzle the olive oil evenly over the tortillas in both pans. (You may have to use your hands or a pastry brush to spread oil evenly over the tortillas.) Place the pans in the oven and allow the tortillas to soften for about 5 minutes. Remove the pans from the oven and check that the tortillas are softened by using tongs to lift up one of them. (You want them soft and pliable. If they are not yet soft, put the pans back in the oven for a couple of minutes. You do not want to cook the tortillas through, which will harden them.) When the tortillas are just cool enough to touch, place one of the folded towels on a plate. Using tongs, place one tortilla on the folded towel. Place another folded towel on top of the tortilla and press lightly to absorb excess oil. Continue with the remaining tortillas. Set aside.

Using a large bowl, make the filling by mixing the chicken, *crema* or sour cream, cheese, and salt until blended. Set aside.

For the sauce, heat the oil in a large skillet over low heat. Add the onions and cook for a minute, stirring. Add the garlic and stir. Continue to cook and stir over low heat until the onion is translucent (about 10 minutes). Add the tomatoes, chiles, and oregano. Simmer this mixture over low heat for 5 to 8 minutes. Remove from the heat, allow to cool slightly, and spoon into a 4-cup glass measuring cup. You should have 3 cups of sauce. If you do not have 3 full cups, add the extra tomato sauce to make 3 cups.

Butter a 9-by-13-inch glass pan.

To fill the enchiladas, place each tortilla on a flat surface and scoop a ¼ cup of filling into the center. Using

your fingers or a spoon, shape the filling into a cylin-
der in the center of the tortilla. Roll up the tortilla and
place it, seam side down, in the prepared pan. Continue
until all the tortillas are rolled up.

Spoon the sauce over the tortillas and place the pan in
the oven to bake until the center of the enchiladas is
steaming hot, about 20 to 25 minutes. Serve with sour
cream on the side, if desired.

Makes 12 enchiladas

Not-So-Skinny Spinach Dip

1 tablespoon unsalted butter
1 tablespoon minced garlic
1 10-ounce package frozen chopped spinach,
  thawed and drained
8 ounces cream cheese, softened
10 ounces Alfredo sauce (contents of one
  refrigerated package)
⅓ cup finely grated Parmigiano-Reggiano cheese
1 cup grated fontina cheese
Freshly ground black pepper

In a medium-size sauté pan, melt the butter over low heat. Add the garlic; cook and stir until it is translucent. Add the spinach and cream cheese, stirring until very well combined. Add the Alfredo sauce and cheeses. Stir until the cheeses have melted. Continue stirring until hot.

Taste and season carefully with the pepper. Serve immediately with chips or crackers.

Julian's Fudge with Sun-Dried Cherries and Toasted Pecans

1 cup pecan halves

3 cups granulated sugar

¾ cup (1½ sticks) unsalted butter

⅔ cup evaporated milk

¼ teaspoon kosher salt

12 ounces best-quality bittersweet chocolate, chopped

7 ounces (contents of 1 jar) marshmallow crème

1 cup (about 6 ounces) sun-dried cherries

1 teaspoon vanilla extract

In a wide skillet, toast the pecans, stirring constantly, over low heat until they just begin to turn color and emit a nutty smell. Turn out onto paper towels and allow to cool. Chop and set aside.

Butter a 9-inch-square pan. Place the sugar, butter, salt, and milk in a heavy-duty saucepan. Stir constantly over medium heat until the sugar is dissolved. Continue to stir vigorously until the mixture comes to a rolling boil and measures 234°F on a candy thermometer. Remove from the heat and stir in the chopped chocolate and crème, stirring until the chocolate is melted and both are incorporated. Stir in the vanilla, cherries, and pecans.

Pour into the prepared pan and cover with plastic wrap. Allow to cool completely. When completely cooled, cut the fudge with a warm knife.

Makes 32 small or 16 large squares

Crunchy Cinnamon Toast

1 cup granulated sugar
1 teaspoon ground cinnamon
½ cup (1 stick) unsalted butter (you may not need
  all of this)
8 thick slices best-quality bread, preferably
  brioche
Applesauce

Preheat the oven to 350°F. Butter 1 or 2 large cookie sheets, or lay silicone mats on them.

Mix the cinnamon into the sugar and set aside. Melt the butter.

Lay the bread slices on the cookie sheets so that they are not touching. Place them in the oven and allow the bread to toast for about 5 minutes. Remove the sheets from the oven, but do not turn the oven off.

Flip the bread slices so that the untoasted side is facing up. Using a pastry brush, brush each slice of bread generously with butter. Carefully sprinkle each piece of bread generously with the cinnamon sugar. You want a thick layer of cinnamon sugar on each slice.

Return the sheets to the oven and watch carefully. In about 10 to 20 minutes, the cinnamon sugar layer will begin to bubble. Remove the sheets from the oven.

Serve immediately with applesauce on the side.

8 servings

Chocolate Snowcap Cookies

4 ounces extra-bittersweet or bittersweet
  chocolate, broken into pieces (recommended
  brand: Lindt; be sure you are using a full
  4 ounces, as package sizes differ)
½ cup (1 stick) unsalted butter
4 large eggs
2 cups dark brown sugar, firmly packed
2 cups all-purpose flour
⅓ cup cocoa (recommended brand: Hershey's
  Special Dark)
½ teaspoon kosher salt
2 teaspoons baking powder
¼ teaspoon baking soda
2 teaspoons vanilla extract
1 teaspoon chocolate extract (available at Sur La
  Table)
1 cup powdered sugar (for rolling)

Place the chocolate pieces and butter in the top of a
double boiler and melt over simmering water. When
the mixture is just melted, set aside to cool.

In the bowl of an electric mixer, beat the eggs until
well combined and light yellow in color. Add the brown
sugar and beat until very well combined.

Sift together the flour, cocoa, salt, baking powder, and baking soda.

When the chocolate mixture is no more than lukewarm, stir it into the egg mixture. Using a wooden spoon, gently stir in the extracts and the dry ingredients.

Cover the bowl tightly with plastic wrap and chill overnight. (The batter must be very well chilled.)

When you are ready to bake the cookies, preheat the oven to 350°F. Put silicone mats on two cookie sheets.

Place the powdered sugar in a large bowl. Remove the bowl of batter from the refrigerator. Using a 1-tablespoon scoop, measure out a dozen scoops of dough (level the scoops with a knife). Put the plastic wrap back over the bowl of batter and return to the refrigerator, to keep the rest of the batter well chilled. (As the batter warms up, it becomes too sticky to work with.)

Roll the first dozen scoops into balls, then drop them one at a time into the bowl of sugar, rolling them around until they are white. Place the cookies in even rows on the first cookie sheet, 2 inches apart. Bake for about 8 to 10 minutes, or until the "cracks" in the dough no longer appear wet. Watch carefully, as you do not want the cookies to overbake and dry out.

When the first batch of cookies is done, remove it from the oven and allow the cookies to set up for 5 minutes on the sheet. Use a metal spatula to carefully move the cookies to cooling racks; let cool completely. Remove the bowl of dough from the refrigerator and repeat with the other cookie sheet. Repeat this process until all the dough is used up.

These cookies can be messy to serve, because of the powdered sugar. Serve them on plates.

Makes 3½ to 4 dozen

Dad's Bread

½ cup plus 1 tablespoon dark brown sugar,
   divided
1 cup old-fashioned oats
2 teaspoons kosher salt
1¾ cups spring water, divided
2 tablespoons unsalted butter
1 tablespoon plus 2 teaspoons instant yeast
2 large eggs
¼ cup Bread Dough Enhancer (recipe follows)
5 to 6 cups bread flour

In a large mixing bowl, place ½ cup brown sugar, oats, salt, and butter. Heat 1½ cups spring water just until it is hot (125°F) and pour over oat mixture. Stir to mix and allow to cool to about 110°F. (A thermometer is handy for this. You do not want the mixture so hot that it destroys the yeast or cooks the eggs.)

In a glass bowl or container, stir 1 tablespoon brown sugar into the remaining ¼ cup spring water. Stir yeast into this mixture and set in a warm spot (no hotter than 150°F) for 10 minutes to proof.

Stir the enhancer into the flour.

In a separate bowl, beat the eggs well. Reserve two tablespoons and then stir the eggs and the yeast mixture into the oat mixture. Place this mixture into the large bowl of an electric mixer and stir to combine.

Attach a dough hook to the mixer. Stir in the flour, one cup at a time, until the mixture comes together. Knead on low speed for at least 5 minutes, until the dough comes together and cleans the bowl.

Butter a large, cylindrical hard plastic container and its lid. Place the dough in the container and, using a measuring tape and a marker, measure on the *outside* of the container the volume of the dough. Mark the container (still on the outside) where double the amount would be. Place the lid on the container.

Allow the dough to rise at room temperature until it is doubled in size (about 45 minutes to an hour). Remove the lid and gently punch down and knead the dough to roughly its original size. Allow it to rise again to double its size, about 40 minutes. Punch down again.

Butter three 8½-by-4½ glass loaf pans. Divide the dough evenly (you can use a scale to make sure the loaves all weigh the same) into thirds. Shape the dough pieces into loaves, and place them in the pans. Butter 3 large pieces of plastic wrap and place them loosely over each pan. Allow the dough to double in size, about 40 to 60 minutes. Remove the plastic.

Preheat the oven to 350°F.

Whisk the remaining 2 tablespoons of egg and brush it over the tops of the risen loaves. Place the pans in the oven and bake for about 30 to 40 minutes, or until the internal temperature reads 180°F and the loaves sound hollow when thumped.

Place the pans on racks, allow them to cool for 5 minutes, then turn the loaves out on the racks to cool completely, covered with a clean cloth dish towel.

Makes 3 loaves

Bread Dough Enhancer

1 cup wheat gluten (available in health food
    stores)
2 tablespoons lecithin (available in health food
    stores)
2 tablespoons powdered pectin (available in health
    food stores)
1 teaspoon ground ginger
2 tablespoons gelatin powder
½ cup nonfat dry milk

In a large bowl, stir all the ingredients until they are
well mixed. Place the mixture into a zipped plastic
bag, and keep it in the refrigerator, where it will last
for six months. Most yeast bread recipes with 4 cups
flour will call for 2 tablespoons. Recipes calling for 6 to
7 cups flour may use up to ¼ cup.

Makes about 2 cups

Love-Me-Tenderloin Grilled Steaks*

4 6-ounce filet mignon steaks, each 1½ to 2 inches
thick (use prime grade from Costco, if at all
possible)

¼ cup garlic oil (recommended brand: Boyajian,
available at Sur La Table)

Kosher salt

Freshly ground black pepper

*This recipe must be made using a digital probe meat
thermometer.*

Allow the steaks to come to room temperature. Preheat
the oven to 350°F. Have your digital probe meat thermometer ready.

Take the steaks out of the package and pat them on
both sides with paper towels, until they are thoroughly
dry.

Heat a large ovenproof grill pan on the stovetop over
high heat. (If the steaks will not fit in the pan without
crowding, you might have to use 2 pans. Alternatively,
you could use a large oven-proof skillet.) When the pan
is hot, add the oil. Heat for about 5 seconds (you do not

want to burn the oil), then lay the steaks in the pan. Lower the heat to medium-high, sprinkle the steaks lightly with salt and pepper, and cook for 1 minute only.

Using tongs, flip the steaks and remove the pan from the heat. Insert a meat thermometer into one steak, place the grill pan in the oven, and cook until the thermometer indicates 125°F (for medium-rare). Remove the pan from the oven and loosely cover it with foil for 5 minutes before serving the steaks.

Makes 4 steaks

Goldy's Chef Salad

Vinaigrette*:*

1 tablespoon Dijon mustard

1 teaspoon granulated sugar

¼ teaspoon kosher salt

¼ teaspoon freshly ground black pepper

¼ cup freshly squeezed lemon juice

½ cup best-quality olive oil

Chicken (optional)*:*

2½ pounds chicken breast, trimmed of fat,
   pounded to an even ½-inch thickness, and cut
   into 8 even pieces

Salad*:*

⅔ cup dates, chopped

2 avocados

5 ounces organic field greens, washed and dried

2 large tomatoes, cored and thinly sliced

2 large eggs, hard-cooked and thinly sliced

½ cup sliced celery

½ cup pecans, chopped

4 ounces chèvre with garlic and herbs, sliced into
   8 pieces

Croutons, preferably homemade

For the vinaigrette:

Using a whisk, mix together the mustard, sugar, salt, pepper, and lemon juice. Whisking constantly, slowly mix in the olive oil.

For the chicken:

If you are using the chicken, preheat the oven to 350°F. Place the chicken in a large bowl. Measure out ¼ cup of the vinaigrette and pour it over the chicken. Allow it to marinate for 15 minutes. Heat an ovenproof grill pan over high heat. Drain the excess marinade from the chicken and discard. Place the chicken in the grill pan, lower the heat to medium-high, and cook for 1 minute only. Using tongs, flip the chicken and remove the pan from the heat. Insert a digital meat thermometer in one piece of chicken. Place the pan in the oven and bake until the thermometer reaches 160°F, approximately 8 more minutes, and the chicken is cooked through. Do not overcook the chicken. Allow it to cool slightly.

For the salad:

Place the dates in a bowl. Measure out ⅓ cup of the vinaigrette and pour it over the dates. On a cutting board, slice the chicken.

Peel, pit, and slice the avocados into eighths.

In a large bowl, toss the greens, tomatoes, eggs, celery, and pecans with the dates and vinaigrette. Divide evenly among four plates. Place evenly divided slices of chèvre, chicken, and avocado on top of the salad on each plate. Sprinkle on croutons.

Makes 4 servings

Sugar-Free Vanilla Gelato

4 large egg yolks

½ cup sugar substitute, such as Splenda

1½ cups whole milk

1½ cups heavy cream

1 teaspoon vanilla extract

Following the manufacturer's instructions, freeze the inner bowl of an ice-cream or gelato maker for 6 hours or more, until it is thoroughly frozen.

Whisk the egg yolks with the sugar substitute in a large bowl, until thoroughly combined. Set aside.

Combine the milk and cream in a medium-size heavy-bottomed saucepan and place over low heat, stirring occasionally, until the mixture comes to a simmer (bubbles appear around the outside of the mixture). Remove the saucepan from the heat and pour the mixture into a large, heat-proof glass 4-cup measuring cup.

Whisking the egg-yolk mixture constantly, pour the hot milk mixture very gradually into the egg-yolk mixture. (The key here is not to cook the eggs.) Whisk until completely combined.

(Using a paper towel, wipe out the 4-cup glass measuring cup; you will be pouring the cooked custard back into it.)

Pour the egg-milk mixture back into the pan and place over medium-low heat. Put a thermometer into the pan and stir constantly with a wooden spoon, until the mixture thickens and covers the spoon. The thermometer should read just above 170°F. Once the mixture thickens, immediately remove it from the heat. It is now a custard. (If bits of cooked egg begin to appear before the thermometer reaches 170°F, immediately remove the pan from the heat.)

Pour the thickened custard mixture through a sieve back into the 4-cup glass measuring cup. Stir in the vanilla. Place a large piece of plastic wrap directly onto the custard to cover completely. (This is to prevent a skin from forming as the custard cools.)

Chill the custard in the refrigerator until it is thoroughly cold, usually 1 to 2 hours.

Following the manufacturer's instructions, turn on the gelato maker and scoop the chilled custard into the frozen rotating bowl. Set a timer for 25 minutes.

The soft gelato will be ready after 25 minutes. If you desire a firmer gelato, scoop it into a hard plastic container with a lid, and freeze, covered, for 20 minutes or so.

Freeze any leftover gelato, covered, in a hard plastic container with a lid. Allow it to soften at room temperature for about 15 minutes before serving again.

Makes about 2 cups gelato

Spicy Brownies

4 ounces best-quality extra-bittersweet (85% cacao)
  chocolate (recommended brand: Lindt; check
  that you are using the full 4 ounces, which may
  involve using a digital scale to weigh)
1 cup (2 sticks) unsalted butter
1 tablespoon minced crystallized ginger
3 tablespoons dark European-style (Dutch-
  processed) cocoa
1¼ cups cake flour, measured by gently spooning
  into measuring cups (high altitude: add 2
  tablespoons)
1 teaspoon ground ginger
½ teaspoon baking powder
1 teaspoon kosher salt
4 large eggs
2 cups granulated sugar
½ teaspoon chocolate extract (available at
  Sur La Table)
1 teaspoon vanilla extract

Preheat the oven to 325°F for dark or nonstick pans,
350°F for glass pans. Butter a 9-by-13-inch baking pan.

Melt the butter with the chocolate in the top of a
double boiler, stirring occasionally. When the mixture

is melted, add the crystallized ginger, stir, and set it aside to cool slightly.

Sift together the cocoa, flour, ground ginger, baking powder, and salt. Beat the eggs until thoroughly combined. Add the sugar, beating until thoroughly combined. Add the cooled chocolate mixture and the extracts, and stir until thoroughly combined. Gently stir in the flour mixture, stirring only until thoroughly combined, about 30 to 40 strokes.

Spread the mixture in the prepared pan. Bake for 30 to 35 minutes, or until a toothpick inserted 1 inch from the edge of the pan comes out clean.

Cool completely on wire racks. To serve, place the pan in the freezer for 10 to 15 minutes. Using a sharp knife, gently slice the brownies and lever them out of the pan with a spatula. Serve with the best-quality vanilla ice cream or gelato.

Makes 16 large brownies

Variations: To make the brownies more spicy, add 1 tablespoon minced fresh ginger root. To make chile-flavored brownies, omit all ginger ingredients and add 1 teaspoon chipotle chile powder to the dry ingredients.